SHADOW STAR

BANTAM BOOKS

New York

Toronto

London

Sydney

Auckland

SHADOW STAR

THIRD IN THE CHRONICLES OF THE SHADOW WAR

BY
CHRIS CLAREMONT
STORY BY
GEORGE LUCAS

SHADOW STAR

A Bantam Spectra Book / November 1999

SPECTRA and the portrayal of a boxed "s" are trademarks of Bantam Books,
a division of Random House, Inc.

BOOK DESIGN BY CAROL MALCOLM RUSSO / SIGNET M DESIGN, INC.

Library of Congress Cataloging-in-Publication Data
Claremont, Chris, 1950–
      Shadow star/by Chris Claremont ; story by George Lucas.
         p.   cm. — (The chronicles of the Shadow War ; 3rd)
      (A Bantam spectra book)
      ISBN 0-553-09598-6
      I. Lucas, George. II. Title. III. Series: Lucas, George.
      Chronicles of the Shadow War ; 3rd.
      PS3553.L255S54   1999
      813´.54—dc21   99-33250
                                                  CIP

Published simultaneously in the United States and Canada

Bantam Books are published by Bantam Books, a division of Random
House, Inc. Its trademark, consisting of the words "Bantam Books" and the
portrayal of a rooster, is Registered in U.S. Patent and Trademark Office
and in other countries. Marca Registrada. Bantam Books,
1540 Broadway, New York, New York 10036.

PRINTED IN THE UNITED STATES OF AMERICA

BVG   10 9 8 7 6 5 4 3 2 1

Dedicated To

ALASDHAIR MAXWELL

&

BENJAMIN SIMON

With a Father's undying love
because they, like Elora Danan,
are the hope
and the future

And to the man who made it all possible,

with thanks for the opportunity

delight for the vision

and gratitude for the trust

in allowing me to share that vision:

GEORGE LUCAS

The Twelve Great Realms

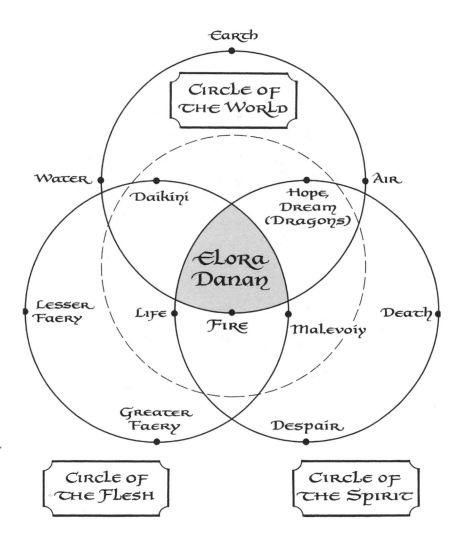

Earth

Circle of the World

Water • • Hope, Dream (Dragons) • Air

Daikini

Elora Danan

Lesser Faery • Life • Fire • Malevoiy • Death

Greater Faery • Despair

Circle of the Flesh

Circle of the Spirit

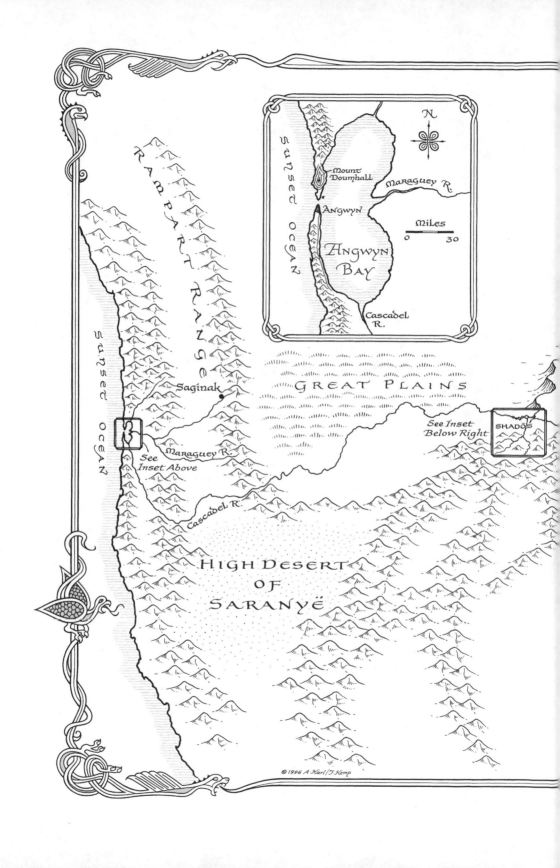

N

Sunset Ocean

Mount
Doumhall

Angwyn

Maraguey R.

Miles

0   30

Angwyn
Bay

Cascadel
R.

RAMPART RANGE

Sunset Ocean

GREAT PLAINS

Saginak

See Inset
Below Right

SHADOS

See
Inset Above

Maraguey R.

Cascadel R.

HIGH DESERT
OF
SARANYË

© 1996 A. Karl / J. Kemp

A Crown not made for Crowning,
A Throne that ne'er be Filled.
A Kingdom not of People,
But of Twelve Crowns Royal.

The Wheel of Fortune Turns,
Time rests heavy on the brow
The Wings of Fate bring fire and flame
Or can Peace be r'stored by Thou?

Alone and lost, through desert and wood
With nothing of her own, no place to call home,
Wanders the Thirteenth Crown
For the Thirteenth Throne
Dominion ever offered, but never claimed.

Born in the Heart of Darkness
Forever Touched by the Shadow
That ever seeks to Claim her
The Voice from the Wilderness
The Dream Undying
The Hope Reborn

Twelve steps around the Circles Three.
No one to save her, Will no one aid her?
Twelve Realms in Conflict, Twelve Hearts to Win.
No one to save her, Will no one aid her?
Twelve links in the Timeless Chain,
That must be bound
The World to save
Will no one aid her?
Only one to save her.

—*a song sung in the pubs of Sandeni,*
in the aftermath of the Shadow War,
attribution unknown

CHAPTER
1

Thorn Drumheller stood in the heart of glory, yet all about him was desolation.

"Elora Danan," he breathed, in a voice so faint and broken it wouldn't have done justice to a ghost, "what have you done? What have you *done?*"

The air was still, but not with any absence of wind. To Thorn it was as if all life, all vitality, had been torn from it. The same held true for its scent. When he had arrived in this most sacred place there had been an edge to every breath, so keen a sensation he feared it would sear his lungs. He had never tasted air so pure, and yet so richly textured. It was a pale comparison, he knew, but he was most strongly reminded of wandering through a stand of old-growth forest, amongst trees whose lives were measured more in centuries than simple years. All that those venerable trunks had seen, all the earth that sustained them had felt, all the history of the beings that called that grove home, was wrapped up in that heady mixture.

Here, was nothing.

So simple a word, *nothing*. He never imagined it could be so terrible.

The sand beneath his feet had sparkled before, its grains scattered thick with shards of crystalline fire that glittered with a radiance all their own, like the embers left from a celestial hearth. The same held for the rock of the escarpment that ringed the caldera, this bowl of a volcano as ancient as it was huge. The crater was more than Thorn could grasp. He simply didn't know numbers big enough. It would take him days to walk from where he knelt to the wall of jagged, saw-toothed peaks that surrounded him, yet even so the ridgeline towered higher than most of the mountain ranges he had seen, including the fabled Stairs to Heaven.

There had been fire in that stone, pulsing as fiercely as the blood did through his own body.

Now, nothing.

Atop every summit of that promontory had stood a dragon and the memory of that sight sent chills along Thorn's spine. He was a Nelwyn, born to one of the lesser races of the Realm of Lesser Faery, whose role in the scheme of things was said to be as modest as their stature. For most of his days he'd been a farmer, a simple, structured life for what seemed a simple, structured man. He had a wife he loved, two children he adored, and believed himself content. Dragons were the stuff of legends and adventures and that had no truck with Nelwyns.

Until one came to him fifteen years ago in the dead of night, in what he thought then was no more than a dream—for that was how dragons, creatures wholly of the Circle of the Spirit, visited those races who lived on the more physical planes of existence— to steal him from hearth and home and set his feet upon the path that ultimately brought him to this place. He had never ridden the back of a dragon before that night. Now he wondered if he ever would again.

Here was where they lived, the seat of wonder and imagination. Here, according to all the stories and beliefs of all the races of all the Twelve Great Realms, *anything* was possible. If Creation had a soul, this was said to be its home, and the dragons were its embodiment.

Only the dragons were no more. Thorn had seen them slain.

And now, the killer was walking straight toward him.

She didn't look the part, and that had nothing to do with her dancer's costume. Her skirt hung low on her hips, generously cut to allow the fullest range of movement, while a bandeau top covered her breasts; both were dyed a scarlet so dark it seemed almost black, the color of night-washed blood spilled in passion, that formed a stark and dramatic contrast to the gleaming silver of her skin. There was no outward warmth to her appearance. She resembled none of the races he knew, not her own Daikini nor any of the myriad tribes of Faery. It was as though someone had captured the essence of moonlight, wrapped it in human form, and given it life.

She moved with the sleek and arrogant ease of youth, propelled by muscles that had yet to suffer the touch of time or injury. Despite all she had endured in her sixteen years, there remained an air of innocence about her, the same sense of renewed hope and possibilities to be found in a highland meadow washed by the first gentle rains of spring.

There was pride to her step as she approached, and such a look of joy and wonder on her face that Thorn questioned if she was mad, or hoped in some small and hidden part of himself that he was instead, that this would turn out to be no more than the most awful of nightmares.

By his side, Khory Bannefin stirred, the timbre of each breath making plain to him how badly she'd been hurt. They had come to this hallowed ground—the Princess, the Warrior, and the Mage—to try to save the dragons from a sorcerer who'd sought to claim their power for his own and through it dominion over all the Realms, who'd set himself as Elora's sworn enemy almost from the moment of her birth.

In that, they had succeeded. The Deceiver had been driven from the field without his prize. But to Thorn, the terrible cost had made their struggle and sacrifice a mockery. Victory had burned to bitter ashes in his grasp. A battle had been won, and as a consequence perhaps all the world lost.

"Elora Danan," he called again in a hoarse cry whose passion flogged him to his feet to face her, "what have you done?"

"What was necessary," she replied.

"You killed them. You killed them all." His words described the act but they could not do justice to the enormity of the crime. Neither language, nor even emotions, existed that could properly do so.

"It was that, Drumheller, or let the Deceiver claim their souls and power."

"You were born to be the Savior of our world." The accusation tumbled from him in a torrent, like water from a burst dam, and he had neither strength nor will to stop it. "Why is it all you do is harm?"

She blinked, and staggered stiff-legged to a stop, as though he'd physically struck her. In the whole catalog of responses he expected to his indictment, there was no listing for tears. They came suddenly, without preamble, a stark reminder of just how young the Sacred Princess was, still far more girl than woman. Her eyes grew round and the cords of her neck stood out from the effort it took to keep from bursting into sobs.

She stood very straight, to her full height, like a sapling that had taken a terrible shock but was determined not to be uprooted, no matter what. When she spoke at last, her voice was low, its cadence measured.

"You're hurt, the both of you," she said quietly, ignoring both his words and the tone of voice that sharpened their cutting edge. "Let me help."

"Works for me," Khory said before Thorn could speak. "I could use some."

A belt of tooled leather decorated with intertwined knotwork encircled the waist of Elora's skirt, fastened by a buckle that blended iron and silver and chips of lapis lazuli in a design that Thorn for all his knowledge didn't recognize. From the belt on either side of her hung a pair of well-worn leather pouches. Elora donic grin, *the question is,* he heard himself say, *are we fools? To accept the world as it seems and never try to determine what it truly is?*

"It was their time," she continued. "It would have happened regardless, whether we came or not."

"So *you* say!" A challenge. He didn't want to hear her, refused to believe. Too many certainties in his life had proved to be false, too many beliefs upended and cast to the winds of chaos. This last was more than he could endure.

Her gaze moved up and past him, toward the peak that had served as the perch for the Lord of this host. He didn't try to follow; he couldn't bear to behold only gathering darkness.

"Calan Dineer told me."

He knew the name, but now it was his turn for his eyes to burn with hot tears as he found no face in memory to match it.

Again, he shook his head, in a vain attempt to deny their loss. "They were the ideal, Elora, the representation of all our hopes and dreams!"

To his surprise, Khory interrupted him. She had always been a woman of few words, husbanding speech as she would any other finite and valuable resource, choosing to use them like her swords, to best effect.

"Dreams perhaps, Drumheller," she said in a clear alto, a step lower than Elora's voice but nowhere near as husky. "But the Danan is our hope. Has been from the start."

"So spake prophecy."

"Every prophecy, mage, of *every* race we know of, whether Daikini or Faery, dragon or demon. All the stories tell of a time of great change, when the hearts and souls of all the Realms will be put to the test. And a Sacred Princess will stand forth as Savior."

"To lead the Realms into a new era of peace and harmony," Thorn finished for her, and again his rage got the better of him. His words emerged like bludgeons and though Elora didn't flinch from them they still had impact. Thorn made a dismissive snort.

"No one said it would be easy," Khory offered, one veteran campaigner to another, while Elora offered the beginnings of a comforting smile, her hand reaching out toward his shoulder. He refused to acknowledge either.

"Someone should have mentioned it would be so hard," Elora said to Khory, turning her back on the man who'd been her mentor and protector almost from the day of her birth. "That, I would have appreciated."

Still on her knees, she worked close beside Khory. Even in the phantom light that remained to the caldera, Thorn could see how pale their companion had become. The resilience had fled from Khory's golden skin. Her flesh lay in folds so stiff over the distinctive points of chin and jaw that they threatened to crack with every change of expression or gesture. He needed no physical contact to tell him how dry it had become to the touch as well, or how chill.

"The Deceiver hurt you pretty badly," Elora told her.

"Trust me, this I know."

"We won't leave you," Thorn said unnecessarily, discomfited by the realization that he didn't altogether trust Elora to say it for him.

"But as you are," the young woman said, taking no outward offense at his remark, "we can't afford to take you."

"Deceiver won't be giving up, that's certes," agreed the warrior. "We've a long road back to Sandeni; somewhere along the way, he'll be waiting."

"Which means, since you're the warrior, before we go we have to make you better."

"Is that wise, Elora?" Thorn interjected. "I mean, to do that here?"

"It has to be here, Thorn. Nowhere else is safe."

"Of all the words to choose from, child, to describe our situation, *safe* is the last on my list."

"We have time," she repeated.

"Can I help?" he asked. "The two of us, working together, will speed the healing." *Especially,* he thought, *since I'm the one who can wield magic.*

"Hold fast to your strength, Drumheller," she said, in a manner far older than her years, that carried with it the instinctive stamp of royalty. It was a voice that was learning to command, and growing accustomed to being obeyed. "We'll have need of it later."

He pursed his lips and huffed, very much a father confronted by an unruly offspring, frustrated by the realization that the child might be right. There was no sign now of the escarpment, as though a curtain of blackest velvet had been dropped before it. He remembered tales told by the sea-roving Cascani traders, of sandy islands surrounded by the trackless wastes of the Mother Ocean and it seemed to him that this was much the same. He wondered if he walked to the boundary of that darkness, then took one more step, whether his feet would find solid purchase beyond. Did it represent the limit of what could merely be seen, or what actually *was*?

On impulse, he dropped to one knee and swept a hand through the sand beneath him. Memory told him what it felt like while the dragons lived, yet every sense now gave the lie to that recollection. The soil flowed around his hand and between his fingers more like water than earth, and he found he could not grasp it. There was no texture to its touch, and even less substance; he might as well have been trying to catch air. With swift, sure strokes of his staff, he began to draw a sigil to serve as the focal point for a minor spell, but left the task unfinished as the marks in the sand disappeared as quickly as he made them.

"What is happening?" he asked, and supplied his own answer in a voice that mingled awe and stark terror. "What happens to the Realm of Dreams, when the Dreamers are no more?"

"Thankfully," Elora said from her position by Khory's side, "the Fates willing, we'll never have to learn."

"It does no good to deny what you've done, child!" he began, only to have words fail him utterly as Elora reached into one of her pouches with both hands and drew forth a single, gleaming egg, which she cradled in her lap as if it was the most precious thing she'd ever held.

"All living things have their allotted span, Thorn," she said, and as she drew a set of fingertips across the surface of the egg, gently stroking it as she would a kitten, flickering coruscations of fire followed from deep within. It was of a fair size, roughly the equivalent of a Daikini's head, and of a weight to match. Its coloration best resembled an opal, with that gem's ability to refract light into a rainbow spectrum of subordinate hues. In this instance, the lines of flame Elora's touch brought into being started out as a blend of scarlet and gold, but as the flames moved farther afield from their source they cast off ripples of lapis and rich purple that reminded Thorn of the colors of a summer sunset.

"Some," she continued, allowing herself a slight smile, her caress of the egg returning as much pleasure as she gave it, "like the mayfly, last but a day. Others walk the waking world for years. For some, that term is counted in centuries. For the world entire, a stretch of time beyond measure or human comprehension. But death when it comes doesn't necessarily mean the end. From each generation comes the seed of its successor. As you were the father to your children, as I am the child of my murdered parents. Even Khory here"—and her smile broadened—"the body of a warrior slain in ages long past serving as the repository for the soul of a demon, had a mama and a papa."

She looked up from the egg and her smile turned ineffably sad, and Thorn knew she was seeing what he'd just tried so hard to recall, the form and texture of the dragons.

"Even dreams get old, Thorn," she said. "They need to be renewed, they need to speak to each race and generation in turn. And be shaped by those races and that generation."

"That's why the Deceiver came, hey?" Khory nodded. "To gain the power to dictate the shape of those dreams."

"And why he was able to breach their citadel," Elora said. "Because, real as they may have looked to us, they were no more than shadows."

A *truth,* Thorn realized with sudden insight, *but not the whole truth.* Elora was holding something back, the same perception revealing a thread of purest fear laced through the body of her thoughts and words. It didn't glow very brightly, which made him wonder if she was even consciously aware of it, nor was it very thick, but it reached through the whole of her being. It was something he'd never seen in her before, and gave off resonances of both the dragons and the Deceiver. *Something happened here,* he thought, *that struck her so deeply she dare not even acknowledge it.*

He considered voicing his thoughts; instead, he chose to keep his own counsel and said, "Speaking of shadows," emphasizing the comment with a wave toward the encroaching darkness.

Spurred to action, Elora set aside her reverie and returned the egg to her pouch, scooching forward until her knees barely touched Khory's side right at the waist.

"Watch our backs, Drumheller," she told him, and he responded with an assent.

"Thought you had no gift for magic," Khory muttered to Elora.

"Depends on how you define the term," Thorn replied in Elora's stead.

"Figured there'd be a loophole. Someways, mage, you lot put lawyers to shame."

Thorn ignored the gibe. "To most," he said, "*this* is magic."

He snapped his fingers and, presto, in the palm of his hand a ball of light appeared, so pure and radiant that Khory had to narrow her eyes.

"A little showy, don't you think, Thorn?" Elora commented. The contrast between light and shadow was absolute, each so intense that they made it almost impossible to see, the glare washing out the shapes and colors of things as effectively as the darkness. In fact, the only way to tell the form of an object was by extrapolation from the shadows it cast.

"For now, perhaps. For later, perhaps not. The point is," he told Khory, "magic is generally accepted to be the conscious manipulation of natural and unnatural forces. Summon a wind or a demon, it's much the same procedure. Cast the proper spell, you'll get the proper result. Elora can't do that. By the same token, thankfully, she's also immune to the effects of those enchantments."

"Except when they're cast by the Deceiver."

"Bannefin," Elora said with a dash of asperity, "I am so grateful for the reminder." During their first encounter, on the night of Elora's Ascension when the girl was thirteen, the Deceiver attempted to destroy her soul and assume dominion over her body. That attack failed, and with Thorn's help Elora managed to escape. But as with the battle here in the caldera, that victory came at an equivalent price. The city of Angwyn, together with all its people and the reigning monarchs of all the Twelve Great Realms who'd gathered there to honor Elora, was ensorcelled, encased in ice. As for Elora herself, her skin had turned purest silver, as though she were a statue cast from that argent metal and miraculously given life.

"You're the patient," Elora said, and her tone brooked no further discussion. "I'm the healer here. Lie flat, shut your mouth, let me do my work."

"This magic that really isn't?"

"My kind of magic," Thorn continued, "is the imposition of my active will on the natural order. The Deceiver represents what I do carried to the furthest and most damnable point. His power is the total dominion of his will over nature. Same powers between the two of us, same skills even, only he has allowed them to totally corrupt his soul."

"I saw you two go at each other, Drumheller. There seemed no difference at all."

He shuddered at the memory. "A taste only, Khory. I've seen now what I can do, and what I might become. I'll have none of it, ever again."

"And Elora?"

"She imposes nothing. She asks for the active help of what powers she needs, with no guarantee they'll be in the mood."

"Well," Elora interrupted, "I'd certainly like to give that a try, if you two would quit jabbering long enough for me to concentrate on the task at hand. Hush, please, I'm serious."

Khory nodded to Drumheller, which he returned, moving around the still form of his fallen companion until he stood opposite the kneeling girl. Sitting on her heels as she was, with her back gracefully curved toward Khory, he was finally able to look down on her. That recognition prompted a shy and rueful twist to his lips as he considered one of the main drawbacks to Nelwyns associating with Daikini, or any of what his people called the Tall Folk, namely the cricked neck that often came from trying to look them in the eye.

Elora laid one hand on Khory's hips, the other on the center of her body, just below her breasts. The woman's heart was sound but the beat of her pulse was slow and sluggish, as though the muscle was growing too tired to continue its work. The physical injuries done her were serious, that had been evident at a glance, and much of Elora's preparatory work involved damping the pain Khory felt, then straightening the broken limbs as best she could. Healing the warrior wouldn't be of much use if the result left her lame. The real damage, though, was within, and Elora suspected the Deceiver had struck with poison spells as well as blows, to sap the strength of body and will, to infect and overwhelm Khory's soul.

A Daikini would have been dead and damned before his body hit the ground. Even Khory's hybrid constitution only postponed the inevitable. If nothing more was done, she was doomed.

The problem was, trying to save her might lead to Elora's infection by the same foul sorcery.

Khory sensed the danger and gripped Elora by the wrist.

"Danan," she said, "enough."

"Elora," Thorn said, kneeling opposite her, "let me."

She was tempted. Thorn had skill and experience, he was a mage and though he'd be the last to acknowledge it, one of the foremost in the Great Realms.

She shook her head and spoke softly, a single word.

"No."

She leaned forward and laid her palms against Khory's bare skin.

The contact was a shock. After all, she was the one who looked like a silver casting, it didn't seem right for Khory to feel as cold as one. Elora stepped aside from her physical self, using InSight to view the scene from a perspective far broader than human eyes would allow. For her, there were no longer any such things as flesh and bone, muscle and sinew. The body was not a solid object but was composed instead of currents and networks of energy, crackling streams of fire, much like what she'd called forth beneath the shell of the dragon's egg, that blazed with a multitude of colors and intensities. In Khory's case, those blazes were muted, hardly more in some instances than faint embers, desperately close to outright extinction. Those were the points closest to the actual wounds themselves. From there spread the spiritual contagion that threatened the warrior's young soul. It was hard to remember that while Khory's body was that of a woman in the prime of her middle years, the soul that animated it wasn't much more than a child, given its life by Thorn the same night that the Deceiver had tried so hard to claim Elora's.

She bent herself to her task, concentrating first on the gross and major wounds, starting with Khory's broken leg. She'd already set the bones, now she had to sing the Song of Making to them, to remind them of what it had been like to be in one piece, united and whole. There was resistance, a strand of foulness that was alien to Khory, glorying in the pain and chaos of the moment, savaging the careful latticework Elora was constructing even as she set it into place.

It would be like this throughout, she realized then. All the good she attempted would be undermined, if not undone outright. She'd hoped to save this worst challenge for last but she knew now there was no hope of that.

She drew back a little into herself, to take stock before making her next move, and that hesitation almost proved her undoing as the strand of infection that was ruining her repair on Khory's leg suddenly reared up to strike at her with the aspect and deadly speed of a killer cobra. In that flash, it wound its own pattern tightly around her own and sent its poison racing up her arm. In a twinkling, it would be over.

In a twinkling, it was.

The breath rushed out of her, as though she'd been punched, with a deep *whoulf* that erupted from the pit of her diaphragm. She felt her blood begin to boil, and thought of the elemental firedrakes she'd befriended, creatures who were close but lesser kin to demons and dragons together, whose substance was as molten as the heart of the world. Where human hearts pump scarlet, hers suddenly cast forth molten, liquid gold, so incendiary hot it gave her skin a roseate glow that mimicked the living flesh of her own race. It wasn't just her blood that burned; every nerve ending, the smallest particle of her being was suddenly turning to fire. She wanted to cry a warning to Thorn, to hurry himself and Khory to safety, or at least cast some kind of warding spell to protect them both, but she couldn't draw even that single breath. She wondered in that moment, as glorious as it was terrible, if this was how dragons felt when they spat their fire.

As the Deceiver's poison raced to claim her heart and soul, it ran full-tilt into that awful storm of flame and was instantly and completely consumed.

Elora wasn't finished, though, not hardly. As the infection had leaped from Khory's body to her own, so did she now cast her inner fire back across that gulf into the warrior. Khory's back arched like a drawn longbow, her eyes wide and staring, their irises of jade subsumed beneath glimmering firegold. She cried out, more loudly than Elora had, not so much an expression of pain but of defiance. It was the sound a warrior makes in mortal combat, summoning the last of her strength from the core of her being as she throws herself a final time into the fray. It was her way of saying, "I will die, or I will triumph, I accept no other outcome."

Elora sensed she herself was glowing, which happened when her own abilities were pushed to their limit. She could see that Khory was as well, though nowhere near so brightly.

Only when the battle was fully joined did she realize that the outcome was nowhere near as certain as she'd assumed. Her fury and her strength made her a formidable foe, but the infection the Deceiver had cast forth into Khory was her match, so tenacious and determined she feared it had a mind of its own. In a way, it did: Khory herself. In the same way that gangrene corrupted the flesh, this spell did the spirit, attaching itself to the darkest potential of its host and using it to gradually seduce the rest. The same resolve and courage, tenacity and battle savvy that Khory was attempting to bring to Elora's aid was also being marshaled against her. The victory the warrior craved was as much over Elora as over the poison that threatened to destroy her. Whatever the outcome, the death would be—at least in part—her own.

A spear of darkest shadow erupted from Khory's midsection to stab Elora through the heart. It pierced her body entirely, but as it emerged from her back the shadow exploded into flame, which instantly consumed the entire length of foulness as if it were no more than a construction of rice paper. Fast as a bolt of lightning, the silver fire rushed back along the course established by the shadow spear, carrying Elora along with it. The ride was wilder than anything she remembered, like plunging down a succession of cataracts, through a gauntlet of jagged boulders that churned the water white with spray and accelerated it to breakneck speed. She didn't try to fight the current or grab for a handhold; both attempts would have been a futile waste of effort. She knew she'd have to stay this course for its duration.

She found herself in darkness, but the texture was different from the shadow that had attacked her. This wasn't brought about by an absence of light, this was an active, dynamic force that defied the laws and structures that were the foundation of Elora's life. With a shock of recognition, she recognized it as the part of Khory's spirit that came from her sire, the part of her that was demon.

The fire plunged into that darkness like a high mountain flash flood, walls rising on either side to form a gorge, creating a narrow channel that forced the torrent to rush ever faster and more out of control. The flames Elora ignited could find no purchase, any more than she could herself; instead, they abraded the shore like a monstrous rasp, tearing at the walls with an inhuman fury, as though Elora's spirit was taking revenge on Khory's for daring to challenge her.

Scars appeared on the surface of the darkness, faint scorings at first, reminiscent of the scratches on polished metal that came from casual, careless use. But quickly, suddenly, those marks became the vicious gouges of a cold chisel, each gash great and small allowing a flash of light and color to burst free. The contrast was dazzling, even though there was a sense of great age to the images, the feeling in Elora that these were not true memories but their final fading echoes. They reminded her of the dragons upon the rim of their stronghold, so noble and majestic and passionate, so essentially wondrous to behold you didn't realize they were little better than ghosts.

The same held true here, save that the memories themselves

were the ghosts, the last vestiges of a soul that had long since departed to its just reward.

Even as Elora had that thought, the foundation her fire had undermined at last gave way and the entire edifice of darkness collapsed in upon her. It seemed to Elora that the world was suddenly composed of crystal and that some terrible mallet had struck the perfect tone to shatter it to bits. The young woman had barely a moment to realize what was happening, and none to contemplate the consequences, as palisades crumbled on every side. Pieces great and small tumbled into the cataract, filling it to overflowing, bursting its banks and barriers of a stream that had lasted for ages, transforming a flood into a maelstrom.

Now, Elora fought, though she feared it was too late. A reflex action, mostly, an instinct as primal and indomitable as Khory's never to be subdued, never to be beaten without a fight. She might have succeeded, too, if not for the weight of memory crashing down upon her.

There was an electric moment of contact . . .

. . . and Elora found herself blinking human eyes, drawing human breaths, and instantly regretting both. The sight before her was a mountaintop citadel, breached and burning, with such flames that sodden timbers went up like kindling and curtain-wall stones thicker than a Daikini was tall cracked wide or crumbled to dust. The stench was of burning flesh; the taste, the harsh metallic copper of fresh-spilled blood; the sounds a cacophony of screams and curses, men and animals; too much confusion. About her, all was chaos.

It was a battle. It was a victory.

Her body didn't sit right on her soul, which was how she knew it wasn't really hers. She wore Khory Bannefin's skin, in those ancient days when the warrior woman still lived her first life. Somehow, the cataract had etched a pathway to the past, an age so distant that both events and people were more the stuff of legend than history.

This can't *be,* she thought. *Khory's original soul was gone— Drumheller told me so, else he would not have performed the Rite of*

Transposition. She held fast to that belief, ascribing to it the same immutable force of the movement of the turning of the world about its axis and about the sun; she made it an absolute of her life, that Thorn Drumheller would do nothing so foul or dishonorable, because the alternative was unthinkable. Her rational mind formed a buttress to that desperate article of faith, reminding her of the taste and texture of the memories, like keepsakes in a hope chest too long sealed.

"Khory was dead when Drumheller found her," Elora told herself. "Her soul had long since fled its casement, that's what he told me; otherwise, he'd never have cast the Spell of Binding to join it with the DemonChild's essence. She was no more than a hollow vessel, stripped bare of every aspect of the woman that was. But this is her body I'm wearing, her life I'm watching. These *have* to be her memories."

The answer came almost as quickly, with blinding logic: "Think of where you are, Elora," she continued, "and who knows, maybe *who* you are as well. In the Realm of Dreams, in the heart of imagination, with a pair of dragon's eggs in your pocket, who knows what's possible?" And she had to marvel then at the spirit of the woman whose life she now beheld, because if these scenes were but faint and pale shades of the pure memories there was a passion and a glory in Khory Bannefin that even the dragons would respect.

She stood on a sloping plain below the fortress, amidst a series of defensive redoubts that her forces had been compelled to tackle each in their turn before the final assault on the keep itself. Bodies were scattered about as thick as snow and at first glance it was nigh impossible to tell friend from fallen foe. Both sides had fought with the ferocity and brutality that had become the hallmark of the war, acknowledgment by all the combatants that there were but two possible outcomes to their conflict, victory or annihilation.

At first, Elora saw none of that. For her, this world was a wonder, unlike anything she'd ever known. Each breath made her giddy. There was *power* here, as young and untamed as the globe itself. All about, she perceived strands and filaments of raw energy, some representing the stuff of natural life itself, others the vast reservoirs of magic available to any with the talent or wit to tap them. She could feel that force crackle between her toes and under her skin like lightning, with such intensity she was surprised she wasn't glowing more brightly than the full moon. It was a revelation to her. The world she knew, even in those of the Twelve Great Realms where such magic still held sway, was a desert by comparison.

She strode across the field as though she owned it, taller than most, bareheaded so that everyone could see her face and know she had survived, her hawklike features distinct even without the raptor tattoo that decorated her left eye and cheek or the hair she'd cropped short in defiance of tradition and style. Her blades were sheathed but that meant nothing. Her speed with them was as legendary as her skill: she could draw steel, slice a gleaming blade through a foe's body, and return the weapon to its scabbard almost faster than sight could follow. Her escort, picked warriors the lot, sworn to her service and the dearest of comrades, were almost as good. She moved over this ravaged moonscape, pitted and gouged worse than any open-pit mine, as surely as if she followed a paved highway and they found themselves hard-pressed to keep pace.

A mist had risen over the course of the night, as land and bodies cooled while the air stayed unseasonably warm from the heat of the burning fortress. She'd heard mutters from some of the Rock Nelwyn that even their own furnaces didn't burn so hot. The moon was waning, which meant it cast precious little light upon the scene—which was just as well; the view would be awful enough come sunrise. She could feel a tightness in her own face, from the strain of keeping herself from howling, and was thankful no one could see the grief and rage that battled there for dominion. She'd been in the thick of this battle, as she had in every one she'd fought, but this had been a rare occasion where she'd emerged without a wound to show for it. Yet she felt as if she'd been struck to the quick, a blow that should have been mortal, that could not be endured.

All the other noise around her faded, she had ears only for the crackle of flames atop the rocky promontory before her. The memory of the screams that had brought the battle to a momentary halt, as the defenders, realizing their cause was truly lost, set their citadel alight.

She cared nothing for the warriors, their end was richly deserved. But this castle had been the prison for almost the whole of the race of dragons. Rather than see their captives rescued, the defenders had chosen to see them burn instead.

For all their might and courage, Khory's army could do no more than watch.

A hand grabbed for her arm but it caught her with fingers only and was easily brushed aside. Another managed a better hold but she sidestepped, dipped her shoulder, wrenched ahead and down in a reflexive move that was as sinuous as it was effective and remained free without losing stride.

Her two captains, Rhys and Taliesin, blocked her path and she simply stiff-armed them both aside. She would not be stopped.

Or so she thought, until a gale-force gust of wind staggered her, forced her back into the grasp of her comrades, and she looked up to behold a dragon executing a pinpoint turn almost right on top of her. The tip of one wing lightly scraped the surface of the ground, the other stretched as high as the crests of the castle flames, giving the impression of a creature so monstrous huge that he could have gathered the entire fortress up in his claws and carried it away as easily as a child would his toys.

Air cracked like thunder as he belled his wings for landing, sending forth swirls and eddies that set the flames beyond to dancing. He was a shadow on shadows, features only hinted at by the firelight, as he dampened the inner energies that normally made him a riot of iridescent color.

Elora recognized him at once, though this face was far younger than the one she knew. She'd last seen it atop the highest promontory of the Dragon's Caldera, as she begged him to help her find a way to save himself and his people.

"Dineer," she screamed, her voice breaking as much as her heart, his name too poor a vessel to encompass the grief she felt.

"I know" was his gentle reply, echoing her pain with his own, and Elora didn't know if the reply was meant for her or Khory. She didn't care. The forgiveness he offered struck her like an iron bar across her shoulders, so much so that she thought she'd break from the force of it.

Within the caldera, Elora Danan bared her teeth. She tasted salt tears at the edges of her lips and saw tears of flame well from Khory's eyes. On the warrior's left side, the rivulets of fire were caught by the wells and ridges of her tattoo, until the entire outline of the design was ablaze. She'd never noticed before but at the core of every framing line was a thread of purest silver, as pristine as her own skin, laced through the indigo ink stain. The flames took on that coloration as well, casting off no heat as they burned high and bright, doing the woman no harm.

Unlike Khory, Elora made no sound as her back arched as deeply, as though both women were bows drawn to their fullest extension. Thorn, watching, didn't see how it was possible for bodies to be so limber. He feared their spines would break but the trance was so deep, the forces raging from one to the other so violent, he couldn't see a way to help. Bad as things seemed to him, intervention would only make them worse.

I'm sorry, Elora said silently in her thoughts. *I should have known better how to save you.*

"I'm sorry," she heard the warrior say aloud, her voice aching with loss and misery. It had been Khory's plan, daring as they all were, to try to rescue the dragons. She'd taken a fearful risk. It had almost worked.

"Their day was done," Calan Dineer told her, and Elora wondered if the words were meant as well for her. He curled his neck, seemingly as boneless as a swan, only far more graceful, until his head was on a level with hers, angling it a bit to the side so one of his glimmering eyes could meet the both of hers. He kept his mouth closed as a courtesy when he spoke, since even the stoutest Daikini heart tended to skip a beat or three in such close proximity to a phalanx of gleaming fangs the size of tree trunks.

"What do you mean?"

"A new age dawns, milady. New dreams must inspire it, as young blood must consecrate it."

"That's not fair."

The tone of his voice echoed the shrug of his great shoulders. "It's war," he said, as if that phrase explained everything.

The warrior turned, and through her eyes Elora surveyed the battlefield, feeling a measure of Khory's sadness at the cost of her victory. Despite the mist-laced darkness, her MageSight revealed the scene as clearly as daylight. She saw faint firefly flashes and marked them as fairies searching for survivors from either side. Close by were clutches of soldiery, mingling Daikini with the taller, lean-as-reeds forms of the elves of Greater Faery and a mix of shorter, broader, more overtly powerful forms representing the races of Lesser Faery. Any comrades found would be gathered quickly away to an aid station, for healing or the mercy of a painless and final sleep. Their foes, however . . .

Elora had seen firsthand what fairies did to those they hated. To her it was an obscenity, that creatures of such delicacy and innocence could be moved to such terrible deeds. She couldn't help but wonder what her victory would truly be worth, if those who won it were transformed by the struggle into brutes.

"No one said it would be easy," she heard from Dineer, a whisper on the wind, his voice a welcome caress. *Are those Khory's thoughts you speak to, my Lord of the Dragons,* she thought with a touch of whimsy, *or mine?*

"Someone should have mentioned it would be so hard" was Khory's reply.

"Think of the cost, aye," the dragon said. "But never forget as well what's been accomplished. That's the miracle."

In truth, that's precisely what it was as a squad of sappers trudged along the line of battle, gathering their tools and equipment. A Rock Nelwyn led them—who better to lay out the gullies and tunnels so necessary in siegecraft than those who spent their days mining deep within the earth—but close behind were three Daikini, themselves dwarfed by a pair of ogres whose specialty was heavy lifting. There were trolls and brownies to act as scouts, though they'd be far from here since brownies hated the stench of death that came with battle and trolls would find that same smell too irresistibly enticing, since they mainly fed on carrion. Fairies made the best messengers, provided the notes were neither long nor complicated; otherwise, brownies generally rode the backs of ravens and eagles. Firedrakes, kin to the dragons themselves, provided the raging heat for the furnaces where the Nelwyns forged their weapons and which likewise kept folk warm through the cruelest of winters. The spirits of field and forest, too numerous for her to name though she and her army were indebted to them all, provided the lasting bounty that kept them fed, and safe haven for their loved ones.

The Malevoiy had preyed on every race. Their only hope of throwing off that cruel and seemingly eternal yoke of oppression was through unity.

All her life, Khory had heard the myriad reasons why that couldn't be done, a litany of despair that stuck in her craw like a jagged soup bone.

She'd fought from the start, but she was one life, one sword, against a legion. In the scheme of things, the threat she represented was less than insignificant.

Eamon Asana, the *ard-righ,* the High King, changed that.

Trumpets sounded a fanfare in the distance, a shift in the wind bringing the sweat scent of approaching chargers, a tremble to the ground marking the thunderous hoofbeats of a squadron of heavy horse, assault cavalry. There was a taste of steel to the air as well, meaning men in armor. Her companions had noticed the newcomers as well, each taking his place on either side of her and a step behind, while the dragon loomed impossibly high overhead, completely blocking out all sight of the castle as the crest of the promontory collapsed even farther, turning it at last into a blazing cauldron.

For Elora, Asana was a revelation. He was a barrel of a man, of moderate height and powerful build. On a bet, he'd managed to lift the war-mallet of the King of Lesser Faery, no mean feat even among the Nelwyns, who'd forged it, and in another wager had crossed blades with Rafiel, the High Elf who was Liege Lord of Greater Faery, emerging from that single combat wholly unscathed, without even a tear to his shirt. His hair was a true mane of ruddy gold and while his features were no match for the unhuman beauty of the Elf King's there was a mark of character to them that brought out the best in people. He had a voice that could cover a parade ground and a way of speaking that made folk want to listen. Passion ruled him but that wasn't such a bad thing because in him that passion was devoted wholly to the good. He viewed his crown as a solemn covenant with his land and with his people, to serve them both and do for them what was best.

This Lord of the Daikini, the youngest of the races of the world, had forged the grand alliance against the oppressor Malevoiy. It was Khory Bannefin, his warlord, who'd led it to victory.

Flanking him were both his fellow monarchs, at the head of escorts of their own. By right and custom, she should prostrate herself before them but they had fought too long together to stand on such ceremony. In their eyes, she had long since earned her place as their equal.

"Bloody business," growled the shorter of the Kings, with a voice rough as grinding stones.

"Aye," agreed Asana. Only his eyes betrayed his true feelings, for they were as haunted as her own. "But it's done, Borugar. Thanks be for that at least."

"It's a watchtower, Eamon" was the other's retort, gnarled hands twisting around the haft of his mallet. If a boulder had been nearby, he'd have crushed it to powder then and there. "The least of our objectives. And d'you see the price we paid for it?"

Rafiel lifted his stag-horned helm from his head—always keeping his right hand free, in case his sword was needed—then pulled at the bindings that held his hair in place, allowing it to tumble in a mahogany waterfall. He arched his neck and gave his head a quick shake, settling his glorious mane as a lion would.

"I know the butcher's bill as well as thee, friend Borugar," said the Liege Lord of Greater Faery. "Didst think t'would be any different?"

"You did your best, Khory," Asana told her from horseback. Proximity to the dragon made the animal nervous, so Khory took the gelding by the bridle and stroked its muzzle gently. "It was a good plan."

"They're only good, my lord," she replied, "when they succeed. Borugar's right. The Malevoiy never fought this hard before."

"They've never faced defeat before." There was satisfaction in the High King's voice. This was a victory he'd richly celebrate.

"Knowing what that means," she said matter-of-factly, "they'll make us pay for it." Eamon's horse danced a moment as a shrill, ululating shriek broke the morning peace. There was a small hubbub off in the middle distance that snared the attention of Rhys and Taliesin. Khory ignored both cry and sight, she knew full well what it meant. The fairies were making sure the Alliance had one less Malevoiy to fight.

"Find me another way, warlord," the *ard-righ* told her sharply. "I'll gladly take it." He jerked the bridle from her grasp, wheeling his mount roughly clear of her.

She smelled the approaching dawn, cast about herself for some herald of the break of day, the smallest paling of the eastern sky, but Calan Dineer blocked her view, his monstrous great wings fully outstretched along the ground to cast a wall of shadow between her and the sunrise.

Elora burned with the passion of Khory's memories. She'd never ridden a wild bronco but she'd seen horsehandlers ply their trade enough to imagine how it felt. This was worse. She found no way for her soul to gain a safe and stable purchase as forces of tremendous power buffeted her every which way. She had to find an anchor for herself, and quickly, or her attempt to heal Khory would doom them both.

She smelled pitch-coated torches, and death. She counted a handful in head-high sconces along the wall but the light they cast was pitiful, barely able to illuminate the patch of wall from which each hung, much less anything beyond. She thought she was standing but didn't understand how solid land could possibly roll beneath her feet like a deep ocean swell. She thought she was going blind, because no matter how hard she rubbed her eyes her vision wouldn't clear. They felt coated in grit as well, as did her entire body, and she wondered if some demon or vengeful sprite had painted a coating of pumice beneath her skin.

In slow motion, she moved; in slow motion, she fell, so that it seemed to take an age to strike the ground. She landed in an ungainly sprawl, one kneecap bruising itself on unyielding stone while her face struck something far softer. She felt a sudden blotch of wetness on her cheek, tasted copper on her lips, and groped reflexively for the blades she carried in belt and boot. They came away empty, she was unarmed, and so she felt instead for the features of the body she'd stumbled on. A wail escaped her as fingertips found the touch of a familiar mustache, a crooked and broken nose, a scar riding outward from the crest of the left cheek.

For that instant, MageSight locked her eyes into focus, and she saw the face of her second lieutenant.

"Taliesin," Elora cried, and Thorn started at the anguish in her voice.

Khory's world wouldn't stop spinning, poisoned in body and spirit. Try as she might, Elora could find no firm purchase for the anchor of her will. This storm couldn't be escaped, couldn't be fought, couldn't be overcome. She could only run before it, with tight hold on her own wits, and pray for whatever skills or strength or sheer blessed fortune was required to survive.

Images bombarded her like volleys of thunderstones, each one alone capable of leveling a fortress wall.

Eamon Asana. Her voice was crying out to him, but he made no reply. The look in his eyes, though, struck her to the quick. It was more sorrow than any soul should have to bear. She challenged him to meet her eyes, but he could not. He left her to her fate.

A fortress. Foul stone under a foul sky. Spiked walls that loomed like small mountains, fit snugly into the crook of a sawtoothed range. There was only one approach, across a plain that was broad and deep and sodden with the residue of those who'd died here. She knew of vengeful monarchs who'd sown fields with salt to ensure that nothing would ever grow again. Here was one saturated with blood, that could bring forth only horror. Awful as this was, she knew it would be far worse within as the gibbering howls of Death Dogs arose from within the gate to herald her approach.

This was the seat of the Malevoiy power.

She thought she would face death here. She was wrong.

They thought they could break her to their will. They were wrong, too.

Sword in hand, she stumbled through the endless, crooked hallways, letting instinct guide her, for in this nightmare domain her physical senses were useless. Every aspect of the fortress was designed to drive intruders mad. She was their greatest enemy become their greatest prize, whom they hoped to turn into their greatest weapon.

Again and again, she lashed out with the obsidian blade she'd taken from the first Malevoiy she'd slain. Each life she took stripped from her one more layer of her humanity. It was a price she willingly, eagerly paid.

Images came in frantic quickstep, to match the pulsebeat of her racing heart, flash after flash, blazing bright enough to sear their image indelibly onto the canvas of her mind's eye, replaced one after the next before the scene could properly register. The sanctum tower. A room at the summit, with walls so thick that windows and doorways were more like endless tunnels, whose low ceiling warred with the expanse of the chamber itself, denying the space beyond its boundaries to make it seem as though the room were buried deep within the earth. Skylight in the ceiling, a ringed, many-pointed star carved from a crystal that admitted no light from outside but generated one of its own like nothing Khory had ever seen.

Guardsmen ringed the wall of the sanctum, more than enough to overwhelm her, but they gave her a wide berth. A copy of the skylight was etched on the shadowstone floor and at each point of the star stood a Malevoiy.

They were expecting her. They let her find this place because this was where they'd wanted her all along.

Welcome, she heard in their voice like nail scratchings on smooth slate.

Her sword point sagged, as she responded in kind to the courtesy of their greeting. With a snarl that provoked a chuckle of approval from her foes she jerked it back *en garde* and raked the warriors for someone to slay. They wisely kept their distance.

Embrace thy fate, warrior. Be One with Us.

These were creatures who'd hunted her race for sport since time immemorial, who'd made the world a slaughterhouse for all its people. She'd hated them since before she knew how to talk, and fought them any way she could for almost as long.

Yet their offer struck a chord in her, mouth curling into the beginnings of a smile at the temptation.

Shadow without, Shadow within, as *something* uncoiled from the pit of her soul, kin to what rippled and curled within the boundaries of the Malevoiy circle.

Defy Us not, warrior, for We have so much in common.

Hate begets hate, she realized too late, *as do cruelty and the lust for blood. Have I fought my enemy so long and hard only to become him?*

She found a crossroads in her mind, two doorways, and remembered the classic warrior's conundrum, the Damsel or the Death Dog. One path led to glory, the other to damnation.

She made her choice.

She was in Darkness. She was dying.

There was no peace to the last moments, she was in such agony she couldn't draw breath enough to give voice to her screams. She didn't understand how flesh could be so burned and broken and yet still cling so stubbornly to life. Her lungs continued to pump, her heart to beat, her mind to observe with preternatural acuity. She didn't know where she was, save that she lay splayed along a wall of stones and that it was far from where she'd been. There was age to the place that put the Malevoiy stronghold to shame, but though she was surrounded by such darkness that even her MageSight was useless she felt nothing of the taint that had surrounded her.

She was alone. She knew none would find her. She didn't mind. She'd struck her last, best blow, and her wolfish smile returned at the memory of Malevoiy screams.

Then, the darkness before her . . . moved.

It twisted and flowed, malleable as mercury, shot through with reefs of violet and deepest purple, colors that only served to emphasize the total absence of light. Looking at it made her ill but she couldn't turn her eyes away. It thrummed with curiosity and expectation, in the presence of something wholly outside its experience. It was a whole catalog of impossibilities and contradictions, every aspect of its being a fierce and heartfelt denial of the natural order of things. It could not possibly be, and yet it was.

And when Khory's feverish thoughts came to that juncture, a wail of bleakest despair escaped her lips.

It was a demon.

It had come to claim her.

She felt an echo then, so faint she first assumed it was imagination, a siren call from the Malevoiy. *Reach out to Us, little lostling,* she heard. *Thy time is not yet past, thou canst still be saved.*

To her surprise, she wasn't tempted. She managed a quirk at the corners of her mouth, the best excuse she could do for a smile, and felt eerily at peace. In song and story, demons were portrayed as fearsomely as the Malevoiy. Indeed, it was said they were the one creature the Malevoiy truly feared. She knew of mages who had truck with them, and seen the blasted, cindered ruins that resulted.

Damned by one hand, she thought, *damned by the other.*

"Better," she decided, trying to speak aloud, "the devil I don't know. I've had my fill of those I've met."

She felt a tingle of sensation at her fingertips as the darkness within darkness made contact. She felt afraid, but it wasn't a bad fear. Like riding into battle, it was an acknowledgment of the unknown, a faith in herself, an acceptance of what was to come.

She felt no more.

Stillness. Elora heard the bellows pant of her own breath, in measured cadence, felt a myriad of impressions—the thunder of her heart, the sizzling fire of blood flowing through her like the molten essence of the world, a line of coolness on each cheek where tears brimmed from her eyes. Her nose was running, too; she'd been crying quite a while.

The fire wasn't only within her. Khory was glowing as well, a pale reflection of Elora's own roseate luminescence. However, those fires were fading in both of them. Her work was done, the infection routed completely, the Deceiver's traps tripped and overcome.

There was a dull ache within Elora's breast, left over from her wanderings through Khory's past. She looked about the vault of her memory but found no sign of what she'd seen. She didn't really mind. The journey had been hard enough, she could wait a bit before reviewing what she'd found.

She offered the DemonChild a smile, received the same in return, and beheld in Khory's eyes a different quality than had been there before. Elora hadn't been alone in her journey; all that she saw and felt, her companion had as well. And, like Elora, been changed as a result.

She wanted to sleep forever. Instead, she felt a Nelwyn hand upon her shoulder, looked up and around to behold Thorn's worried face.

"I'm sorry," she said, "that all you could do was watch. It must have been so hard."

"Simple solution, silly girl. Don't do it again."

"No fear, old duffer. But it worked. We won. She's all right."

"Glad I am to hear it, Elora Danan," Drumheller said softly, with the utmost seriousness. "There's no more time. We've got to go. *Now!*"

CHAPTER
2

SHE COULD SEE THORN CLEARLY. BEYOND, AND ALL
around, was nothing, a darkness so absolute and impenetrable Elora couldn't help but shudder. A body length above
them floated the ball of radiance that he had conjured earlier,
still so blinding that only a momentary gaze in its direction
left spots before her eyes worse than staring straight at the
noonday sun. Its glare lit the three figures huddled close
together and that was all.

She could still feel solid ground beneath her but all her
eyes revealed was featureless ebony, without the slightest
boundary to demark the horizon or differentiate earth from
sky. The scene tugged at her memory, the way a fish might
nibble on a lure, trying to decide whether or not to take that
fatal bite. She hoped in vain, however, for nothing came of

that faint and evanescent tease. She looked to Drumheller, to voice her frustration, only to be checked by the look in his own eyes. The setting struck a chord with him as well.

"What," Elora prompted, but it was Khory who replied.

"The dungeon," she said.

Elora's mouth formed an O of comprehension. "Where you were imprisoned, Thorn? In Angwyn?" Unspoken was a question for Khory: *Where you were reborn, a demon's soul bonded to a Daikini body?* It was forbidden sorcery, the spell that had brought her into being, considered by many to be the blackest of arts, piled thick with prohibitions and punishments, that would result in summary execution for Thorn and Khory both if the truth were ever revealed. In the process, as he passed a portion of his human essence into Khory's body to remind it of the sensations of life, so was that offering replaced in turn by a similar fragment of the demon.

Supposedly, demons were as fundamentally and irredeemably evil as Thorn's Spell of Transposition was profane, yet Elora felt no sense of that from either him or Khory. In the same way, while the darkness surrounding them made her draw her body closer in upon itself, she recognized as well that it was only her imagination that was populating it with beasties. There was a hush to this corner of the world that made her wonder if this was how things were in the moment before the first sparkling flash of Creation.

"Yes," the Nelwyn Magus said, concern for their welfare overwhelmed momentarily by the sense of wonder and insatiable discovery that was at the core of his being. "In the oldest stories," he continued, "dragons are said to be the firstborn of Creation. Some say it was their flames which lit the first celestial fires. Demons are their bastard stepchildren, who refused to see the Universe settled into orderly patterns. They are shaped and defined by chaos; the more solidly a thing is built, whether spell or house or even a world entire, the more eager they are to smash it to bits, just for fun. Yet from that chaos always comes a rebirth, making them an essential part of the balance they seem hell-bent on destroying."

"That makes no sense."

He smiled broadly and almost permitted himself a chuckle.

"Now you know why sorcerers go prematurely gray and we're almost always cranky, trying to puzzle out the inherent contradictions in the shape of things." His grin faded a bit, his tone turned more serious. "This place, it's like Khory was before the spell. Alive, but not. Rich with potential but lacking the spark of animation that would bring it into being."

"A house," Elora said, "with nobody home."

"Something like that," he agreed.

"Are we overstaying our welcome?"

"Here? Never. This is the Realm of Dreams, Elora, in the Circle of the Spirit. Supposedly, the only way to visit as an outsider is *in* your dreams."

"Yet we've come to it in the waking, walking flesh."

He nodded. "That wouldn't have happened if it weren't meant to be."

"Does that apply to the Deceiver, Thorn? He beat us to it. He almost claimed the power here, the future of all the Great Realms"—and she patted her pouch for emphasis—"for himself. Even if the dragons were at the end of their lives, as Calan said, how could he have breached their defenses?"

"A reason, I fear, for us to make our way quickly home—to find out. And to forestall him from coming back to try again."

"Place isn't so important, mage," Khory noted with a minor outrush of breath as she levered herself to a sitting position, grimacing in mock pain as she rolled the muscles of her arms and shoulders to life. She pulled her legs up as well, crossing them at the ankles and leaning elbows on her knees. "Any more'n was I before you worked your magic."

"Darkness," Thorn said, his voice sounding a little lost and suddenly so lonely that Elora took immediate, reflexive hold of his nearer hand. "An eternal void, without shape or form." He shook himself, throwing off those thoughts as a dog would a coatful of water. "That's how the old texts describe things before the Realms."

"If all was nothingness," Elora asked, "who was there to take notes?"

"Thank you." The sorcerer sighed. "One more gray hair I didn't need."

"Makes you look distinguished."

"Wasn't someone saying," Khory interjected, "it was time to go?"

"If we're ready," Thorn said, with an assessing look at both companions.

"We'll have to go back pretty much the way we came," Elora said. "That means passing through the Malevoiy Realm."

"Can't be avoided. They're the point of contact between the Realms of the Flesh and Spirit."

"And they'll know what's happened here."

"Elora, child, every sorcerer worth the name, every creature and being in all the Realms with only a drop of magic in their soul, knows what's happened here, even if they can't find the way to put that knowledge into words."

"We'll deal with that when we have to. It's the Malevoiy who are right across our threshold. They'll want these eggs as much as the Deceiver, won't they, and for pretty much the same reason? Control the dragons, you control the shaping of the Age to come?"

"It makes sense."

"You don't *know*?"

"For sure?" He shrugged and shook his head. "No. Answer me something, child, will you? From your heart."

"Anything."

"Don't be so hasty."

"I trust you, Thorn."

"Hear me out first. These eggs, is it better to risk them falling into the wrong hands, or take the chance that they may be lost forever?"

Her mouth opened at once to give her answer, but her brain thankfully trod both feet upon her mental brakes, leaving her sitting a long moment with jaws agape until she slowly remembered to reel them shut.

"What do you mean, 'forever,' Drumheller?"

"Simple word, simple meaning. Strong as I am, any ward I cast can be broken, especially since the Deceiver seems uncomfortably familiar with our personal histories."

Elora shuddered visibly and again felt the quicksilver sensation of memories slithering through her grasp. Something had happened during her battle with the Deceiver, but there were too many shadows in her recollection; she'd been so caught up in her attempt to save the dragons, and then the act and aftermath of their destruction, that all the collateral events had been shoved aside into a jumble pile she had no desire to sort through.

"Strong as *you* are, Elora," Thorn continued, "you're still barely grown. Still learning about yourself, your abilities, and, more importantly, *liabilities*. And Khory, for all her skill as a warrior, has none in the arcane arts. We're all of us mortal. We can be hurt, we can be broken in ways too horrible to contemplate. We can be killed. Therein may be our salvation."

"Come again, mage?"

"When you were a baby, I cast a Spell of Protection about you, keyed to draw its strength from your own."

"I remember. It saved my life."

"What I propose is much the same. An interlocking lattice of guardian wards, to keep the eggs from being opened by any but we three."

"I thought you said any spell you cast could be broken."

"Good as I am, I stand alone. That means I have limits. But Khory is part-demon and you draw on reserves of energy and inspiration that encompass the whole of the Twelve Realms. Imbue the spell with a portion of the life force of we three together, and I'll wager not even the Deceiver can find a way to untangle that knot. Or," he added, recalling the legend of a King who'd faced the challenge of a puzzle that couldn't be solved, "hack his way through it. The three of us cast the spell, the three of us must release it. Of our own free will."

"Suppose, Drumheller," Khory asked, "there are but two?" *As in,* Elora thought, *what if one or more of us should die?*

"That's the risk. Our choice. Our responsibility. Is it better to risk the egg entrusted to your care falling into the wrong hands, or to lose it forever?"

Khory smiled but there was little humor in her expression. It reminded Elora of a predatory cat, facing a particularly intriguing hunt.

"It's one sure way," she said, "of ensuring our own survival."

Elora snorted. "Assuming everyone knows what we've done. Or doesn't have other plans." Then she turned back to Thorn. "But suppose *we* fall into the wrong hands."

"Can we be coerced into opening the wards, you mean?" She nodded, biting her lower lip as her imagination supplied the gory details of such a fate. "Yes, child, we can. Nowt to be done about that. If magic won't do that trick, there are devices and drugs aplenty to fill the bill. Except"—now it was his turn to smile and it was one she'd never seen from him before, as formidable in its own way as the DemonChild's, and she thought as dangerous— "my wards won't allow it. Of our free will, we enter into this compact. Of our free will, and *only* our free will, can it be broken."

"That's a lot of trust, Drumheller," Khory said quietly.

"Where better for such a gesture than this sacred ground?" he asked. "And who better to ask it of?"

Elora reached out to him with her right hand, aware that she was blinking rapidly in a vain attempt to forestall a torrent from her eyes, and when he took it she reached for Khory with her left. She was snuffling, and knew she must look positively wretched, but she didn't care. There was an ache in her chest, as though her heart had become a thunderstone of lead, but it wasn't a bad feeling. Her thoughts were a jumbling cascade of all the moments of her life that had led her to this moment. Mostly, they were of the injuries she'd done her friends, the slights given, the torments inflicted. Faces were etched in her mind's eye with blinding clarity, of those who had fought for her, sacrificed for her, died for her.

She was glad she couldn't speak. She was certain whatever she said would be wrong.

Who am *I,* she thought, *to deserve such companions?* And with that thought, an echo from the time she'd spent in Khory's memory, a sense of the same humility, coupled with a determination to prove herself worthy of so signal an honor, from the woman Khory once had been, as she viewed her company of warriors.

"I'm willing," she said simply.

Khory nodded assent. "As am I, Drumheller."

"So say we all," he finished, and as one the three of them

squeezed the hands they held. "To begin," he continued, "we'll need the eggs."

Elora reached into her traveling pouch. As always, thanks to the enchantments Thorn had woven into the fabric of the leather, what she required came immediately to hand.

"There's just the one," she said in confusion, thrusting her arm into the pouch all the way to her elbow.

"It looks different than before," Khory noted. "Bigger."

"Take hold of it, Elora," Thorn suggested. "Tell us what you feel."

Her eyes glazed over a moment as she did so, cradling it as gently as before. "I don't understand," she said, blinking to clear her gaze. "They're both here. Somehow, they've joined. How can that be?"

"Magic," Thorn replied with a grin.

"Of course. I should have known. Silly me for asking."

"Make fun if you wish. I'm still right."

"Do we banter, mage," Khory interjected practically, "or do we work? It's you who's been saying time's too precious to waste."

"Can you fit it in your lap, Elora?" She wriggled hips and bottom, to sit them a tad more comfortably on her heels, and found that her burden lay quite naturally in place.

"Lay your hands on it," he told her, and moved them slightly until he was satisfied with their placement.

He spoke then in the language of wizards, a tongue like no other. They had the form and shape of words, they could even be recorded on parchment, but only when uttered by those who wore the mantle of sorcery did they truly come into their own. It was like someone striking a great bell in the core of Elora's soul, that sent out resonant waves of energy to course through her in mingled streams of fire and ice. The sounds made were beyond human hearing, the images that came to her in a great, thundering rush were of granite blocks grinding into place, of raw iron hissing as it made its way from ladle to mold. Pops of sensation exploded throughout her awareness, each an impurity being stripped from the molten metal during the cooling process. A needle stabbed through her, gathering a glittering streamer of brightly colored fire that she recognized as the essence of her own life force. It arched before her, becoming more like an arrow, and she watched entranced as it descended to the egg to spin a cocoon of rainbows, flashing around and around the circumference of the egg before stabbing outward to her fingers. From there, the line bounced back and forth, creating a cat's-cradle latticework of breathtaking complexity with such speed that Elora found it nigh impossible to follow.

Despite the fact that the bindings covered every bit of the egg's surface, Elora found she could still see through to the shell, and the sight she beheld there was such a wonder that it made her gasp. The fiery colors left by the stream of energy were matched, and surpassed, by a similar display from within the egg. It was like watching a pair of lightning storms, one the complement to the other.

She was so bedazzled by the show that she barely registered Khory's hands covering hers. The other's palms were broader, her fingers not quite so long as Elora's; they snagged and tugged a small bit at Elora's skin from the calluses raised by a lifetime's work with the sword. Thorn's were the hands of a farmer, Khory's those of a warrior. Though Elora had done her share of physical labor, and fighting, her skin was still mainly that of a Princess.

The energy Thorn drew from Khory was of a wholly different texture and not so long ago the mere sight of it would have hurled the life from any decent soul and raised a shout of terror from Elora herself. The dominant color was a scarlet that echoed the color of Elora's gown, that of blood. It defined Khory's being as the land did Thorn's. But laced thickly through those streamers was another hue that defied description, and even sanity itself, whose very presence in a living being seemed an act of both rebellion and utmost violation. No human eye could look upon such a primal chaos without being driven instantly, irredeemably mad; even Elora had to grab tight to herself to keep from being desperately ill. If dragons were the stuff of dreams, then demons—unbelievably, their closest kin—were the font of nightmares. By rights, these two elements, a demon's soul bound to a human body, should have been anathema to each other, and the resulting conflict should have sealed her doom.

Thorn, however, made it work by leavening the mix with a measure of his own nature. He'd added to Khory's physicality a portion of his wizard's strength, the ability to overmaster even such creatures as demons, and in return taken unto himself a similar share of the DemonChild's being. Here, it was the fact that the DemonChild was hardly more than an infant that made success possible. A creature fully grown would have been too powerful, the patterns of its behavior too ingrained; the attempted spell would have proved instantly fatal.

Khory's string was composed of equal strands of demon and human, laced through with a portion of Thorn's soul to bind them together. In Thorn's case, the patterns of his life force were similarly colored by threads of purest demon.

At first, she thought he was simply laying each weave atop its predecessor but as she watched, all those myriad filaments appeared to take on independent life of their own. They wriggled and rolled before eyes that went wide with astonishment and then amazement and finally delight, entangling themselves in a weave of such marvelous complexity that Elora couldn't begin to pick it apart. The colors likewise merged, yet at the same time each remained distinct so that she found herself dazzled by two antagonistic perspectives that presented her with each distinct and individual element and also the conjoined whole. The fires leaped and danced within her grasp and she deliberately tensed the muscles of her arms to make sure her body was still awake, suddenly desperately afraid she might drop the egg and thereby ruin everything. Her heart was thundering, her skin felt ablaze, her body pushed to its limits, as though she was equally caught up in the madcap passions encircling the egg. She couldn't tear her eyes away but knew that Thorn and Khory were gripped by similar sensations. It stood to reason, she realized; since their life forces were empowering Thorn's binding spell, their bodies would pay the price. She wondered suddenly if the mage had underestimated the power required for the task. What price the safety of the dragon's egg if their own hearts burst in the process?

Light blazed, blinding her, and she cried out in startlement.

Then, without any warning, the flash from her lap was

answered by an infinitely greater explosion from all around them. One moment, they were in darkness as absolute as death itself, the next cast into the heart of a radiance so absolute and pure that it could not be endured. Elora thought wildly that this must be what it was like to be struck by lightning, actually to *become* lightning—her imagining confirmed a heartbeat later when the three of them were struck by as primal and all-encompassing a sound.

She called it thunder but that was like calling the core of the world *hot,* or the midday sun at high summer *bright.* It cracked like a whip yet was at the same time so sonorous that it shattered her to the core.

Once more, she found herself in darkness, and at first she gloried in the amazement of being able to "find" herself at all. That betokened awareness, which came from thought, which meant that she was alive. She did nothing for the longest while, content to remain snug within the darkness the way she used to huddle within a cocoon of quilts when she was a child. She heard a quiet finger-snap from her right, where she remembered Thorn was sitting, and his globe of radiance once more popped into being. He'd raised it a little higher than their heads, to illuminate their faces. There wasn't any more to see in the darkness that engulfed them and so he saw no need to make the globe excessively bright. They'd endured enough on that score already.

Elora dropped her head, to confirm by sight what her tactile senses had previously reported, that the egg still rested safe and sound in her lap. It looked quite unremarkable, without the slightest outward hint of the energies that now protected it.

Without a word, she slipped the egg back into her traveling pouch.

She offered no comment to the others about what had just happened, afraid that doing so would somehow diminish the moment.

A sudden, nervous demand for reassurance sent her hand back to the pouch, to feel for the egg and make certain it was all right. But what came to her grasp, and made her brows purse with surprise, was the lean, cylindrical shape of a sword hilt.

The blade she drew forth was slightly shorter than the broadswords she had seen, and possessed a shallow curve in the manner of weapons from the eastern isles, beyond Chengwei. Scabbard and hilt were both utterly plain, lacking in any ornamentation, because the blade itself needed nothing to enhance its terrible beauty. In the light of Thorn's globe, steel gleamed like chrome silver, and when Elora held the blade out from her body it seemed most like an extension of the natural curve of her arm.

"This is yours," she said, handing the scabbard over to Khory and then reversing her wrist so that the blade itself lay along the top of her arm, its hilt toward Khory, edge pointing away from Elora. She didn't require proof as to its sharpness, every instinct she possessed screamed to the young woman that the sword was the deadliest such weapon she had ever held.

Khory took the blade, nodded approvingly at its workmanship.

"Nelwyn forged," she noted. "But the alloy's more than metal. There's enchantment to this blade, the elves of Greater Faery had their hands in its making."

"The dragons heated the forge," Elora started to say and then corrected herself as that memory shifted into proper focus. "Calan Dineer heated the forge, with his own breath."

"And added a dollop of his own life's blood to the melt," Khory finished. "I can taste it."

"How?"

"He's dragon, I'm demon, we're kin. I'd know his kind anywhere, girl"—and suddenly she fixed Elora with a sharp and assessing gaze that made the younger woman squirm—"same as he'd know me and mine."

In a movement so swift and sure the blade left an afterimage in its wake as she spun it through the air, Khory snapped the tip of the sword to the top of the scabbard and shot the weapon home. Then, with both hands and surprising formality, she held the sword out to Elora.

"*Her* sword, Princess," she said. "I have one." She meant the straight blade that hung from her belt, an old campaigner's weapon taken from the body of an honorable foe betrayed to an untimely death the night Khory was born and the city of Angwyn ensorcelled.

"I can't take it," Elora protested.

"Whose hand found it? Nothing in that pouch comes to you by accident, girl. You walked a while in old Khory's boots, saw her world through her eyes, in this place where dreams can be made flesh. Now you find her blade. Happenstance? I think not." The warrior took a breath. "Some blades have souls, same as people. The how an' why of it, that's not for me to say. Can't say as I even care all that much. I know it for truth, though, as does Drumheller. I can use that blade, aye, as well as any. So can Drumheller."

He coughed. "Within my own limitations," he demurred.

"Too modest y'are by half, sorcerer," Khory chided him. "Get over it. We can use it," she repeated to Elora, "but it's meant for *you*."

Elora took the blade, but only because Khory didn't give her any other choice. She slipped the scabbard beneath her belt over her left hip, in the style of the eastern islanders, wholly unaware— as her companions were not—of how easily her body shifted to accommodate it, of how both hands came to rest, one ready to brace the scabbard and hold it steady while the other drew the sword itself.

"Now what," she asked, turning to Drumheller.

With no more warning than the hiss of steel as her blade was drawn, Khory swung for Elora's throat. Thorn's mind registered the attack but it happened so quickly his cry of outrage and warning perished stillborn as Elora met it with a parry of her own. Contact didn't come with the flat *tang* of steel on steel, this struck a purer note, as a chime on crystal, and flashed a spray of sparks that left the Nelwyn dazzled and blinking. Both women used the momentum of their blows to surge to their feet, managing to remain completely balanced as they rose, trading a couple more blows as they did. Khory had the advantage of height and strength; moreover, her straight blade was longer than Elora's curved weapon. If the girl had any edge at all, it was her quickness, but that was essentially crippled by the all-enfolding darkness surrounding them. She couldn't move beyond the painfully small circle of radiance cast by Thorn's glowglobe because she had no idea of where it was safe to place her feet.

Taking a risk that left Thorn gasping, Elora slapped her bare hand against the flat of Khory's blade to push it aside, while spinning herself into a swift pirouette along the length of the sword that brought her well within the circle of Khory's reach. The warrior might be able to punch her, but for this fateful moment she couldn't touch Elora with her sword. At the same time, Elora brought her own weapon around. It was only a one-handed strike, she needed the other to keep Khory's sword arm at bay, but the blade itself was so sharp even a whisper of contact would be sufficient to end the duel.

She'd forgotten, in the heat of the moment, that Khory had a pair of arms herself. Elora was caught by the wrist and as quickly disarmed by a casual twist she thought would dislocate her entire arm.

At long last, Thorn found his voice.

"Stop," he commanded, using that single word like a cudgel to get the attention of both combatants.

Elora's response was a glare of outraged defiance that dared Khory to do her worst. The DemonChild, by contrast, offered up the broadest of grins as she sheathed her sword and offered Elora's to her.

"What," Thorn cried in a rushing stammer that made plain how upset he was, "in the name of the Abyss was that all about?!"

"Won't be an easy journey home" was her taciturn reply. "Wanted to see if the student remembered her lessons. And," she concluded, "if the teacher's wounds were truly healed."

Elora was breathing too hard to make any comments, though her thoughts were enough to make old campaigners blush, her heart pounding so hard from fright and exertion that it gave her a small headache.

"With the dragons gone," Khory said plainly, "there's no more direct route from their Realm to the Waking World. We'll have to return the way we came, through the domain of the Malevoiy."

"You figure," Elora asked, "they'll be waiting?"

"Them, and others. You, they want, moonchild, they made that plain." And Elora shuddered at the memory of her encounter with the Malevoiy. "Me, my face"—Khory shrugged—"they'll likely remember."

"Not fondly," Elora said. Khory's comment was another shrug and then she turned her eyes to Thorn.

"You'll have to be ready to fight, too, Drumheller," she said.

"Whatever needs doing," he replied, "provided neither of you frightens me like that ever again."

"You didn't hold back, did you," Elora asked of Khory, "when you first attacked?"

"Where you're concerned, always."

"You always hold back?"

"You're alive."

"And you're too arrogant by half."

"You're the one who knows about arrogance, that's certes."

Elora bristled visibly. She didn't like being reminded of the girl she'd become before Thorn rescued her from Angwyn. Spoiled and mulish, without the slightest regard for anything or anyone around her, everyone's worst perception of a Princess, good for absolutely nothing. She'd started life with a band of stalwart friends to stand beside her and then, in a flash that turned her dreams to nightmares, lost them all. She found herself cast from one side of the world to the other, into a land of strangers who cared not a whit for the girl herself but whose goal was to use the Sacred Princess Elora Danan to advance their own political ends. The Deceiver displayed much the same ambition, to supplant her spirit and soul with his own and exercise her power himself.

Since the only people who ever had faith in Elora had been taken from her life when it had barely begun, it was small wonder she grew into an adolescent who had precious little faith in herself. Especially since she'd never been able to banish the nagging fear that somehow their deaths, the destruction of Tir Asleen, the Cataclysm that rocked all the Great Realms a decade before, were somehow her fault.

"Stop," Thorn said again, more quietly this time, yet somehow his words rang out with far more compelling force. "We're in this together now, as we've never been before; we just made that free choice. Stand or fall, win or lose, it's together, or not at all. We can't accept that, and the trust that comes with it, we're done before we start. Better off staying where we are and play the victim."

"Harsh judgment, Drumheller," Elora said.

"It's what the moment calls for, lass. Khory needed to take your measure, and her own, although"—and here he fixed his gaze on the warrior—"a tad more tact and possibly common sense would have been appreciated by all concerned."

"You've shown us the way we have to bend, mage," Khory told him. "Howzabout yourself?"

"Perhaps it comes of the realization I truly can't do this alone. Not escape this trap successfully, nor defeat the Deceiver. Staying where we are, we'll never know."

"How do we go, Thorn?" Elora asked. "*Where* do we go?"

"The Chengwei speak of journeys to the end of time as beginning with a single step." He rose to his feet, which placed his gaze on a level with his companions' waists. "Shall we take ours together and see what happens?"

"Bare steel?" suggested Khory, but the Nelwyn sorcerer shook his head.

"Not to start."

"You expect the Malevoiy to abide by any rules of hospitality?"

He grinned and for that instant a surprisingly carefree, almost wild, spirit flashed from his eyes.

"You've both demonstrated how quick you are on the draw. We'll let them make the first move."

He reached up toward the glowing globe of energy he'd cast, but Elora's hand intercepted his. She stepped right beneath the orb and opened her palms to it, caressing its surface as it descended in answer to her invitation much as she had the shell of the dragon's egg. She took a deep breath, streamers of radiance erupting from the globe to her nostrils, and it appeared as though she was inhaling its very substance. Once again, her silver skin gave off a soft glow, lit from within by the energies running rampant within her. There was a faint, contented smile on her lips, the kind of pleasure folk find in stroking cats. She exhaled through her mouth, a puff of scintillation that faintly echoed the fiery outrush of a dragon's breath, and released Thorn's globe.

It shone no more brightly than before, yet both of Elora's companions recognized the lasting endurance of its radiance.

"Leaving a candle in the window, are you," Thorn wondered aloud in a gentle voice, "to show us the way back?"

"Something like that," she replied. "But also to remind the darkness that it isn't alone."

"You think it's afraid?"

"More, lonely." Inspiration touched her, tardy companion to the impulse that compelled her to energize Thorn's globe, and she reached into her traveling pouch to draw forth a stuffed bear that had clearly seen better days. It had been repaired more than once, by a seamstress who hadn't always known what she was doing, but those tears and gashes were the least of its injuries. The bear had been scorched all the way up one side, as though by some terrible fire, and one of its crystal eyes was gone. It had never been a handsome creature, its strength—like its creator's—lay in its character. There was a solidity to its features, a sense that here was a trusted friend and boon companion. The eye that was left sparkled beneath the radiance of Thorn's globe and brought a proper smile to Elora's lips now as it had the first time she saw it, because it somehow made the animal seem alive to her.

"He's seen better days," Thorn marveled.

"I wouldn't know" was Elora's reply. "This is the best he's ever been for me."

"You were asleep when I brought him to you."

"Carried from your farm in Nelwyn Vale to Tir Asleen on the back of a dragon," she recalled aloud, but kept silent the other part of the tale he'd told her years ago, that the dragon in question had been Calan Dineer. "That must have been an adventure."

"I thought it was a dream."

"Sometimes I wish it had been. And that I'd wake snugabed and on my birthday. I remember screaming; I think that's when I broke my voice." Elora had what was called a whiskey voice, husky, almost a little hoarse, deeper and more resonant than you'd expect from a girl her age. "One moment," she continued, "I was in my bed, safe asleep; the next I was naked in the waryard of the King's Keep in Angwyn, with the whole world shaking around me. The bear was in my arms." She made a sudden, wryly humorous quirk of the lips, quickly there, as quickly gone. "No one could pry him loose. Not without breaking my arms and fingers. He was my protector."

"As I charged him to be." In memory, Thorn recalled how he'd held the gift before him and looked square into its crystal eyes, talking to it as he would a stalwart comrade in arms. His words then were *"All that I would be, were I here, let him represent."*

To his surprise, he heard Elora repeat them now.

"All that I would be, were I here," she told the bear, as Thorn himself had a decade and a half before, "let you represent. Keep this place safe, as you did me, till I return. Or in my stead, the rightful inheritors."

And as one of Thorn's brownie companions had said to him then, so did he now to Elora. "Do you know what you're doing, child?"

"I'm caretaker of the dragon's egg, Thorn."

"Then shouldn't the bear stay with it?"

"What is hope but the essence of a dream? Khory's called me the Hope of the World, that's how my name translates in the old Dracic tongues, the language of the dragons. I feel like this is my home, as much as the physical world of the Daikini. I can't leave it empty. I'm taking away its heart and soul for safekeeping, it seems only fair and fitting and right for me to leave a bit of my own behind. Isn't that why you left the bear with me, back in Tir Asleen? To stand surrogate because you couldn't be with me in person."

"I should have."

"Most likely then you'd have died, along with Sorsha and Madmartigan and all the rest, and maybe me as well in the bargain."

"Time to go then?" Khory asked.

Thorn nodded and Elora started to. Then, on a final impulse, she pulled her scabbarded sword from her belt and thrust it into her traveling pouch.

"Elora," Thorn protested, "you'll need that weapon!"

"*A* weapon, yes," she agreed, and the reverse of her gesture brought forth a length of polished wood that was longer than she stood tall, "but not that one. The time isn't right."

"You know how to use that?"

Elora flashed an evil grin to Khory, who chuckled in response.

"Your Sacred Princess, mage," she said, "she's chock-*full* of surprises."

Together, forming a rough triangle with Khory in the lead, Elora flanking her behind and to her left to cover her blind side, while Thorn brought up the rear a little off to Khory's right, they stepped from the light . . .

. . . and the darkness that surrounded them abruptly vanished, as if it had never been.

They found themselves atop a jumbled mound of rocks, as though someone had taken the whole of the Stairs to Heaven, the greatest mountain range on the world of the Daikini, and smashed it with a sledgehammer, leaving only the detritus you'd find at the bottom of a quarry, the cast-off bits of stone that were of no use to anyone.

The vista should have been breathtaking, for they stood as high as the summit of many of the peaks they knew. In the Dragon's Realm, form was minimal, but substance piercing. Every sense was heightened to a fever pitch, bombarding the consciousness with more information than it could process, so that the body was engaged in a constant struggle to keep from being overwhelmed by this magnificent delirium. Adding to those sensations was an even more glorious passion, a fierce hunger more keen than any infant's for life in all its wondrous variety.

The Realm of the Malevoiy, by contrast, was nothing *but* form. In surface impressions, it very much resembled the Daikini world Elora had known her whole life, although the overall landscape was far more barren. What struck her most, however, was the lack of substance, the sense that all the physical aspects of this realm had forgotten their purpose, in the way that people of a certain age tend to misplace the details of their lives. There was a great and fundamental weariness to this domain, as if the very act of physical existence was growing to be more trouble than it was worth. And from that descended a primal desolation because the elements that drove this Realm at its zenith were blood and cruelty and an insatiable hunger for violence. Glory here was found in savagery and destruction—not the mad chaos of the demons but something far more wicked. Conquest was the order of the day, whether it be a single soul or an empire. It was a place, and a people, utterly without mercy.

Now, there were no more fields of conquest. The Malevoiy had seen and done too much, and they'd become bored. Their land simply took its cue from them.

Illumination of a sort came from a ghostly radiance that most resembled dusk, where objects were defined as much by shadow as light. By that same process, everything was leached of color; even the dramatic hues of Elora's gown registered to her eyes merely as gradations of gray-washed carmine. As for her argent skin, Elora thought that if she stripped herself naked and leaned against any wall of stone, she would disappear, her flesh indistinguishable from the landscape around her. She wondered then if that "disappearance" applied to more than the purely physical. This was a place where a person could easily lose herself, and while the predators who ruled here might claim to be as old as time itself, she felt certain they had not forgotten how to hunt. Or the heady taste of a prey they'd successfully run to ground.

"You've been here before," Thorn said, the timbre of his voice, its lack of resonance, reminding her that sound traveled as weakly through this ancient atmosphere as light. "Which way?"

She angled her chin toward a circular stand of ruins in the middle distance, just beyond the base of the broad, shallow slope that stretched down and away from the summit where they stood.

"So far? Take us an age to reach there."

"Distances deceive in this place," she told him. "It won't be quite so long."

"You don't much like this Realm."

I will die here, she thought suddenly. *I will kill here. It will be good.* She gave her head a quick and violent shake, to banish the cruel and brutal images of fangs and blood and laughter, then ran her tongue across her teeth, upper and lower jaw both, to make sure they were still flat. When she was there last, en route to the Dragon's Realm, the Malevoiy had made plain that they wanted her for their own. What she hadn't expected, what truly terrified her, now as then, was that she found herself tempted by their offer.

The best way to travel was over the fallen rocks; they could spend a score of lifetimes in a vain attempt to navigate a passage on the ground through the cracks and hollows between. That meant the occasional scramble up or down a vertical face, or a heart-tugging leap from one boulder to the next; more than once, Elora and Khory were forced to improvise a means to carry Thorn with them, for this blasted landscape was far more suited for Daikini limbs than Nelwyns'.

"No welcoming committee," Thorn noted, when they paused for a rest.

"Be thankful for small favors."

"What are they like, the Malevoiy?"

"Creatures of dust," she said quickly, "for a Realm crumbling about them. Less than ghosts, Drumheller." *Yet,* she thought, *they remain the sum and substance of our every nightmare. And rightly so.*

" 'Twelve rings affixed on three,' " she continued, mainly to herself, remembering the words spoken to her by the Malevoiy, " 'to be bound entire by one, that is the scheme and riddle of things.' "

"Twelve Great Realms," Thorn said, making the connection. "Making up the three Greater Circles of Being—the World, the Flesh, the Spirit—anchored and bound by the Thirteenth Realm—you," he finished.

" 'How can the pieces hold fast,' the Malevoiy asked me, Thorn, 'without a center to anchor them?' "

"That's the challenge."

"They'd have me walk their road to accomplish it, in fire and blood, to make the world their private boneyard once more."

"You ask me, child, you're proving remarkably adept at finding your own path, in defiance of logic, advice, entreaty"—he paused a beat for emphasis—"or compulsion."

A skibble of grit along the surface of the huge slab on which they sat heralded the return of Khory from a scout ahead. Both Thorn and Elora were a trifle startled to see her, since neither had noticed her departure. She came to them in a fast crab-crawl, as low to the ground as she could manage and still remain on her feet. She held her body angled a little away from them, the better to keep sight of the ground behind her.

Neither Thorn nor Elora had to ask if there was trouble; Khory's manner made that plain as midday.

"Ambush" was what she told them as she slid herself flat by their side.

"Whereaway?" Thorn asked of her.

"Fair-sized cadre, Maizan Black Rose, close about the World Gate." This was not good. The Black Rose were the most formidable arm of one of the most formidable fighting forces the world had ever seen, infiltrators and commandos, whose specialties were assassination and terror and whose martial skills beggared description. Their courage needed no further hallmark than the fact that they were there, and neither did their ability—both for the trackers who followed their trail and for the sorcerers who obtained them entry to this Realm. Their loyalty was absolute, to Castellan Mohdri, who led the Maizan. And that meant to the Deceiver, who wore Mohdri's flesh like a tailor-made suit.

"Layered deployment," Khory finished, "staggered too thick for us to sneak past or fight our way through."

"The Malevoiy allow this?" Even as she spoke the words, Elora found them hard to believe.

"The Black Rose are here, girl, it must be so," Khory replied.

"I guess we didn't hurt the Deceiver as badly as we'd hoped," Elora said, "when we drove him from the Dragon's Realm."

"A prudent commander always has a backup."

"Since that World Gate's closed to us, Elora," Drumheller asked, "can you sense another? Hopefully, close by?"

Elora pursed her lips, furrowed her brow. The air was flat and still, not even their hardest breaths were able to stir it. She found herself licking her lips often, in a futile attempt to detect the slightest hint of taste, thankful for the least residue on her own skin.

In any other Realm, she'd be able to spot the natural lines of arcane energy as easily as a good scout does a trail. Here, she felt like she was sleepwalking.

"That way?" she hazarded, though she wasn't really sure.

Khory didn't care, she took Elora's words as gospel.

"Then we go," she said, and hustled both companions to their feet.

"Why the rush?" Thorn asked.

"Too big a cadre for simply an ambush," Khory told them. "Even for us," she added, forestalling a smart comment from Elora. "They've numbers enough to cover the Gate and send out rovers to keep us from trying another."

Without asking permission, the tall woman scooped Thorn off his feet and onto her back, wrapping his arms around her shoulders, his legs her waist. Elora had grown so much the past couple of years, she was giving Khory serious competition in the height department, yet she found herself hard-pressed to keep up with the warrior's furious pace. There was no hesitation to Khory's moves—she scrambled over every obstacle with the uncanny agility of a mountain goat. When she didn't think of what she was doing, when she let her body define its own rhythm, Elora was equally surefooted. But her trust in herself wasn't quite as absolute as her companion's; every so often, she couldn't help but think about what she was doing. That was when she made mistakes. A slip of the sole, a stumble, a stubbed toe, some shredded nails and barked skin. Each slowed their pace, each proved a delay they could ill afford.

They came to a fair-sized gap, too deep and sheer a drop for climbing, bridged by a line of disturbingly dainty pillars. Without a word being spoken, Elora knew what was coming. The problem was, the tops of the pillars themselves barely presented sufficient room to stand. If a successful crossing was to be made, they'd have to hop from one to the next in a single, continuous sequence and hope that enough momentum was generated by a running start to carry each of them all the way to the far side. They couldn't go together, either, one would have to lead the way.

"Who goes first?" she asked.

"Depends on where the Maizan are," Khory replied, searching the scree for any sign. "Behind us, it's you. Ahead, me."

"Flip a coin? Hope for the best?"

"Can you do this, Elora?" Thorn asked in total seriousness.

"Is there an alternative?"

"Khory can carry you."

"What about you?"

"Two trips," Khory said.

"Bollocks."

"Sometimes, child," Thorn said with a parental sigh, "you talk like a stevedore."

"Sometimes, Drumheller, you deserve it. I can make the crossing."

He looked at Khory for confirmation. Elora wanted to slap him, her cheeks burning with outrage at how automatically he dismissed her opinion. Khory gave him the barest of nods, while her eyes offered Elora an apology.

Elora gathered up her skirt, fastening it fore and aft to her belt to make a rough pair of leggings. They didn't bind her stride in the slightest—she had full freedom of movement. She looked around for any sign of pursuit, or manifestation of the Malevoiy, and was disturbed to find neither. She tried to gulp some big breaths of air to supercharge her lungs but found it wasn't worth the effort. She couldn't sweat here; her heart was pounding, her body beneath the skin was hot with exertion, yet all the mechanisms for cooling had apparently broken down. This Realm simply would not tolerate extremes of any kind.

At some point, if they remained and continued at this pace, she knew she'd collapse. She wondered what would happen then . . .

. . . and spun around full circle where she stood at the faint sound of chittering laughter. Save for her two companions, she appeared to be alone.

"So," she said under her breath as she readied herself to make her charge, "you *are* here."

We are Malevoiy.

"So you said when we met."

Thou art the Danan.

"Likewise."

Hast thou come to claim thy destiny? To embrace Us?

"Who says the two go hand in hand?"

There was the driest of chuckles, like the crackling of dry tumbleweed.

The Danan must bind *all,* or she binds none.

"There must be a balance," she hissed, repeating what she'd been told her last visit. "It must be restored."

Thou art the key.

With a cry that wove together rage and defiance—and provoked a stronger laugh from the Malevoiy that was itself laced through with approval, they liked this feral aspect of her—Elora threw herself forward, honing her focus totally to the length and force of her stride as she rushed toward the precipice. There was no turning back, she'd have no second chance and she gloried in the all-or-nothing danger of that moment. She bared her teeth in a snarl and uttered a cry that would have rocked the foundations of the world if the air had the body to carry it, as her trailing foot thrust her over the edge.

Five great leaps, like a sequence of giant steps planted square in the center of each pillar, and she was across.

Thing was, she'd built up so much momentum that she found it impossible to come to a graceful stop. She'd pushed herself too hard at the end and had almost sailed right over the final pillar, managing to catch just enough of a purchase with the ball and toes of her foot to kick herself across the final stretch. Her leading foot struck awkwardly and she came down too hard on her heel, with a sharp thud that jarred her all the way up her leg and made her teeth *clack* together. A surface layer of stone powdered from the landing, so that her leg shot away to the side. There was no time to think, only the barest matter of instants to try to break her fall so she wouldn't break any bones. Reflexes twisted her body with the manic, boneless agility of a cat and a rude grin of triumph split her face as she came down hard but safely.

Elora's elation was short-lived however as something tight wrapped itself around both ankles and her legs were yanked hard out from under her. Elora managed to break this fall with her arms, so her breath wasn't wholly knocked out of her, but she hissed from the scrape of rock on flesh, as though her skin were being raked by coarse sandpaper. It made her regret not taking the time to change out of her dancing costume.

Her first thought was that the Malevoiy had decided to intervene directly, but she knew instinctively that wasn't so. This wasn't their style. What they had in store for her was seduction more than outright conquest; they wanted her to join with them of her own free will.

Her first act was to try to scissor her legs loose of their bindings, only to find her legs wrapped tight to the knees. She sensed rather than saw another tether arcing toward her and levered herself to the side, pivoting over her bottom like an infant and moving away in a three-point hobble on hands and knees that took her quickly to where she'd dropped her staff. Her outstretched hand caught it by the end just as a Black Rose assassin leaped from his hiding place and lunged for her, evidently figuring that his hands would suffice instead of the tether she'd managed to dodge. Elora scythed the staff toward his shins and he made no attempt to hide his contempt for her as he leaped over her attack. The expression froze on his face as she shifted her grip on the staff far faster than he could follow and hammered it forward straight to the pit of his stomach. His torso was armored, which meant she didn't do him any real damage, but she had worn the same armor—adapted from garments she'd taken off one of their fellows—and was well aware of its strengths and weaknesses. The protection it granted the wearer was balanced by the need for flexibility. So, while she didn't drive the air from his lungs, as she would have against an unprotected foe, the man's own momentum doubled him over the staff, as though he'd run headlong into a post. For a couple of seconds, he was vulnerable. It was all the time Elora needed.

She brought the staff around like a bat, with the full strength of her shoulders behind the blow, to crack it across the length of his skull. He dropped like a poleaxed steer.

Sadly for Elora, he hadn't come alone.

Neither had she.

A second tether caught the far end of her staff and yanked it from her grasp, hard enough to make her wrists ache. Unfortunately, the Black Rose had no chance to capitalize on his advantage, as one of Khory's knives caught him full in the chest with the force of a cudgel, to drop him where he stood.

Khory's legs were longer than Elora's, which had made her

crossing a tad less helter-skelter. Seeing what was happening, she was able to pick up speed as she went, so that she reached Elora's side in a full-throated charge. As she made that final leap, Thorn swung himself free of her, hitting the rock in a hedgehog roll that brought him quickly to where Elora lay. With both hands free, Khory drew her sword and swung for the body of the nearest Maizan. The armor they wore was cured leather sandwiched over a layer of finest-quality chain mail, which made it proof against most attacks. Khory possessed more than human strength and a blade to match. She opened her foe down the whole of his chest and moved on to the next before his lifeblood had begun to spray from his gutted heart.

Thorn was busy with a blade of his own as he hacked at Elora's bindings, which imprisoned her now to the hips very much like a mummy's wrappings.

"Be careful," she cried. "They're using tanglefoot! If it catches hold of you—!"

"I know the risk," he barked at her and then uttered as rich an epithet as ever she'd heard from him as the best of efforts yielded only the most minimal results.

"What's wrong?"

"This damnable place" was his reply, as he cast a quick glance all about to check on the opposition. Khory's assault had drawn the bulk of the Maizan's attention but their breathing space wouldn't last for long. "My blade's coated with an enchantment to counteract the properties of a tanglefoot line but some aspect of the Malevoiy Realm mutes its effectiveness."

"They're not fond of extremes," she told him, "except their own."

"They ought to love Khory, then," he said with an appropriate dollop of acid to his tone. It was strange to behold a fierce clash of arms no more than a half-dozen body lengths away yet hear only a muted sound of steel on steel, the grunts and bellows of the combatants, the piercing cries of the fallen, as though the battle were actually occurring far in the distance.

"You don't know the half of it," Elora said, while thinking, *and be grateful for that.* "How many are they?"

"Hard to tell, Khory's moving too fast, I'm finding it difficult to focus."

"The Realm, you think, affecting our MageSight?"

"Anything's possible."

Suddenly, he cried out, pitching himself away from Elora as though he'd just thrust a hand into blazing tar. In his growing fury to see her released, he'd come into direct contact with the tanglefoot line and now the end of the filament he'd severed had wrapped itself around his wrist, beginning to climb his forearm.

Now it was Elora's turn to react solely from instinct, just as she had when she'd landed. She lashed out with both hands to grasp the tanglefoot on Thorn as she might some deadly serpent, ignoring his shout of warning and the free hand he used to try to bat her away for fear she'd only imprison herself all the more. That was the nature of tanglefoot; like wisteria, it loved to cocoon everything it came into contact with. With anyone else this ploy would have spelled immediate and total disaster, but the properties of the tanglefoot derived from magic, and magic didn't work terribly well in the Malevoiy Realm. Moreover, and far more importantly, Elora herself was imbued with a total immunity to spells and enchantments. They could affect her, but only temporarily.

That was what she was counting on. If she was wrong, she figured, she'd be no worse off than before.

She caught the leading end of the filament wrapping Thorn's arm, just as it tried to make the jump to his chest to bind limb to body, and called on the Nelwyn to cut the line free. Thorn did as he was told and both of them were rewarded by the sight of the severed vine shriveling to dust in their grasp. Even as she looked back to her own legs, Elora could see that the tanglefoot looked far more brittle down around her ankles, where it made its initial contact, than her thighs. Thorn's mistake was in cutting the wrong end.

Thorn's shout of warning came at the same instant as her own inner flash of alarm. Elora swept up her staff above her head just in time to block a sword swipe aimed at her companion. It was no mean attack, the impact nearly jarred both arms from their sockets, but her parry gave Thorn the opportunity to pitch a length of tanglefoot back at their Black Rose assailant. In a trice, the man was off his feet, one arm stretched across his body and bound to the opposite shoulder, a leg twisted up beneath him.

Then came Elora's mistake, in thinking this Black Rose was out of the fight. Freed of the last of her own bonds she rolled lithely to her feet, intent on joining Khory. Thorn was trying to catch sight of the World Gate and as well any Maizan reinforcements. Elora wasn't sure if she caught a movement out of the corner of her true eye, or perhaps some instinctive equivalent that Khory and Thorn's tutelage had implanted in the back of her head flashed a warning. Whichever, she spun around in time to catch a blur of motion from the fallen Maizan's free arm aimed toward Thorn.

With her, at that moment, thought and execution were one. Her staff formed a blur of its own as she spun it in her grasp, and set a faint whistle in the tired air as she used it first to bat aside the nearest of the steel spikes he'd thrown and then to complete the move by cracking the end of the staff upside his head hard enough to knock him out. At the same time, she stepped sideways to put herself between the Maizan and his intended target, adding a hipcheck to Thorn's shoulder to knock him clear of danger. There was no time, less chance, to count the number of spikes; she knew she'd caught a pair with her staff, one deflected, the other stuck in place. She felt a third *whizz* by her ear and registered a tickle of severed hair from its passing.

Then, quite without warning, all the strength went out of her legs and Elora dropped to her knees, with no more integrity than a castaway puppet. She couldn't understand why she found it so impossible to move and thought for the first few moments that she'd been caught by another tanglefoot or some such snare. But that didn't explain why it was suddenly just as difficult to breathe until she found Thorn's dumbstruck look of horror and followed his gaze down her torso to find bare skin streaking as red as her dancing costume. There was a burning sensation along her right ribs and the suede of her bandeau top had been slashed almost all the way in two. It was a nasty cut, and messy; it was the source of most of the blood she saw but wasn't the wound that did the damage.

The last spike had stabbed her right beneath the curve of her rib cage, angling up and in to strike deep into a lung. That was why she couldn't breathe and her mouth was filling with a bloody froth. All at once, Elora felt like she'd been plunged into an ice bath and a pit of fire; half of her was going numb while the rest was being stuck through with white-hot pokers.

Her vision blurred, Thorn's face flowing like wax into the features of the Maizan, and Elora saw such a look of desolation and stark terror that her heart couldn't help but go out to the man, even though she knew he was her enemy. In his zeal to serve his lord and master, whom he knew as the Maizan's own Castellan Mohdri, he'd struck down the object of his lord's desire. Mohdri—the Deceiver—wouldn't take kindly to such a mistake, and Elora knew the assassin's fate was as sealed as her own.

Time for her ticked ever more slowly, yet around Elora the action hurtled past at a headlong rate. A trio of Maizan moved in her direction, attempting to take advantage of the situation. Thorn scooped up Elora's staff and, wielding it more effectively than Elora, drove them back, striking with pinpoint precision at ankles and knees, elbows and the knob of the jaw, knuckles and toes, all those hard-to-reach, hard-to-protect places of the human body where hits are more likely to annoy than outright disable. For Thorn, that was sufficient. His goal was to keep them occupied. Khory's was to finish them.

The warrior's sword was plain steel, albeit as finely forged and honed and cared for as metal could be, yet in her hands it left a trail of light in its wake, an afterimage of fire as though it were managing to set even the ancient, weary air of the Malevoiy Realm ablaze.

It's not flame, Elora realized, chiding herself for being so slow and wondering why finding it hard to breathe should make it equally hard to think as well. *That's blood. Maizan blood.*

The Black Rose were feared from one end of the continent to the other. They had no peer, so the stories went, in the arts of skullduggery and those of mortal combat. They possessed as many ways to prick a body as their namesake blossom had thorns, and each was reputedly fatal.

Khory was outnumbered a dozen or more to one, yet the battle was no contest.

We taste thy life, Danan.

The voice was withered, ancient and desiccated, one small step removed from powder. It spoke in so dry and distant a tone, anyone hearing would have thought the Malevoiy was discussing nothing of consequence. Elora knew better, because she was listening, not simply to the words, but the emotions behind them. There was an all-consuming hunger, a great and terrible desire, the like of which could never be comprehended by any mortal creature from either side of the Veil. She felt such passion that she knew the slightest expression of it would crumble this entire Realm to nothingness.

Enjoy it while it lasts, she thought and felt a tickle of amusement from the Malevoiy.

We would savor it a while . . . longer. This is not the time, not the place, for thy life to meet its end.

How kind of you to care.

We know naught of kindness, Danan. Thy survival is Ours.

What do you want of me?

No more, no less, than all the world. In return, We offer Our strength.

I can manage on my own.

There was a silence, she couldn't tell for how long; there seemed to be no connection between the presentation of events within her head and what occurred outside. Time held different meanings, almost as if she existed in two distinctly separate worlds with no way for her to cross between. She wondered if the Malevoiy had abandoned her and was torn by warring emotions in response, as relieved at their departure as she felt devastated.

That was the cue they'd been waiting for, the chink she'd opened in her own inner armor.

Thou art the Danan.

So you keep saying.

The Thirteenth Realm, that Binds all the others.

A chill laced its way through her, that had nothing to do with her physical wound.

That binds *all* the others.

Including you.

Without Us, there is no fulfillment of prophecy. Without Us, there can be no salvation.

She was conscious of her breath tearing at her in a succession of quick, panicky gasps, as desperate for air as a baby for milk. There wasn't a lot of obvious pain but she had this overwhelming urge to cry, in a way she'd never allowed herself to when she was growing up in Angwyn. In those days, tears for her were a weapon, a means to garner attention and gain her own way. The aching misery of loss, the gnawing sense of abandonment and aloneness, she tucked deep away, a twisted version of some potentate's private treasure trove.

There was fear in her now, and it held a resonance of those awful days. Back then, it made her a brat. Here it drove her surging and yowling to her feet, with an animal cry of blind rage that was answered by one of alarm from Thorn.

In her imagination, she saw herself fly forward, unhindered by her wounds to join her friends in battle. Reality turned out to be simpler, yet more complicated. She lasted upright for all of a couple of steps before stumble-staggering into Khory's grasp.

"I can do this," she tried to protest aloud.

"Never doubted it," Khory agreed, while scooping Elora into her arms.

"Put me down," Elora told her. "You can't fight carrying me."

"Fight's done," Khory said. "We tarry; so are you. Which way?" The last was directed at Thorn, but it was Elora who answered.

"To the left," she said, marveling at how she could be curled up against Khory's breast yet feel as though her skin encompassed the whole of the Realm around them. She could feel the weight of her own body and those of her companions, like a knot of weary muscle beneath her shoulder. Farther up, past her nose, a succession of staccato footfalls made their hurried way over her face, identifying themselves to Elora as the remaining Black Rose, in hot pursuit. The assassins came armed with sorcery as well as steel and their progress left a trail of spikes along the orbit of her eye. Elora's inner world tilted, the way a skiff rocks in a heavy swell, and her stomach lurched with nausea, forcing her to fight the urge to be sick all over Khory. The Black Rose were a danger only if they caught up to them; otherwise, they were merely a distraction.

Down her flank, across from where blood still flowed freely from her flesh wound, she recognized the distinctive burr of power that signaled the nexus of a World Gate.

Too bad, she thought and wanted to giggle, *I can't tell Khory and Thorn to rush over to my left hip, that's the way home.*

"To the left," she said again, hoping she was mouthing comprehensible words because her attempt to point the way resulted in a directionless flail of her arm.

"Along the ridgeline?" Thorn asked, and she grunted a thankful assent.

There was no dignity to their flight—this was a headlong race for their lives. Khory didn't bother asking permission; she hooked Thorn by the collar and dumped the Nelwyn unceremoniously atop Elora, ignoring both his protest and her moan as he scraped her slashed side and twisted his body into an awkward hump to avoid contact with her chest wound. He tightened one hand around a strap of Khory's own harness and the other about Elora's belt. The look in his eyes made plain that he would release neither hold until they were safe.

The Black Rose knew their destination but such was Khory's speed that only a couple of them were able to reach the Gate before her. Without breaking stride, she plucked Thorn from his perch and slung him full in one assassin's face. The Nelwyn was as much surprised by her ploy as the Maizan but Thorn was far quicker on the uptake, boxing the man's ears, then eyes, as soon as he landed on him. As Khory rushed past, she unlimbered Elora's staff, using it with a skill that eclipsed the girl's to trip Thorn's target and bring him down.

The second warrior had only a heartbeat or three's time to prepare for Khory's onslaught but it proved sufficient time to prepare a counter. She'd covered better than half the distance between them when he unlimbered a mace on an extended chain, a spiked ball roughly the size of a large Daikini's fist at the end of a set of links anchored to a haft of ironwood and metal. The ball was too light to damage anyone wearing proper armor, that wasn't its purpose. Instead, weight had been sacrificed in favor of mobility, the advantage of which could readily be seen by the way the Maizan whipped the chain in a vicious circle about his head. He held the haft in both hands and put the full strength of his powerful shoulders into the spin, producing such velocity that the ball would have screamed through the healthy air of home; here it produced a faintly keening moan that seemed to Elora, held fast in Khory's arms, like the wail of a lost soul. There were barbs as well, set at random intervals along the chain. The intent of the weapon wasn't to bonk its targets on the noggin, but to wrap the chain about them. A hearty tug by the Maizan would drive the barbs into clothes or flesh, making it near impossible to escape.

The Maizan was a master of his weapon, striking with such speed and accuracy that Khory was forced to backpedal frantically to keep from being struck. Even so, she had to use Elora's staff to parry the mace as the Maizan suddenly snapped it toward her head like a whip. Her intent was to use the staff to deflect the attack off to the side but a twist of her foe's wrists and a snap of the chain, again more like a whip than linked metal, did the reverse and disarmed her, raising a nasty bruise on her cheek where the butt of the staff connected in passing.

Khory feinted and withdrew, again and again, trying to find just the smallest opening for an attack, but the Maizan refused to rise to her challenge. He would move as she did, but only enough to make sure she kept a fair distance from the Gate. Try as she might, she was unable to pull him from his defensive position and both knew that the longer this took, the closer came his companions. Elora sensed rather than saw Thorn's approach from behind them; it was confirmed by faint shifts in the Maizan's stance and the focus of his gaze. It was also clear to her that the assassin didn't consider Thorn a significant threat. He was probably armored as well against spells as against material weapons; also to his advantage was the fact that Thorn's enchantments probably wouldn't be terribly effective in this deadened Realm anyway. In this kind of encounter, sadly, the Nelwyn's stature was a definite liability.

So, too, was Elora's wound.

The Maizan reeked of confidence. To him, the battle was all but won.

Elora guessed what Khory had in mind to try next. It didn't take a genius and she was fairly sure the Maizan had reached the same conclusion. During her next charge, Khory wouldn't back off. Instead, she'd take the Maizan's best shot, gambling on her own skill and strength to enable her to survive long enough to finish him.

It was an all-or-nothing ploy, but circumstances allowed them no viable alternative. Or so everyone thought.

Khory began her advance and the Maizan sidestepped to meet her. He actually grinned with anticipation as he hurled his mace.

At that moment, Elora wrenched herself loose of Khory's grasp, surprising both of them with the strength left in her as she used the sleetstorm of pain exploding from her abdomen as a goad to drive her forward. Khory was her fulcrum, and Elora's sudden, unexpected motion threw her off stride, forcing her to concentrate on staying on her feet, even as she made a frantic, failed grasp at the younger woman.

At the same time, Elora took the mace full on the shoulder. It was a costly stratagem, because she wasn't wearing any armor at all. She felt the bite of the spikes as they scored her flesh, knew there was worse to come, didn't really care as her outstretched arms wrapped themselves about the following chain. The weight of her body did the rest as she tumbled to the ground, that and the sick realization from the Maizan that he, like his comrade earlier, had just wounded the very object of their mission.

Shock stopped him dead and a moment later Khory finished him with a blade across his throat.

"I'm sorry," Elora managed in the faintest of whispers from where she lay, sprawled across his mace chain, as the man dropped to his knees and then his face, the light fading from his eyes as he fell. Yet there was a part of her that felt the glorious chitterings of the Malevoiy, to taste blood once more, to feast on yet another spirit brought to the slaughter, and she repressed the urge to bare her own teeth in sympathetic celebration.

She knew both Thorn and Khory would yell at her for what

she'd done; the fact that neither did as Khory peeled her off the chain and scooped her up once more only made matters worse. She had neither breath nor energy left to speak. It was all she could do to keep her heart pumping.

Like the Gate they'd entered through, this was a round of steps, cut into the wall of a perfectly circular pit that ended in what appeared to be a pool of molten silver, the same color as Elora's argent skin. The stairs made one complete circumference of the pit before disappearing beneath the pool's surface.

Khory wasted no more time. Once more, she gathered up Thorn and took the stairs in headlong, catlike bounds, reaching the pool itself just as the remnants of the Black Rose cadre started down after them.

The surface of the pool didn't stir in the slightest as they passed. Though it appeared solid, the sensation was more like gossamer than air. The only difference was that, suddenly, without missing a stride, they were climbing a set of stairs identical to the ones they'd just descended.

Now, Khory's strength and endurance were put to the test as she used her momentum to carry them forward and up. Her long legs proved their worth as she mounted the steps two and three at a time, at a pace that would have broken almost anyone else.

Elora didn't much care. Along with the last of her own strength, her skeleton seemed to be leaching from her as well. She felt utterly boneless, transformed to a creature of undulant taffy. Thankfully, she'd also apparently lost the capacity to feel pain. She recognized the series of jounces and bumps produced by Khory's ascent but none had any meaning to her. Her brain simply filed them in her mental copybook and forgot all about it.

She saw the first of the Maizan emerge just before they reached the summit, heard the whistle of a crossbow bolt close by her ear, heard a sharp command to belay, the risk was too great to their prize and enough damage done on that score already.

She felt a tickle in her nostrils and before she could help herself drew as deep a breath as she was able. It was very nearly her undoing because it produced a fit of frothy coughing accompanied by an awful tearing sensation deep within her belly.

She didn't care. She was actually smiling as Khory laid her gently down and Thorn hunkered over her, quickly laying out all the weapons and tools he'd need for the coming struggle. His expression was as grim as Elora had ever seen; this was a fight he was determined to win. Khory took position between them and the World Gate, bared sword held ready in both hands. Elora noted these actions, with that same portion of her mind that had recorded her earlier pains.

She took another breath, not as extreme as the first but just as delicious, and reveled in the teeth of a winter breeze filling her with air as fiercely cold as fresh snowmelt. There was a heady scent of pine on the wind, tart and minty, and from some impossible distance she thought she tasted a skein of woodsmoke from someone's hearth.

This to her was true glory. What the Malevoiy offered, the Realm where they dwelled, was no more than shadows.

She heard the clash of arms, blinked once to pull the scene into focus, beheld Khory at the lip of the World Gate, trading sword blows with a Maizan, while another of the Black Rose assassins tried to get a clear shot with his crossbow.

She blinked again, but this time her eyelids refused to open, and in that precipitate rush of darkness, came silence and a welcome oblivion.

CHAPTER
3

SHE BURNED. SHE DREAMED. SHE FLEW.

Her skin was dry and desiccated as some grub's husk, so she hacked at it with blunt fingers until they sharpened into claws and then she cheered as flesh cracked to powder and the chrysalis brought forth her ultimate incarnation. She spiraled up and away from the Elora she'd been, unwilling to take a backward glance, far more excited about what lay ahead than what had come before. She felt like molten metal cascading from the pour into its mold, full of potential yet lacking any defining sense of what its final form would take. Her imagination brought forth all manner of choices: she thought of becoming taller, more beautiful, graceful as an elven queen, as strong and resolute as Khory. She thought of the mother she'd never seen and wondered what part of herself echoed those features, that person, and considered that it might be best to be more like her. She thought of not being human at all and remembered the delight she'd found sharing her consciousness with her companion eagles, Bastian and Anele. Their code of honor was as clear as their lives seemed uncomplicated but it wasn't that simplicity she envied, it was their union.

Friends she had, dearly won and more treasured than an emperor's ransom in gold and precious stones, but that was all they were to her. None held the special place in her heart that Anele did for Bastian and that she hoped, prayed, demanded, her parents had for one another. Thorn would die for her, she knew, as would Khory and the brownies and a whole host of folk, some of whom she knew but most she never would; that wasn't enough to ease the sudden and overwhelming ache in her heart. Part of her felt shame for such a desperate longing, as though she were diminishing the loyalty and sacrifice of those who'd pledged themselves to her. She knew that wasn't so, yet she also couldn't deny the misery of her own need.

She became aware of claws and fangs, not as a part of her body but as an extension of her inner being. The pure metal of her forging was darkening, stained with colors beyond human ken, ebon and angry blotches that ate away hungrily at her, leaving a void that was quickly filled with passion and cruelty. All her emotions, in fact, twisted a fatal turn off-center so that desire became lust and anger, rage; there was a yearning for love still, but that love looked more to the shadows for sustenance and fulfillment. It found joy in the infliction of pain, delight in the flashfire of terror from prey that knew it was trapped and doomed.

In her mind's eye, Elora beheld the Maizan once more, falling over and over and over again to his knees after Khory's blade left its scarlet trail across his throat, then to his face as his head bent sideways at a crazy-quilt angle because she'd cut so deeply there was nothing left to anchor it in place but the man's spine. There was an obscene beauty in that fountain spray of blood and a keen regret that Elora herself had played no direct, physical part in his death.

She heard what passed for laughter, a chittering of appreciation, a yearning to see more, that she first thought was a presentation of the Malevoiy. Then her lips curled back from bared teeth and she shook herself from top to toe, eager to cast off the last remnants of her prior existence and embrace what was newly offered her. She noted pinpoints of light in the darkness around her, all in pairs, heard the scrabble of claws on slate as the pack approached, felt the gusts of charnel pants from their breath. The shapes gradually resolved themselves into beasts on four legs, with brutally powerful shoulders capable of nigh-inexhaustible endurance. Their fur was thick at the neck, for protection, so no lesser creature could get at their throats, and their mouths were filled with fangs so long and sharp that a single bite was usually all they needed to finish their quarry. They bore the semblance of living things, but they were none of that, the product instead of foulest sorcery.

They were Death Dogs, the Malevoiy's favored pets.

They waited eagerly for Elora to become one of them.

A splash of radiance tore across her vision from the side, bright enough to blind, yet for all that wild energy it was unable to cast any lasting illumination across this diabolical scene. It caught the Death Dog nearest Elora full in the chest and blasted all the way through him, dissipating only when it emerged from the other side. The dog shrieked and Elora's throat tore as she echoed its cry. It reared on its hind legs, creating a momentary parody of a human standing erect before toppling backward, its shadow substance eaten away from within by that pure and irresistible light.

The eyes gathered close around Elora, as though the pack were trying to coalesce into a single mass in her defense. Again and again, she beheld those murderous bursts of energy, felt the sympathetic pain of a Death Dog's passing. There were two sources; she could tell that from the trajectory of the incoming bolts, but what they were remained hidden. The dogs had no knowledge of fear; their response to any attack was a monumental fury that would only find release in the butchering of their tormentor. To that end, they could be infernally patient, for they drew their sustenance from Elora herself. While she accepted the bond between them, even if only a partial one, the pack could not totally be destroyed. Moreover, the dogs could see what she did, that the bolts of light were gradually weakening. Their attackers still possessed the power to inflict grievous harm but their resources were finite and that end was in sight.

Elora turned to an aspect of her older self, the part of her she considered forsaken, and called on her MageSight to reveal who was slaughtering her pets.

She hissed at the sight of them, refusing to accept that two such diminutive creatures could cause such harm.

They were brownies, shaped much like Daikini but hardly taller than a garden flower. The one on the left wore a pair of swords, carved from the fangs of a Death Dog he'd slain. He hadn't emerged from that struggle unscathed. There were scars all across his chest, she knew, though she couldn't see them now and the expression on his face of implacable resolve was heightened by the pale slash that ran across his right cheek from chin to hairline. There was a fan-shaped spray of silver at the summit of the scar; otherwise, his hair was the same dark chestnut as his eyes. He wore it long, fastened at the nape of the neck by a wrought silver knot.

His clothes were leather, finely tanned hides that fit as well as a second skin, except for a blouse of cotton and an overshirt of finely woven wool. Over his boots went deerskin leggings that rose to mid-thigh; over all went an ankle-length coat of oiled, waterproofed canvas, with pockets aplenty inside and out to contain tools of the trade and loot. Slung across his back was a quiver, in his hand he held a bow; as Elora watched, the brownie drew and nocked an arrow, and let it fly. As it left his grasp, a surge of glittery fire followed, from eyes to hand to the shaft of polished wood, transforming it on contact from something solid to one of fire and sending it shooting to its target with the speed and force of a lightning bolt.

This was Rool.

Beside him walked Franjean. Where one wore skins, the other favored silk. While one appeared more at home in some mountain wilderness, the other apparently favored an Imperial court. One was Frontier wild, his companion the personification of style and elegance. But his weapons were as deadly, his aim as sure, his heart as strong, his soul as true as Rool's.

You, Elora cried, in a voice more resonant of Malevoiy than Daikini.

She'd never dreamed a single word could embody such hostility and utter, all-embracing contempt, much less that it could come from her. She didn't care. These . . . *things* that were less than pecks were no fit foe for her, and even less prey. It was an insult to the order of things that they even existed much less did such damage to her lovelies.

dare!

To her loathing, she added rage and the regret that the Death Dogs would make such short work of them.

"For you," said Rool, "we dare anything."

"So, Elora Danan," noted his companion in a voice so lacking emotion of any kind he might have been discussing the morning weather, "has it come to this?"

The brownies looked gaunt and she realized that was because their bolts of energy were fueled by the essence of their own lives. For each dog they slew, a portion of themselves perished along with it.

She flashed fangs at them and all the dogs who remained followed suit, breaking the darkness now with points of gleaming ivory to go with their bloody eyes.

Again, the image of the Maizan warrior fell before her but this time Elora found herself looking far more closely at the scene than before. There was courage in him, in abundance and without question, for he walked ground that was unknown to even the greatest of Daikini magi. Commitment to a cause and a leader, a determination to win the day. Calculation, in his assessment of Khory's skill and his own; confidence in his own ability to cope with her. Nothing really that Elora could label Evil, not even as a reflection of his master. That was why Thorn called their foe the Deceiver, for his ability to mask his true nature and purpose and thereby obtain the services of those who would otherwise stand resolutely against him.

The warrior was a proud man, and so young, not that much older than Elora herself. He was full of dreams.

Then, before he even knew what was happening, Khory took them all from him.

The pain was nothing compared to the realization of loss, and failure. There was such confusion as the tension fled from his limbs. He was a Black Rose. He had killed, without hesitation or mercy in the service of his Castellan. He thought he had accepted the reality of his own death. But the moment itself left him full of pleading and denial. He sought purpose in his sudden sacrifice. He found himself alone, in the dark.

Elora's head snapped up, her arms as well, and the Death Dogs took the gestures as their cue. Pace by deliberate pace, they flowed outward from her, moving to the side as well to flank their foes. They hoped for flight, hungered for even a brief chase before the kill, but the brownies stood their ground.

Again, Elora burned from the inside out but this time there was a difference. It was as if she'd plunged herself into the molten heart of the world, all trace of physicality cindered in an instant, her only grasp on coherence the primal sense of self. She could think; therefore, she had to exist. From that thought—the instinctive "I am"—came form and a kind of substance. She stretched long and lean, more sleek and sinuous than an eel. She wasn't alone, either. As she cast her senses wide, habit labeling the myriad and overlapping perceptions as sight and sound and scent and taste and touch though they were in fact none of those, she found that the fire was home to score beyond score of similar creatures, gamboling about with wild delight. They popped in and out of view, winding themselves around and occasionally right through one another in gleeful disregard for all the laws of nature she'd been taught.

I *know* you, she cried, the words cascading from her in streams of vibrant color and texture against the greater backdrop of eternal fire.

Know you, replied one, and the cry was quickly taken up in a madcap chorus, **know you know you know you!**

It was worse, and yet more wonderful, than being swarmed by puppies as the firedrakes crowded close around her, overjoyed that she had chosen to join with them at last.

The First Realm is fire, she whispered, meaning to speak to herself and discovering too late that wasn't possible here.

Fire fire fire, she heard, and then, **burn burn *burn*!**

The World burns, she continued, remembering the last time she'd encountered these sweet yet unimaginably deadly creatures, so formidable and uncontrollable that even the most powerful of magi, on either side of the Veil, gave them a wide berth. Very rarely, hubris or desperation would prompt some benighted, hugely ambitious soul to try a Summoning. There existed spells and incantations sufficient to command even creatures as untamed as these— but they allowed no margin for error. The conjuration had to be perfect, and the strength of the sorcerer equal to the task. Elora had seen what little remained of those who'd failed, proud castles reduced to charred stumps of stone, the land around them turned to black glass by the unimaginable heat. She alone was able to call firedrakes to her side and restrain their natural urge to set all Creation ablaze. They had spared her life on one occasion, and she had saved a clutch of theirs on another. She counted them as friends but wasn't sure if the term truly applied. She suspected nothing that made sense to her carried over to them, and likewise in reverse.

The World burns, she repeated. **We burn. All things burn.**

When she swam with the firedrakes before, it hadn't hurt. Now she was conscious of sharp, stabbing pains throughout her body. The 'drakes took no notice of her distress but continued their playtime.

Fire stands at the beginning of things, she said, continuing their catechism, wondering all the while why coherent, structured thoughts continued to come to her in a form that had no use for them. Firedrakes were creatures of random impulse, wherein concept and action were one. Because of that, all their thoughts tended to be simple and active; they moved too quickly for reflection. **And at the end . . . ?**

Wings exploded from her back, a tail from the base of her spine. Limbs elongated, her neck and skull as well, losing none of the liquid grace of the firedrakes but gaining the majesty of a solid form. She grew tremendously in stature and in the process gathered into herself the fire that surrounded her.

Once more, she found herself returned to the dark place where the Death Dogs dwelled and recognized it now as a corner of her own soul. The pack was closing inexorably on the brownies, who stood back-to-back with weapons raised and ready, determined to sell their lives as dearly as they were able.

She wanted to fly but knew it was too soon for that. Instead, Elora let loose a great and terrible cry to announce her presence. She knew the Death Dogs would turn on her, to try to reassert the dominion of that part of her which was bound to them. She also suspected, in that kind of knock-down-drag-out knife fight, she might not prevail. So she didn't give them the chance.

She opened her mouth and hosed the ebon space before her with the fire she'd brought with her from the heart of the fire-drakes' world. She was a dragon now, and this was one of the things they did best.

There were no eyes facing her when she was done, no gleam of fangs. Nor, sadly, any sign of her brownie friends. She had won a measure of freedom. She was alone.

The fire faded, within her as without.

The dragon became a young woman, huddled on a patch of icy flagstone in the tattered remnants of a dancing costume whose scarlet color matched the blood that covered much of what cloth and leather did not. She reached for her bear, desperate for comfort and companionship, but her hand found only emptiness within her traveling pouch. Belatedly, she remembered where she'd left it and why and cursed herself for such a foolish gesture. She wanted to sob but the effort was too great and she hurt too much.

She'd never felt so cold, she couldn't stop shaking—which was strange because as far back as she could remember the extremes of weather and environment touched her as lightly as spells were meant to.

Darkness loomed, crashed down on her like a rogue wave at the seashore. She was caught in its fierce undertow, jounced and bounced so hard that awareness fragmented worse than any shattered mirror and before she knew what was happening all those broken pieces were swept beyond her reach.

In desperation she grabbed for one . . .

. . . and heard the sound of panting, mistook it at first for some poor puppy after a hard run.

She flailed for another . . .

. . . and worked her tongue past teeth that seemed to have grown fur to touch faintly lips gone so dry they felt dusted with shards of stone.

Her eyelids fluttered but didn't open—that took more strength than she had available. The panting, she realized, was her, and it took all her effort. She was too tired to turn to InSight and meld her consciousness with another's; even considering the idea exhausted her. She had a sense of something flickering off to the side, a sensation of warmth along that side of her body, concluded there was a hearth blazing away across the room. The fire did her little good, though, she was as cold here as in her dream. She wondered how she looked and thought, with her gleaming, argent skin, she'd probably be mistaken for a true statue.

She wasn't naked, she felt the presence of a long nightgown, loose at the collar and sleeves but rucked snug around her legs where she'd moved and twisted in her sleep. The weight she felt across her body was a thick down comforter. There were additional points of pressure on an upper arm, one side, across her belly that she concluded were dressings of some kind. She remembered the battle, much as she didn't want to, it wasn't hard to catalog her hurts.

She twitched her lips as something cool and damp pressed down on her forehead, sucked fiercely on the cloth as it was placed within her mouth.

"Not so much, child," she heard Thorn say, her lips pursing hungrily as the cloth was removed. Her needs were as simple, her wants as direct, as a nursing baby's. There was a sprinkling fall of water as he dipped the cloth in a handy bowl, squeezed off the excess, and returned it to her.

"I'm afraid you can't handle a proper drink," he went on. "We have to feed you a bit at a time, no more than that."

She grunted in disgust and tried once more to crease an eye open. She had a multitude of questions.

"As you may, or may not, have surmised," Thorn related, while continuing to bathe her face, the column of her throat, gently pulling aside the top of her gown to bare her shoulders to the collarbone, "Khory won the day. We emerged from the Gate atop a highland tor in the Shados, beyond the Cascadel." The Shados were the mountain range that filled the horizon below the city of Sandeni, and the Cascadel the greatest river of the western half of the continent. From headwaters amidst these comparatively young peaks, it made its way west better than a thousand leagues to Angwyn Bay and the Sunset Ocean beyond. What made it invaluable to traders and travelers was the fact that it was navigable for almost its entire length, allowing quick and easy passage from the coast to the heartland of the continent and back again.

The same applied east of the Wall as well, with rivers running downhill from Sandeni to the Tascara Sea and from there through Chengwei to the ocean. Chief among them was the Quangzhua, the Mother of Waters, a river so mighty it was believed by the Chengwei to be the source of all the water in all the oceans of the world. The fact that the river was fresh water and the oceans salt was considered of no consequence. To the south, for the whole of the Quangzhua's length, rose the greatest mountain range in the world, the Stairs to Heaven, with peaks so high it was said that a body could stand at their summit and touch the stars themselves. Many had tried to scale those heights, to learn if that were so, only to discover—some at the cost of their lives—that the mountains rose beyond the point where there was air to breathe, to a place where the cold was unendurable and nothing living could be found, on either side of the Veil.

Splitting the continent from crown to midriff at a point roughly two-thirds the way across from Angwyn to Chengwei was the Wall, a tremendous plateau that stretched from the Shados to the top of the world. To behold it was to wonder if at some point in the distant, unrecorded past when giants walked the earth, some titanic force had somehow *lifted* one side higher than the other, thereby forming a line of cliffs that stood better than a thousand feet high.

Throughout most of known history, the Wall had been precisely what its name described, a barrier blocking all travel from east to west. True, there were passes and trails through the Shados, but only the most enterprising of traders would follow them and then only at the height of summer, for those few scant weeks between last snowmelt and first snowfall. Daikini, being inventive by nature and fiercely stubborn by temperament, took that as a challenge and found another way.

Sandeni was where both river systems—the Cascadel and the Quangzhua—had their source. The beauty of water was that a merchant only had to deal with one race of the Veil Folk. Naiads ruled lesser tributaries but their influence varied in direct proportion to the size of the stream; the great rivers were the province of the freshwater Wyrrn, as the oceans were of their seafaring cousins. By contrast, anyone making their way cross-country on land found themselves forced to deal with a whole host of the Veil Folk, each tribe of which had its own price and terms for allowing unobstructed passage. What suited one might prove wholly unacceptable to the next, and all seemed to take inordinate pleasure in vexing strangers no end, especially Daikini.

More than once, Elora likened it to the notion of a huge, ostensibly comfortable mansion, wherein dwelled a multitude of folk, each in a separate room, most of whom wanted nothing to do with their neighbors. Few would acknowledge in the slightest that they shared a common cause and responsibility. So long as their individual room was maintained, they cared nothing for the rest.

The problem now was that, thanks to the Deceiver, the house was in danger of collapse. And while attitudes had begun to change, hands finally held out and grasped in friendship, Elora desperately feared this rapprochement had come too little, too late.

"Where . . . ?" she began, amazed to find that speaking that single word left her breathless and borderline exhausted.

"Fort Tregare."

Her first sight of it, she remembered, had been through the eyes of one of her eagles. A natural meadow stood on a promontory at a crooked bend in the upper reaches of the Cascadel, at possibly the last place where the fast-flowing river was fordable. It was a natural stronghold, dominating both the river and the valley through which it passed, the best and most direct route through the Shados to Sandeni. Forest had been cleared in a great fan shape to provide better than a half mile of open ground, and the timbers used to construct the fort itself. The stockade rose twenty feet above a stone-and-earthen redoubt that itself stood ten feet high. Its basic shape was of a pentagon, with blockhouses at each of the five joints. Within was an open square twice the dimensions of a jousting yard, ringed by a host of structures: barracks for troops, quarters for families, storehouses, barns, an armory. Dominating the enclosure was a broad, multistoried building that functioned both as the fort's inner keep and a hostelry for travelers.

When last she'd seen the fort, there'd been a scattering of individual homesteads, as stoutly designed and constructed as the citadel itself, off by the tree line where additional land had been cleared for crops. As she replayed her own memory of the scene, she found it accompanied by an addendum from Thorn's. The farms were gone, reduced to charred and smoldering timbers.

The outside corners of her eyes began to burn and she chose to blame it on a wayward wisp of smoke from the hearth as Thorn dabbed the tears away. She'd tried that for herself, only to discover her arms were as weak and useless as her voice.

"Don't talk," Thorn cautioned.

"As if," she husked, "I could." All her efforts for a couple of minutes after that were devoted to recapturing her breath. There were blank spots in her awareness, grace notes marking the passage of time, telling Elora that she'd fallen asleep without her even noticing, sometimes right in the middle of a thought.

"Let that be a lesson to you, child," Thorn said quietly. "You're hurt." His tone told her what the bland words did not, that her condition was grave beyond description.

"You need rest," he continued in that same parental, professorial tone. "You need to recover your strength."

"Because, let's face it," Elora couldn't help herself as her face brightened at the sound of this new, yet familiar voice, "you are of no use to *anyone* as you are."

She tried to see Rool but the brownie had positioned himself (deliberately, no doubt, rot him) beyond the track of her eyes.

Moving her head, she discovered, was out of the question. Even the smallest attempt set the bed to swaying worse than a hammock in a hurricane and left her afraid she'd be desperately sick.

"So *you* say," offered Franjean in a suave riposte from the opposite direction. "Myself, I'm thinking she'll look quite stylish on a dais in a gallery. 'Sacred Princess, reclining, au naturel, in silver'?"

She wanted to hit him but all she could manage was a rude squeak.

"Someone leave a kettle on the boil?" asked Rool in all innocence.

"More like a mouse, daring us to the hunt."

"We are slayers of Death Dogs," Rool pronounced. "We do not hunt mice."

"That's enough, the pair of you," chided Thorn. "Look at Elora, you'll do her an injury with your japes, making the poor girl laugh so. Have a little mercy."

Suddenly, Rool was standing by her collarbone, peering down intently at her face. She'd misplaced her memory of how quickly the brownies could move, more proof of her infirmity because usually she could spot them when they did.

"Laughter, you say?" He scoffed, assuming a dollop of Franjean's manner. "Don't appear so to me, though I'll concede the barest ghost of a grin twitching the tip of her mouth."

Franjean joined him, the pair of them dressed as they'd been in her dream.

"Hah," he said, his tone dismissive. "Don't see a grin, ghost or otherwise. Face is turning t'other way altogether."

"That's the trouble with Daikini. Their mouths, they're built for frownin'."

"I dreamed . . ." she managed to say. "I thought I . . ."

"You did," Rool said, his mien turning serious. "There's a Hook in you, Elora Danan." He didn't have to say whose hook, the way he capitalized the word spoke volumes. This was a power so feared he dared not speak its name. "Pack comes at your calling, sits at your feet, kills at your bidding, shows you the nature of the beast. Bad business."

"You defied them."

"Too dumb to live, that's us," said Franjean.

"Think we'd let the likes o' them lay claim to our Princess?" said Rool.

"No more"—and she gritted her teeth, determined to forge her way through the entire thought—"than I would allow either of you to come to harm."

The effort almost shocked her dead asleep. As it was her eyes were mostly closed, her vision blurring with fatigue by the time she was done. That's why she told herself it was some trick of the moment, a flaw in her perceptions, when she looked past the brownies' ready smiles to the concern in their dark and hooded eyes. For the first time, she saw doubt.

She didn't know how long she slept but was thankful there were no more dreams. As consciousness returned, creeping across the landscape of her mind like a tide upon the shore, she enveloped herself in purely physical sensations, noting—like a student in her copybook—the crackling pops of wood in the hearth, the tang of hardwood smoke, the gloriously toasty feeling of being enveloped in rich, thick goose down.

She was still cold. Not on the surface, but deep inside, to the pit of stomach and heart and soul. Somehow, she'd been cracked in two, as the continent was by the Wall, only she was wrapped in layers where the land was laid out flat. All the efforts being made to comfort the outside of the young woman had no effect on the heartland of her. There was found a roiling, ugly mass of foulness and putrescence and Elora quickly found it could no more be ignored than banished.

To her credit, weak as she was, she tried both. She called on the meditation exercises taught her by Thorn to calm her thoughts and soothe her spirit. She reached out to the one special power that was her own and spoke to her body, reminding her torn flesh of what it had been like to be whole and unscarred, hoping that the act of healing her physical being might likewise help her soul. She dealt with the wounds in their turn, examining each for any infection and then purging what poison she found.

It proved a clumsy, halting process. To Elora's dismay, while the full force of her will could be focused as intently as ever she quickly discovered she had no stamina. She would complete one session of treatment and promptly forget what was next on her agenda. A seductive languor would come upon her and suddenly whole stretches of the day, or night, would vanish in what seemed to be a flash. There was no sense of sleep, no recollection of any dreams, but the shuttered windows of her room would be bright with sunlight shining through the slats one moment, the waryard beyond resounding with purposeful noise. The next, however, when she would have sworn on her life that she'd done no more than blink her eyes, all was still, the room around her painted in layers of midnight shadow, save for the glowing embers banked high in the hearth. Sometimes, her consciousness would flee right in the middle of a thought or, far more embarrassing, she'd find herself finishing a sentence begun the day before in conversation with someone altogether different.

She understood fever, she understood exhaustion, but in neither case had Elora ever felt anything so profound. To her annoyance, none of her friends apparently had the slightest interest in helping her free of it. Three times a day, Thorn would visit her bedside, to check the clarity of her eyes, the sound of her breath, the force of her pulse. From his own bag of tricks, he offered herb tea to take the edge off the pain of her wounds and her own healing enchantments, and a rich wayfarer's soup that was more stew than broth to build up her strength. If she was interested in talking, he'd stay to listen but since she usually just didn't have the energy, he'd mostly take his leave, with the stock admonition that she drink plenty of fluids to keep her system hydrated.

The brownies were just as solicitous, which wasn't like them in the slightest. Usually, they could be counted on to pester her to the point of madness. She decided to ignore them.

Once she began her own attempts at healing, however, Elora quickly feared she'd made a terrible mistake. Songs of Mending that had in the past knitted torn flesh seamlessly together, that had banished all taint of infection from her body, seemed suddenly to fall on deaf ears. Her power more often than not was like water spilling in a madcap cascade from a duck's back without the slightest impact. Time after time, she would close the flaps of a wound only to wail in frustration as the bindings refused to hold. Desperately, she scaled back her field of influence, until she was working on fields no larger than a brownie's hand, to no avail. Her best efforts only seemed to make matters worse, taxing her system to such an extent that her fever returned with a vengeance.

Gradually, without realizing it herself, Elora slipped into a coma, a sleep so profound that some of those caring for her muttered that she would never awaken. Only Thorn and Khory and the brownies knew differently, that Elora had withdrawn inside herself to marshal all her strength and resources for this battle. But that knowledge was torture for them, because there was precious little they could do to help—a realization that prompted its own share of angry words between those longtime companions in arms.

"Y' just gonna let her fade away t' *nothing?*" flared Rool to Thorn, as the Nelwyn gently bathed Elora's brow with a damp, cool cloth.

"I'm open to suggestions" was the infuriatingly calm reply.

"Fangs, Nelwyn, *you're* the sorcerer here. Tell me what herb t' find, what talisman t' steal, it's yours. Cast some bloody spell or other! *Save* her, damn your eyes!"

"She's immune to magic, brownie!" Thorn said in return, his voice too flat and controlled, bespeaking an anger only barely restrained. As it was, power crackled from the corners of his eyes and the knuckles of his clenched fists, and there was at the back of his throat an aspect of roiling storm clouds preparing to hammer the ground with a monstrous thunderclap.

"You've known that from the start," the Nelwyn continued in that same dangerous tone, "as long as any of us. My enchantments have no hold on her, save perhaps to add a portion of my own strength to hers. But even there, Rool, she has to ask. If she doesn't reach out for aid, I can't force it on her."

"Damn foolish way t' live, an' you ask me," offered Franjean.

"No argument."

"What happens if she dies, then, Drumheller? What of the world, if its Savior is no more?"

"I don't know, Franjean." For the first time, a doubt surfaced in

Thorn's thoughts, a niggling little thing as annoying as a seed stuck between his teeth, and as infernally difficult to dislodge: *suppose prophecy is wrong, suppose we've made a mistake, suppose she isn't the one.* Angrily, he thrust that burst of heresy aside, only to find himself confronted by a wish that was far more bleak, because it came wrapped in the stale, tired air of the Malevoiy Realm: *perhaps it would be better for us all, if she did die.*

With all his own strength of will, he denied both thoughts and banished them.

Yet they would not go away.

As for Elora, once more she burned, and once more she flew, and it was glorious beyond imagination. Her wings thrust her through the molten heart of Creation as easily as through the mantle of air that englobed it. Moving from one to the other was as simple as diving into a pool of water and each felt more comfortable to her than any home she could remember.

Her first thought was to label this a dream but experience taught her that it was far more. Dreams were the special province of the dragons, which were how they traveled to the other Realms and touched the lives of all who dwelled therein. Here was where the World That Was could be transformed by the hopes and imaginations of the dreamers into that which Might Yet Be.

For Elora, this visit, that meant a world without strife, where there was no war, where the fate of everything no longer rested on the shoulders of one girl who considered herself painfully ill equipped for the role. No one wanted her, no one could demand things of her, no one had to die because of her. She was safe here, she was at peace.

She was alone.

There were no more dragons, she'd seen to that. And if the egg she carried in her travel pouch wasn't allowed to hatch, there never would be again. No people, either, because each face she conjured came from the vault of her memory and carried with them a reminder of tasks left unfinished and responsibilities abandoned. Simply the world, a playground all her own, to remake as she pleased.

A flaw in the smooth curve of the horizon caught her eye, a

shrug of great shoulders shifting the plane and camber of her wings to bring her closer. At first she'd taken it for a knucklebone ridge, but that was only because she was so far away. The closer she came, the more stark and dramatic the arrangement of the range. There was no gentle transition leading up to them, plains giving way to foothills, to lesser highlands, until at last the climber came to this summit line of peaks. Instead, the mountains reared violently upward from the surrounding landscape, almost like spearpoints, bringing first warning of an invading army. Even more strange was the fact that they stood alone, on terrain that otherwise stretched flat and relatively unmarred in every direction for as far as Elora herself could see from on high.

Something about the sight poked at Elora's recollection but the specific memory proved fiendishly elusive. She beat her wings skyward, to get a view from above—which revealed a central valley, not so impressive from her perspective but quite the opposite, she mused, when seen from the ground—but she couldn't bring herself to overfly the mountains directly. It made her nervous.

Interesting, she told herself, as she swung through a lazy succession of tacks back and forth through the air to return her to the earth, how the natural arrangement of these peaks and valleys reminded her of the design of a castle fortress, with the valley as its central courtyard.

The thought made her chuckle and she concluded that the opposite was more likely true, that the designers of those classic strongholds had taken their cues from nature. She never realized that, for all the time she was close to the peaks, she never once turned her back on them; that during her descent, she always turned toward them, never away.

When at last her feet touched the ground, her dragon form melting from her to reveal the human figure at its heart, she was a fair distance removed from the range. The mountains remained an imposing sight at the horizon, but she didn't stand in their shadow. Somehow that, too, seemed important.

As a dragon her energy had seemed boundless. Returning to her normal self brought with it a painful reminder that the truth was otherwise. No sooner did her feet touch the earth than the rest of her followed suit as her body collapsed out from under her. She lay sprawled a fair while, soaked with sweat, racked with chills, obsessed with the need to draw breaths in and let them out.

She'd landed by a stream, she lay on rich earth, she was enveloped by air, all that remained was fire to complete the four Great Realms that comprised the First Circle of Being, that of the World.

Elora cast forth a piece of herself into the ground like a fisherman would cast a line into a lake, letting it fall fast and free to the molten heart of the globe. She thought to find friends there, the community of demon firedrakes who'd adopted her, was saddened to discover that the world's core was as uninhabited as its surface. The Second Circle, that of the Flesh with all its myriad peoples, had yet to touch this place.

She had more important concerns than philosophy, foremost among them her own survival. She grasped a fistful of fire and brought it up to her, grinning with irrepressible delight at how the radiant ball of liquid rock blazed before her. The raw heat was indescribable; if she let fall even a drop it would fuse the ground to glass on contact. By rights, the hand that held it should have burned to ash in an instant and all the surrounding vegetation set alight. But Elora had swum through the heart of the world and not been harmed. She had bonded with each of the Great Realms of the World in their turn, offering a portion of herself to them and accepting part of them into her in return. Many thought that since she was the Sacred Princess, that meant accepting the fealty of the Great Realms as their sovereign but hers had never been the power to command. In that regard, Thorn was far more powerful than she. With the proper spell, he could bend the most primal and powerful of forces and entities to his will. Even demons, should the need arise.

Elora couldn't force anyone to do anything. She had to ask for help, occasionally persuade, but most of all make friends. Unfortunately, at that particular task, she felt woefully inadequate. Everyone looked to her for salvation, yet the harder she worked, the worse things got.

Do not despair, Danan. There is no need.

She stirred where she lay, tried to rise to her feet, but only managed to lever herself onto an elbow at the sound of that familiar, tantalizing, desiccated voice. While she'd been lying there, the sun had vanished, her glade now cast in shadows so deep they were more appropriate to nighttime than dusk. A glance upward revealed the reason why. The mountain range had grown, or moved. What had been a safe and secure distance removed was now on her doorstep, slopes rising so high and steeply that she couldn't even see the crest of the promontory ridgelines, much less the summits beyond.

Come to Us, child. Join with Us. Let it be thy foes who art brought low, for now and evermore.

With those words, her fatigue was gone. Her breath was still short, the hollowness to her chest still remained from her collapsed lung, and she knew that nothing substantial had been done to heal her wounds. This was enticement and promise. All she had to do was rise to her feet and a path would be revealed to her through the mountains. With each step would come Malevoiy strength until at the last she reached the central valley.

We are the old, thou'rt the new. Learn from Our experience, Danan, let Us be reborn with thy youth. Take of Our stronghold and make it thine own. Here wilt thou ever be safe. None can do thee harm, all wilt pay thee homage. This war shall end, in a twinkling, in a trice. Victory will be thine. So much to gain. So small an act to bring it to pass.

It was the longest speech she'd heard from the Malevoiy and it made sense. She stirred her feet, starting to shift position and balance so she could stand erect, and realized that she'd have to set aside her ball of molten incandescence. That gave her pause.

On the one hand was salvation as a gift. Offered freely and apparently with no strings, but she knew there'd be a price. In the other, she held deliverance of her own making. No guarantees here, of victory or life itself, and in its own way the price exacted would be far higher.

She didn't want to make the choice, she didn't want to make any choices.

She heard a growl, low and rumbling, that resonated through her bones as much as her ears. There was warning to it, and challenge, and a heritage of enmity reaching back over a score of aeons, to the moment the Circle of the World gave rise to that of the Flesh. It was a gauntlet the Malevoiy recognized and It responded with a snarl of Its own.

Foolish ancient, Elora thought wanly, *this has nothing to do with you.* The insight surprised her. *Both warning and challenge are to me.*

She moved her head as best she could, swept her eyes around her for a glimpse of the source of the growl, but found the world as empty as before, save for herself and the Malevoiy. There was a path now, into the mountains. Simply looking toward it made her blood sizzle with anticipation and she suddenly could swear she heard the faint and distant baying of a hunting pack of Death Dogs. They wanted to follow her, not as prey but as their leader.

"No," she said aloud in the softest of tones, meaning her refusal to be final and absolute, but her thoughts betrayed her with a qualification: *not yet.*

Anger got the better of her then and she paid for it in full measure. With a reflexive snarl that was mainly frustration she thrust the fire she'd caught into the center of her chest, into her own heart.

At first, she couldn't scream, for all the muscles of her body had suddenly turned to adamantine steel. Each pump of her heart cast forth a jet of flame, surging down the great vessels right to her toes, then back again the other way to the crest of her skull, which she was certain would instantly explode and thankfully end her torment. She rolled herself into a tiny hedgehog ball, then felt her whole body arch like a drawn bow until she was poised on heels and head like a baby having a hissy fit, at last giving voice to the fire threatening to consume her with a bellow that encompassed the whole spectrum of pain, as it did of pleasure.

In that selfsame instant, blind instinct drove Elora to hurl herself into the raging torrent within herself and battle her way to the crest of the surging wave of fire. There she had to ride it, as in childhood from her tower she'd seen the young men of Angwyn do the surf off Point Redoubt. The stakes were absolute. All those lads on the coast risked if the wave got the better of them were thumped skulls and the occasional broken bone. Untamed as it now was, this fire Elora had summoned would surely consume her. It was a purely natural force and as she'd learned too often to her sorrow, she was as vulnerable to them as anyone.

To her advantage, she'd spent much of the past few years as an apprentice to Torquil, master forger of the Rock Nelwyns, a distant cousin of Thorn Drumheller whose people worked with stone the same way Drumheller's branch of the family did with soil, as farmers. She'd proved herself a gifted student. Indeed, of all the cardinal elements, fire came most naturally to her.

There was no time for due thought or consideration, and not the slightest margin for error. She knew that she now possessed the power required for healing even a mortal wound but she couldn't dally over any of them. The task had to be accomplished with this single rush of blood and flame, one complete circuit of her body from heart to heart to make herself once more physically whole. Thankfully, her earlier failures now proved beneficial, allowing her plenty of opportunity to examine the wounds and determine the necessary treatment.

No problem was the first thought to make itself clear amidst the chaos, surprising her silly because it was accompanied by a laugh, *no worse than juggling a multitude of balls—only to have them grow spikes in midair.*

And juggle she did, supremely well, with a joyous abandon she hadn't felt in what seemed like ages. Rage paled within her, the mountains of the Malevoiy receding almost to insignificance, there was neither doom nor destruction to her work. By her own force of will, she shaped this fire into a force for creation, strengthening some patterns, reweaving others altogether, treating her own body the way she would a pour of molten metal. There came a moment, late in the process, as the wild tide swept through her head, when she faced the choice of every forgemaster, whether to bring forth pure metal, unsullied by any impurities or flaws, or find a way to turn those same potential liabilities to his benefit, as with an alloy. She could purge the Malevoiy taint from her soul, with such a blast of fire that it would never return.

Thou art the Danan, the Malevoiy had said, and a gust of rage sparked such prominences of flame at how like Its voice her own sounded speaking Its words that she almost lost her balance and tumbled from the crest of her wave. After a brief, fierce struggle, she managed to restore herself to a semblance of grace for the final surge of effort. The experience left her shaken, but more determined than ever to prevail as she repeated the rest of what the Malevoiy told her: The Thirteenth Realm—that binds *all* the others.

The Malevoiy were no domain, like the Nelwyns or the brownies, or even the firedrake demons. They were a Great Realm entire, the pinnacle of the Circle of the Flesh, the point of linkage between that Circle and that of the Spirit. Cast them aside, Elora's cause was lost.

Thought and action occurred as one, just as her wave crashed once more into the heart that was its source.

It was a memory of Torquil that pointed the way for her, working the fingers of one hand through the bushy tangle of his beard while his other hand fingered the pipe he always carried but almost never smoked.

"Purity's an ideal," he said, his voice deep and rough-hewn, as befit his barrel chest and hands that could bend steel as easily as forge it. For all of that, like all Nelwyns, he stood barely half Elora's height. "So's perfection. Something we strive for, but like as not never achieve. Tha's f'r the best, an' you ask me. How c'n y' have perfection, when y've a mind to consider the possibility of somethin' new an' mayhap better? The most pure an' perfect thing c'n carry within it the seeds of its own destruction. Someroads, it's the flaws that make the difference. An' make a body interesting."

Life is growth, she thought to herself, or so she believed until she realized her lips were moving.

"Growth is change," she continued, breath hardly stirring across the tongue that shaped the words.

"Change is chaos," she finished.

"I hope that's a good thing, Elora Danan, what you just said." A familiar voice, but not one immediately placed beyond the realization that it was neither Drumheller nor the brownies. "But I'd have t' warn ye, my master, he'd challenge yus square on any proposition that chaos were good."

The voice came from one side of her. From the other, her hand registered sensations that were at once cool and warm, in both cases damp and of a fair weight, resting on her palm. Hot breath blew up her arm, accompanied by a gruff underbark, exhorting her to open her eyes and rejoin the world.

She did precisely that, saw who was there, and promptly closed them, wishing for the strength to curl herself into a tiny ball and retreat under the covers until both she and the young man perished of old age.

"Oi," she heard, "wha's all this, then?"

"Go 'way," she wailed.

There was a long moment's silence, while her admonition was considered, then the sound of boots and claws moving from the bed.

She reached after him, but her hand got tangled in the duvet, forcing her to call out.

"Luc-Jon, where are you going?"

The young scribe had already reached the door to her room. The fire was hot embers, and only a few candles were lit, plying the space mainly with shadows, but her MageSight revealed his features as though he stood in noonday sunlight. She saw puzzlement but no anger, nor any sorrow at her abrupt dismissal.

"Seein' as y're awake, 'Lora, I figured I'd summon Master Drumheller."

"If I'm truly awake, he'll know it and come along himself in his own time. As will the brownies."

She wanted to sit up but wasn't sure she had the strength. More to the point, she didn't want Luc-Jon to see her wearing her sickbed nightgown. Bad enough, her face and scalp were on view.

"I look a fright," she muttered, using her fingers as a comb and finding tangles even in her close-cropped hair.

"Life is chaos," agreed Luc-Jon, offering her own catechism back at her.

She gave him the response he deserved by sticking out her tongue and trying to disappear into the deepest recesses of bed and covers. Unfortunately, his hound demanded some attention of his own, which Elora was delighted to provide.

"Puppy!" she squealed in delight as a pair of massive paws, very

close to the size of her own hands, landed beside her on the bed. Luc-Jon's wolfhound levered himself up and over to run his great tongue across Elora's face, which brought forth a terrible attack of the giggles.

She wrapped her arms around the hound's neck, burying herself against his wiry, grizzled heather-gray fur, and hugged him close with a strength that matched his own. He obliged by lowering his chest to the bed, pinning her beneath chin and one long leg.

"Someone looks fair proud of himself," chided Luc-Jon as he hunted up a chair.

"He's feeling cocky," Elora said. "He thinks he's got the girl."

The hound cocked an eye her way, which made her wonder how much of what was said this ancient breed of hunters could actually comprehend. There was no real comparison between these hounds and other dogs, any more than between dogs and wolves; for all their outward similarities, they were very much a breed apart. In the oldest of olden days, the Great Highland Wolfhound—for that was the breed's official title—was conceived for one supreme task, to stand against the Death Dogs of the Malevoiy. And ultimately against the Malevoiy themselves.

"It was you, puppy," she murmured, pitching her voice deliberately for the dog alone, too quietly for Luc-Jon to hear. "The growl I heard when the Malevoiy reached out to me."

His eyes were the pale blue of an arctic ice sky, unique to his canine species. Hers, also blue, were more of a sapphire jade, the only spot of natural color on her otherwise argent body.

"Puppy's the reason I'm here," Luc-Jon said.

"Such a compliment."

He blushed and seeing his reaction, so did she, praying the shadows of the thick quilt hid the sight from him.

"Don't be like that, Elora Danan. Y've had the whole stronghold in a state, what with y'r takin' sick again when everyone figured y' were on an uptick."

"I feel better."

"Y' look it, an' tha's no error. Anyroad, y' weren't in any proper sleep this last time, an' nowt tha' Drumheller nor the physicians could do would break y' from it."

"How long?"

"Fair part of a week, all told."

She made a face, then took a conscious experimental breath. There was no pain, none of the phlegmy hollowness, the copper-tasting bubbles at the back of her throat as the wound produced a bloody froth. She filled her lungs until they were close to bursting, then held them as long as she could, which turned out to be not very long at all. On the plus side, she felt no ill effects from the attempt, nor any aches and pains beyond the stiffness caused by staying too long abed.

"I'm hungry," she announced.

"Considerin' how long y've not eaten, tha's no surprise. What shall I bring yus?"

"Porridge to start, with raisins and cinnamon, and then . . ."

"We'll see how you feel," announced Thorn with his entrance, balancing his joy at seeing her awake with the more professional mien appropriate to one of the foremost magi in all the Realms.

For the time it took to produce the porridge, Thorn subjected Elora to a comprehensive medical examination, employing the purely physical skills of a physician as well as the more esoteric and specialized tools of a sorcerer. Both disciplines pronounced her fully recovered.

Sadly, that pronouncement didn't prevent Elora from nearly falling flat on her face as she clambered out of bed, intent on the bathroom and a long, luxurious soak in steaming water as she scrubbed herself clean. Thorn caught her as she stumbled and supported her easily to her destination. That was where Nelwyns invariably surprised other folk, who assumed that strength walked hand in hand with stature. Every now and then, some Daikini—usually pig-drunk and at the urging of equally soused comrades—determined to have some fun by picking on one of Thorn's race, only to find himself generally upended in a horse trough and wondering what giant had swatted him upside his head.

The tub was delicious, sized large enough so that she could actually float in it. Sensibly, however, Thorn had provided a stool for her to sit on in the water, to keep her from drowning. He also stayed in the room with her.

The bath was hot enough to produce a fair volume of steam yet as always Thorn proved impervious to the elemental extremes around him. Both Nelwyn and his clothes appeared completely unaffected by the humidity and Elora knew both would be dry to her touch. For a rude moment, she was tempted to splash him just to see what would happen, but common sense got the better of her. He was probably expecting it anyway.

"I can manage here on my own," she protested.

"Certainly as well as you managed to alight from your bed and cross the room," he agreed. "You're no longer sick, Elora, but you won't be fully recovered until you've regained your strength."

"Yes, Uncle," she grumped, using the term of endearment she reserved for him when she was in a mood.

"I've cared for you, girl, since you were in diapers," he said, by way of explanation. "It's an old habit I'm loath to give up just yet. Sorry."

"Sometimes that may not be enough." She'd meant that in jest but the words held an unintentional edge of seriousness that made Thorn nod.

"Doesn't mean I won't keep trying, Elora."

She had no answer that made her feel comfortable so she took refuge by dunking herself beneath the surface. He wasn't joking about her recovery, the bath soon provided proof positive of that. Before she'd soaped the top half of her body she felt like she'd been working a full day in Torquil's forge, shifting massive blocks of ore and slabs of finished metal by brute body force alone, without the aid of winches and pulleys. She was actually grateful when the Nelwyn shrugged off his surcoat, rolled up his sleeves, and took a scrub brush to her back. When he went to work on her scalp, with shampoo and massage, she began to purr.

She felt pampered and delicious—this was a treat she didn't want to end. Because the sensations were all positive, because she felt safe and secure, but mostly because she was still underestimating how deeply fatigue was ingrained in her body, she didn't notice when her awareness began to drift. Thorn did, of course, he was on the lookout for just such a lapse but seeing that she was in no real danger he took no action.

For Elora, the water changed texture around her, flowing where it had been still, burbling where it had been silent, refreshingly cool where it had felt warm near to boiling. There was life around her, as well, made plain by the tickling of fingerlings and minnows along the length of her body and between her toes. Her perceptions had widened from her tub to the Cascadel running past the fort.

She felt the water racing over the riverbed and, at the same time, was one with the earth that formed that bed. She felt grains of dirt being carried downstream, perhaps ultimately to form some of the silt banks that bedeviled boatmen trying to navigate their way to and from Sandeni. She felt new channels being etched in the river bottom, which in turn created wild new currents and rills to make these upland rapids even wilder and more untamable. At the same time, the water picked at both banks, at earth and stone together, gradually wearing them down to widen the course of the river. It wouldn't rush so quickly then, it might even prove manageable.

There was a heaviness to the earth that was new to her, a strange and continual sort of pounding. Intrigued, she pushed her perceptions upstream, noting as she went a growing absence of all but the smallest of fish. The farther she progressed, the more curiosity turned to outright concern and she felt Thorn's awareness focus alongside hers. He was still content to let her take the lead but now he was an active partner in their journey, ready to bolster her strength with his own or, if need be, cover any retreat.

They both noticed when the water turned foul, and not long after she identified the reason why. Waste matter, a lot of it, transforming this once-pristine stream into such a monumental sewer that it would be years before nature could flush it clean again.

At the same time, Elora's perceptions caught little evidence of landborne life. No deer close at hand, though this was their normal range, no elk, not even rabbits; all that could be classed as prey had fled, and as well the predators who hunted them. Save one.

She stopped, so suddenly that Thorn was caught off guard.

In the tub Elora lay still, barely breathing with but an intermittent pulse, while Thorn knelt, hands gently cupping her head.

They weren't alone in the room: Franjean and Rool hunkered watchfully on the counter by the washbasin while Luc-Jon stood just inside the door, the promised bowl of porridge growing cold in his hands. At Luc-Jon's feet, pretty much filling the available floorspace, crouched the puppy, but his attitude was deceptively casual. He was as alert as the others, as poised for action.

Far upriver, an astral projection of Elora crept ashore. By rights, in this form, she should be absolutely undetectable, especially given her inborn immunity to magic, but she took no chances regardless.

"There's nothing here," Thorn reported, after casting wide his own InSight.

"I know," she agreed. "That's just it. There's *nothing*. Not only are there no animals for as far as we can perceive, where are the peoples of Lesser Faery? Why haven't any naiads reported the poisoning of the river? It's their home, Drumheller, and we've the Liege Lord of Lesser Faery in residence at the fort, the overlord of their entire Realm. At the first sign of this, someone should have come screaming. No dryads, either, the trees around us are hollow, without any spirit at all. They're—just wood. No brownies, sprites, fairies, boggarts. What there is here is what we see with ordinary sight. Nothing more."

"How do you want to proceed, Elora?"

She smiled, broadly in spirit, reflected by the barest quirk at the corner of her physical mouth in the tub. The fact that he sounded so casual told her with banners how concerned he truly was for her welfare. She responded in kind.

"Carefully, old duffer." She looked around them, but saw nothing out of the ordinary. "What's so special about this stretch of the river, I wonder? Why draw us ashore here?"

"Isn't the road yonder?" he asked.

She nodded and was taking her first step toward it when his astral hand caught her arm, the shock as strong, the warning as urgent as if real flesh had come into contact.

"Wait!"

She heard nothing but that was no surprise. Her enhanced senses notwithstanding, Nelwyn ears were still keener than

Daikini, even in phantom bodies. Dimly, at a fair distance, she caught the rhythmic tread of boots moving in a quick military cadence that she identified as a jog trot. A dozen men, of good size, approaching from upriver. In the darkness, separated from the road by both forest and underbrush, she'd never get even a glimpse of the strangers, much less a useful look at them. But she stayed in place. Thorn had made no move since his first warning and instinct prompted her to follow his lead.

A new sound presented itself as counterpoint to the marching feet, that of tiny bells, a baker's dozen of them, thirteen in all, the pattern and stroke of their chiming telling Elora they were part of something being carried.

"They move fast," she commented as the party drew abreast of them.

"Be ready to run" was Thorn's reply and she had sense to confine her own response to a furrow of the brow, a purse of the lips.

With a start, she realized the night had fallen silent once more around them. Nothing disturbed the suddenly still air.

A faint *chuff* stirred the evening, the sound of a palanquin being set on the ground, followed by a ripple of bells as its passenger rose from his seat. The marchers began a chant, one that Elora had never heard before, low and sonorous, far deeper in pitch than she'd ever imagined a human voice could project, striking resonances more in common with a horn.

Whatever the men were carrying was tall and it took long, solid strides, planting its legs like pilings that could never be dislodged. Despite the evident risk, Elora shifted her position, moving forward from her hiding place and to the side, deliberately masking Thorn from view, hoping her immunity to magic would stand her in good stead. The stratagem was sound, but unfortunately there was a risk—that the stranger might seek them out with ordinary sight. Her astral form was as striking in appearance as its physical counterpart. Even in these heavily shadowed woods, she stood out like a beacon.

Time stretched. She had no idea how long she crouched motionless, tense as a drawn bow along the whole folded length of her, only that the strain had begun to make her intangible form ache. She didn't want to think how her true body would feel when she returned to it. The only minor comfort was that Thorn at least wouldn't chide her for her wanderings, and that he'd probably be just as sore.

A single rippling *cha-ching* marked a stir from the stranger, a shift in his massive weight. Somehow, this pause was worse than what had come before, and Elora was glad she had no weapon at hand. The temptation to race shrieking into battle—to satisfy the urge to do *some*thing—would have been near irresistible.

Then came another cascade of chimes, the *chuff* of retreating footfalls, the creak of wood and line from the palanquin as the bearers once more took up their burden. Without any verbal cue or command, they continued on their way, at that same implacable trot. In fairly short measure, they faded beyond Elora's hearing and, not long after, beyond Thorn's as well.

He didn't relax, not in the slightest, but tugged her elbow back toward the river.

"Quickly," he told her. "Quietly. Let us begone. And be more careful than before," he cautioned, in a tone that made it an absolute command, "because we'll have to pass them on our way home."

"They're gone, Thorn."

"And believe me, child, you don't want them coming back."

"What are they?"

"Barontës. And if the tales are true, a Caliban. The one are lesser sorcerers, forming a coven around the creature they serve. The other, the ultimate warrior wizard, as adept with enchantments as with blades."

"Like the Black Rose, you mean?"

"If only. Come. We're gone."

But to both their surprise, she pulled from his grasp and, ignoring the phantom creaks of phantom joints frozen in place, stepped forward from their hiding place, closer to the road.

"Elora Danan!" Thorn cried.

"Something happened here, Thorn."

They stood in a moderate clearing, accessible from road and stream yet possessing decent cover. The tree branches didn't begin until well above double the head height of a tall Daikini, which made the location good for cookfires. The earth was soft and loamy between her phantom toes, it had been recently turned.

"Someone died here," she said.

She lowered herself to her knees, then to her belly, stretching herself full length as though the ground were the softest of feather beds. To his credit, Thorn stayed silent, recognizing the quality in her announcement that made plain this was no casual discovery. Then, Elora tweaked her concentration just a little, loosening the mental bonds that anchored her to the world, and sank beneath its surface. Save for the density of the medium and the total absence of light, it was much the same for her as swimming underwater. The main difference was that water moved around her as she passed through it, its currents and eddies constantly affecting her course, whereas the ground stayed relatively fixed.

She didn't have far to go. Barely a body length in fact when her outstretched hand came across another.

It was a man, Daikini, strongly built. His death had caught him unawares, leaving no marks on his body or recognition of what was happening on his face. Elora assumed from that, he'd died in his sleep. In short order, she confirmed her worst fears, that he hadn't died alone.

MageSight guided her on her way, illuminating her way better than sunlight. The bodies were arranged in a line, along a fairly lengthy trench, buried quickly and without ceremony, so that most were piled one upon the other. All had been stripped of their outer garments and weapons; a few gave evidence of a struggle that must have been as fierce as it proved ultimately hopeless. She thought then of the creature Thorn had named, the Caliban, and wondered what part it had played in this massacre.

The men looked familiar, faces and figures briefly seen—no more than a glance—enough to register on her memory but lacking names to properly identify them or labels to tell her when and where. Until she came across one she knew.

"Fergal," she breathed, staring into his clouded eyes and trying not to note the snarl on his lips or the awful gaping wounds that marked his limbs and torso. He was a patrol sergeant, mainstay of the regiment. The kind of soldier who would never win prizes for deportment, whose uniform rarely stood the muster of a full-dress parade, but who also knew the Frontier like it was his own private preserve. In a scrap, it was said, there was none better to stand at your back. On patrol, though an officer had official command, those with sense, who truly knew their business, deferred to Fergal. It was whispered about the fort—no one who wanted to keep their features or their teeth was dolt enough to say so to his face—that he was mixed blood, that he could count an ancestor or three from beyond the Veil. Those who served with him counted that as a badge of honor, and pride. It was generally they who led the charge against any detractors.

His skill, his knowledge, his blood hadn't saved him. Or his men.

Elora's eyes burned with grief and fury . . .

. . . and the ground around her trembled ever so slightly at the Caliban's approach.

She came up fast and silently, slithering eel-like into the air to rejoin Drumheller. The night seemed to ring with chimes, telling her the Caliban was close and coming far faster than she would have expected given his bulk. His bearers, the Barontës, flanked him on either side, curling toward their position like the horns of a bull.

The path to the river was still clear. If they hurried, escape was possible.

It was a superb trap, she almost fell for it, but Thorn caught her eyes before she could take a step and told her all she needed to know.

She leaped on him, gathering Thorn close the way she used to hold her stuffed cuddly bear at bedtime, and plunged the pair of them back into the ground. Taking his cue from her, Thorn wrapped his arms around her neck, stumpy legs as best he could about her waist, allowing her the freedom to kick with arms and legs together.

A blast of rage thundered after them, as tangible to their phantom forms as an avalanche, and it took a fair chunk of Thorn's will combined with her own to keep them from being tumbled from their course as it overtook them. A hand came after and Elora prayed it was only imagination, and a hefty dollop of fright, that tipped its fingers with claws as long as she stood tall, sharp enough to slice soul from body.

She stayed well clear of the river, for she sensed as did Thorn that they would find some kind of net stretched across its width downstream, probably more than one, each more fine than the last, until they were snared. She wondered about their approach, and how early they'd been spotted, and with each question her estimation of their foes rose another significant notch.

Her special affinity for fire brought her unerringly to a rill of magma that coursed its way through the planetary mantle as its counterparts of water did across the surface. She could have made the whole journey through rock but this route was far quicker and a part of her was screaming all the while that time was of the essence. She slipped and slid her way along, following the course of the stream to the right, to the left, up and down, all the while at speeds that made the term *breakneck* seem tame by comparison, the child in her suddenly and surprisingly reasserting itself to shriek with delight at the madcap nature of their passage.

She perceived a beacon, far above and ahead, recognizing it as the grouped life forces of the inhabitants of the fort. She had perhaps a moment to marvel at the wondrous mix of intensities and hues that she realized had never been seen before in this World—where Daikini stood with Faery in common cause and common friendship—and then had to bend all her efforts to twisting free of the torrent before she was swept past her destination.

For those in the bath chamber, there was no warning. Elora lay in the tub, water cooled to the same temperature as her body, with Thorn supporting her head, the both of them barely breathing. Suddenly, the silence was shattered by the sound of lungs gulping in a tremendous breath of air. Elora's skin flushed a dark and angry rose beneath its hallmark silver, Thorn's turning likewise with the fierce onrush of blood. The water began to bubble boiling hot and those closest to the tub sprang back, Luc-Jon making a desperate grab for Thorn to yank him clear before the Nelwyn could be burned.

With Drumheller safe, the young man immediately turned back for Elora but she was already vaulting free of the tub, to land in a huddle in a far corner of the room, away from the others. When Luc-Jon turned toward her she warned him back with a flail of her hands, as though she couldn't yet trust her body to behave. It radiated such heat that water flashed to steam upon her skin.

"Drumheller," she called, concern making her normally broken voice sound even huskier than ever. "Thorn, are you all right? Luc-Jon, is he well?!"

"I'm fine, Elora Danan," came the Nelwyn's reply, emphasized by a chuckle of relief. "Bedazzled, I confess, but otherwise altogether well."

"I've never done that with another," she confessed. His head turned away at a decorous angle, Luc-Jon held out a robe, which Elora gratefully struggled into, belting it tight around her waist and closing the fastenings at its collar. She found it hard to look at Luc-Jon, either, suddenly uncomfortable that he'd seen her naked.

"Done what," asked Luc-Jon, and Elora saw that he felt much the same.

"Ridden a rapids of fire, my boy," Thorn told him, marveling at the experience, shaken by the cause, "through the bowels of the earth, in flight from a creature too terrible to name."

Luc-Jon began to grin and say, "Sounds like a story worth the writing," when his wolfhound sprang to his feet, as though the war tocsin had just sounded the call to arms. True, a trumpet could be heard, but that was merely to announce the approach of friendly forces.

"What's that?" Elora demanded of him, seeing Puppy's reaction.

"Only the lookout" was Luc-Jon's reply. "Most like, the scouting force back from the upper reaches of the Cascadel."

Before he finished his sentence, Elora bulled her way across the room and out the door, the hound right on her heels.

She was on the second floor of the hostel, in one of their best suites, and she took the stairs three at a time, racing outside to find herself at the opposite end of the waryard from the main gate. In her mind's eye, imagination revealed what couldn't yet be seen: a troop of a hundred cavalry emerging from the tree line a mile or so distant from the fort, approaching double file in good order, the situation as normal as could be.

She didn't pause. Somehow, she found the wherewithal actually to increase her speed, drawing on the fullest depths of her reserves without care of the cost as she sprinted across the sprawling yard, sparing breath she could ill afford in cry after cry at the gatehouse.

"Elora *Danan*!" squawked a protest in one ear, the elegantly clad brownie it came from struggling for purchase on her shoulder and a handhold on the neck hem of her robe. A flick of the eyes revealed that Rool rode on her right-hand side. She didn't need to pose any question, their next words anticipated them.

"You move fast," Rool told her proudly, "we move faster. Jumped aboard as you went by." Then he sounded a tad scandalized: "Didn't even notice, you! Just because you've been sick, think you can forget all we taught you?"

"Had enough of this, you going gallivanting about all by your lonesome," said Franjean, picking up an unspoken cue from his partner. "Makes us look bad, it does, like we can't properly discharge our duties. Don't matter where or when or why—you go, we go with, an' there's the end to it! Can't do a decent job as your protectors, with you always trying to leave us behind!"

"So what's the problem, hey?"

"Sound the alarm," she bellowed to the guardhouse, ignoring her diminutive companions, "close the gates! It's a trick! Those riders are impostors!"

If the sentries heard her, they didn't believe. Not right away. Some heads turned at the sound and sight of her, this slim, lean, silver figure racing flat out for the gate with a wolfhound at her side. It was Puppy, did the trick, as he let loose a howl that raised the hackles on every neck. Few had ever heard such a noise, because precious few—even among the troops—had ever seen these magnificent beasts at war, but all recognized the sound, those of Faery as well as the Daikini. And hearing it, found themselves reflexively grabbing for weapons.

The hound bayed a second time, and this time his clarion call was taken up by his fellow pack members. One, then two, a half-dozen, the whole of his extended family, some taking up the charge to join him while others hung back to form a second line of defense, their movements as purposeful as those of the troops they served.

Even though the sounds and actions within the fort were hidden from outside view by its massive walls, some element of Elora's headlong dash must have communicated itself to the approaching patrol, for they spurred their mounts into a gallop, as intent now on reaching the gate as Elora.

The young woman didn't slow her pace in the slightest, even when a few of the sentries stepped forward to block her path. All but one she dodged, with a ridiculous ease that left the soldiers flat-footed in her wake. This last, a woman, was treated to a body check that popped her instantly to the ground, hard enough on her backside to dislodge her grip on a halberd spear as long as Elora was tall, topped by a curved blade that extended it by an arm's length. Most spears were designed as stabbing weapons, to be used in massed formations of infantry. This was meant more for a woman's use, utilizing agility and speed more than raw strength; in trained hands it was much like wielding a sword with double the normal reach and more. It could be especially effective against cavalry.

Elora spared herself time and breath for one last cry, over her shoulder because she refused to slacken her pace by even a step, and this was with the voice she'd learned in Angwyn, watching the King, and later in battle, listening to his daughter Anakerie. It was a voice of Royal command and to hear it was to obey, instinctively, immediately, and without hesitation.

"Close the gate!" she yelled, noting that the onrushing riders had spread out into a rough arrowhead formation. Their own spears were still held upright, maintaining the fiction that they were friendly. Elora's, she held across her front at a diagonal, the blade pointing up and back over her right shoulder.

Behind, so far away it seemed the fort had receded to the very horizon (she should be so fortunate), she made out the belated sound of the alarm tocsin, shouted orders, the bustle of soldiery reacting too late to the attack. Someone at long last had recognized the cavalry charge for what it truly was. Then, Elora thrust all awareness from her but that of the task at hand. She reached once more to the earth that had so often sustained her and set loose another charge of magma from her heart, giving fire to her blood and strength to every muscle.

With a bellow of defiance, she swung her spear for the rider to her left.

He ducked, sensible fellow, and the blade whizzed past his ear in a clean miss. Sadly, he wasn't her intended target as she reversed the grip of her hands and thrust the butt of her staff up and sideways into the body of the man who headed the spear-point of the charge. Caught unawares, the solid impact stopped him in his tracks, the shock transmitting itself down the shaft of the spear and into Elora's shoulders like a direct physical blow. She thought her arms might pop from their sockets. Instead, the rider was catapulted from his saddle.

She gave no thought to the man she'd deliberately missed. He had troubles of his own, as did many of his fellows, as Puppy and his pack went for mounts and riders both. She heard a cry, panic and pain mixed, topped by a snarl as the trooper was tackled by Elora's wolfhound. All around her, the attack dissolved into chaos, the irresistible momentum of the charge disrupted by snapping jaws and rearing, terrified horses. At the same time, the brownies made their own contribution, loosing arrow after arrow from their bows, imbuing each shaft with that portion of their life force sufficient to make them strike like battering rams. With the horses, they weren't as blunt, choosing lances that stung rather than bludgeoned and letting the animals themselves take care of the rest as they reacted to what must feel like the ultimate bee sting.

Elora had no hope of actually stopping the attack, even with the brownies' and Puppy's help; the odds against them were simply too great and the ground too advantageous to her foes. True, the first section of the charge had been thrown into chaos and the momentum of the assault broken, but she was engaging only a fraction of the total force. The rest speedily regrouped, fanning out from Elora on either side, bypassing her in favor of their true objective.

However, precious time had been lost. Not much in objective terms, hardly more than a minute, but militarily that proved a fatal delay. Archers had reached their firing posts on the parapet, their great longbows capable of punching steel-tipped yew shafts through plate armor at a hundred yards and more. A squad of infantry formed ranks outside the gate, advancing to Elora's support, ready to sacrifice their own lives in her defense. But the gate itself remained infuriatingly open, and the thought chilled Elora that perhaps treachery was involved here.

That thought was nearly her last as a frantic backpedal barely cleared her from a wild sword swing, a miss so close that her robe was sliced open across the whole width of her belly. She was already swinging the butt of her spear around to crack the man upside his head when another, burlier figure rose from the ground. Luc-Jon wrenched the warrior's sword from his unconscious grasp and took a stance at Elora's back. The next few moments were for them both a continuous flow of movement, bobbing and weaving, spinning high, crouching low, Elora using her spear as club, as scythe, breaking bones when she had to, drawing blood when there was no other choice. The battle became for her a kind of dance, possessing a grace and murderous beauty all its own that at once repelled and excited her. Facing the abyss of death, she had never felt more alive, eyes sparkling, the most madcap of grins on her face. By her side, Luc-Jon wielded his sword with a rough-hewn skill that matched his appearance. He'd win no points in a tournament for style, but none of his foes came close with their own blades, while his in turn tended to find its way unerringly through their defenses.

A trumpet sounded, and the ground trembled slightly with the sudden cavalcade of hooves. Behind Elora, the clash of arms picked up in intensity as cavalry from within the fort broke forth to join the fray. With their assault, at long last, the gates of Fort Tregare finally swung shut.

With their arrival, the tide of battle turned for good.

CHAPTER
4

JUST AFTER SUNSET, THE COLONEL CALLED A COUNCIL OF
war. Originally, Elora had wanted no part of it. As the battle
before the main gate wound down to its inevitable bloody
and brutal conclusion—as it became clear that the attackers
had no intention of surrendering but were determined instead
to sell their lives as dearly as possible—the day's exertions at
last caught up with her. She began to sway and tremble, her
muscles losing the ability to support her body's weight. A
spear she'd wielded as though it weighed nothing suddenly
became heavier than lead in her grasp. One of the attackers,
seeing an opportunity, made a charge for her, only to be blindsided by Luc-Jon. The pair of them went down in a tangle of
limbs and Elora's heart leaped to her throat with fear for her
friend, as she saw how clearly he was outmatched. The

attacker raised a knife—and Luc-Jon's hound crashed into the man with the force of a battering ram, using powerful shoulders and chest to drive the warrior to the ground and then closing his great jaws about the man's head. A single shake was all the hound needed to end the fight and then he took Luc-Jon by the scruff of the neck, to drag him close by where Elora stood.

She collapsed to her knees beside the young man, trusting to hound and brownies to watch over her while she tended to Luc-Jon. He looked a mess, as no doubt did she, but his hurts were superficial. Little of the blood that was splashed across skin and clothes was his own and what blows he'd taken in the fight had left him mainly with aches and bruises.

A shape moved between her and the sun but Elora didn't need to see the woman's features to recognize Khory Bannefin. The warrior stalked in a quick circle around the girl, a half-dozen paces out from where Elora knelt, close enough to offer decent protection, far enough distant to allow decent room to maneuver.

"*Alive,*" she heard someone cry in a voice hoarse from trying to make itself heard over the din of the brief and brutal conflict. She couldn't place either face or name to it but from the tone of command she assumed it was one of the officers. "Colonel wants prisoners, Shando!"

"Doin' our best, Cap," came the reply, from a sergeant she knew.

"Bloody hell," snarled Khory with rare vehemence, and a shiver trilled up Elora's spine at the realization that the warrior's anger was directed at her.

"Lady Khory," Luc-Jon tried to say in Elora's defense, but Khory cut him off.

"I'm no lady," she snapped. "Sit and be silent."

Khory gave him no time to think, no room for argument. Before Luc-Jon knew it, he was once more on his rump. Only his hound wasn't cowed in the slightest by the warrior's fury, but Elora also noted that the dog always looked in the direction opposite from Khory's gaze, automatically covering her back as she was Elora's.

"I'm sorry," Elora started to say and then cut herself off because she wasn't. When Khory turned to glare at her, with a gaze that would do a basilisk proud, she met the tall woman's gaze without flinching.

"Bloody *hell*," Khory growled again. "What were you thinking, Elora Danan, playing hero like that?!"

"I saw what was happening. I had to stop it."

"You like to got yourself killed, girl."

"If I'd done nothing and these attackers had seized the barbican and the gate, would we be any better off?"

"That's not the point."

"Oh. Forgive me. I forgot. I'm the Sacred Princess. I'm the Savior of the World. Fates forfend I should ever lift a hand in my own cause."

"Don't play the snip with me, girl. You don't have that much luck left that you can afford to press it so—and, yes, after the Dragon's Realm you should think more on the consequences of your acts before indulging yourself."

"The same applies to you, Khory Bannefin, and to Drumheller."

"You went to the Dragon's Realm?" Luc-Jon asked in a voice barely louder than a whisper.

"Mind your tongue, boy," Khory told him, "and your business." Then it was back to Elora. "It's different with us."

"Not if you're killed."

"Listen for once, will you? And heed my words. This is my craft. You need blood shed, or lives taken, *I'm* the one to do it, not you."

"You weren't here."

Khory ignored Elora's reply and looked instead at Luc-Jon. "You hurt?"

He shook his head. "Not so's it matters."

"On your feet, then. Give a hand with Elora Danan."

The hound rose, too, with that smooth, effortless, almost liquid grace unique to his kind. Elora hated being singled out for special attention, but she couldn't deny that she also appreciated the help. There was nothing smooth or effortless or especially liquid about her own ascent; she clambered up in fits and starts, marked by pinpoint bursts of pain at every joint. She was grateful for Luc-Jon's arm about her waist. Though she'd managed to drape her own across his broad shoulders, she had no illusions about how much good it'd do if she started to fall.

In the aftermath of battle, troopers from the fort had been busy. The enemy slain were being dragged to a communal grave, the few survivors manacled and placed under guard. Even so, Khory took no chances. She gave the scene a wide berth, with herself and the hound between Elora and their foes. Luc-Jon was not only responsible for helping her, his own eyes ranged the field beyond, just in case any attackers had been missed. As they made their deliberate way toward the main gate, Elora noted a fair number of Sandeni soldiers among the dead, precious few in the hands of the healers, and asked about that.

It was the sergeant she'd heard earlier, Shando, who answered.

"Not much for mercy, the Chengwei," he told her, his own demeanor as wary and alert as Khory's, his sword loose in its scabbard, right hand close by and ready, "in a fight or after."

"Chengwei," stammered Luc-Jon, "so far from home and in these mountains? Shando, are you sure?"

"You know your business, scribe. I know mine. Weren't no raidin' party neither, no band o' deserters nor renegades," he continued, forestalling Luc-Jon's next question, "these were proper soldiers, professionals." Shando looked ahead at the towering ramparts of the fort, mouth twisting as though he'd suddenly tasted something vile. "If they'd seized the gate . . ." The way he said that left no doubt in anyone's mind as to the consequences. "E'en so, even with the warning—an' f'r tha', 'Lora Danan, me an' mine, we're more grateful than y' can know—it were a near thing, this scrap. They got more like these follerin' along behind, well we're in f'r a rare fight an' tha's no error."

"They have more," Elora said flatly.

"Best tell the Colonel."

"Drumheller's already doing so," said Khory. "This one's for where she belongs, bed."

"I'm all right, Khory," Elora protested.

"Let her go then, lad," the warrior told Luc-Jon. "Let's see her walk unaided."

"She'll fall!"

"The hell I will," growled Elora.

"Then my point's proven."

"Y'll need the rest, lass," Shando advised her gently. "We all will. The way this lot fights"—and he waved a hand toward the Chengwei—"it puts the Maizan t' shame. We stand against them, it'll be a brutal, bloody business. We'll need all our strength—*watch out there!*"

A pair of riders, each leading a remount right as they left the gate, barely missed Elora's party as they peeled right and thundered around the periphery of the stronghold to intercept the main road back to Sandeni. They were couriers, stripped to the bare minimum of clothes and equipment—light chain mail for defense, sword and daggers for weapons, hardtack and canteen for food, plus a rucksack of oats for their mounts, and a light racing saddle— trusting in their animals' speed and endurance to carry them past any danger.

Khory spat a mouthful of dust as she watched the riders disappear around the farthest balustrade.

"Only two riders," Elora noted, mainly to herself, "both heading downriver, to Sandeni."

She twisted slightly in Luc-Jon's grasp, to allow her eyes to take in the wide expanse of forest that filled her view of the other direction, from where the Chengwei had come.

"Shando, how many other patrols are there?"

"Four more all told, the best part of a reinforced comp'ny."

"They get no warning of what's happening?"

"Colonel's orders, m'lady. Tha's why he stands 'neath the eagle standard, t' make those kinds'a calls. Y'r pardon, 'Lora, but I best be returnin' t' me duties."

They stood now in the shadow of the gate itself, with armed troops on every side.

"He can't just abandon them, Khory," Elora said as the sergeant moved off.

"There are other ways of sending messages, lass," the warrior told her. "Quicker and more certain, especially given our allies, and the circumstances. The Colonel's a good man, he knows his business. Let's leave him to it and see you safely home."

Elora refused to acknowledge her exhaustion; the awful paradox was that she was so far gone with fatigue, she found she could neither sleep nor eat. Her nerves were still jangly from the ferocious outburst of energy that had propelled her out the gate, try as she might she couldn't find a way to relax. Worse, the very taste and scent of food—even the forest stew that was her favorite—made her ill.

At the same time, obstacles to sleep piled up around her higher and faster than snowdrifts in a midwinter blizzard. Orders had been issued to all the fort's master craftsmen and women and within the hour the waryard was bustling with activity. Teams of quartermasters scurried through the great underground storage bunkers beneath the fort, to make a comprehensive inventory of the stronghold's reserves of food and other supplies. The hearths along blacksmith's row blazed hot and high, as troopers came by in shifts to have their blades sharpened and their armor repaired. At the same time, scores of molds were put to use to forge replacement weapons for those sure to be lost over the course of the battle to come so that the yard rang with the constant din of hammers tempering that freshly minted steel. Teachers and some of the parents did their best to calm the growing apprehension in the many children—far too many, Elora realized, the fort's population of noncombatants swollen near to bursting over the past weeks with refugees from the Frontier towns upriver—while others worked in the hospital, rolling bandages and packing first-aid kits for use on the front lines.

Livestock represented one of the greater problems: how much would be needed to sustain the fort in case of siege? How many head of cattle and sheep could the defenders afford to keep alive, how much could be slaughtered and placed in storage, what to do with the numbers that remained? There were howls of protest from farmers and ranchers at the sacrifice of their stock, and precious little faith in the vouchers handed out in return, even though they were promised compensation for their loss at full market value. Some demanded the Colonel drive the combined herd downriver and when he refused, citing the need to keep every fighting man and woman at the fort, they demanded permission to take the herd themselves, and their families with them.

To that demand, reluctantly, the Colonel acceded and another set of frantic preparations was begun among the refugees for a departure the next morning at first light. In the meanwhile, Elora added all the myriad sounds of the barnyard to the catalog of her misery.

When Drumheller poked his head around the door of her room as the last bits of outside light faded to darkness through the slats of her window shades, Elora was actually relieved.

"Whassup?" she asked him from underneath a small mountain of down pillows.

"Colonel DeGuerin requests the pleasure of your company, child."

She shifted position and triggered a modest avalanche of bedding.

"You saw everything I did," she said.

"Perhaps. But I wasn't the one who sounded the alarm."

She considered a moment, pursing her lips in thought, and then began a wiggle toward the edge of the bed. She was still too sore and tired to consider leaping to her feet. In passing, she blearily noted Rool atop the headboard, making no secret of his amusement at her state as he reviewed her progress. She rewarded him by sticking out her tongue, which made him laugh. Franjean struck an elegant pose on the nearby cedar chest and indicated the neatly folded cloth that rose beside him almost to the height of his own head. It was a *caracalla,* a warrior's scarlet war cloak, of a melton wool so tightly woven it was as impervious to the elements as oilcloth. This one had clearly been made for Elora by the brownies, their fingers as nimble and talented with needle and thread as with picklocks, gaining them renown as tailors to match their fame as thieves and cutpurses. Though it weighed the proverbial ton it hung with surprising comfort from her shoulders, cut so superbly that its clasp didn't need to be closed to stay anchored in place.

"You've outdone yourselves, my lads," she complimented them. "This feels delicious."

"The weave's laced through with ironcloth," Franjean told her. "Not as strong as the pure fabric or steel mail but it'll deflect its share of attacks."

"Certainly easier to wear." Elora snugged the cloak close about her body over her nightgown and was about to slip her feet into shearling-lined boots when she looked up at Thorn. "Can I at least make myself presentable?"

He smiled. "I think we can afford the time."

She allowed herself a half hour for the change, not because she wanted to keep the Colonel waiting but because she wanted to make the right impression on him and his officers. She chose to wear a jumper rather than pants because her intent was to retire to bed as soon as he was done with her. The key was a steaming hot bath and a session with a scrubbing brush that left her skin tingling clean. Thankfully her close-cropped hair, that owing to the Deceiver's enchantment had grown as absolute a black in color as her skin was purest silver, was easily managed.

The council was in the Colonel's office; all the chairs had been cleared away and his desk covered with a fair-sized jumble of maps. Around it crowded his battle staff—senior officers, senior noncommissioned officers, the Chief of Scouts, the surgeon, the chief quartermaster, the chief armorer, plus representatives of the civilian residents and most importantly of the Veil Folk who'd allied themselves with the Daikini of Sandeni—and they greeted Elora's arrival with a mix of emotions and responses. Among the Daikini officers, disdain and an instance or two of dismissal if not outright hostility; whatever her title and reputation they considered her little more than a slip of a girl, with precious little to offer their deliberations. The noncoms knew her better. Shando quirked his lips in what passed with him for a smile of welcome. Tyrrel, Liege Lord of the Realm of Lesser Faery, was more open with his own greeting, striding over to embrace her with a hug that left her near breathless.

Ranulf DeGuerin was more reserved and circumspect in both regards and Elora understood in that instant why his men respected him. Whatever his feelings, he kept them superbly masked as he indicated a place for her and Drumheller opposite him at the table.

The air in the room was close, too many people, too much agitation, and, though few here would admit it, too much fear. There was only a handful of candles, Elora noted, most of the illumination provided by Faery globes, spheres of clear crystal that glowed when charged at the heart by the touch of magic. The atmosphere was electric with tension, like the sky with summer lightning in the advent of a storm.

DeGuerin himself was the supernally calm center of this growing tempest. He was the kind of man most folks called *compact* because to describe him as short—which is what he was, standing at full height better at Elora Danan's shoulder—would be sure to provoke a fight. By the same token, any such fight, he'd be sure to win, because every aspect of his body bespoke solidity and strength, as though someone had cast the trunk of an oak in human form and set it walking across the world. His beard and what was left of his hair were the color of coal, very lightly dusted with snow, and his eyes were dark as well. He'd served the Republic for thirty years and while the rigors of that duty had been etched indelibly on his face they were tempered by equally deep lines of laughter and good humor. From Shando, Elora had learned that his men would follow him anywhere, secure in the faith that if there was a way to bring them safely home, he'd be sure to find it. At the same time, precious few considered themselves arrogant—or fool—enough to face him over a game of chance or strategy. He was a man who liked to win, and who was very good at it.

"On behalf of the Republic of Sandeni," Colonel DeGuerin said quietly, "I bid you welcome, Elora Danan, to Fort Tregare. Though as I recall, this isn't the first time you've graced us with your presence."

She flushed, the rush of blood touching her argent features with the palest hint of rose, casting memory back a few scant months to the nights she spent here in the company of a troubadour named Duguay Faralorn. Through him she had found in herself an ability to sing and through those songs to inspire powerful emotions in her audience. Like many she had known, Duguay turned out to be far more than he seemed. He wasn't human at all, but an otherworldly entity of transcendent power called the Lord of the Dance, who had sought to win her to his side as his eternal partner. Instead, it was she who'd won his heart and as a consequence in the Dragon's Realm he had sacrificed himself to save her and her companions.

"It was kind of you to remember, Colonel," she replied.

"Nothing of the sort. It was a rather remarkable performance. Capped, I believe, by a tumult at our main gate that involved you."

"And some Maizan," she finished.

"Then as now, we are in your debt."

"How may I help?"

She wasn't conscious of swaying, and only barely noticed an answering flick of the hand from DeGuerin, she was mainly concerned with stifling a sudden great and unexpected yawn. A moment later, an orderly stepped up behind her, campaign chair in hand. Gratefully, she sank onto the leather-covered seat and pulled her cloak more snugly about her, acutely conscious of how sickly she must look to the others.

She met Thorn's gaze, intense and concerned, and managed a wry grin.

"More tired than I thought," she said.

"Hardly a surprise," he answered, "considering."

"In that case," the Colonel said, "we'll be brief."

He set both fists on the table and leaned his weight on them, giving his attention first to the maps, then to Elora.

He didn't request her own recitation of events. Instead, he looked at her from under his dark brows, reminding her disconcertingly of a Highland wolf, and asked simply: "How many?"

She took a breath to settle her thoughts. An answer leaped to the tip of her tongue but she kept it captive a small while longer, letting her body curve against the back of her chair as she considered what she wanted to say. Some of the officers thought she was being disrespectful; she didn't care. She was returning to the earth, reaching downward with that part of her spirit which resonated most strongly with the world beneath her, feeling once more the tread of countless feet upon its surface.

She blinked once, twice, restored her posture.

"If you kill a hundred of them," she said, "for every one of us within these walls—warrior and civilian, man, woman, child,

Daikini and Veil Folk—they'll hardly notice the loss. A thousand, perhaps, might give them pause. Nothing less."

"Impossible," snapped one of the officers. "Who could muster such a force?"

"The one thing the Chengwei have never lacked," replied the Colonel, "is manpower."

"But to march an army through these mountains? Colonel, they'd have had to cross the Stairs to Heaven themselves!"

"Evidently they found a way, Lieutenant."

"But to bring such a force this far undetected?" questioned another.

"Frontier's been pretty much deserted these past months," said the Chief of Scouts, a lean, laconic man whose dress was as individual as his manner, a haphazard combination of military uniform and outback buckskin. Of them all, he was the only one to wear his hair long, gathered together in a queue the same way Rool wore his and held by a similar clasp.

"A raiding party, I can understand, slipping past our patrols. This is an army!"

"Din't slip past nothin', Cap," growled Shando. "Ran right over the patrol what found 'em."

"Your point being, First Sergeant?" prompted the Colonel.

"Weren't newbies, that lot, sir, none of 'em. Were a good troop, well led. They knew the ground, they knew trouble. They had experience fightin' the likes of us"—meaning Daikini and specifically the Maizan—"an' the likes of them." He poked a thumb toward Tyrrel. "Meanin' no disrespect, Highness."

"None taken, First Sergeant," said the Faery sovereign in acknowledgment.

"So how come they got so dead so quick? Not a one of 'em managed to get hisself clear?"

"There's a more disturbing implication," interjected Thorn. "Originally, our enemies hereabouts were renegade forces of the Realm of Greater Faery." Lesser Faery consisted of those races among the Veil Folk who lived mainly in the world, on the Daikini side of the Veil. Fairies, sprites, boggarts, trolls, ogres, nixies and pixies, naiads and dryads, Nelwyns like Thorn Drumheller—and, of course, brownies—to name but a few of their number. The peoples of Greater Faery resided on a different plane of existence; the world was someplace they chose to visit, and then only rarely—it was never their home.

"As a consequence," he continued, "and thanks to our alliance with Tyrrel and his folk, all Sandeni patrols should have included representatives of Lesser Faery, to warn their Daikini companions of any magical attack and provide a more secure and efficient means of communication with headquarters." He looked to Tyrrel. "I take it you felt nothing amiss in this instance."

Tyrrel slowly shook his head. The thought hadn't occurred to him.

"So," said Thorn, putting a period to his ruminations. "Their powers are arcane as well as temporal. Moreover, they have the means of keeping their deeds close and well hidden."

"How long?" Colonel DeGuerin demanded of Elora, but it was one of his staff who answered.

"From where the girl and Master Drumheller encountered the patrol"—he consulted one of the maps to be sure—"better than a week. Possibly even closer to a fortnight. Plenty of time to prepare proper defenses, and possibly bring up reinforcements."

"A day," Elora countered flatly. "No more than two."

"This is our business, young woman," said the officer who'd just spoken.

Elora felt like she'd been thrown into the suttler's store and told to fill her arms with supplies; given a scant minute to grab hold of everything she could possibly carry, she clutched at ideas with frantic speed, trusting instinct to guide her as she gave voice to her thoughts without even the barest moment to evaluate what she was saying. When she was first at the fort, she'd spent many an evening listening intently to the Colonel and his officers relaxing after dinner. They never noticed the serving girl who hovered in the shadows, ever-ready with the wine as they talked strategy and tactics until all hours. Now, she put all the knowledge she'd gathered from him—and Drumheller, and Khory, and others along the highway of her life—to the test.

"A hundred men, no matter how skilled, can't hold the main

gate of this fort for a week. Even if they torched it, and the wall as well, that week's more than enough time to effect repairs. True," she acknowledged, "the main body of the Chengwei army is farther back. There's no way to hide the tread of so many feet, especially as they close in. But put a force between them, a proper regiment, heavy cavalry most like, and it's a whole different game."

"Your sorcery tell you all that, girl?" scoffed the officer.

My wits, she almost said, but fortunately managed to bite back her reply. *I have no sorcery.*

"Suppose the commando assault had proved successful," Elora continued to make her case, ignoring the interruption. "Right away, we're on the active defensive, fighting desperately to retake positions already lost, or repair what's been destroyed. We're so caught up in one threat—because we believe we *know* how far away the main body is, and how much time that likely gives us— we've no resources to spare against another. Even if we defeat the second strike force, we've lost troops and matériel and especially time that can't be replaced. When the final assault comes, we'll be that much weaker."

Her gaze met the Colonel's and found confirmation of her analysis. He'd come to the same conclusion, had entered the room hours ago with it. He'd brought her here, invited her to speak her mind, as a test of her own ability.

"Your response, Elora Danan?" he asked her. *To both the Chengwei threat,* she realized, *and the implicit challenge of his officer.*

She shrugged her shoulders, pursed her lips. "Truth to tell," she confessed, "I haven't a clue. As you say," she told the officer, "this is *your* business. I've only just begun to learn the craft."

She evidently struck the proper note of respect and contrition because the mood among the officers eased a fraction. Before they got too comfortable with themselves, however, their commander cast their presumptions to the dust.

"As it happens," he said, "the Sacred Princess's strategic and tactical analysis squares with my own." His use of her title was intentional and deliberate, to remind his staff of her proper place in the scheme of things, one that stood far higher than their own.

"Only an idiot throws away a force of this caliber to no purpose, and whatever we may think of this Chengwei commander, he is no idiot. The fact that he was able to cross the Stairs to Heaven at all is proof of that.

"I believe we can expect a significant assault at any time. Convey that alert to the watchtowers. Anyone who sleeps at his post had best pray the Chengwei slit his throat because I guarantee to make him wish he'd never been born.

"Our one advantage is that this second force shouldn't have much in the way of siege equipment. Bridges to span the moat, ladders for the wall, battering rams for the gates, that should be the extent of it. Anything more will slow them down too much. So, fortunately, no catapults of size, no engines, no assault towers. They'll come later.

"And when that main force of Chengwei does arrive, I want them to have to reach our walls over a carpet of their own dead."

It was a sober speech, and a somber group that broke not long after to continue preparations for the fort's defense. Only four remained with the Colonel as he set glasses on the table and opened his sideboard for a bottle of fine cognac and his humidor of cigars. With an air of tradition, DeGuerin poured each of them—Shando, Tyrrel, Thorn, and Elora—a double thimbleful. Then he raised his own glass and though he was looking toward them his gaze encompassed far more than this room and those within.

"I could ask for better odds," he said, "but not comrades." His eyes turned to Elora and she rose to her feet. "And certainly not a better cause. It is both honor and high privilege to stand with you, Lady," and he touched the rim of his glass lightly to hers, the crystal sounding a pure, clarion note at the contact, "and with you, my friends."

Shando drained his glass in a single gulp, then withdrew, taking refuge from the emotions of the moment in his duties as First Sergeant of the Regiment.

"My folk are already at work," Tyrrel told the Colonel. "Come morning, our foes will have an easier time crossing a bog than the field beyond the moat."

Elora shook her head, savoring the heady tang of the cognac as it scorched flame over her tongue and down her throat. It was a little like swallowing a firedrake and she had to restrain herself from an attack of giggles.

"By midday," she said, "the ground will be bone dry, with the Caliban and his pet monsters waiting for any of your folk foolish enough to venture forth to try to reenergize the spells. Would they come so far, Colonel, without preparing for every contingency?"

"They're a methodical people, the Chengwei." They were the oldest Empire in the Daikini world, and the most arrogant race. They dominated the eastern half of the continent and if not for the presence of Sandeni would have long ago fulfilled their manifest destiny and pushed their borders to the Sunset shore. Too often in past days, a new Khagan would claim the Jade Palace in the Imperial Capital of Daido and proceed to forget the lessons of history, or believe he was brilliant enough to overcome them. Once more, armies would follow the sun and a new generation would spend its best and brightest on the highland plains before Sandeni as the Republic sanctified its freedom with blood.

With the rise of Angwyn in the west, a balance of power had been achieved across the continent. No longer did Sandeni stand alone and the Chengwei seemed to discover the value of coexistence. Sadly, though, old hatreds die hardest of all and the sudden fall of Angwyn to the Deceiver created a political and military vacuum the Chengwei had evidently found irresistible. With the Maizan pressing from the Cascadel side of the Wall, this must have seemed the perfect opportunity to catch the Republic between the jaws of a monumental nutcracker, especially considering their contemptuous opinion of the Maizan, whom intelligence reports said the Chengwei considered prairie nomads, barbarians who would prove a foe of minimal consequence.

In that respect, the Chengwei were in for a rude surprise. But that realization was of little comfort to the defenders of Fort Tregare.

"By all means, Highness," DeGuerin finished to Tyrrel, "do your best, but as the Sacred Princess says, keep your folk within the walls when the enemy arrives."

"Truly the Caliban, Drumheller?" Tyrrel asked of Thorn. "In all my years, I've felt no sign of its feet upon the earth."

"By rights, by legend, you're not supposed to. Like a demon, the Caliban walks beyond the boundaries of the Twelve Realms. Like demons, the price of its summoning is . . ." Drumheller's voice trailed off, his words inadequate to encompass the horror of his imagination.

"What is it?" Elora inquired. "Before this, I'd never heard of the monster."

"It's a name rarely mentioned," Thorn replied, "for fear it might hear and answer the call. It slays those who work with magic, and claims their power for its own. Hence, the Barontës. It travels with its own sorcerous circle. Some tales call it the one foe the Malevoiy respect and possibly even fear. Others say it is their creature. On one thing the stories all agree, no one who ever faced the Caliban in battle survived to tell the tale."

"How do you kill it?" the Colonel asked.

Thorn looked lost. "I don't know," he said.

"Can it be killed?" wondered Tyrrel aloud, to receive the same reply.

"I don't know."

"Colonel," asked Elora, "what about the women and children? There must be something we can do for them."

DeGuerin shook his head. "I'll tell you what I told the ranchers and homesteaders earlier today, lass; I can't spare the troops for an escort back to Sandeni. Even if I could, time's too short. Chengwei cavalry would quickly catch them on the open road. I'm sorry."

After that, there was little more to say, so Elora took her leave.

Luc-Jon was waiting on the porch, along with his hound. Without preamble, without even a word, Elora pressed herself against him, gathering him as close as she could in a fierce embrace that the longer it lasted, the less she wanted it to end. The young man didn't know what to do with his hands at first. The naked declaration of her feelings startled him, stripped him at first of the ability to respond. His own initial touch was far more gentle, even though her own strength left him near gasping. Her rangy figure was deceptive, masking muscles he suspected could lift him from his feet without exceptional effort.

There was no flex to her as his own hold tightened. She might well have been cast from the pure metal she so closely resembled.

By contrast, each breath filled his head with the scent of her. A soft perfume from the soaps used in her bath. A clean, windswept tang to her hair that reminded him of highland woods on a crisp spring day with the breeze rippling through the trees. An underlying taste that was uniquely her own and that he knew he would never forget.

"It can't be so bad," he offered by way of comfort, after what seemed like an indecently long while.

"No, it can't," she agreed, her voice muffled against his cloak-covered shoulder. Then, she pulled away, breaking his grip on her as if it were nothing, and when she spoke again both eyes and voice were haunted. "But it is," she said.

And she told him why.

"You need sleep," he recommended, as they walked hand in hand through the compound.

"I've had my share and more."

"You need food."

"I've eaten. I'll be fine, Luc-Jon."

"I didn't think I'd see you again so soon."

"I'm just sorry for the circumstances." She uttered a small sigh and scuffed the hardpan dirt of the parade ground with the toe of her boot. "There are times I really wish disaster didn't follow quite so close on my heels."

The Chengwei didn't come that night, nor the following one, and Elora began to hear mutterings throughout the stronghold that she'd sounded a false alarm, though none of those comments came from any of the garrison. Among the troops there was a deep and lasting fury, at the way the raiders had dishonored the mur-dered patrol by using their uniforms. The frustration here came from waiting for the enemy to make the next move, when every desire in these proud, professional soldiers was to seize the initia-tive and take the fight to their foe.

The civilian residents of the fort, the refugees, quickly began to chafe under DeGuerin's strict martial regime. He was preparing for a seige they doubted would come. Some even scoffed at her report of the main force itself, speculating that the raiders who'd attacked the fort were no more than what they seemed, a band of overly ambitious renegades. It didn't seem to matter that all the decisions were the Colonel's, based on his own assessment of the situation; somehow, it seemed more natural to heap all the blame on the Sacred Princess.

As a consequence, Elora stayed pretty much to herself. She stuffed herself to bursting, scarfing food like a starving wolf as she rushed to rebuild her strength after her fever, and she slept. Time and again during the day she cast her consciousness into the earth, seeking any sign of the approaching Chengwei, only to find an eerie and uncharacteristic silence. When she reported the experience to Thorn Drumheller, the best description that came to her was of an aural fog, that occluded sound the way its counterpart did sight. She'd never experienced the like and though she had no tangible evidence to support her assertion she was sure its presence was both artificial and malevolent. At the same time, she never allowed her spirit self to stray too far nor to roam free of her physical body for too long. She remembered how close the Caliban had come to catching her; she didn't want to give it even the ghost of another chance.

By day, she was most often found with Luc-Jon. As a senior apprentice scribe, his place was to be present at whatever meetings and conferences his master could not attend, to make a comprehensive record of what transpired and, if required, draft any letters. He had a clear, legible hand, and a quick one, so he was in demand almost as much as his master. He also served in the local militia and, while he was still among the more junior officers, his troops had grown to rely on him, to trust his judgment, the way they did the old campaigners among them.

He smiled when Elora pointed that out.

"You grow up here in the outback, along the Frontier," he said, "bein' a quick study an' a good one is a matter of survival. I stay close t' my master t' learn his craft, which I consider my true vocation. I watch Shando an' Colonel DeGuerin an' Lord Tyrrel t' better my skills at theirs. I prefer the one, I need t' other."

"Survival."

"Beats the alternative, don't'cha think?"

"I hope I'm wrong," she said. Then, a bleakness came over face and tone. "I wish . . ." she began, only to allow her voice to trail off.

"Don't we all," Luc-Jon echoed with a sigh, shifting position on the log they were using as a seat, in a vain attempt to make himself a tad more comfortable. They were dressed much alike, in ironcloth and moleskin, wool and leather, stout boots and padded surcoats. He wore iron mail, hers was a metal of Nelwyn forging, sandwiched between two layers of leather so as to allow a fair freedom of movement yet also provide a good defense. Her tunic was a spoil of victory, taken from a Maizan sorceress she'd fought, colored the dark burgundy she favored but cut in a style she considered a bit too daring. It fit as snugly as a noble lady's corset, showing her figure to good advantage, especially since she didn't seem to require the heavy sweaters that kept everyone else warm. There was a short skirt that covered crotch and buttocks and was slit on both sides to the waist. Bare-legged, the design would be scandalous, but Elora wore pants that over time (and with the aid of the brownies' nimble fingers and deft needlework) had come to fit her like a second skin. The tunic could be closed at the collar but was more naturally worn open, just enough to hint at the hollow between Elora's breasts. The lapels rose in an elegant flare to a standing collar that cradled the back of her neck, reinforced to shield her from any blindside blows, either blade or cudgel. The long sleeves were narrow, designed for combat, the overall impression of the ensemble meant to convey a person of dangerous beauty, as able to slay as to enchant.

Around the young woman's waist was a belt of well-worn leather, three fingers thick, from which hung her pair of traveling pouches and an empty hanger for a sword. Elora was dexterous with either hand but preferred to hang her main blade like most folks, for a right-handed draw. That way, Khory Bannefin had taught her, any opponent would be less likely to spot an attack from the equally skilled left. To that end, she wore a dagger sheathed flat along the back of her belt, plus one in a sheath on her right and a last one tucked into her right boot. Anything else she needed, she'd either improvise from whatever was close at hand or draw from her pouches.

Luc-Jon was as formidably arrayed, minus the magic pouches, only his hanger held a broadsword.

"Where's that troubadour you were with?" he asked, after watching the yard a while.

"Duguay Faralorn, you mean?"

"Aye. Way he looked at'cha, an' acted, I got t' figurin', well, y'know . . ."

She slid her eyes toward him, beneath lids narrowed suddenly to slits.

"He was my companion, Luc-Jon."

"That's a word with its share o' meanings."

"What's that supposed to mean?" she snapped defensively. "He was a friend. He taught me his craft. He died. For me."

"I meant no offense, Elora Danan."

"The question was offensive, Master Luc-Jon. I *am* offended."

With each line, she took a giant step back toward the girl she had been, spoiled rotten amidst a life of pampered luxury at the Royal Court of Angwyn. In a matter of heartbeats, the girl became once more every inch an Imperial Princess, pride and arrogance rippling from her like the great warcloak she wore so well.

To his credit, Luc-Jon didn't flinch from her gaze and when she rose to take her leave he caught hold of her arm to stop her. Elora's reflex was to break his grip but Luc-Jon wouldn't let go. To his amazement as she pulled away he found himself yanked to his feet by a strength that most probably surpassed his own though he had the edge on her in height and bulk.

"I'm sorry," he said simply and directly as her action brought them face-to-face.

"He was a friend," she repeated. "I don't have many. It's not safe," she finished, without bothering to hide an edge of bitterness mixed with honest rage.

"Anyone ever tell you, Elora Danan, you're worth the risk?"

Their hands were bare, despite the Highland chill, and when he caught her by the fingertips, the most fleeting of touches, a tremor rippled deep through the heart of her being. All the breath went out of her in a *whuff,* as though she'd been struck in the belly, and for a timeless moment she forgot the need to draw in another.

She blinked rapidly, refocusing her gaze down toward her hands, brow furrowing in modest confusion to find them both clenched into fists, turned inward protectively against her tunic. She wasn't angry, or spoiling for a fight, more like she'd just made contact with the surface of a hot stove and was trying to keep herself from being burned.

Her skin was tingling, awash with goose bumps from top to toe. Because she could think of nothing else to do, that under the circumstances was even remotely safe, Elora reached out and grabbed Luc-Jon by the waist, pulling him against her in a close embrace, resting her cheek on his shoulder until equilibrium returned and she could figure out what came next.

He seemed equally as confused, because she sensed more than a little hesitation before his own hands wrapped themselves across her shoulders. She felt him reach up toward her head, perhaps to stroke her hair, and was horribly conflicted when he thought better of it, suddenly yearning for a further touch yet grateful for his discretion.

Be a friend, she willed silently, *please be my friend.* And for now, nothing more. It was far less than she desired, but far more than she could handle.

"How fares your master?" she inquired, taking refuge in what she hoped was an innocuous pleasantry.

"Much the same." He chuckled. "Much like yours."

"And his library?"

"Even with all the recent troubles, he's managed to get ahold of some new volumes. As a collection, it's nothing compared to the great Athenæum in Sandeni but it contains its share of surprises."

"Could I see?" she asked suddenly.

He pulled his head back for a look at her face.

"No problem."

"What're you after?" Luc-Jon wondered as Elora prowled the eight-sided room. It would have been taller than the walls of the fort itself had the main floor been set on ground level instead of twenty feet below. The layout of the library matched the cardinal points on a compass: primary walls at north and south and east and west. There were two entrances, one at the third level of shelves off the Master Scribe's study, and another that could be reached by descending to the house's storage cellars. The construction was ancient stone, quarried chunks of granite so superbly hewn and slugged into place that no chinks marred the seam, even after the passage of so many, many years. Interestingly, at some point long before the arrival of the current occupant, the library's exterior had been covered in planks, to match the rest of the fort. To an outside observer, the building looked remarkably ordinary.

"Knowledge. The secrets of creation. My creation. My purpose." She stroked the palm of her left hand along the balcony railing, at the same time reaching out to lay her right flat against the stone.

"There's *power* here," she said, meaning magic.

"The books," Luc-Jon acknowledged. "There's iron in the rock, some other things in the mortar, they all serve t' keep a kind of order here, t' make the volumes safe t' handle an' read."

"Wards, you mean?" she asked, while thinking: *That's part of it, yes, but there's also something else, more than just the books.*

"Aye."

"I wonder what makes this place so special? I mean, it's clear from the age of the stone that the tower itself has been here *ages!*"

"Older'n the fort, that's fact. It was here when the first Pathfinders an' trappers roamed up from the flat. Sort'a became a natural refuge."

"From the elements, you mean?"

"Only partways. The Veil Folk, they give this spot a fair berth. E'n now, you won't see any o' Lord Tyrrel's clutch come within a score o' long paces of where we stand."

"Why? Do the wards keep them away?"

The young scribe shrugged. "For that, 'Lora, you're better makin' inquiries o' Lord Drumheller."

"And as likely to get an answer that is no answer. He's gotten far too good at dissembling."

"Ain't fear, if that's what'cher askin'. What keeps the Veil Folk at a distance. 'Leastways, never seemed to t' me. Respect is what I'd say, the same as we'd show on holy ground."

"Hmnh. Luc-Jon," she asked, taking a slow turn all the way

around to take in the entirety of the tower and its contents, "is there anything here that relates to . . ." Thought and words stumbled together, reluctant to give voice to the sardonic, insatiable image that haunted her past and hunted her present.

"That Which Is Never Named," he finished for her, and she nodded.

"Up the very top." And he gestured with his chin toward the uppermost balcony, right beneath the circular skylight of cut, prismatic rock crystal.

"I'd have assumed such things would be buried deep," she noted as she clambered up the steps cut into the wall, observing as she did that the library had essentially been grafted onto a preexisting design. The wood balconies had been laid atop ledges already in place; nothing of permanence had been added. No marks had been made in the stone, not even to hold anchors for the bookshelves, and she suspected none could.

"Wrong thinking" was his reply. Despite the growing separation between them as she climbed, some trick of acoustics created the impression that Luc-Jon was close beside her, allowing them to continue to converse in normal tones of voice. "That close t' the earth, y' never know what might catch theyselves a taste o' what's within an' then come calling, lookin' t' settle scores or make their bones or set off an avalanche. There's not so much threat from the air, so why ask for trouble?"

"Fair point. But they're not locked away or anything?"

"Where's the sense in a library where y're no' allowed t' read the books?"

"What about thieves? Rival scribes perhaps, looking to add to their own collections?"

She'd meant that as a jest but Luc-Jon took the remark in all seriousness.

"Trust me. Without permission, y'd no make it past the door. As f'r a book like that, the precious few who'd want anyroad t' do with it carry a stink about their spirit strong enough f'r e'en the likes o' me t' notice. An' Puppy would of a surety. It's safe enough, Elora Danan, an' that's no error."

Like all tomes relating to the Malevoiy, this one was huge, thick as the width of her hand and in all likelihood as heavy as she. The massive straps were stiff with disuse and she tore a nail struggling one free of its buckle. In frustration she stepped away from the shelf and was about to call down to Luc-Jon when her eye was caught by a much smaller work, poking out from beneath the pile of larger covers.

This was meant to be carried, meant to be read, every physical element a testament to the care taken with its construction, from the quality of the paper to the deerskin cover and bindings. There was a simple peg latch, and when she opened to a page at random she felt a minor thrill that told her of a series of interlocking spells to protect the book from the ravages of time and weather. In every respect, whoever had done this work had wanted it to last.

The language itself was unfamiliar to her, but that wasn't a surprise. Unlike most of the titles she'd seen, this one was spare of illuminations. By contrast, she knew from experience that the Malevoiy volume would be so thick with them on every page—all designed to protect the reader from harm—that the actual content would be minimal. This was the opposite, so densely packed with text laid out in so idiosyncratic a style that she wondered if it might be some kind of diary.

Then, without warning, her breath caught in a gasp of astonishment as she came upon a series of line-art sketches, some full figures, some merely head shots. She found Khory Bannefin's face and smiled at how little the years had changed her. And farther on, the *ard-righ,* the High King Eamon Asana. There was a picture of the two of them, ostensibly in some kind of military conference, for they both wore armor, and pennants flapped in the breeze behind them. Yet there was an aspect to their stance, the cock of Khory's head, the way Asana's hand rested on hers, that told Elora there was more between the two than the comradeship of warriors, or the mutual regard of Monarch to warlord.

She felt dizzy and twisted her body where she stood to put her back to the wall of the tower as she sank to the floor. First reaction was irritation, as she assumed the feeling was a residue of her recent illness. After that, there was no more time for thought, as her world collapsed into a kind of chaos.

The room around her didn't so much spin as lose all solidity. Stone suddenly turned as malleable as candlewax and she felt it give on every side, bending and rippling as though it had assumed the aspects of the ocean. She reached out an arm and her eyes went wide to behold a limb that stretched longer than a war spear; she looked down, to find her legs shriveling to the size of a doll's limbs and the consistency of twigs. She didn't dare move, and yet some instinct, the most terrible of fears, honed by a lifetime of combat, bellowed that she had to. The fault was not in the world, that inner voice counseled, but in herself, and being in herself could thereby be overcome.

She heard footsteps on the stairs, tried to cry out to Luc-Jon. She might well have succeeded but she couldn't tell if she made a coherent sound. Shapes blurred before her eyes, taking on a cruel duality, the way things do when you let both eyes lose their focal point, except in this case Elora didn't observe double images of the same reality. Somehow, a completely different vision was superimposing itself on her perceptions, replacing ancient stone with rough-hewn logs, the sight of open air above the great, circular skylight with a ceiling not much higher than most Daikini stood tall, illuminated by rough torches. Hurried feet on the stairs gave way to a deliberate tread across an earthen floor, and the face that loomed before her was not Luc-Jon, but Eamon Asana.

"No," Elora cried, and her ears heard Khory Bannefin's voice.

"No forgiveness, Khory," the High King said. "I will not shame us both by asking for that which you will not give. Any more than I can offer mercy."

"What have you done?"

"What must be done, to bring this conflict to an end."

He didn't expect her lunge, he always was too confident of his own abilities, and by rights she'd been fed enough opiate to put a company of warriors to sleep. In truth, he'd been surprised to find her even conscious and so was caught completely unawares when the edge of her dagger opened his face to the bone from the knob of his jaw to the chin. He bellowed, with good reason, and used his fist to finish the job of sedating her.

Elora fell as Khory did and was sick on the floor, because she knew what came next, that the warrior would wake to find herself a prisoner of her deadliest enemies, knowing that the King she trusted, the man she loved, had sold away her life and soul for the promise of peace.

The taste of bile in her mouth almost made her sick all over again but at least when Elora pushed herself upright she found that stone was once more dependably solid, her world back the way it was supposed to be.

She heard the sound of boots on steps and her heart leaped to her throat as she skibbled a hand over to the knife scabbard on her right only to find it empty. She started to call Luc-Jon's name just as he came into view and relief was more welcome than a spring rain when she saw that his face was unscarred.

He carried a flask and a towel and used them both to wash her clean. She took the towel and used it to wipe the floor as well and finished with a hefty swallow of water from the flask. Her knife, she noted, was tucked securely into the scribe's belt.

She owed him an explanation and, with the book's help, gave it to him.

"You know they call him the Haunted King," he told her when she was done.

"No."

"Not so much anymore," he continued, "but in ages past there were stories told about him, plays written, pictures." He waved his hand to encompass the library stacks. "The greatest King in Daikini history until he betrayed his greatest friend."

"What happened after, do you know?"

"Eamon Asana lived to a ripe old age and it's said that to know him was to watch a man become a living ghost before your eyes. Not that he became invisible but that gradually he came to lose everything that made him human. No one's even sure he actually died. Nowt tha' was his was left standing t' remember him by— except"—and here, Luc-Jon smiled a grin he'd learned from Elora, a wry quirk of the mouth—"the World itself and all its myriad peoples. There's some in the old writings who claim that our troubles descend from that betrayal, that the foes in those old days—those who must remain Nameless—weren't properly defeated. Are they right, Elora Danan?"

She had no proper answer for him, beyond a shrug.

"Ancient history," Luc-Jon suggested.

Another shrug, as she swung her legs over the edge of the parapet and leaned on the railing to gaze down the tower. From this height and angle it appeared far deeper than from the bottom looking up.

"Is there such a thing," she asked at him in return, almost a retort, "for races that are immortal, or others for whom time is as easily traversed as space is for us? Compared to the Veil Folk, the lives of Daikini are nothing. We dance our little while and then we're dust and how much of the knowledge learned during that time vanishes with us? When do we have the chance to transform it into true wisdom, Luc-Jon? Thorn Drumheller's young as Nelwyns go, chances are he'll know your great-grandchildren. I saw a dragon for whom these people"—and she shook the book at him—"weren't just pictures in a book or actors on some stage, they were *real*! Comrades in battle! *Friends*!"

"Less time, perhaps," he replied, taking a seat by her side, "a greater incentive to do more. Age don't connote wisdom, not always, not in everyone. Authority, yah, I'll grant'cha that. But somewhile y' get comfortable in the pattern of things. Y' work a certain way because that's the way it's always been done. Y' resist change because y' don't see the need.

"Y' plant the same crop year after year, Elora, the soil eventually dies. Y' run a wagon down the same exact path journey after journey, y' come t' wear ruts in the road so deep the wheels won't turn. Who knows, from what y're sayin', mayhap a change was begun in those ancient days that wasn't completed?"

"Everyone has a theory, Luc-Jon. I have to be sure."

"The way you mean the word, lass, I dinna think it's possible. Y're no' a god, Elora Danan. Y' see the world mainly as we do, through your own two eyes, five feet an' a bit off the ground."

"I don't want to make Asana's mistake."

"Who said it *was* a mistake? He was High King, yah? Wi' a war t' win. He takes the offer, he has a semblance of peace, the chance t' build somethin' lasting f'r his own folk and the other allied Realms, yah? What's the cost, a few lives, a few souls? Versus how many if the war goes on? An' f'r once, 'tis the King who pays the price, no' the commons. Betrayal, aye, in full measure. But also a rare courage."

"You're worse than Drumheller."

" 'Tis a failing of scribes. We read so much it's easy to act the part o' teacher." He stirred his hand beside her but made no move to touch. He looked down as she did but his eyes were slightly unfocused, his gaze turned more inward, to his own memories.

"I've had to lead men in battle these past months, Elora. The answers there weren't always what I thought they'd be."

She said nothing for a fair while and Luc-Jon's lips pursed with anger at the thought that she wasn't listening.

"They never are," she spoke at last, then looked sharply at Luc-Jon as he chuckled. "What?" she demanded, letting some irritation show.

"Just watchin', is all." The answer was unsatisfactory and an upward prompt from her eyebrows demanded more. "Whenever y're frustrated, kind'a like Puppy worryin' an itchy patch o' skin . . ."

She made a nasty face at him at the image, which she didn't find at all complimentary.

". . . y' start tracing circles. Same pattern every time."

She looked down and saw it was so. Three interlocked rings, surmounted and bound together by a fourth.

"It's how I feel sometimes," she told him. "Spinning in circles, getting dizzier and more lost with every revolution."

"Talk it through. Might help."

The pitch of her shoulders told him eloquently, you asked for this, almost as though it was a dare. Then, she began, quite simply: "The physical world, this globe we Daikini live upon, spins daily on its axis like a top. At the same time, the moon revolves around us. The world and moon together, in turn, revolve around the sun."

"And the sun, what does it revolve around?"

"Who knows? Other than the dragons, and maybe Drumheller.

The Liege Lord of the Dragons, Calan Dineer, told him all this when I was just a baby. Years later, Drumheller told me. The point is, everything moves in relation to everything else. As they do so, the relationships between them change, the balance of powers shifts and flows.

"You know about Magus Points, yes?"

"Where the lines of magic intersect, both in our world an' those beyond the Veil," Luc-Jon replied. "I'm not completely dim, lass, thank y' kindly," he said with a chuckle. "Bein' a scribe, it's no' just about scribblin'. It's about books. It's about knowledge. We seek out what's been lost. We try to learn it f'r ourselves, an' then pass it on to those who come after."

He leaned over and tapped a knuckle on the diary she'd uncovered.

"That one's mine," he said with a measure of pride. "First book I found"—and his smile broadened—"an' near my last as well. Got too cocky, got a scar t' show f'r it. Weren't f'r Puppy . . ." He didn't need to finish.

"I'd hate to think of what the scribe who found that Malevoiy text had to go through." She spoke lightly, but there was an undertone of awe. If the challenge matched the prize . . .

"Giles the Red, they called him, so my master tells."

"Your master knew that scribe?"

"They were mates. Giles Horvath. He lives in Sandeni, teaches at the University."

"I've met him!" she acknowledged, though she was hardpressed to match the quiet, almost reclusive academic she recalled with someone worthy of such a nickname.

"F'r scribes, the tales of our Book Quests are our badges of honor. We pass 'em about at gatherings as we do the knowledge we've accumulated."

"That makes you sound like troubadours."

"We're more private, like. We don't perform. The big book, though, that's a story I've never heard told, from either man. Anyroad, I want t' hear the rest o' what you were sayin', about the Magus Points."

"Magic is strongest where the lines of power intersect," she repeated what he'd said, for emphasis. "At the strongest of those points is where we find World Gates, passageways to the other Great Realms that lie beyond the Veil. On one side of the Veil, the Realms and races who're anchored more to a purely physical state of existence, like us and Lesser Faery. On the other, those who tend more toward the spirit."

"Greater Faery an' the Malevoiy?"

Elora nodded. "But why," she continued, "should those lines of power be limited to just this one world? Perhaps they run through the cosmos as well? If we look back through history, we see that the Magus Points aren't fixed. It may take generations, but they move." She pursed her lips as her musings led her to an unexpected inspiration. "I wonder, could the point of change referred to in the prophecies about me occur because the world itself is about to pass through a Magus Point in the heavens?"

"How could you know that for certain, or chart such a thing?"

"Haven't a clue. But it makes too much sense to ignore. And it would help explain why time is so critical."

"How d'you mean?"

"If we're building to a specific moment, a specific place in the scheme of things, then this really does become a once-in-a-lifetime opportunity—only we're not speaking in terms of Daikini lives, but of the Veil Folk. As you said, was that opportunity missed ages ago, with Khory and the *ard-righ;* could this be our chance to set things right?"

"Or consider—would it be better to leave matters well enough alone, as they are now?"

"I don't know. I don't know."

This time, it was Luc-Jon who reached out to offer comfort. This time, when they came together in an embrace, there was an all-too-real awareness of the bodies beneath the clothes. She tilted her head, and saw a scattering of crow's-feet around his eyes and a quality within them that hadn't been there before. She thought of her forge and the swords she made, of how gleaming pure the metal was in the mold, and how deceptively strong it appeared. Fate had taken a hammer to Luc-Jon's soul these past months, folding and tempering him as Elora did her steel, adding substance to the shape and a resilience that would allow him to bend without breaking. She'd thought him as much boy as man when they'd first met; that had changed.

To their surprise, they made the next move as one. That was why, the moment their lips touched, they backed away, not so much startled by their own temerity but by the realization that the other had just had the same idea. In that instant, the stakes suddenly rose higher than either was yet prepared to wager.

Again, as though they were twins, both dropped their eyes simultaneously and offered shy, inane expressions of excuse and apology.

The great book Elora left, the little one—with the Master Scribe's permission and blessing—came away with her, to show to both Drumheller and Khory.

They had a little time left before Luc-Jon went on duty with his troop; impulse took them to the watchtower by the main gate, which had the most commanding view of the Frontier approaches to the fort. It was a decent climb, since this tower stood as high above the ramparts as they did above the ground. While Luc-Jon swept the tree line and what could be seen of the horizon beyond for any sign of the enemy, Elora looked the other way, down at the layout of the fort itself, and wasn't surprised to find that it echoed the shape and alignment of the scribe's tower. The fort itself was nestled in a hollow, if the term applied to a geological formation that had to be miles across, and Elora had a sudden yearning for the companionship of her eagles. In the great scheme of things hardly any time at all had passed since she'd last seen Bastian and Anele, barely a fortnight in fact, yet in Elora's heart it felt like forever. It wasn't simply their company she missed, though, but their wings. She wondered what the shape of this land would look like from their perspective, if the lay of the ridgelines that formed this valley would echo that of the tower.

She looked down at her hands, removed one glove, and looked again. One palm bare, the other sheathed in worn, serviceable deerskin. She closed each slightly, curling her fingers just enough to make the creases and folds of her skin visible. She flexed her hands, stretching them as tight and taut as she could. The lines were indelible, in hand and glove both. The precision of their definition depended on how she looked at them.

"Patterns," she whispered to herself. "It has to be the same here. The power exists in harmony with the earth, as it does with air and fire and water. But those are all mutable elements; nothing about them is fixed. The land doesn't flow so easily. Once its pattern is established, that's how it tends to stay. So—for the power to define the land, for the land to reflect those patterns of magical energy the way this valley does, and Sandeni as well, they must have been laid down ages upon ages ago, when the very World itself was forming."

"Your intuition does you credit, Elora Danan," said a new voice from behind.

She whirled, and in so doing slammed her backside hard against the railing to pin her left hand, shocked speechless inside at the reflex which had sent her grabbing for a dagger at Tyrrel's words. The Liege Lord of Lesser Faery was friend and ally, yet she'd reacted to him as a deadly foe. For once, she was grateful for her argent skin, so pale in the daylight that none could tell when the blood rushed from her features.

"Another piece for my puzzle, m'lord," she replied. "To add to my collection."

"Why so upset, then?"

"I don't feel any closer to the answers. And I know already I don't like the paths I see before me."

"As opposed to those already taken?"

"My lord?"

Tyrrel stood a double span of arms distant from her, the position of a wary man who is unsure of his companion but also respectful of her abilities. She'd gained a measure of height since their first meeting, months ago, but he still topped her in mass and strength of body. She didn't need to glance around to spot the glittering motes making lazy circles about the watchtower, each a fairy, each ready to immolate themselves in defense of their Monarch. An attack by an individual fairy could be survived; in their case, size was a crucial difference. Despite their ferocity, there was a limit to the damage one alone could inflict. Even a score of them might leave their prey alive. In war, however, fairies swarmed by the thousands, the tens of thousands. The merest touch of iron would doom them but even plate armor was no defense, because it was impossible to craft a suit that did not have a chink these tiny creatures could slip through.

Elora always considered it strange that most Daikini had a much greater fear of the elves of Greater Faery. Perhaps because they were most like the Daikini in stature, that made them somehow more worthy of respect. The smaller creatures of Lesser Faery were generally considered objects of amusement, rarely given a first thought, much less a second. Yet Lesser Faery was one of the Twelve Great Realms and its myriad races in their way, far more formidable than most would give them credit for. Elora knew so from cruel experience, memories all her own, as well as those she'd seen of Khory's.

"What do you mean, Tyrrel?" she demanded of him when he made no reply to her initial query, only this time she dropped the honorific, deliberately reminding him of her own stature.

"There's summat about you that's changed, Elora Danan. A taste t' your spirit that hasn't walked this world since, I don't know when."

"The days of Eamon Asana?" she prompted. Tyrrel made a face, features quickly flashing through an expression of heartfelt contempt; at the same time, he made a warding sign with both hands and spat. Elora heard a faint buzzing that might have been mistaken for bees, but she knew better. Tyrrel's bodyguards had pulled closer about the platform in response to their Monarch's burst of agitation.

"Do not speak that name, child," the Monarch warned. "And have a care which path you choose to walk."

"Is that a threat?"

"A warning. You don't know everything, Elora Danan."

"I know this, Tyrrel. There are *Twelve* Great Realms. I can't pick and choose between them, which to include in the binding and which not."

"Consider then, perhaps we should let this binding pass us by?"

"And leave the world as it is? Look about you, Tyrrel, and tell me if this is what you truly want?"

"Beg pardon, m'lord—!" It was Luc-Jon, bless him for his timing.

"You're not interrupting, lad. We were just finished, the Sacred Princess and I."

"They just called up from the main gate. There's a message pouch."

"Good. It's past time."

"Still no sign of the Chengwei," Luc-Jon continued, trying to defuse the tension with a change of subject.

"Colonel DeGuerin's had his own scouts out lookin' for 'em, as I've had mine. Been starting to worry why I've had no word."

A trooper clattered up the steps, handing the oilskin package to Luc-Jon, who turned to pass it on to Tyrrel.

Elora struck first, with a swiftness that would have done Khory proud. There was no margin for error, or for hesitation. Each move had to be precise and sure.

She blindsided Luc-Jon with a shoulder check that knocked him off his feet. As he tumbled, she yanked her knife from its scabbard behind her back and used it to slap the package from his grasp. Continuing the same motion, she flipped the blade across her body, to bury its point in the opposite wall a narrow fingerwidth in front of Tyrrel's nose. Sensible man, he flinched from it, opening a decent space between himself and Elora. While Luc-Jon was still falling, she used her other hand to grab for the pommel of his sword, grateful that he kept his equipment in such pristine condition that it slid free of its scabbard without a snag and only a whisper of sound, three feet of tempered, double-edged steel, honed to a killing edge.

Elora felt a burst of pinprick stings about her face and bare hand and down her front. The first of the fairies, believing their Monarch to be threatened, had rushed to the attack. The fiercest attack was directed against her hand, which held the sword. They meant for Elora to drop the blade, before it could be used against Tyrrel. If necessary, to save him, they'd strip her flesh right down to the bone.

Fortunately, the sword wasn't for him.

Elora swung her arm up and over her head, grasping the hilt

with her other hand at the apex of the curve and putting the fullness of her strength into the blow as she sliced straight through the oilcloth while it was still in the air. She let momentum carry her around for a second cut, this one lateral, to bury sword and package deep into the watchtower. She didn't strike wood, however. The sound of contact was the sharp *ding* of metal on metal, as she pinned the pouch hard against one of the massive iron spikes used to fasten the massive structural timbers together.

That was when the screaming started, frantic ululations pitched so high they registered to Luc-Jon as an instant headache. Elora's eyes creased to slits and Tyrrel collapsed to his knees like a man who'd just taken a cudgel across the shoulders, clutching his own gloved hands to his head in wordless agony. All about the waryard, the animals pitched a variety of fits. Cows bellowed and bulls rammed the nearest wall. Horses turned skittish, nostrils flaring wide and eyes showing their whites as they bugled both challenges and calls to flight. Cats puffed double their size and bared fangs while every dog in the place howled. The sole exception was Luc-Jon's hound, who charged the watchtower at a flat run.

Puppy was at their side in moments, bounding up the stairs even as Luc-Jon tried to gather his wits, announcing his arrival with a basso growl that got everyone's instant and undivided attention.

He had no interest in any of the people present, be they Daikini or Faery, his eyes went straight to the pouch, and at the sight of it his stance shifted into one of attack.

Flames of purple fire burst around the sword like prominences from the surface of the sun. They formed fingers to clutch at the steel in a vain attempt to do it harm or at least push it loose, but the magical energies could find no purchase on the sleek, polished metal. The flames took on defined and recognizable forms, changing color and intensity all the while. They burned ever more brightly, with the manic desperation of creatures fighting for their lives; paradoxically, as the colors grew increasingly dark, the strength of the blaze appeared to increase. Where flames and sword were in actual contact, the blade grew pitted, their attacks scoring the steel as acid would.

Ignoring Luc-Jon's shout of alarm, Elora stepped forward to

close her bare hand around the blade below the sword guard. She felt a burning sensation across her palm where the edge drew blood but she didn't mind; when this was done, a moment's healing would see her good as new again. She sang a Song of Remembrance, reminding the steel of how it had felt when it was touched with fire. Of the glorious moment when, rushing headlong from cauldron to mold, it was one with the molten heart of the world.

The sword began to glow. Red-hot to start, then quickly white, and finally a pristine radiance shot through with silver, so intense a glow that both Luc-Jon and Tyrrel were forced to hide their eyes to save themselves from blindness. By rights, Elora's hand should have been reduced to ashes by a heat as terrible as the light it cast.

Instead, it was the creatures in the oilskin who died, with nothing to mark their passing but a harsh burn scar up the pillar that supported the tower's beacon.

Elora was breathing hard, winded worse than after an exercise session with Khory. There was tremendous tension across her collarbones and the top of her chest and the cords of her neck were stretched taut. The battle had been as intense as it was brief, the opposition so formidable it had to be vanquished quickly. And completely. She closed thumb and forefinger of her bare hand about the flat of the blade and slid her hand along its length to the point. She broke no skin this time, but left instead a faint trail of crackling silver fire. Then, transferring the hilt to her bare hand, she laid the sword flat against the burn scar, letting its steel seek out any taint of infection that might have escaped to the wood.

There was no response, acknowledged by her grateful sigh of relief. She reversed the sword and laid it along the length of her left arm before holding it out to Luc-Jon.

He tilted the blade so it flashed in the sunlight.

"There isn't a mark."

"As clean as the day it was forged," she agreed. "And happy to be so."

"What did you do, Elora Danan? Are you all right?"

"Tired."

She turned to Tyrrel and went to one knee before him, bowing her head in a formal show of respect.

"There was no time for explanations, my lord," she told him.

"That pouch."

"Your scouts, those who survived."

"You killed them."

"I ended their torment with what mercy I was allowed. I freed them from bondage. I saved what they would have slain."

"I am their Liege, Elora Danan. They would not turn on me, nor do me harm. Their fate, in any case, is mine to decide."

"Tell that to the Caliban. He would have claimed you, too, given the chance. He took a try at me, Tyrrel"—she rose to her feet—"I know his taint. It was on that pouch."

"Abomination," Tyrrel hissed, and Elora wasn't sure whether he was referring to the Caliban, or to her.

"How could such a thing be done," the Faery Monarch growled, "and me remain unaware?"

"I don't know. My contact with the fairies was brief, but they were transformed beyond all recognition. One touch, Tyrrel, the merest contact, would have condemned you faster and more certainly than the kiss of iron. It didn't feel like any magic I've ever encountered, more like a kind of . . . chaos."

"A demon?"

"I hope not. But these are the times we live in, Majesty, where the rules that order our existence are splintering before our eyes. Would you still leave well enough alone, when the power exists to make a change?"

"Can you guarantee that change is for the better?" Tyrrel's face rose, his eyes fixing on a distant point above and far beyond where Elora stood. "Boy," he snapped, meaning Luc-Jon.

"Forgive me," he amended as the young man straightened to attention. "I mean no disrespect, Lieutenant."

"None taken, milord."

"Summon Colonel DeGuerin. Have the tocsin sound the call to arms. The Chengwei have arrived."

CHAPTER 5

THE LAY OF THE LAND ABOUT THE FORT WAS SIMPLE, and from a military standpoint a defensive joy. The Cascadel itself acted as a natural moat to the east of the fort, its current too fast, the river itself too wide and deep to be practically forded, especially since the opposite shore consisted of a series of step-back cliffs too high and steep to support any assault force. A similar escarpment rose past the fort to the west in a shallow curve that created a fan-shaped flatland valley roughly twice as long as it was broad. It wasn't so much that the terrain was impassable—paths could be found for small parties on foot or horseback. However, for the mass movement of quantities of troops and goods there was only one path, along the shore of the Cascadel, where the convergence of the two ridgelines created a natural funnel.

When Elora followed Tyrrel's gaze, nothing leaped to her eye at first, until she was attracted by a flicker of movement on the crest of farthest rise to the south.

"Horsemen," she reported, "and standards," as she noted flags and pennants opening to the breeze.

"The Chengwei commander and his staff," agreed Tyrrel. Around them, Fort Tregare bustled like a breached anthill, civilians scurrying to the safety of their bunkers while troopers hurried to take up positions on the ramparts.

"Ahead of their troops or following behind?" she wondered.

"There's your answer, lass."

A troop of horse broke from the tree line, to turn parallel to the forest and trot from the shore of the river toward the point where the ridgeline made its presence felt. There were perhaps forty in all, arrayed in a column of twos atop mounts that were smaller of stature than the horses Elora was familiar with but no less sturdy, their shaggy coats proof against the cold and storms of the mountains they'd traversed to reach here. The uniforms were more brightly colored than those of their Sandeni counterparts, baggy trousers and segmented armor as opposed to chain mail and molded plate. Curved swords instead of straight, single edge instead of double, wicked-looking axes slung across the back, short spears as well as lances. In start contrast to the compact recurve bows favored by the Maizan, these warriors used an asymmetric longbow that was taller than they, with longer arrows to match, the shaft laid and sighted at the bottom third of the bow's length rather than the midpoint where Elora had been taught.

"What are they doing?" she asked.

"Marking turf" was Tyrrel's reply.

"Determining the lay of the battleground" was DeGuerin's, as the Colonel joined them atop the watchtower. "Laying claim to their piece of it, making sure it's clear. Here come the rest now."

The assault force emerged from the trees to the sound of massed drums, a tattoo of such power that Elora concluded each soldier had his own personal drummer to mark the cadence. They advanced along a single broad front, forming a rectangle five deep by two hundred across. Fifty paces behind them came a second identical formation, and a third and ultimately a fourth.

"Four thousand men," said Tyrrel in a tone that made plain his disbelief. "They're serious."

"Cavalry only," said DeGuerin with a dismissive shake of the head. "All they've got is whatever they can carry."

"Plus whatever it was killed my folk." And the Monarch of Lesser Faery indicated the burn scar Elora had placed on the beacon post. "We've that to contend with, don't forget."

"Find me a way to deal with him, then," the Colonel said, to Tyrrel, Drumheller, and Elora together. "In the meanwhile, I'll fight the way I know how. They won't strike at a single point, the vanguard'll most likely divide when they're close, hit us on two walls and hope to split our forces. Same for the second wave. The last two, they'll go where they'll do the Chengwei the most good."

"From what you told us, sir," Luc-Jon questioned, "I expected more."

"Men, you mean? They've got us in numbers right now, lad, and I suspect they've plenty more waiting in the wings. Isn't just numbers to contend with, either. That commander and his men, they know their business. The fact they neutralized our every picket, Daikini and otherwise, makes that plain."

"How do we stop them?"

"By keeping them as far away from the walls as possible. So much for your bog, Lord Tyrrel," he noted with a mirthless smile.

The land was dry as old bones, each step the approaching soldiers made sending up whorls of dust from earth that at sunrise had been too sodden and saturated with water to support even a child's weight, much less that of a man armored for battle.

"Archers to their places, gentlemen," DeGuerin said to his officers, and the order was as quickly passed as carried out.

To Elora's eye, the range was extreme, but the Colonel had trained and equipped his men superbly well. At his command, bowmen rose as one, stepped to the ramparts, and let fly. The air whistled with the flight of their arrows, three full flights in the air before the first struck home. The Chengwei pulled a "turtle," raising small, circular shields to form a roof over their heads. Infantry were better suited for this kind of engagement. Their shields were rectangular and in many cases equipped with hooks and grooves so that the edges could be linked together, denying the arrows any convenient points of entry. At closer ranges, and flatter trajectories, the pull of the standard longbow was such that a war arrow could punch straight through most thicknesses of armor, even that of a shield. Here, however, so much distance had to be covered that the shafts had only the force of gravity to sustain them in flight, thereby minimizing their penetration ability.

Sight as always traveled far faster than sound. Elora beheld the moment of contact a heartbeat before she heard the faint *thok* of steel points embedding themselves in solid wood. It reminded her of archery class and the sound her own arrows made as they struck the target butts. She also could make out the sound of a second, softer impact and thrust from her thoughts the images of what that had to mean, even though the proof was plain before her eyes as holes began to open in the ranks of the enemy. The vanguard began to leave a trail of bodies, some moving, others forever still. The troops that followed simply marched over them, while the decimated vanguard contracted in on itself to fill the gaps, five lines becoming four and then three, sacrificing depth to maintain the width of its battlefront.

The second wave came in range, forcing the archers to split their marks. They continued to take a fearful toll on the enemy but the overall effect began to be diffused. They had too many targets, and no effective way to deal with them as a whole. Despite their efforts, a significant force of the enemy would likely reach the walls.

"Kill them," DeGuerin said in quiet exhortation. "Kill them all. Quickly. While we can."

Now, the second and third waves of Chengwei began to return fire and cries of alarm and pain rose along the ramparts and from farther within the fort. The vanguard had been reduced to little more than a single ragged line and the casualties of the second formation were almost as horrendous, yet their advance continued at that same inexorable, relentless pace, marking such perfect cadence with their drums they might have been on a parade ground instead of a battlefield.

"Mounted crossbows," the Colonel ordered, and word was swiftly passed along the palisade. "Target the rear echelons."

"Why don't they withdraw?" Luc-Jon asked, unable to keep the horror from his voice.

"They're making a point," the Colonel said, as calmly as to a classroom. "As are we."

"Where are their ladders?" Elora asked suddenly. "No ladders, no grappling lines, how do they expect to climb the walls?"

"It was never their intent."

From the two corner towers fronting the battle line, the sound of heavy equipment being swung to bear made itself heard above the din. The mounted crossbows were larger versions of those carried by infantry bowmen, capable of hurling far larger missiles— more like javelins than standard bolts—with far more force and significantly longer range. They could also fire in multiples of three. At DeGuerin's signal, they opened fire.

The results were devastating. No armor could deflect their points and at this point-blank range they punched through the entire depth of an advancing formation, taking out men in whole handfuls rather than singly. Counterfire from the attacking force was weakening visibly; any Chengwei who raised a bow was likely to find himself the focus of a half-dozen arrows in return. Safer, they apparently concluded, to hunker down beneath their tiny shields and pray for a miracle.

It didn't come.

If there was glory in this battle for the Chengwei, it was the kind born of utter futility. None of the attacking force returned to their lines, the field before the fort belonged to the dead, the dying, the wounded. As daylight faded to dusk, reconnaissance parties slipped from a sally port, to collect any salvageable weapons and give aid to those still living. A rider under flag of truce was dispatched to the tree line to inquire whether or not the Chengwei had any interest in collecting the few survivors. The enemy sent him back with the flag aflame, and the rider minus his head. From that moment forth, the Chengwei were left to lie where they fell.

. . .

"I'll need you tonight," the Colonel told Elora, as his staff shared sandwiches and hot drink over the latest strategy session, "with that special sight you and Drumheller share, so you can see in the dark."

"Understood, Colonel. You think they'll attack at night?"

"However they come, Elora Danan, I'd rather learn of it before they scale our ramparts."

"Tyrrel's folk could help in this," she suggested.

"And I'll welcome it as I do yours."

"You have doubts?"

"Not to their loyalty, Highness. But the Cascadel patrol was massacred with none of us the wiser, not even Tyrrel, who is conscious in ways I can't even begin to imagine of the life and death of each and every one of his people. His scouts were likewise slain, or turned to Chengwei purpose, and again he remained wholly unaware. That tells me the Chengwei have found a way to harm the Veil Folk and keep their purposes hidden. If true, maybe fairy sight won't see the next attack when it comes, or they'll be deceived into looking the wrong way. That's a risk I can't afford.

"Luc-Jon," he said to the scribe, "the Sacred Princess is yours to mind. That's your sole military mission during this campaign. In the absence of Khory Bannefin, you keep her safe."

"Where is Khory, Colonel?" Elora asked. "I've not seen her since before the attack, nor Thorn Drumheller as well." *Nor,* she thought with a sharp pang of apprehension, *the brownies!* She remembered their pledge to stay by her always and knew only the most urgent of tasks would have drawn them from her side.

"I pray, somewhere safe." *But that isn't,* she thought, *where you sent her.* His next words confirmed that suspicion. "More than that, I cannot say. Get a meal, the pair of you, and then some sleep. You'll be called for by midnight."

Dinner was a hearty stew, ladled forth from massive drum kettles that had been set up in the open yard close by the cookhouse. Bread was fresh and there was a choice of drink, though the wine had been so diluted with water it was little better than juice. While many yearned to get stinking drunk tonight, none was willing to pay the consequences. There was precious little formality among the troops and no ceremony at all. These were professionals and they would face what came as their training and experience had prepared them. They hunkered together in their units and kept their weapons close at hand and one or two among them would always have an eye or ear cocked toward the wall and the watchtower, for the slightest warning of an attack.

Among the civilians, who for the most part hadn't seen the battle, the mood was brighter. To them, what mattered was the victory. In their ignorance—or perhaps out of their desperate hope—they took the wrong measure of the enemy. The soldiers knew better and as Elora and Luc-Jon found some space to sit and share their meal, they heard snippets of conversation from every side.

"Why dint they break? They must've seen there was no hope, why dint they bloody withdraw?"

"Countin' how many we could mass on a wall, I'll wager. How many bows, how fast we could shoot, an' how far."

"Four thousand men, just for that?"

"Not ordinary men, neither. They knew they was dead the moment they started their advance, they came on regardless."

"Damme, I hadn't seen *tha'* wi' me own peeps, I'd no' believe it."

A chorus of somber "ayes."

"They're spooked," Luc-Jon muttered.

"*I'm* spooked," Elora agreed.

"So what do we do then?" she heard asked.

"What DeGuerin said," came the gruff reply. "Kill 'em."

"Kill them all?"

" 'S'na' like we have much choice, boyo. We sent 'em a herald under flag o' truce an' look you how they sent him home, the bastards, with his head in a bag."

The next round of comments were so profane that Elora, who thought she'd heard it all in terms of soldiers' language, blushed.

She started to sing.

She didn't push the moment, but kept her tone relatively close, reaching out only to the clutches of men nearest her. It was a saga, with a clear melody and a strong refrain, of a battle against hopeless odds. She didn't remember where she'd heard it, but the voice that led her in her head was deep and rich, with the rounded burrs of a Highlander. She sang of a dark time, with hope all but beaten from the world, when life was short and brutal and too often defined by the spiked mace of oppression. The Daikini were a people in chains, at best slaves but more often considered common prey, to be hunted and slaughtered for sport.

From that awful darkness came a man with a dream, that there was a better way for the world to be ordered. He had more passion than was good for him and a tongue to charm the devil, and a sword arm to serve when persuasion and diplomacy failed.

They were three comrades in arms, the like of which the world had never seen, before or since—a Daikini, an elf, a Nelwyn. They weren't Kings when first they met, that came later. One was a slave who would no longer serve his masters, the other a thief who lost the pleasure of plucking purses in a world that stole the souls of the living, the last an artisan who yearned simply to create beauty.

Fate brought them together, circumstance turned that meeting into a pitched battle for survival. When it was done, the rock and snow about them strewn with Death Dogs and their ensorcelled handlers, plus (most terrifying and impossible of all) the corpse of one of the Malevoiy themselves, the shape of their future had been defined.

Elora was on her feet, conscious of eyes turning toward her from every which way, a few voices hesitantly taking up the refrain of her song. She executed a series of pirouettes in time to the music playing in her head, building force and speed with each until her warcloak billowed out from her shoulders. Then she slipped its clasp, catching it in one outstretched arm, holding it through a last revolution before letting it fly off to Luc-Jon, who caught it as smoothly as if the sequence had been choreographed and rehearsed. Watching, he realized this was one of Elora's great gifts, the ability to improvise a performance with such a strength of character and personality that her audience couldn't help but be swept up in the action. At the same time she created indelible portraits of the subjects of her song—Eamon Asana, conflicted yet committed, who never desired the crown ultimately placed upon his head yet who would not abandon the responsibility that came with it; Rafiel of Greater Faery, who lived utterly for the moment, every decision made and acted upon with the speed and suddenness of a bolt of light; Borugar of Lesser Faery, a man of absolute precision, not so much deliberate (for when necessary he could move as quickly as Rafiel) but exact.

Humble men from humble beginnings, who stumbled onto greatness.

Arrayed against them, an Imperial dominion that acknowledged no equal.

Their cause was hopeless, yet they didn't care. They adapted, they improvised, time and again they found a way to win.

And so, Elora sang to the assemblage of Fort Tregare, *will we!*

Musicians among the civilians picked up the tune she'd begun a cappella and with their participation, Elora allowed herself more freedom to dance. In the torchlight, in her Maizan colors, she was a figure of blood and silver, at one and the same time so unearthly she seemed more icon than real yet imbued with a human passion that could not be denied. Her voice filled the waryard, topped only by the chorus, which itself grew in force and defiance with every repetition. She yanked a pair of torches from their sconces and for a series of verses left trails of sparks and fire in her wake, using her own special powers to inspire the flames to burn so brightly these alone were able to illuminate the entire compound.

Without missing a step, she tossed one brand to Luc-Jon, returned the other to its cradle, and came away with a pair of swords, the air ringing with the sound of steel on steel as she brought the blades together.

She sang of struggle, of commitment, of hardship, of glory. Ultimately, she sang of triumph.

Three men, who alone were less than nothing, who found it in themselves to change the shape of a world and its future.

She dropped to one knee, and plunged two swords point first into the ground on either side.

The song ended as it began, with only her voice, and the silence that followed was complete.

Someone at the back began to chant her name, "Elora! *Eh-lor-ah!*" and it raced through the crowd like wildfire, first as an expression of acclaim for her performance but quickly changing, growing in intensity as it did so, into a war cry. An expression of defiance, a challenge to the Chengwei to do their worst; they'd find within these walls a foe well worthy of the contest.

She drew herself to her full height, facing the headquarters building and Ranulf DeGuerin himself, who was watching from his porch and cheering as lustily as any of his troops, making sure he was seen by all to do so. She raised both swords high, and blades were raised on every side to join them. Without a care for their razor edge, she flipped them simultaneously end over end, to catch them bare-handed by the blade and extend them hilt first, one toward the soldiers, the other to the civilians. Shando grasped the one, and from among the settlers stepped a woman in the homespun of a farmer's wife. Without a visible cue, but again giving the eerie sense that they knew precisely what was called for, Shando and the woman raised their blades at an angle to the full extension of their arms, crossing them two-thirds of the way to the swords' points. DeGuerin provided the third sword, striding into the heart of the assemblage to form the third of the cardinal points of this human compass.

Luc-Jon assumed Elora would provide the fourth point but it was Tyrrel who now made the trio a quartet, adding his straight-edge cutter to the construction. It was then that the young man realized Elora stood beneath the tent of weapons and that she had a sword of her own in hand. This blade was curved, much like an unstrung bow, and if there was steel in its makeup that metal was subsumed beneath a sheen of silver that matched the color of Elora's skin.

With a war cry of her own that sounded like it came from no human throat—indeed, it sent chills through the souls of all who heard it, not so much of fear but of awe because this was a clarion call heard only in dreams, sounded by dragons—Elora Danan thrust her own sword straight up through the heart of the four above her.

The shout that answered, from every throat in Fort Tregare,

would have done the dragons proud. They meant it to be heard to the farthest reaches of the heavens, and perhaps it was.

Elora lowered her sword, the others followed suit, and the five of them stood a while longer, rocks upon which a storm of passion broke again and again as the crowd vented its fear and proclaimed its heart.

She felt DeGuerin's hand gently come to rest on her shoulder.

"I couldn't have asked for better, Elora Danan," he said. "I am in your debt."

"Nothing's changed," she marveled.

"Not so. Death is a soldier's lot, we know that one and all when we take the oath, and occasionally it comes in a lost cause. Moments like that, we fall back on our pride, as warriors, as members of this command, as citizen-soldiers of the Republic of Sandeni. If we must die, in this place and at this time, then we will do so with honor, even if none but we know of it. That is what had been forgotten tonight, until your song reminded us, and for that you have my gratitude."

At dawn, the Chengwei came again, but not to go blindly once more to the slaughter. They staked out a battle line just beyond the maximum range of the mounted crossbows in the corner towers and sallied forth skirmishers to trade volleys of harassing fire with the archers on the ramparts. The attacks were neither concentrated nor intense; in fact, it was their random and unpredictable nature that made them so dangerous. You never knew when an arrow was coming, whether on a flat trajectory to the wall or a high and arching one meant to strike the yard beyond, and so had to be constantly alert, on guard either for the sight of an inbound shaft or a shouted warning. Absent that, there was the hollow *thok* of a steel point into wood or earth, the softer sound of an impact on flesh, followed by a cry of pain that could mean a casual wound or a mortal one.

The archers on the walls gave better than they got, since they had the advantage of position and better cover. This wicked game of attrition cost the Chengwei far more than the defenders, but not so dearly that their commander considered either disengagement or a modification in tactics.

The real trouble began at night, when the Chengwei snipers moved closer still to the walls. Their archers split into two distinct teams, one along the line they'd established by daylight, their positions marked by braziers of hot coals that they used to ignite their fire arrows. They had no real hope of setting the walls themselves alight but who knew what they might hit beyond them: a stack of hay, somebody's tent or wagon, perhaps even a roof? Every arrow that found a mark was a distraction, every distraction drew warriors from the wall and served to keep the defenders awake and busy; the more that happened, the more physical and emotional reserves were sapped for the days and battles to come.

The problem was that the braziers were themselves ideal targets—which was where the second group came into play. They were pure snipers, with superb night vision, whose job was to deal with anyone on the wall. The moment a defender rose from concealment to mark his target, the poor soul became one himself. And because these Chengwei were beyond the light cast by the braziers, or any capable of being cast from the fort, they were near impossible to spot.

The Colonel's initial response was to put Tyrrel's people on the wall, to use the exceptional night sight of the Veil Folk to mark targets for the Sandeni archers. Here, though, his and Drumheller's suspicions about some magus-level sorcery directed at the Veil Folk to protect the invaders found a measure of proof. For the fairies, of all sizes and shapes and kinds, there was nothing wrong with their sight; they viewed the night as clearly as they did the day——only they couldn't clearly see the Chengwei. Some field of distortion enveloped the invaders, that made the fairies ill to look at them.

Only Elora Danan appeared immune.

Reluctantly, because the job was dangerous, DeGuerin sent her to the wall with the best of his archers. She was the spotter; they would do the rest.

It didn't take the Chengwei long to realize a new factor had entered the engagement and their own snipers began searching

Elora out in earnest. She and her team had to move constantly along the wall, hoping to keep the Chengwei guessing as to where she'd strike from next, praying all the while they'd never realize the main Sandeni asset was a single girl.

In a way, the danger was far greater for the warriors who followed her. Once she marked a target, she could duck behind the safety of the rampart. If the Chengwei had spotted her at the same time, her archer would be met by an incoming arrow as he rose to let fly his own. The first such casualty took a bolt under the outstretched left arm that held the bow, the barbed point punching up and out through the hollow of the collarbone. Elora's own reflex was to follow the warrior to the hospital and try her best to heal him, but Shando held her back, telling her what the Colonel had, that she was needed here. Another was wounded soon after, messy to look at but otherwise of no major consequence, by a shaft that tore straight through his flank. The third to fall did so without a sound, dead before he had a chance to hit the floor of the parapet.

For Elora, it was little solace to know bodies were falling just as certainly below. She wanted to leap atop the rampart, or into the heart of the enemy camp, and somehow find a scream, an incantation, a song which would end this conflict. DeGuerin had made the stakes brutally plain. The General Staff in Sandeni had never taken seriously the possibility that a force of such size might come at the Republic from below the Stairs to Heaven. Why traverse the greatest mountain range in the world when you could attack across a far broader and more accessible front over the plains? Consequently, both defenses and strategic plans were inadequate to a threat of this magnitude. Even if the campaign ultimately failed, it would demand resources desperately needed to face the Maizan horde riding forth from Angwyn, and yet another Chengwei army undoubtedly advancing along the traditional invasion route.

Tregare was a key, absolutely critical to both sides. Bestriding as it did a natural choke point along the Chengwei line of march, the fort would have to be eliminated for the army to proceed. By the same token, if it held, the Chengwei plan would fail. DeGuerin had no illusions on that score—the odds against his command were simply too great—but he knew that each day's delay was another day his comrades in Sandeni could use in preparing the city's defense.

Elora Danan said the Chengwei would not notice a hundred dead for every one of his, but that a thousand might possibly give them pause. So, DeGuerin resolved to aim for that figure. To make the invaders bleed and learn once and for all time that when they took up arms against a free people they did so at their peril.

To that end, for DeGuerin and his command, Elora realized, the Chengwei attackers became simply The Enemy, without any existence other than as foes to be slain or driven to surrender, as she was sure the Chengwei viewed them in return. Elora couldn't do that. Each one to fall on either side had parents, siblings perhaps, or children. Dreams, for certain. Each was a light of life—until she snuffed it out.

Elora looked around suddenly, a foolish move that almost got her killed had not Shando and Luc-Jon together yanked her flat. She paid them no heed, nor the arrows that whizzed close overhead or broke themselves on the stone of the parapet. She was thankful her face was hidden because she didn't want to have to explain its look of startlement as she swept the waryard and the far ramparts for the source of the voices she'd heard calling to her.

There was nothing to be seen, of course, because they hadn't originated on this side of the Veil.

The Malevoiy had called out to her, chiding her stubbornness, offering aid, offering the power to end this conflict. And she had been tempted.

"Sodding bastards!" Luc-Jon raged quietly as they crept along the rampart. "They're so close, Shando. If we slipped a small force out the side gate—!"

"Learn, boy, an' live! 'Tis what they want, don't'cha know? Aye, that's why there's three levels t' their encampment. Archers close, but so far forward from their main force that we might be tempted into a spoiling assault t' bloody 'em an' maybe drive 'em back a ways. Thing is, y'look close at that third picket line, their nags be all saddled, lances one by each. The first shock of arms'll see those troopers mounted an' on the move."

"We have to find another way, then. Elora Danan can't take much more of this."

"I'm fine," she protested.

Luc-Jon put his back to the rampart and pulled her close, searching her eyes before turning his gaze back to Shando.

"It's murder, Shando."

"It's war, boy."

"Was the Sacred Princess born to be a killer?"

"Haven't a clue, Luc-Jon, anymore'n you do. I take my days one by each an' bless the Maker f'r ev'ry new dawn I see. It's not in me t' think so well as some, mayhap like y'rself. I got no truck with the fate o' worlds, what matters are my men. I want t' bring 'em home, alive an' whole. If that means the Sacred Princess has t' get her hands bloody, same as us who fight in her defense—!"

"Hoy, Shando," came a call from farther along.

"Yah, Racay?"

"Take a gander. Nowt much t' see but some interesting sounds carryin' our way from the Chengwei camp."

Experience suggested this was some kind of trick so initial glances were quick and wary, mostly taken through the narrow arrow ports that were cut through the ramparts. The soldier was right about the noise, a growing cacophony could be heard from the distant encampment, the cries of men—some in panic, others trying to restore order and discipline—interspersed with the shrill screams of horses frantic to escape.

With a tremendous *whoosh,* an entire line of tents erupted into flames. A large central pavilion was where the conflagration started. It was consumed so quickly and fiercely that those watching concluded the canvas must have been soaked with oil or pitch. The fire jumped to neighboring rows, as though someone was racing along the neatly described avenues, laid out with appropriate military precision, torching them all.

Then a roar was heard that every soldier on the rampart recognized, and made more than a few take a reflexive step toward safety.

"Can't be," Luc-Jon breathed, unaware that he'd gone as pale as Elora.

"Can't fake that noise," Shando said, the stillness of his tone indicating he was as disconcerted as the young scribe. "That's an ogre."

"Two of them," Elora corrected, as their massive forms appeared as silhouettes against the flames. The anchor ropes of the picket lines had been cut. In the face of a massive fire and creatures they numbered among their mortal enemies, the horses responded accordingly; they bolted, which added magnificently to the confusion.

Surprise soon ran its course, and as the defenders watched, the Chengwei troops rallied. The ogres took a fearful toll, no less than you'd expect from fearsome brutes whose average height was double that of a tall Daikini, whose hands could grasp a human skull like it was a child's ball and crush it more easily than a grape, whose rage and raw strength beggared belief. They were territorial creatures, staking out a range much as bears or great cats would, and generally solitary except when they were gripped by the urge to mate. They weren't so much intelligent as cunning but their physical assets were so formidable that most folks gave them the widest possible berth. No spread, regardless of how rich and fertile the land, was worth intruding on an ogre's turf. Only the greatest of fools picked a fight with them.

Once that fight started, there was only one possible outcome.

Bugles and drums sounded, resulting in a purposeful deployment of forces away from the fort and to the support of their embattled comrades. Troops advanced at the run, in a haphazard collection of armor and weapons, their officers allowing no opportunity to properly prepare for battle.

The distant flames were fading, depriving all save Elora of a decent view of the end game. For everyone's benefit, she presented a running commentary. The ogres had begun with their usual weapon of choice, huge, spiked mallets that were as tall as the average Daikini and weighed as much. They were meant for smashing walls; flesh and armor hadn't a prayer of standing against them. One was flailing about with a body in his other hand. Arrows and javelins filled the air, so that the ogres quickly assumed the macabre appearance of living pincushions but given the stamina of their race even these appalling wounds took what seemed like forever to have any visible effect.

A Chengwei leaped to the fray and buried a war ax into the back of an ogre's leg to sever its hamstring. Crippled, the monster dropped to one knee but not before a backswipe of his club made the soldier responsible little more than bloody pulp. Off-balance and deprived of effective mobility, this ogre's end came quickly.

Having determined that only a single foe remained, the Chengwei swarmed over the ogre like ants, without regard to their own survival. A shake of massive shoulders sent troops flying in bunches, a swing of the mallet sent most of them to their final rest, but there were always more to take their place, to grasp the arrows and spears that had found their marks and shove them deeper still.

"Well now," Shando muttered, "whassup here, hey?"

Someone was at work at the nearer encampment as a lantern described a short arc through the air to scatter fuel and flame throughout the interior of one of the many tents that sheltered these troops. Once more, the fire spread from one to the next with lightning speed, following a trail of accelerant to engulf the entire site quickly and completely.

Elora beheld a single figure, striding with purpose on the periphery of the conflagration, lacking the mass and stature of the ogres but in her own way far more deadly, as those who rushed to face her learned to their sorrow.

Cries filled the air from midway between the two burning camps, as the reinforcing troops realized their own stronghold was under attack. There was a burst of disarray, officers and men torn by indecision about where they were needed most. The ogre seized that moment to shake himself free of his own attackers and take the initiative.

Inspiration struck Elora Danan but when she turned back to the waryard to give it voice she discovered that Colonel DeGuerin was far ahead of her. A troop of fifty was mounted below in the full armor of heavy horse, with swords and bucklers, battle-axes and javelins. Another hundred of infantry stood poised to follow, some carrying short swords, others the double-handed claymores with blades almost as long as they stood tall.

Without drum or bugle to announce their attack, the gates were swung silently open, a single outthrust hand from the Colonel giving the signal for the advance. This was their ground, where his regiment lived and trained—none knew it better. These men and their mounts needed no daylight or torches to see their way, the stars were more than adequate on this moonless night.

The Chengwei archers were silhouetted against their burning camp but DeGuerin's cavalry had no interest in them, they were left for the infantry that followed. He led his troop through their ranks at a gallop and onward in a curve that took them clear of the fire. Most soldiers let out a great shout when they attack, just before the initial clash of arms, to summon forth a transcendent surge of energy to propel them through that fearful moment of collision and as well to strike a measure of fear and terror into the hearts of their adversaries. The Sandeni assault was carried out in silence, DeGuerin's answer to the Chengwei commander, his own demonstration that the fort's defenders likewise knew their craft. Arrows were of little use in close combat and the invaders were cut down like wheat before a scythe.

DeGuerin's troop opened its formation, from the standard column of twos to an arrowhead shape. As well, their gait increased into the headlong rush of a full-fledged charge, aimed at the heart of the Chengwei force floundering between the two ravaged campsites. Only at the last, when the thunder of approaching hoofbeats carried warning of their approach, did he order the bugles to sound. On that cue, spears were leveled and the fate of those Chengwei sealed.

In strategy, there's but one practical defense against an assault by heavy horse—the armored cavalry—and that's to face it behind an embrasure of defensive spears better than twenty feet long, whose butts are embedded in the ground. The trick is to deceive the horsemen into committing to the attack, and when they're too close, and coming too fast to stop, raise the spears into position so the cavalry can impale themselves on them.

The Chengwei had no such opportunity.

The tremendous shock of contact—fifty powerful beasts weighing a ton apiece moving at better than thirty miles per hour—smashed through the Chengwei line like a plow through soft earth. Any possibility of mounting effective resistance was trampled beneath the hooves of DeGuerin's chargers and the blades and spears of his men. While the Chengwei were still reeling, scrambling to arrange themselves in some semblance of order against the follow-on assault they knew was imminent, the Colonel hauled his force around and gave it to them.

There wasn't so much momentum behind the attack this time and even a minute's preparation could make a difference. DeGuerin's troop struck like a hammer and the Chengwei force broke again before them, even as a ragged cheer went up from the main encampment, signifying the death of the second ogre, but not without effort and a share of casualties.

A bugle sounded the recall from the ramparts of Fort Tregare, a rocket was launched skyward to convey the same message. DeGuerin's force obligingly disengaged, leaving the enemy the field of battle and their dead, the infantry coming last to cover their withdrawal.

Khory was waiting at headquarters when the troop cantered home, a few horses with empty saddles, a few men riding double. The infantry hadn't been hurt as badly, the element of surprise and odds totally in their favor meant that their own engagement had ended almost before it truly began. This was a far more significant victory than the day before but in stark contrast to the response then, precious few cheers greeted the warriors as they returned. Folks took their cue from the soldiers themselves; the men knew they'd done a good night's work, they also knew it was but the first of many and that a gift like this wasn't likely to come again.

Elora didn't wait for a summons from the battlements; she took off around the ramparts while DeGuerin's troops were still returning, Luc-Jon hustling after her, trying to close the gap left by her unexpected head start.

She didn't find just Khory in the Colonel's sitting room, but Thorn Drumheller as well, with Rool and Franjean ensconced on the sideboard beneath one of the windows, one brownie keeping watch while the other carved up a piece of marzipan fruitcake baked by the Colonel's wife. As always, though they talked the parts of fierce rivals, Franjean split their bounty equally between himself and his companion. Elora was struck right away at how weary her friends looked. Brownies and Nelwyn were coated with trail dust and Thorn sat gingerly in DeGuerin's easy chair with the bowlegged presentation of someone who's come straight from a hard ride. Given his diminutive stature, Elora knew that meant precariously perched on Khory's saddle, between the warrior and the pommel.

The Colonel's wife rushed in with a tray of fresh stew and a carafe of water, plus a mug of steaming broth. That was what Thorn reached for first, drawing a measure of comfort from the warmth of the rugged, serviceable stoneware.

He caught sight of Elora in the doorway and creased his face into a small smile.

"I hear you've been busy," he said companionably.

"You've missed your share of excitement." The words were innocuous, the underlying subtext anything but.

"You're upset."

"No less than you'd be, were our roles reversed."

"The Colonel felt this reconnaissance was necessary, child . . ."

"I'm not a child, Drumheller. Not the way you mean!"

"Then I stand corrected. But I also agreed with him."

She wanted to say much, much more, but she didn't trust herself to keep her anger in check. She also wasn't completely sure *why* she was so angry and she felt uncomfortable proceeding further without that answer, either.

"How did you bring two ogres into the fight?" one of the officers asked of Khory.

"Leave a proper trail, you can get 'em to follow you pretty near anywhere."

"But I thought the Chengwei had driven out all the Veil Folk."

"Ogres are like bears," Thorn explained from his chair as he relaxed into the plush cushions, giving the impression that the broth he savored was melting his bones. "They can be blessed stubborn when they're of a mind. They also weren't too happy about the absence of game—not Veil Folk, not animals, not Daikini. All we really did was provide the connection between all that frustration and upset and the probable cause."

"Not so nice for the ogres," Elora muttered. "Or the Chengwei."

"Welcome to war, girl," Khory said, cutting herself a piece of cake.

DeGuerin didn't sit, but took a stance in front of Thorn that allowed him easy sight of the Nelwyn, Khory, and Elora. His senior staff spread out behind him, just as eager for Thorn's report but with nowhere near their commander's expressionless poker face.

"Well?" the Colonel prompted.

"Leading elements by morning," Thorn replied. "More than likely the better part of a week before the entire force is on-site."

"Is it truly as large as . . ." someone began to ask but the rest of the query was forestalled—and died stillborn—by Thorn's shallow nod.

"They're not bothering much with outriders and flankers," Khory said flatly. "They don't feel the need. Small force ambush won't do 'em any harm, won't hardly be even noticed, so why worry?"

"The arrogance," another officer exclaimed. "Gods, for the chance to teach 'em a lesson!"

"You did," Khory said flatly. "On your doorstep. They won't care."

"What about the Caliban and the Barontës?" asked Elora.

Thorn pursed his lips. "They are creatures of magic. We drew their attention, you and I, because I was using magic. And while you cannot wield those powers in the same way, Elora, it is integral to the fabric of your being. We came at the Chengwei as Daikini would, using nothing more than stealth and guile."

"But you took the brownies!"

"We needed their services, and their ability to go places Khory and I cannot."

"They look right at us, those lummoxes," Franjean chortled, "didn't see a thing."

"No challenge there," agreed Rool. "Playing hidey-seek with the likes of the Caliban, that was *fun*!"

"Came walking by once, he did. Thought he sensed something. Did a lookabout, came up dry. Could'a stripped them bare, they'd never have noticed."

Rool provided a reality check to his friend's exuberance. "Chose instead not to press our fair fortune. Had what we were sent for. Did a rabbit back to Drumheller. Won't go back."

"Don't be such a ninny."

"You should share some of his sense, Franjean," said Elora. "That's the Caliban's style, to make you believe he's missed you and catch you by surprise during your next incursion."

"You're two days late, Drumheller," the Colonel said idly and at his comment the breath went out of Elora in a rush. She hadn't realized he'd been gone *that* long.

"We found something that required further investigation. And then Khory insisted on finding the ogres. It led to a somewhat more roundabout journey home."

"What something?"

"I'm not altogether sure. Tyrrel tells me his people of Lesser Faery couldn't easily see the force opposing you."

"It made their heads hurt," Elora told him. "And dizzy, like they were seasick. By day, it wasn't so bad, just annoying. By night, though, they were worse than useless."

"Franjean and Rool had the same complaint. We managed to isolate the source—a freight wagon, big as a house, with some sort of fantastic mechanism inside. Whatever it is, the Chengwei are taking precious few chances. It's sited in the heart of their army, within the grounds of their commander's pavilion. As you can imagine, the location is well guarded, and not just by soldiery. There arc Chengwei sorcerers, thick as proverbial thieves, and none of less than adept rank. At that level, magi generally like their creature comforts, they view them as well-earned perks; usually that means a full complement of novices and initiates to do all the scut work—but we didn't see nary a one. These Adepts cooked their own food, did their own cleaning."

"Heaven forfend." Elora managed to sound duly scandalized.

"I grant you your amusement, Elora Danan, but this is a serious matter. Whatever that wagon carries is of sufficient importance to bring about a fundamental change in the behavior of these men."

"But you've no idea what it could be, Drumheller?" the Colonel asked.

"The brownies couldn't get close, for the reasons I've said. I couldn't because of my stature; the Chengwei don't hold much truck with Nelwyns. And given the quality of the opposition, I also suspected that not even my cloaking spells would be proof against their power. It was trial enough utilizing them to counteract the influence of that mechanism."

"But it was possible, yes?" Elora insisted, grabbing tight to that sliver of hope. "You were able to do so?"

Thorn nodded. "I was, for brief periods, at great effort. And only, I suspect, because the device itself was not in active operation."

Elora was aghast at the implications. "If it can do so much while it's at rest—?"

"Heaven help us," Thorn agreed, "or anyone, when it's actively brought to bear. Khory volunteered to make a reconnaissance. In fact, she was our only hope."

"You were successful?" The Colonel nodded to her.

"I got close, I got away, I believe undetected. At least we heard no alarm raised. But that may have been their intent all along, to give us a glimpse of their toy and allow us to return with the news."

"It's a weapon, then? And that formidable?"

"From the glimpse and the listen I got, I'd swear it was a clock. Something that ticks, for certes. And yes, a weapon. As to how formidable, the magi I listened to spoke of it as being the key to ultimate victory. The army is there to keep it well protected and to enforce Chengwei rule on the conquered territories."

"Cocky bastards," commented an officer.

"Supposedly," Thorn said to DeGuerin, as if they were alone in the room, "it destabilizes magic. Even at a distance, I could taste the chaos emanating from that infernal device."

"You mean disrupt spells, cripple sorcerers such as yourself, limit the effectiveness in battle of the Veil Folk, that sort of thing?"

"Some of the above, Colonel, perhaps all, certainly more than you've listed. Elsewise, why make the investment in men and treasure?"

"Magic doesn't refer to just the Veil Folk, or parlor tricks like Thorn's," Elora interrupted, words coming out of her in a rush, propelled by a burst of anxiety she was struggling to understand and explain as she went along. "It's one of those catchall words that covers a tremendous spectrum of forces and states of being. There's 'magic' in the way the world holds itself together, in the soul of each Daikini, as much as in the mage who thinks himself ready to tackle a demon. Might as well try to dam the Cascadel or the Quangzhua," referring to the two greatest rivers of the continent, one flowing west to the Sunset Ocean, the other eastward through the heart of Chengwei.

"There's been talk of doing both."

"And what of the consequences?"

"You believe they mean to turn this infernal engine on us, Thorn?" the Colonel asked the Nelwyn mage, who responded with a shallow nod.

"That'll weaken the walls a tad," Shando interjected, since he knew the physical structure of the fort better than most, "since spells've been used to strengthen the mortar and cement, t' bind the logs more tightly t'gether and protect 'em from weather an' the like. Beyond"—he shook his head—"they'll have t' reduce this yard the same as it's allus been done, by siege an' storm."

"It's Tyrrel's folk who'll suffer the most," agreed Thorn.

"Cut them loose, then," Elora cried. "Give them leave to go while there's still time."

"I'll lay odds, Elora, that's where we'll find the Caliban and his Barontës."

On that note, DeGuerin ushered his staff out the door, to consider the further defense of their position in light of this new intelligence.

Within his study, that left himself, Thorn, Elora, the brownies, Khory, Tyrrel, and Luc-Jon.

Elora's eyes flashed across the quartet who'd formed the Colonel's scouting party.

"What are you planning?" she demanded of Thorn.

"You said it yourself, child. Our fairy allies cannot stay."

"But if the Caliban's waiting to ambush them—?" She paused. "What am I missing?" she wanted to know.

"What're you askin' *him* for?" screeched Franjean, sorely tempted to pop a marzipan cherry Elora's way, only to think better of it and take as big a bite out of the sweet as he could manage—an impressive achievement considering he needed both hands just to hold it.

"Sorcerers don't know everything," commented Rool.

"Only brownies!" finished Franjean triumphantly.

"So what is it the Chengwei are playing with?" Elora inquired of them, figuring to teach them a modest lesson in humility. She should have known better.

"A nasty," said Franjean, with a flick of his elegant cuffs to show his contempt.

"There's eloquence for you."

"What more needs knowin'? It's a bad thing, it's coming our way, we should go somewhere else."

"By way," finished Rool, "of yon World Gate."

"I beg your pardon."

"World Gate," Rool repeated, motioning toward the scribe's tower with his chin. "Over there."

Elora sank to a chair and laid her head on crossed forearms atop the table before lifting one fist and lightly pounding it on the back of her head.

"Elora?" asked Luc-Jon in concern.

She ignored him, repeating the phrase "I'm an idiot," over and over, in tandem with her fist, until Luc-Jon caught her hand.

She looked sideways at him.

"I thought you knew," he confessed lamely. "I mean, it's na' common knowledge but when you were talkin' about the sacred circles an' power an' such, I assumed . . ." His voice trailed off as she turned a gimlet eye to the Nelwyn.

"Can we do that?" Elora asked Thorn.

"By rights, no. There is no longer a Magus Point here. This Gate is dead, as is its counterpart in Sandeni, as the one atop Tyrrel's Tor is dying."

"So there's nothing to be done," said the Colonel, and something in his tone caught Elora's attention, brought her head up.

"You were considering evacuating more than just Tyrrel and his people," she told him.

DeGuerin nodded. "The civilians, the refugees, have no place here," he explained. "And I'll not leave our women and children to suffer at Chengwei hands."

"Why leave anyone?"

"Each day we can hold this position, Elora Danan, is one more day for Sandeni to prepare its defenses. One more for the weather to close, for the first of the winter storms. Each Chengwei we kill, or who dies along the road, is one less to threaten our homes."

"Even if you die?"

"We're professional soldiers. That's part of the contract. These others, though, they're who we signed on to protect. They should have no part in this." He considered something, looked to Thorn. "Forgive me, Drumheller, but you said the World Gate in Sandeni was also dead?"

"I did, didn't I."

"But by your own words, that was how you reached the Circle of the Spirit, through that World Gate."

"Yes. We, and the Deceiver both."

"How? Magic?"

Thorn didn't answer him directly but looked instead to the brownies.

"What's the status of that Gate now?" he asked them.

"Dead as ever," Franjean told him. "From the moment you passed through."

"Was it magic, Drumheller?" DeGuerin asked again, applying a veneer of command to his words to make sure this time he got a response. "Did you cast a spell?"

Thorn uttered a snort of sardonic amusement. "Not me," he said. "Not possible, though there are records of sorcerers who've tried over the ages. To create a World Gate or reenergize one whose time had passed. There mostly, they were working in places that still possessed a residue of power. Sometimes it worked, most often not. For here, or Sandeni, I doubt I have the proper skills, or the strength. And even if it were possible for me, that level of arcane manipulation would stand out like the brightest of beacons. It would bring the Caliban down on us for certain and very likely provoke the Chengwei into unleashing their device."

He smiled and the expression sent a minor chill curling about the base of Elora's spine.

"However," he finished, "we may have an alternative."

"What makes you think I can do any better, Drumheller?" Elora challenged, unaware that she'd placed her back flat against the wall.

"Faith. And"—with a smile—"a hearty dollop of blind desperation. It's you or no one, Elora Danan."

"Work it out amongst yourselves, how best to go about this," the Colonel ordered them, all business and in a hurry. "If it can be done, I want you ready by midnight; I want the evacuation complete by dawn. If not, I need to know before I set people's hopes to rise."

"One thing, Colonel," interjected Tyrrel.

"Highness?"

"Beyond the Veil, there can be no steel, no cold iron. For the Daikini who accompany us, that likely means no weapons of any kind and only what possessions can be carried on folks' backs."

"Their lives will be in your hands then, milord."

"Aye. Make that clear."

"No small thing, to ask Daikini to walk beyond the Veil," Luc-Jon muttered, "when legend has it that those who do are ne'er seen again."

"Aye, that's us," grumbled Franjean back at him, "monsters all."

"Given the history between our two races, especially out here on the Frontier," the young man said, " 'tis a lot to ask, and a lot to take on faith."

"That's what this war is all about, in a way," Thorn said gently, stating what was for him a primal truth. "On the one hand, those who would impose order by blood and blade and fire, according to their lights. On the other, those who have faith in the community of beings."

Elora sank down on her haunches, letting her knees fold until she rested on the floor.

"The Gate may be too old," she worried. "It may not want to remember what it used to be."

"Only one true way to find out," the Nelwyn told her. "But if you lack faith in yourself, Elora Danan, how can you expect to truly inspire others? You'll have to lead them, you realize, along with Tyrrel."

"Aren't you coming with?"

Thorn shook his head, savoring his latest mouthful of stew. "Someone has to provide the Chengwei device with a decent adversary."

"That's madness; you're talking suicide! I won't allow it!"

Thorn laughed with genuine delight. "I haven't heard that tone from you in a good while."

"If you stay—!"

"You will do as you're told!" The Nelwyn hadn't moved from his seat. There was nothing at all imposing about him, almost lost in a chair designed for someone twice his height and girth and more, using a chunk of bread to mop up the juices left in his bowl. He was as worn as his clothes, more ragamuffin than man, and not much more impressive after a wash. His hair was tousled and, like his beard, in need of a trim. Yet when he spoke, he gathered about himself an air of authority that fit him as naturally and well as any Monarch's crown. Elora Danan might be the Sacred Princess spoken of in prophecy but in every way Thorn Drumheller was her equal. When he knew he was in the right, his was the will that proved unbreakable.

"Who else but you, Elora," he continued in that same outwardly conversational manner, laying out his sequence of truths as Colonel DeGuerin would the day's regimental duty schedule, "can calm the fears of the Daikini you'll be leading? As well as those of whomsoever of the Veil Folk you encounter as you go? Tyrrel is Monarch of Lesser Faery, his sway over the elves of Greater Faery is a matter of courtesy alone. The brownies will accompany you, as will . . ."

Before Thorn could finish, Luc-Jon broke in, stepping forward and stiffening to a relaxed form of attention, one hand on the hilt of his sword.

"I ask your pardon, Magister," he said, using the formal term address for sorcerers of Thorn's rank, "but I'll be staying at the fort." He stated his reasons for Elora's benefit, Thorn understood without being told. "This is my home, y'see, and these my friends and comrades in arms. The closest I have t' family, closer'n blood kin I've known. The Colonel himself gave me a commission an' I've managed to earn the trust an' regard of my troops. An' my master." His eyes flickered around the room, touching briefly on every other face present before returning to Elora. "Funny thing is, I think they'd understand my goin', they'd na' think it the act of a coward. Which is why I haveta stay. I'm sorry," he finished but he couldn't hold his gaze on Elora's eyes, which were suddenly bright with tears she stubbornly refused to shed.

"All right then," Thorn said. "Khory will accompany the withdrawal."

"No!" Elora snapped, the intensity of her emotions pushing her from her huddle against the wall to stand before her mentor.

"I'll be fine, Drumheller, I can take care of myself, I don't need a minder."

"I'll be the judge of that."

"The hell you say. Who watches your back then?"

"As targets go, I'm not so easy, believe me."

"Remember our oath, Nelwyn, and the spell we cast?"

"Every moment."

"If you die, Drumheller—!"

He shook his head, still radiating such insufferable calm that Elora wanted to hit him. "If the dragons must be lost," he said, "for this generation or for all time, then so be it. On the other hand, I can think of no one who can better take their place than you.

"We can't all stay, Elora Danan, we can't all go. Keeping you safe is paramount."

"He's right," Khory said with a quiet finality of her own.

Elora ran a hand through her close-cropped hair but it didn't make her feel any better. What she really wanted was to wind long ringlets around her fingers.

"Have you ever wished you could turn back the clock, Thorn?" she wondered aloud. "Wished you could go back and start over, with the foreknowledge to sidestep the original mistakes that led you to this damnable place?"

"Unfortunately, there are always new mistakes to be made."

"I suppose. But I still can wish . . ."

The scribe wasn't thrilled by the disruption of his home, any more than the refugees when they were told how much they'd have to leave behind. Among the troopers waiting with their families, the mood was mixed, passion given full rein or hidden behind stoic masks, kisses and embraces that looked like they'd never end, tears. The overarching sensibility was of finality; for these households, it was a last farewell. This was the only miracle they'd be allowed.

Elora kept increasingly to herself as the witching hour approached. She couldn't bear the looks in people's eyes: awe and wonder that she could do this, resentment that she couldn't do more. She couldn't decide what was worse, the hope she saw in those who'd given up any chance of escape, or the grief from those about to be forever parted.

The Master Scribe's library tower had been cleared of its contents, the books removed under Luc-Jon's direction. Some went to a subcellar of the house to be locked away, while others were parceled out to a trusted selection of those who'd be going through the Gate, to carry them to the Athenæum, the great University library of Sandeni. What was left went into Elora's traveling pouches, among them the massive Malevoiy text. They were the most important works in the scribe's collection, and by extension the most dangerous—either in and of themselves or as the objects of another's desire. Elora refused to lay that burden on anyone else's shoulders. She would care for them, and assume the risk of doing so, herself.

The only access to the tower and its World Gate was, sadly,

through the house itself and that route, too, had to be cleared of furniture and breakables. The scribe himself hadn't wanted to leave. This was his home, had been for twoscore years and change, he wasn't about to abandon it for anything. Until Colonel DeGuerin had a quiet word with him. The scribe still wasn't happy, but he'd do as he was told.

When the time came, Elora asked to be left alone in the tower. She started at the topmost level, right beneath the skylight, noting again how perspectives conspired to make the tower seem more like the deepest of wells. Even with her MageSight, she had to strain to see the floor below.

At a relaxed, steady pace, Elora followed the circular ramp down to the bottom, allowing her right hand to trail along the wall from time to time. Her booted feet raised a faint *skrunch* sound as she strode from the base of the ramp to the center of the floor, and canted her head back for a view of the skylight. When she looked up instead of down, the distance didn't appear anywhere near so extreme.

She took in a slow, deep breath, let it out, and watched the cloud of frost hang briefly in the air. Cold was an abstract to her, as was heat. She was aware of both sensations yet was far more resistant to them than most folks from either side of the Veil. The perpetual chill outdoors that had its origin in the magic the Deceiver had employed against Angwyn and now tainted even the heights of summer meant little to her; she was as comfortable in a shift as in a sweater and would survive long after those around her had frozen to death.

She rubbed the palms of her hands on the thighs of her trousers, mainly because of nerves. That prompted a wry smile: unique she may be but in so many ways she remained refreshingly normal. She scrubbed her fingers through her brush-cut hair and her smile grew into a teenager's grin at the reminder of how the sight of her scandalized the proper ladies of the fort. Even those women among Colonel DeGuerin's command didn't wear their hair so short, and precious few men, either. Elora missed the opportunity to style long hair, but only a little. She liked the way she looked. It made her feel wild and untamed.

To business, she told herself, and knelt into a crouch, one knee up, one down, to place both hands flat on the dirt floor.

There was no response but that was to be expected in so old and quiescent a Gate. Asleep so long, its power would be hard to wake and most likely as cranky as a sleeping bear when it did.

Elora sounded a low clear note from the bottom of her vocal register, allowing her perceptions to pace the sound as it bounced off the circular walls and faded up toward the skylight. She called forth her own memories of passing through World Gates, transposed them into words, and cast them forth. She allowed the song to find its own rhyme and meter, and her body to follow. She was drawn to her feet and that act of rising was much the same as pumping the handle of a well for with her came the first stirrings of the power of this ancient place.

She described a series of circles with her body, one arm and the opposite leg outstretched as if in a fencing lunge, moving so smoothly and easily over the floor she might have been wearing skates on ice. She made contact with the wall, her pace quickening, becoming recognizable now as a dance to match her song.

She returned to the center, pirouetting along the same axis as the ramp that wound its way down the wall. She turned outward from it in a growing spiral and in her wake a trail formed in the dirt that flashed with tiny bursts of silver, as if the young woman were leaving pieces of herself behind. She sounded that same, deep note again and this time the tone didn't fade. The walls picked up the resonance and answered in kind, filling the tower with a reverberation of such power it was felt more than heard, to the core of Elora's being. She couldn't help her expression of delight, the concentration on her face yielding slightly to wonder and awe at the majesty she was drawing forth. She had to consciously and continuously remind herself not to get carried away by the glamour of the moment. Bears were majestic, too, but only a suicide chose to wake one in hibernation. This wasn't the quick-fire power she was used to but that didn't make it any the less formidable once aroused.

She wondered as well if, once aroused, it would be so eager to return to sleep?

The act was necessary, the cause just, but she hadn't really given serious thought to the possible consequences.

She shook her head, reminded of the interlocking wheels that were the symbols of the Great Realms. Nothing happened in a vacuum was what Thorn had always tried to teach her. Every choice has its repercussions, and rarely where you expect. But there was also her experience in Sandeni to act as precedent. If he was right and she was the key to open these Gates, they would slip shut once more after she passed along her way.

A final sweeping turn brought her to the foot of the ramp and she didn't need a look to reveal the design she'd inscribed on the floor. It was a perfect match for the sigil she and Thorn had used in Sandeni. Anyone looking down from the topmost tier of the tower would perceive the ramp as descending forever, with such precision that it looked as though it had been laid out by architect and engineer.

However, Elora's song wasn't done. It gained strength as she climbed and she flushed with passion. She no longer left sparkles in her wake, but a trail of incandescence, the way a blinding radiance will leave an afterimage across the mind's eye. The air hummed with energy, making the hackles stand to attention on her neck and igniting a brush fire of tingles over every inch of her body. The sensations were too exquisite to be endured and she wanted to tear off her clothes, to become one with the forces she was unleashing.

Propriety and self-preservation combined to save her as she reached the very apex of the helical ramp. A cry welled within her but she wasn't the one to give it voice. The tower spoke, with a shout like a thunderclap, sharp like a body blow, that initial explosion setting off a perpetual series of growling afterbursts. Elora staggered and nearly fell, dazed by the tumult, and she understood in that instant all the old stories about gods and giants striking at each other with their great and terrible hammers.

When next she looked down to the base of the tower, there was no floor. Only a surface, supernally smooth and featureless, that most resembled a vat of heavy oil save that it was lit from beneath by a glow that echoed Elora's argent coloration.

She sagged against the wall and stood braced there a little while, reflecting on what she'd done.

"I have no magic," she said in the barest whisper, summoning forth the memory of an exchange with Drumheller.

"Not in the way most folks define the term, no" was his reply. "In a sense, you *are* magic."

"Hooray for me."

"Through my spells, I can command forces and powers. That, you cannot do. By the same token, you are likewise immune to those spells and those powers. Your gift instead, child, is to summon forth the magic in others, to draw them to you like a beacon would a fleet of ships. The question is, to safe harbor or to the rocks that will spell their doom."

She had been younger then, so she had ended the conversation the best way she knew how—by sticking out her tongue. She felt that urge again.

Her steps wove a bit, side to side, as she made her way to the tower's upper entrance, where Thorn and the others waited. She wasn't tired, but the intensity of the rush had taken its toll.

Thorn was waiting and as she stepped through the doorway, both brownies leaped from his shoulders to hers, snugging close to her neck, where they could best keep watch against any blindside attacks.

"Hooray for me," she said dryly.

"Told you so."

"Everyone ready?"

"As they'll ever be."

"Thorn—!" she tried to begin, but that was as far as he'd let her go.

"I've already had this out with Khory."

"You should listen to her. For once, old duffer, you should listen to *me*!"

"I always listen. I merely don't agree. I need to stay. You must go, and Khory with you."

"I can take care of myself."

"Fine. Then she can take care of the rest of the column. Time's wasting, Elora."

She nodded. "Tyrrel and his folk first," she announced.

Elora stepped aside, fitting herself into an alcove just beyond the doorway, as a faint *thrumming* made itself heard, interposed with the *flutter* of insectile wings. A few solitary beads of light formed the vanguard, flitting through the narrow hallway and into the tower. They formed a line on a level with Elora's eyes, about three feet apart from each other, each of them linked by a spiderweb of energy. They were taking no chances. The string placed them in constant contact with one another, so that if the scouts ran into trouble they'd be able to communicate it instantly to Tyrrel.

Moments stretched while they waited for word from the fairy Pathfinders. Absently, Elora plucked her knives from belt and boot and slipped them into her traveling pouch. In their place, she drew forth a pair of curved swords, her own forging from her days not so long ago when she served as apprentice to Thorn's cousin, Torquil, of the Rock Nelwyn. Plain, unadorned scabbards and fitments, the metal of the blades folded hundreds of times, pounded and honed to the keenest edge known. Torquil had provided the ore but Elora had refined it, creating an amalgam that matched the strength of steel but was forged of noble metals, making them safe for use beyond the Veil.

One she thrust into her own belt, the other was for Khory.

With the all clear came the bulk of the fairy host, a cloud of iridescence that seemed to consist of all the fireflies in Creation, generating every color imaginable. They flew, they walked, they crawled, they were carried. They were smaller than a finger, they stood as tall as a child. They were naked, they wore all manner of clothing. They resembled Daikini in general form, perfect in every respect save size; they were nothing like Elora's kind. They passed her in a steady stream for the best part of an hour, under the watchful gaze of Drumheller and their Monarch, without a word spoken.

They were considered creatures of the Veil yet the overwhelming sensation Elora received from this multitude was of loss. They were being driven from their homes as much as the Daikini who would follow. Their present was as unsettled, their future just as uncertain.

The first of those Daikini looked even more uneasy. They were bunched in the entrance to the house, by the scriptorium, gathered into a close huddle, children in the center. Elora tried to jolly them with a smile as she sidled by; she'd have a better chance of a response preaching to stone. Intellectually, she'd done a rough total of the column, it was another thing altogether to actually behold it winding its serpentine way back and forth across the waryard. Luc-Jon met her on the porch, lugging a bulging satchel, which he explained was full of letters and mementos from those who'd remain. She wanted to grab him away to some hidden corner, and steal time enough for a private farewell, but that wasn't possible. He put on his bravest face and traced the line of her jaw with his fingertips, sending a fierce thrill straight down to her toes. She cast decorum to the winds right then and there, grabbing him by the melton wool of his hood that lay flat and bunched up close about his throat and pulling his lips to hers.

It was the best kiss she'd ever given (or received) and it prompted a scattering of applause and good humor from the onlookers. More to the point, it left Luc-Jon bright-eyed and breathless, dazzled beyond speech.

"You live, you hear!" she told him, and though her tone was as young and excited as his, her eyes as glittery, there was also the force to her words of a royal command.

"I'll do my best," he joked, so she dropped all pretense.

"You—*live!*" This time, it was a command and the force of custom plus her own indomitable presence rocked him back on his heels.

His reply was in kind, and just as serious.

"I shall do my best," he told her, and it was only when she released him that he realized he'd straightened to full attention.

When Khory chose that moment to approach, Elora grabbed the second blade from her belt and tossed it to her, in a single smooth, graceful motion. Khory matched it, snatching the weapon from midair and drawing it from its scabbard. The blade ran the length of her arm and followed the natural curve of that limb. When she reached to full extension, it seemed like a living part of her.

Elora expected the warrior to hand over her own straight-edge broadsword for safekeeping in Elora's traveling pouch, but Khory demurred, slinging the heavy blade diagonally across her back, right shoulder to left hip.

"Tyrrel won't like that," Elora cautioned.

"Tell him it's the demon in my nature, being contrary," she replied with a laconic twist to her mouth.

"Time to go, then?"

"They've lost enough nerve, by the looks of 'em," Khory said, meaning the gathering crowd. "Let's roll before they're dry."

Elora took a last look at the fort and its garrison and hurried inside as her eyes began to burn hot with unexpected tears. A farewell wave from Shando on the battlements had been more than she could bear.

Unaware how much like Khory's her stride had become, her own legs just shy of the warrior's in length, Elora made her way to the front of the line, deliberately presenting a face of good cheer and resolve. Tyrrel awaited her in the doorway, his wooden sword—whose keenness placed it in good company with steel when it came to cutting flesh—held at the ready. His weapon came from a markedly different design philosophy than Daikini blades; fairy swords were much shorter, the length of a forearm rather than the full yard that was the Daikini standard, and shaped like a slim leaf, with a serrated edge. At her approach, he raised it flat across his chest in salute.

A mother and children stood near the head of the line. The woman was having a difficult time coping with toddlers and an infant barely a year old, grumpy because it was well past his bedtime. She was grateful when Elora snugged the baby into her own arms and amazed at how quickly the child slipped into sleep.

"My own nannies," Elora confessed to the woman, "could never get me to be so cooperative." Then, to Tyrrel, "My lord, shall we?"

"I bid you welcome, you and yours, Elora Danan, to my Realm. I wish on all of us safe journey and Godspeed."

Elora led the way down the steps and onto the landing at the bottom. The floor remained so utterly motionless it could easily be mistaken for solid ground yet radiated sufficient light from beneath its surface to illuminate the entire tower. With a backward glance and a smile of encouragement, Elora continued her descent as the landing proceeded to another set of descending steps. She passed into the floor without raising a ripple, even as a burst of alarm hurried back along the people following her.

Elora didn't bother with any words of reassurance, none would listen. Instead, she maintained her deliberate pace, sensing that the others had come to a stop, ignoring the mother's frantic outcry for her baby as the eerie substance of the floor passed Elora's ankle, her knee, her hip. The next step would put the floor at the baby's chin, the one after would immerse them both.

Elora never heard the woman's wail of loss. She was already gone.

Before shock had a chance to turn to outright panic, she was back, ascending the stairs to the landing, only now the baby was awake in her arms, gurgling contentedly and utterly unharmed.

"It's safe," Elora called out, in a voice that filled the tower and would have served her well amidst a pitched battle. "I know you're afraid, but this is our only salvation. Trust me," she said, and held out her free hand to the baby's mother.

The woman grabbed her more tightly than any vise. Elora didn't mind.

Once more, she began her descent and passed through the boundary layer of the floor. And, as always happened with World Gates, where the normal rules of existence and nature never seemed to apply, found herself immediately climbing up out of an identical pool on the other side. The woman went all goggle-eyed, while a toddler made sounds of delight and amazement. Her brother, another toddler, shorter and younger, burst immediately into tears, which gave the mother something constructive to do.

The contrast with the Realm of the Malevoiy was absolute, striking at all her senses with an immediacy that nearly stopped Elora in her tracks. Her strongest feeling among the Malevoiy was of a world and people who existed as the barest of memories. There was a ghostliness to every shape and substance, like a tomb that had been too long sealed, wherein even the air had gone taste-less and stale.

The Realm of Lesser Faery reached as far as possible in the other direction. The air was so crisp and clear that every breath scoured her lungs with flame. It hurt, tremendously, but this was the kind of pain that actually felt delicious. In every direction, for as far as she could see, her eyes beheld a greensward of such rich-ness all the labels for colors she had stored inside her skull suddenly became useless. Meadows of grass interspersed with wildflowers covered gently rolling hills and in the moderate dis-tance stood a forest the like of which could not be found on the Daikini side of the Veil. This was a world very much like their own, yet possessing a vitality and a passion so fierce that even as any Daikini would rush to embrace it, they would be as surely consumed. In simplest terms, it was the difference between stand-ing before the warmth of a candleflame and beneath the untram-meled fury of the sun itself.

There was beauty here to make the heart ache and, of course, it was the children who responded best as Khory shepherded the last of the column through the Gate and she and Elora, Tyrrel and his fairy host, plus some of the adults among the Daikini, tried to form their unwieldy group into a semblance of marching order.

"We've a ways to go," Elora told them, though her attempts at the stern demeanor of a leader were subverted by giggles and shrieks of laughter and delight coming from the nearby field the children had appropriated for their own. They were playing tag, kids against fairies, and the meadow was patterned with color and light as the tiny, winged creatures zoomed this way and that to evade the eager but mostly clumsy attempts of the youngsters to capture them. Now and then, the fairies would swarm on a child, scooping him or her into the air for a brief ride that would be remembered for a lifetime.

"Tregare to Sandeni afoot," someone posited, "that'll take us weeks!"

"Time and distance don't mean the same on this side of the Veil," Tyrrel countered. "More likely, we'll reach the Sandeni Gate in a few days."

"Assumin' yeh know the way."

The Monarch of Lesser Faery creased a smile. "This is my Realm, sirrah."

"Is there food enough for the journey?" another asked.

"My people will provide," Tyrrel told them, which ignited a frisson of anxiety among the refugees. The oldest of wives' tales told of the dangers of eating or drinking anything in the Realms of Faery, that doing so would enslave a person's soul to them forever.

"We are the Liege Lord of Lesser Faery," Tyrrel cried in his best parade-ground voice, using the formal pronoun to remind them of his status, "Monarch of one of the Great Realms. In Our domain, Our will is law. You are welcome here. There is nothing to fear, not from Our subjects, nor from anything that lives or grows on these lands. Eat and drink your fill, you will be safe. Of that, you have Our most solemn pledge."

"Not altogether true," Elora told him wryly as she and Tyrrel took the point, out beyond the head of the column.

"You doubt Our word, Sacred Princess?"

"Never! I just mean, once you've had a glimpse of paradise, it can't help but change you."

"Paradise," he snorted. "Forgive me, Elora Danan, but it only looks the part. An epoch ago, an epoch from now, it would look exactly the same, as would we."

"Is constancy so bad a thing?"

"I admire a fly frozen in amber but it's a helluva way to spend eternity. Still, for all my complaints, we're better off here than in Greater Faery."

Tyrrel gestured with thumb and chin, off to the most distant horizon. Elora narrowed her eyes, assuming for a moment what she saw was some trick of the light. Marching all along that rim of the world was a magnificent escarpment, mountain peaks that more closely resembled spires, arranged in a serried rank that had to be so tall they'd dwarf the Stairs to Heaven back home. Most strange about them was the eerie sense that they were a mirage. Elora was sure she could see right through them and decided it was because they weren't composed of stone at all but a kind of crystal. To her eye, they had no solidity, but existed in a flat plane, as if the sky were a transparent canvas on which some artisan had etched a design in acid.

"Is that real?" she asked.

"I'd tell you to go see for yourself, youngster, but then you prob'ly would."

The truth of his observation made them both chuckle.

"Greater Faery, is it?" Then, after a bit more consideration. "How cold it seems."

"The Realms reflect the nature of their inhabitants. Because we of Lesser Faery spend as much time on your side of the Veil as on ours, because many of us make our homes among the Daikini, this land reflects that interaction. The High Elves of Greater Faery keep mainly to themselves."

"You don't approve."

" 'S'na' a question o' that, lass. Drumheller was born a farmer and a Nelwyn; look at him now. Find me another Nelwyn in all memory who would willingly stand at the scene of a Daikini battle, to cast his life into the hazard alongside them Tall Folk, with the knowledge he has of what's coming."

"Don't remind me, Tyrrel, or I'll be back to join him."

"No, you won't."

"You doubt me?"

"You're the one who opens dead World Gates, Elora Danan. Without you, the way to Sandeni is closed for these folk. Is that fair payment for their trust?"

"Sometimes, Tyrrel, your words can be as remorseless as Drumheller's."

"But you know them to be true."

"I know them to be true," she echoed, in the barest of whispers.

"You've changed, milady, just in the few months since we've met—and that's my point. *Change,* Elora Danan. *Growth!* The constants of life. You Daikini have the shortest spans of all the Realms, yet with that mayfly existence comes the ability to alter the shape of your world almost beyond our recognition. We accept the world as it is, your kind tend to see it as a challenge. So mayhap"— and he looked back along their line of march—"the main good that comes out of this trek is your kind gets to see why we treasure the world and mine comes to accept that you're not all monsters."

"Monsters?"

"Aye, Elora, to the dryad whose grove is cleared to make room for a farmer's field, or worse yet a road. To the naiad whose stream is dammed for irrigation or befouled by the refuse of some new town. Of a surety, we can retreat behind the Veil, but that'll make us just like them yonder." Another gesture toward the mirage mountains. "And you'll lose the passion we offer."

The column's route took them close by the woods and excited cries were raised as a Royal pair of deer appeared from the shadows, the King of the Forest and his consort. The stag stood taller than most warhorses, with more points to his antlers than could easily be counted. The couple matched the refugees' pace a while, until the King was satisfied this incursion represented no threat to his people, then vanished into the forest in a single, powerful bound.

With Tyrrel's permission, a few campfires were lit as dusk spread across the sky. The rest were provided for by Elora, as she sang a variation on her Song of Remembrance, this time to a collection of rocks and stones, reminding them of how they'd felt when originally cast forth from the molten core of the World. Under Khory's supervision, trenches were dug for latrines as camp was made close by a meandering stream.

Its water was like liquid crystal, a fair substitute for both wine and beer. There was no meat to be had, save what had been brought with them, and, having seen the King of the Forest, precious little enthusiasm for going hunting. Fruits and vegetables proved, surprisingly, a most acceptable alternative.

As full night fell, the stars were visible. They were the same as could be seen on the Daikini side of the Veil, but the purity of the air allowed them to be presented in all their majestic glory. Even Elora was touched by the vision and a yearning to discover if those tiny dots of light above were truly suns like their own, circled by worlds such as this. A stillness came over the campground, as families tucked themselves in, the air dancing both with the firefly light of fairies keeping watch and the sounds of jokes, idle comments, endearments, entreaties. Wrapped in her warcloak, Elora wandered among the tents and lean-tos, savoring these ordinary realities of life. There was sadness in the air, for those left behind, and anger for possessions that had been lost—in some cases, the work of generations—but in such a land of peace and beauty these negative emotions didn't linger long. She saw youngsters, too excited by this journey yet to surrender to sleep, gazing in rapt astonishment at some of the Veil Folk, drawn forth from the surrounding woods by just as strong a curiosity. Places were made by fires, fairy mead offered by hands that were webbed or bore six fingers, the gesture returned with flasks of hearty dark beer or highland wine. A grandfather waved his hand toward the sky and pontificated to a clutch of children the complete history of this constellation and that, while nearby one of Tyrrel's people, who looked scarcely older than her audience though she'd seen easily twice the old man's years and more, did much the same.

She heard a guitar from one camp, fiddle from another, the roiling beat of a tiompan drum from a third, voices raised tentatively in song. She wandered over toward the guitar, accepted the instrument when it was proffered. Of their own volition, her fingers plucked at the strings, a random collection of notes at first that soon resolved themselves into an improvised melody. This was toe-tapping music, irresistibly infectious, and she let inspiration drive her forward, determined to lure some of her audience off their duffs and into a dance.

A father of middle age was the first to accept her invitation and she modified her playing to suit his ability as she saw that ambition had an edge in him over skill.

Then, suddenly, came a gasp from the crowd, the Daikini stopping dead in his tracks, as a spectral figure emerged from the fringes of the fireglow. Even Elora was taken aback, her fingers stumbling on the strings. Tyrrel rose to meet the newcomer, with a formal courtesy he rarely showed, and bid her welcome.

She was elf and she was noble, taller than anything human had a right to be and whipcord thin. There were no obvious curves to her, yet at the same time she cast forth an aura of womanliness that matched even the most matronly Daikini present. Her hair hung to her ankles, caught by carved-jade clasps at the nape of the neck, the shoulders, and her waist, and wound into a loose braid beyond. If it were left unbound, Elora knew every strand would be precisely the same length, so that her hair would form a totally flat and even edge. Her skin was so pale it distantly echoed Elora's silver coloring, her eyes touched by the faintest hint of cerulean, whereas Elora's were a blue so dark there was almost no difference between iris and pupil. Her face was oval, her features possessed of the kind of grave beauty that men found haunting. The only bright spots on her were the gems that were dusted in runic patterns onto the fabric of her skinsnug gown, ankle-length and long-sleeved with a shallow scoop neck. The material itself was a gossamer so fragile to the eye it seemed the slightest touch would shred it. The gown flowed with her movements and created the sense that the elven Princess was shrouded by mist.

In perfect harmony with Elora's tune, and a grace that made the heart ache to watch, the Princess spun her way once twice thrice across the clearing to where the Daikini stood dumbfounded in the face of such a vision.

She offered him her hand and a smile.

It was quite a scene, Elora perched on a flat-topped boulder, guitar in hand, her skin gleaming like polished metal in the torchlight. Before her, a Princess of Greater Faery scandalizing her unseen brethren in the nearby shadows by doing what none of her kind had ever considered before, reaching out her hand in friendship to a Daikini. And that Daikini, torn between visions of this moment as a dream or a nightmare, wholly unsure of what to do and terrified that no matter how he chose it would be wrong.

Elora's smile was lazy, and a tad wicked, and the song she began was a match. The only thing it had in common with her initial piece was that it was for dancing and that it was as close to irresistible as she could manage. To the audience, it seemed at first that she played in vain because nothing much happened. The elven Princess stood stock-still, and whispers could be heard like the rustle of a background breeze, wondering if she'd lost her nerve, if she regretted stepping into view like this and how could

she withdraw without shame? Virtually the same was said about
her partner.

To their surprise, it was the Daikini who made the first move.
He had a good smile and he used it without trying, letting it light
up his face as he gave full vent to the wonder he felt at the sight of
the Princess. He bent his torso a little to the left, allowed Elora's
beat to bring him back to the right; he let his feet follow suit, and
Elora made it easy with a strongly defined melody line. Then, out
of nowhere, a sharp burst of chords sent the pair of them into each
other's arms and from there on, they were magic together.

They each brought something to the dance, the Princess offering a measure of her supernal grace, the Daikini an unexpectedly
unbridled passion; from Elora Danan came the music that bound
them together and offered the opportunity to transcend culture
and heritage and especially the prejudices that had kept their races
apart for so long.

From off to the side, from somewhere among the watching
Daikini, came the wail of uilleann pipes, harmonizing off Elora's
melody, to be answered—almost as if on cue—by the riffling staccato drumbeat of a tiompan from where some of Tyrrel's folk
were gathered. A great grin split Elora's face and her fingers struck
at the guitar strings so fast their movements were a blur. The
moment had become timeless, she cared nothing for the fate of
Tregare or the perpetual winter that threatened the world, or the
threat of the Deceiver. She existed for the joy and beauty created
by this music and cast it outward to the audience as the sun would
its rays of light and warmth.

The song built to a crescendo and then, with a last tremendous
chord, Elora brought it to an end, the sheer intensity of the act
driving her to her feet.

There was a wondrous silence, as the whole gathering
attempted to catch its collective breath. Elora's lungs pumped like
a bellows, face flushed with sweat, eyes sparkling with crystalline
brilliance, her body radiating such a glow of energy that you'd
think her silver skin would turn molten. The dancers were no less
transported, the Daikini with his hands around the Princess's
waist, she with hers cupping his face, their bodies curved bone-

lessly together in such rare rapport that the difference in their height actually seemed an asset. Her hair had come undone and as she leaned forward it cascaded around them like a cloak, hiding what happened next from the view of all, which was no doubt what the lady intended as she made this public moment one that was both private and as intimate as if they were alone.

In all likelihood they would never see each other again but that didn't matter. They would also never forget what happened here and it would be a memory both would treasure.

A cheer bellowed from the crowd and as if that was a signal the whole campsite went mad with applause, filling the air with a deafening roar of approval. With an echo of the Princess's grace, the Daikini took a step away, still keeping hold of her hands, and bowed formally at the waist, as elegant a gesture as any practiced at court. Her response was in kind.

As they parted, Elora finished her mug of water, repositioned herself on her seat, and began once more to sing. This was a gentle roundelay, offered like a sorbet to cleanse the palate between the main courses of a meal. When it was done, she slid smoothly into a song of moderate tempo that spoke of longing and love, and she smiled to herself as she caught the Daikini looking over his shoulder toward the Princess, before gathering his wife into his arms and strolling from the fire to find a shadow of their own.

On that impulse, her next tune was mischievous, a playful, roguish romp the audience knew so well that many chose to join in.

When Elora finally called it quits, after so many encores she actually lost count, her voice was a ghost of its true self and her clothes sodden, leaving her certain she'd lost a serious percentage of her body weight to sweat. She clambered off her perch and rubbed her sore butt, waggling her hips in an effort to restore lost circulation and writing a mental note to herself to include a sheepskin pad in her next performance so she'd at least have a comfortable seat.

She had no sense of the Princess's approach, only of her presence, and turned toward a face that loomed a third again beyond her own height.

"I hated you for Angwyn," the Princess said without preamble, and with a directness rare among her kind. "My mother and father remain there still, bound by the Deceiver's sorcery. I held you to blame."

Elora said nothing.

"I always thought," she continued, her voice reminding Elora of the chiming of crystal bells, and which gave the plainest of words the sparkling melody of birdsong, "I should do you harm when we met. To take from you a pain to equal my own."

Again, Elora held silent.

"But you are not the enemy."

"I never have been," Elora said at last. "I pray I never will be."

"You are the light, she is the shadow. Forever at odds, forever one. In her, naught but despair. In you, foolish hope. Yet from that hope"—a flashfire smile, a sidelong flick of the eyes toward the Daikini—"a . . . revelation."

"Life should be full of them. Keeps us on our toes."

Long six-fingered hands cupped Elora's face with a touch so faint it could be felt only as the barest tickle of sensation, yet she also knew that within that deceptively frail frame was a strength that beggared description. She'd seen High Elves take hold of Daikini with bodies built like barrels, all of it muscle, and break their bones like twigs. A flick of the wrist here could snap her neck, a handclap crush her skull. It wasn't so long ago that some of this race had actively sought her death.

Instead, what came was a kiss, as formal a pledge as oaths sworn in blood, as absolute a commitment as any written treaty.

"I stand with you, Elora Danan," the Princess told her. "Against all foes, to whatever end may come."

"Because of a dance?"

"Because of what that dance showed me, about myself and these Daikini with whom we share our worlds. Because I would rather embrace hope than despair."

"Thank you."

"Our trust is not lightly given. Be worthy of it."

Gradually, after the departure of the elven Princess and her retinue, the human intrusion into the nightly chorus faded to silence, allowing Elora the chance to catalog the sounds of nature. The breeze rustling the tips of branches, the crowns of trees, a sharper, more emphatic stirring that told her of creatures hopscotching their way across those limbs. A crash in the middle distance as something was stirred to flight, a yowl of disappointment from whatever had hoped to make it dinner. No sense of insects, the sound of their buzzing was masked by the fairies' wings, but plenty of birds, twirps and chitters and trills, the *whoot* of a solitary owl.

Over everything, a sense of peace. Of every element of life and nature living in harmony. Elora understood now the attraction the Realms beyond the Veil had for the Daikini, and the terror. There was nothing in their own Realm to equal this; at first glance, those who crossed the Veil must have thought they'd wandered into paradise. It was more wonderful than anything Elora had imagined . . .

. . . and she knew, as well, and with a profound sadness, that if she came here to live it would drive her mad.

With that thought, and the smile that went with it, she fell asleep.

Immediately, her eyes opened. She knew it was a dream, that didn't make the shock any the less.

The topography hadn't changed but that was the only thing.

The greenery was gone, overlaid by a sheet of ice, and she remembered the ancient hero stories that told of the days when gods and wizards could do such terrible things, with an incantation and a puff of enchanted breath. Suddenly, this had become a world that had never known the slightest touch of warmth, or joy of any kind, a place whose undeniable beauty gloried in its equally harsh brutality. Elora didn't know if survival was possible here; in truth, she never wanted to find out. The term that immediately came to mind as a description was *wasteland*. Nothing could prosper here. The best that could be hoped for was an all-too-brief denial of an inevitable end.

She didn't need to look around to confirm that her camp had suffered as the land. Everyone in it, Veil Folk and Daikini together, had become a macabre piece of ice sculpture, cast headlong into oblivion without the slightest comprehension of what was happening.

Elora realized this must have been what happened to the people of Angwyn, years ago on the night of her Ascension, when the Deceiver made his first attempt to claim her body for his own. Drumheller and Khory and she had barely escaped the city as a blast wave of incalculable power literally froze it in its tracks. Ever since, she'd believed those people slain; now she suspected differently. Every life contained a portion of magic. It didn't matter whether or not the person was aware of it, or could access it the way wizards and sorcerers could; since all the Great Realms were interlinked, that was the nature of things.

"Figured it out, have you?" The voice was familiar, though as cold and pitiless in its way as this land had become, as Elora turned and found herself facing . . . herself.

"Confused?" her twin inquired with a chuckle that held no amusement, and Elora wondered if she'd forgotten what it was like to truly laugh.

"Not really. I've been expecting you."

"Liar. But a credible try, I'll grant you that."

"We danced together in the Realm of Dreams, you and I, Deceiver. I carry with me the fate and future of that Realm. Hardly a surprise to find you walking dreams of my own, much as I might wish otherwise."

Elora watched the other's face as she spoke, noted the downward twitch of the mouth, remembered the expression from her youth when she didn't get her own way. That moment of recognition chilled her in a way this ice field never could.

She prayed none of that showed on her face, and sought a bit of refuge in an examination of her mortal foe.

The Deceiver stood taller than she, which suggested to Elora that she wasn't done growing. Here, too, came another sheet of rime ice to coat her heart, at how naturally she accepted that this face of the Deceiver was not false. There was a heaviness to the body that likewise reminded Elora of how plump she'd been as a child, although in the Deceiver it was offset by an almost-palpable sense of physical and arcane might. Her hair was the strawberry blond Elora had flaunted before her transformation and there was a touch of cruelty to her features she hoped she'd never see in a mirror of her own. That the Deceiver was a beauty was undeniable; for that creature, though, it was merely one more weapon in an already considerable arsenal.

Her costume flouted that fact. It resembled what Elora was wearing, in the same way that Elora the young woman resembled the Deceiver as one full grown, and like the Deceiver all of its accents were twisted toward what Elora thought of as the Shadow. Elora's was made of cloth and leather, and it showed the wear of hard use; by contrast, the Deceiver's gleamed like polished lacquer, a finish so glossy it was almost a mirror. It fit her and moved like fabric yet appeared to possess the hard texture of a beetle's carapace, without any joints or segments. The image came to Elora's mind that the other woman had been dipped and painted with a kind of liquid armor that gave the Deceiver as much the appearance of a statue as Elora herself—with the young woman cast from purest moonlight and her mortal foe from absolute shadow.

Where Elora's figure was suggested, the Deceiver's was emphasized, so tightly you'd think it would be hard for her to move. Yet she prowled with the grace and coiled menace of a hunting—and hungry—cat. Her eyes missed nothing and behind them was a mind of cunning calculation. Low on her bare hip, the Deceiver wore a curved sword. The hilt was ornate, topped by the carved head of a dragon, and the guard was decorated with precious stones, but Elora recognized it as the twin of the one she carried.

"Who are you?" she breathed.

"Do you ask because you fear the answer, or seek to flee from it?" There was mockery in the Deceiver's tone, the echo of how Elora herself had dealt with servants in Angwyn. The memory was like the flick of a lash across her face.

"Everything about you is a lie!"

"Then you have nothing to fear."

"What do you want?"

The Deceiver made a pitying face. "Elora," she chided, as though to a disappointingly backward student, "with one breath you condemn me as a liar, with the next you demand answers?"

"Humor me."

"As you wish. I demand your future to save my past. Satisfied?"

"You want me dead, to replace my soul with your own."

"There's no other way."

"To *what*? Stop talking in riddles and misdirection. If you want my help, ask for it straight out! Why is that so hard?!"

The question took the Deceiver a step back, making clear to Elora that she was someone who rarely asked—in all likelihood, rarely had to ask—for anything.

"Very well, then," the Deceiver said with a kind of finality. "The world stands at a crossroads, one path leading to a destiny bright with promise, the other to fell disaster. All it needs is a push in the proper direction. I possess the will and the foreknowledge to provide that push. I lack the power." That confession didn't come easy. "I require you to provide it."

Elora bridled at the presumption of the phrase "I *require* you," but she kept that emotion from her face. She pulled her gaze back a tad from her foe, no longer meeting the Deceiver's eyes straight on but taking in the totality of her stance, her attitude, the way she moved, in an attempt to discern what would come next.

Aloud, she made a simple observation: "At the cost of my own life."

"You've risked it time and again for friends. Countless others have made the supreme sacrifice in your cause. Can you do no less in return?"

The Deceiver was constantly in motion, from side to side across Elora's field of vision, each step making a harsh *crunch* on the hoarfrost-encrusted ground. She would come closer, then slip away, feint after feint, without obvious pattern save to provoke a physical response from Elora.

All the while, the Deceiver kept talking in her honeyed tones, presenting her case as methodically as any minister would state policy.

"Why should I believe you?"

"If you have faith in yourself, you must have faith in me."

"I've seen you wear many faces, Deceiver. Why shouldn't this be just another mask?"

The other woman was starting to show some irritation. Arguments didn't sit well with her and defiance even less.

"Yours is the power to listen, girl, to see behind all masks, is it not? I'm sorry for all that's happened"—another admission that came hard and to Elora's surprise she realized that the sorrow was genuine and heartfelt—"it wasn't supposed to be like this. I cast the auguries, I examined my own memories, everything was planned. Everything was properly prepared. It had to be you because you and I are *one*! I could reach across the years and reclaim my own past, while keeping the knowledge of my life to come—every pitfall, every risk, every threat. Every—*enemy*! I want to go back and start over, and I will have the foreknowledge to sidestep the original mistakes that have led to this damnable place!" The last was a snarl so full of rage and intensity it would have done an ogre proud. Strangely, the emotional storm passed almost as quickly, replaced by an eerie calm.

"And you were just a baby," the Deceiver said. "You had so little soul to lose."

Elora staggered, as if she'd been physically struck.

And that, she cried in her mind while refusing to give her foe the satisfaction of hearing aloud how deeply she'd been hurt, *made it all right?*

Her mind tore the scene in two, one part of her observing the here and now, the rest viewing excerpts from her earliest childhood, that fateful night in the ancient Daikini fortress of Tir Asleen when the calm and loving certainties of her world, indeed the world itself, were rent asunder. Friends were cast into oblivion and the proudest fortress in that Realm was reduced in a heartbeat to scattered rubble. Elora herself awakened shrieking from a sound sleep, calling out to parents she never knew, to companions she'd never see again, for salvation that never came as she was wreathed in fires that burned hotter than any Nelwyn forge and propelled to the far side of the globe. Her gown was scorched tatters as she gathered herself into a huddled bundle on the cobblestones laid out before the Palace Royal in Angwyn, the air about her flashing with rainbow lightning. Her body was curled protectively about a stuffed bear, likewise scorched and looking like it had just waged the battle of its life, and over the days that followed no one could pry it from her grip.

Thorn Drumheller had made the bear for her, as a birthday gift. And since he could not be present for her birthday celebration, he'd left it for her to find. He'd told her the story on their travels but some part of her had always been aware of what he'd done, that's why she'd kept the bear close ever since. It was her talisman, her cuddly, her paladin protector. Thorn had charged the bear with the strongest spell he knew to keep her safe and then, because he also knew that no outside spell would have an effect on her, wove the enchantment through the bear into the fabric of her own being—so that it would always be her strength that sustained it. The more powerful the sorcerous threat against her, the stronger she would resist, drawing on her own reserves.

"That little Nelwyn *peck!*" the Deceiver cried, and Elora realized with a shock that the pair of them shared the same insight into those long-ago events, more completely than identical twins. In all her years, she'd also never heard that slur voiced with such viciousness, making it to Elora's ears the ultimate obscenity.

"The world isn't as you remember," Elora told her, "else you'd have known."

"All this is because of *him,* don't you see? If the bastard had left well enough alone, I'd have claimed my prize, the future would have been assured. Those deaths are on his head, my girl, this desolation is his fault!"

"No." For Thorn, Elora remembered, had not come to Tir Asleen of his own volition, he'd been brought on the back of a dragon.

"Time to make amends, you can still do that much at least. Set things right."

"No." The same dragon, she remembered, that had visited her own dreams and brought her to his Realm to bear witness to the moment of his death.

"Are you so full of yourself, so absolutely certain that you know best?"

"No." Hers was the hand Calan Dineer trusted to end his ancient life with honor and dignity. Hers were the hands into which he entrusted his offspring, the future not merely of his Realm but of all the others.

"Are you in a rut then, you stupid girl, to say the same thing over and over and over, like some dumb farmyard beast?"

"No."

"No no no no no no no," the Deceiver taunted in a mocking singsong. "Is that the best you can say for yourself? Don't answer, let me guess." She clenched her hand into a fist and her armor obligingly grew barbs at knuckles and finger joints so that the merest scrape would rive steel and open ordinary flesh to the bone. "I possess the might of ages, Elora Danan. I have committed the most unspeakable of acts—without hesitation, without mercy—to bring myself to this moment, to claim what is mine by right. *I am the Sacred Princess, I will be Savior of the World.* Too much is at stake. I will not be denied. I will have you."

With a great war cry, the Deceiver rushed forward, arms upraised, apparently to strike. Elora held her ground and didn't shift her stance in the slightest to counter the attack, knowing that even a single blow would likely be the end of her.

At the last, she turned her eyes to the Deceiver's. Their gaze met for the most fleeting of contacts . . .

. . . and then Elora stood alone, amidst the tranquillity of the Faery wood, soft grass underfoot and a riot of life within close reach. The air managed to be chill and warm all at once and the breath she took was sweetness.

It was as if the confrontation had never happened.

"As if," she finished, "it was no more than a dream."

Without turning, she spoke to Khory.

"I was looking into a mirror just now."

"I saw," the warrior replied. Elora didn't need to turn to know that Khory stood with bared blade, the curved sword Elora had forged for her, held with casual deceit down and to the side. It would be no effort at all for Khory to swing her weapon from rest to the attack, and Elora had honed the edge so sharp that she'd likely never really feel its kiss as it slashed through the column of her neck.

"Did you know, you and Thorn?" she asked aloud. *That it was me,* she thought, but said, "That she would come for me?"

The shallowest of nods was Khory's silent reply. *But to which question,* the young woman thought.

"Is that why he sent you along to watch my back?"

"Something like that."

"Should I have fought her?"

"You did, in your own way."

Elora found it hard to turn her back to the field where she'd faced the Deceiver, half-afraid that the moment she did her foe would once more appear to strike her down. Khory was evidently of a similar mind because her eyes constantly searched the field and tree line beyond; she never strayed more than a body length from Elora and her blade remained at the ready.

"I meant—!"

"I know what you meant, Elora Danan. To fight in *my* way. That may not be the answer. Moreover, even if it was, you're not ready."

"So *you* say!"

"Speak more like that, headstrong and willful, you become more like *her.*"

Elora turned to face her companion. "Is she"—she couldn't bring herself to mouth the pronoun, to say *me*—"who she says she is?"

"She is the Deceiver, Elora Danan. That's the only name you need to know. The only one that matters."

CHAPTER 6

TIME DANCED TO DIFFERENT BEATS BETWEEN THE REALMS of Lesser Faery and the Daikini—a passage of but three nights in one turned out to be better than a week when the column finally reached its destination. The route Tyrrel chose lent itself to travel and the pace was easy, so spirits rose with every passing day. It delighted Elora, during her many strolls along the line of march and through each nightly campsite, to see these two races set aside their differences and find increasingly common ground to share between them. Wives exchanged recipes and story after story of how confounding and exasperating their menfolk were, while the mothers among them shared poultices and remedies for household ailments. The men gathered in groups, some talking of farm-ing, others hunting, or the best mix of hops and barley for beer. They talked of craft and of sport and of the weather. They talked of their children and found to their surprise that they shared the same hopes and fears. Despite their appearance, in the ways that really mattered they weren't all that different.

Elora told herself she wouldn't sleep from now until she was safe within the walls of Sandeni but her body took that decision from her. She'd slept hardly at all prior to this evacuation and the work of opening the ancient Gate at the fort had been as hard as anything she'd ever done. In truth, she'd long since concluded the only thing keeping her going was sheer stubbornness. Alongside came the sneaky suspicion that exhaustion might have been what brought on the Deceiver's attack, with Elora's natural defenses at a low ebb. The young woman thought, with a tired smile, that the outcome of that confrontation probably surprised the both of them. It had also taken its toll.

How she managed to make it through the following day, she didn't know. Events and people always seemed to be slipping in and out of focus, often in the middle of a conversation. More than once, the first clue Elora had that she'd drifted into a fugue state of waking unconsciousness was when the person opposite her would assume an expression of tender solicitude. Next would come a pat on the arm or shoulder and a comment about how tired she looked, Elora's immediate and voluble protests notwithstanding.

By nightfall, she found herself without an appetite. She considered making her usual rounds of the camp, but chose first to set herself against the trunk of a convenient old tree. She vaguely remembered sitting down . . .

. . . and that was that.

The next she knew Tyrrel was looming like a giant over her with a bowl of steaming porridge in hand, garnished with fresh fruit and flavored just the way she loved, with cinnamon and sugar. It wasn't yet official sunrise, although the whole of the eastern sky was light, and Elora noted, as she blinked her bleary eyes reluctantly into focus, that she'd slipped into a loamy hollow between a pair of massive roots. She stretched as long as she could manage, delighting in each joint that popped; she couldn't remember feeling more deliciously comfortable in any proper bed. Or refreshed.

"Is this how fairies feel after a night's rest?" she inquired.

"Summat," replied the Monarch of Lesser Faery. "We cheated a wee tad, though."

Elora Danan cocked an eyebrow in silent query, the rest of her intent on savoring the wondrous smells and tastes rising from the bowl Tyrrel handed over.

"Normally, we'd cast a glamour t' ease your pains but spells don't work on you, lass, so we had t' find another path t' help."

"I can manage on my own, milord."

"Pish-tosh, milady. Last I saw, 'twas a struggle t' place one foot b'fore t'other. The state you were in, any decent healing would'a taken time we couldn't afford. This was a better way."

She caught the undertone of his apparently innocent words.

"You know what happened the other night?"

He nodded grimly. "The Deceiver"—and Elora noted that her name was as much a slur from his lips as "peck" had been from hers—"can mayhap walk Our Realm unchallenged, but not unnoticed." Then Tyrrel deliberately lightened both mood and language with a return to their original conversation. "Some of my lot, we cast an enchantment on the ground instead, t' make it nice an' comfy."

"Worked for me."

" 'Twas the idea, lass. An', with your permission this time, we'll do the same t'night. Not the ideal cure for what ails you, but a fair stride in that direction."

"I can hardly wait."

Her tone was light, her thoughts anything but as she busied herself with breakfast. Her sleep had been wondrous; in a whole host of ways she felt physically reborn and more mentally alert than she had since her return from the Dragon's Realm. Strangely, that was what disturbed her most. It was the pea in the old legend of the Princess's beds, the burr beneath her saddle, a blunt and unexpected—and no doubt unintentional—reminder of the first and foremost of Drumheller's warnings to her. She was fundamentally immune to magic, that was so, but she was also a living, breathing human being. She could be hurt, she could be slain. She could be conquered but she could also be seduced.

If the Deceiver truly is my twin, she considered, *my other—future— self, why doesn't she know that? Why from the start has it always been victory through blunt force of arms?*

Something told her the answer was a key of some importance. Too bad she had no notion of the lock to fit it to.

That thought led her to the Malevoiy and she was gripped by a sudden chill that nearly undid all the good caused by her meal.

They know *that,* she thought with certainty but no evidence. *They know where I'm weak, they're counting on that to their advantage.*

There was a stream nearby and a stretch of it had been por- tioned off for bathing. Elora decided she needed a swim, as much to clear her head as for cleanliness. She dived in as Khory emerged, the warrior moving to a point on the bank where she could watch both the surrounding landscape and Elora.

As the young woman swam a series of fast laps to the bank opposite and back (registering as she went that Khory had strung her bow and slung her quiver over her shoulder) Elora considered her companion. The word that came to mind was *elemental.* In form and feature, Khory Bannefin was pared down to her essence, her body tempered in much the same way Elora honed her swords. There was grace and power in every movement, the kind possessed by the most dangerous of predators. She might be able to dance as well as any noblewoman, and look quite striking in Court attire, but she would never lose that martial aspect of her personality. Every interaction for her was a form of combat, it didn't matter whether the weapons were edged steel or barbed repartee. Her features echoed her eagle tattoo, sharp and piercing, too angular for beauty, too distinctive for comfort.

Elora wondered suddenly if she was lonely. She wasn't an easy person to know and though she kept the truth well hidden that she was a demon's soul inhabiting a Daikini body (as sure a guar- antee for summary execution as Elora knew of in *all* the Great Realms), there was enough of a hint deep within her eyes to make most folk turn away. Elora hadn't paid much attention to other people when she was growing up. After all, she was the Sacred

Princess, living a life of ultimate luxury in a tower built especially for her; everyone she ever met had but one task, to serve her.

She planted her feet on the streambed, bracing them against the swift flow of the current as she considered that string of memory. She'd been twelve then, going on thirteen; now she was midway through her sixteenth year and it seemed like she'd become a wholly different person altogether.

Looks, manners, attitude, character—even without the Deceiver's spell that had transformed her physically into a figure of silver, she felt like next to nothing remained of the girl who was. That Elora had never slaved for hours in a Nelwyn forge, with the calluses and blisters on her hands as eloquent testament to how hard she'd worked. That Elora had never gone hungry.

And yet, there was a direct line from this moment to that, and from that to the infant lying on a sacrificial slab in dread, damned Nockmaar, the fortress of the sorceress Queen Bavmorda.

She looked down at herself to make a comparison with her companion. She was gaining height on Khory. Nothing that fit a year ago came even close today, which kept the sewing needles of the two brownies, Franjean and Rool, almost constantly busy. Her curves were gentler, the statement of her being more ambiguous. There was no mystery to Khory Bannefin, and no pretense. She was precisely what she appeared to be and dared the world to accept her on those terms. With Elora, people weren't quite so sure. She was finding within herself the capacity to play a host of roles, none of them a lie but none of them the entire truth, either.

"You're learning," Khory noted as Elora trudged ashore, tingling from her exertions.

"I beg your pardon?"

"How to be a King."

"I *beg* your pardon?"

"I know you, Elora Danan," the warrior said with the slight quirk of the lips that passed in her for a smile. "Saw you looking back this way, saw the thoughts behind the look."

"You can do that, read my mind?"

"Read your face."

"I thought I kept my expression pretty well hidden these days."

"As I said, you're learning. I just know what to look for."

"How, Khory? Forgive me, but before Angwyn you didn't exist! Three years and change, that's all the time you've walked the world in that body. How could you possibly know me, or even people in general, better than we do ourselves?"

"Never considered that," Khory confessed. "Just took it for granted when it happened. I see things, things happen around me, I know what to do. No active thought, no consideration, no hesitation." She shrugged. "Mayhap the original Khory left more than just her body behind when her end came?"

Elora sighed. "Or maybe worlds can go mad, just like people. You spend your whole life accepting that life is based on a series of rules, that everything and everyone has their proper place in the scheme of things—only to discover that you may well be a violation of every one of those precious rules. As are all your friends."

"That's war for you. It holds nothing sacred."

"She wanted me to attack her," Elora said suddenly, as the sight of a dragonfly skimming the surface of the stream reminded her of the Deceiver.

"Seemed so to me, aye."

"If I had, would you have struck me down?" Elora turned to face Khory, who made no answer as the young woman gathered herself into her clothes.

"If it ever comes to that—" Elora started to tell her.

"Hush," Khory told her quietly, casually, yet with the underlying force of a battlefield command.

"I know my purpose, Elora Danan," she went on.

"I just—!" Elora tried again, was cut off again.

"I don't need you to tell me my duty. Leave it at that."

Elora wondered what she'd said wrong, and shooed a big beetle off her trousers. It flexed its gleaming carapace, then popped a fat set of wings from their housings and zoomed away almost faster than her eye could follow.

She didn't try, though, she was puzzling over the image of its gleaming casement. The Daikini armored themselves in embossed leather and steel—either mail or segmented armor or molded plate. Sometimes, in the worst extreme, a full suit of plate could weigh as much as the knight wearing it. Those of Lesser Faery mainly took their armor from the natural world about them—nutshells sometimes or suits of bone, depending on the size of the wearer. The elves of Greater Faery attired themselves much like the knights and warriors of the Daikini—cuirass and gauntlets, with segmented pieces for the limbs and extremities—but with one crucial difference. Their armor was ceramic, albeit treated by castings and spells to be as resilient to attack as iron. The pieces were polished to the highest possible gloss; they gleamed even by starlight.

The Deceiver's armor had no such segments. It was as flexible and all-encompassing as a second skin. Elora had seen it before, she knew she had, but she couldn't quite place where—

—until a memory of Khory's broached the surface of Elora's recollections.

After her betrayal at the hands of Eamon Asana, imprisoned in the Malevoiy fortress, the faces and figures that haunted her had all been dipped in that same eldritch lacquer.

"The Deceiver," Elora breathed in horror, "wears the armor of the Malevoiy!"

She whirled at the sound of chittering laughter, her hand already closing on the hilt of her sword. Nothing untoward stirred in her view. The brook burbled, birds sang, the normal sounds of the encampment rustled the air. The most intrusive noise Elora could hear was the thundering of her own heart, accelerating so quickly it made her head pound and her chest ache.

She took the deepest breath she could, and recognized that the laughter came from within the depths of her own soul. The Malevoiy had hooked her as surely as any fish, she carried them with her like a plague. It was only the most tenuous of contacts thus far, they dared not play her too sharply for fear their line would break. That was her sole advantage. There would be other hooks and stronger lines. Their goal was to fight her to exhaustion and then gaff her. The trick for her would be to play them just as cunningly.

But how?

. . .

Roughly midway between Angwyn in the west and Chengwei in the east, a huge escarpment split the continent in two, as though in the most ancient days some titanic force had pushed the land in opposite directions. One side up, the other down, to create a sheer wall of cliffs that ran from the Shado Mountains toward the north pole.

There was no easy way around, since the Shados were a lesser offshoot of the Stairs to Heaven, the greatest mountain range on the planet, so for most of recorded history the Wall—as it came to be called—formed a nigh unbreachable barrier to travel and commerce. However, the point where the Wall merged with the Shados was also where two great river systems began their lateral run to opposite oceans. Flowing westward across the Great Plains and by the High Desert of the Saranyë to its ultimate destination in Angwyn Bay was the Cascadel. To the east, a score of lesser tributaries descended toward the Tascara Sea, emerging from there as the Quangzhua, which defined and nurtured the heartland of the Chengwei Empire. Both rivers were exceptionally navigable through most of their run, the challenge was finding a way to link them.

Thus was born the trading Republic of Sandeni.

The earliest foundations were laid atop the Wall—the most easily defensible position—and as a consequence the bulk of the city-state's commerce was with Chengwei. The strategic value of the city wasn't lost on the Empire and within a generation came the first of many invasions from the east. Likewise, for the Chengwei, the first in a long line of defeats. The Sandeni were a polyglot mix of races, bound by a fierce independence and the grudging acknowledgment that only through mutual cooperation would they have a chance at survival. Some were slaves, others freebooters, all had ambition and a recognition that they were at heart outlaws and rebels. The established rules and strictures of Daikini society didn't work for them; they had to find new and better ways of living together. Thus was born the only nation in the world where all its citizens were guaranteed equality as a matter of right. There were no slaves in Sandeni and the only limits placed on the heights a person could achieve were desire and ability.

One other element made Sandeni unique in the Daikini Realm—and that was its near-total absence of magic. In the dawn of Creation this had been a place of exceptional power, the intersection of so many lines of magical energy it formed the Realm's preeminent Magus Point, complete with a World Gate. Perhaps because of that stature, its fall from that grace was comparable. Some thaumaturgic historians theorized that the loss of that power might have been coincident with the raising of the Wall, either as cause or effect. If so, the event predated not only Daikini records but the memories of the Veil Folk as well for no evidence was ever found to either prove or debunk those suppositions. What that meant for the Sandeni was that they were denied the use of spells and like enchantments to scale the Wall. In this instance, the ultimate natural barrier required an equally natural solution.

The Sandeni rose to the occasion, with a water-driven funicular railway, a series of tremendous elevators capable of lifting goods and passengers from the plains to the summit of the Wall. As the city expanded, atop the Wall and out across the plains below, water continued to be their source of mechanical power, driving trolley cars and all manner of associated devices.

The core of the city was its Citadel, the descendant of the fortress that withstood the original Chengwei onslaught. Here was the seat of government, the only truly representative assembly in the Daikini Realm. Atop the Wall, the city fanned outward from the Citadel, its broad main avenues resembling the spokes of a wheel emanating from its central hub. Where a broad moat had once served as the last line of defense it had long since been replaced by an equally impressive plaza, dotted with small groves of trees and beds of flowers, the ideal spot for a weekend stroll.

Off toward the left, looking eastward from the Citadel, was a finger-shaped island that at first glance looked utterly abandoned, overgrown with trees and foliage, its location forming an unmistakable intrusion in the otherwise harmonious layout of the esplanade. There, the Citadel's moat had not been filled in or covered over with the stone platforms on which many of the government buildings had been constructed. The island retained its wholly natural state, so much that tourists often mistook it for an arboretum. The banks opposite the island had been replaced by stone levees, which made the river race even more quickly to the Wall, where it emerged as one of the spectacular series of waterfalls that cascaded down a thousand feet and more to feed the Cascadel below. The purpose for this layout was deterrence, creating a gap too wide to jump and a current far too swift and dangerous to risk any kind of crossing.

The only access to the island was a narrow causeway, barely wide enough for two Daikini to walk abreast. A pair of crystal obelisks stood sentry at the island end of the bridge, linked by a length of silver chain of hardly more substance than a woman's necklace. Atop them crouched a pair of watchful, predatory chimera.

This was the only place in all the city where even a ghost of its former magic remained. Once upon a time, it had housed the embassies of the Veil Folk. In the catacombs beneath those long-abandoned ruins was the Sandeni World Gate.

The Gate itself opened into a subbasement of one of the ancient buildings and as Elora led her party up a series of staircases she marveled at the enchantments which cared for it, even after so many, many years. Though the furnishings were spare, the rooms themselves sparkled, as if a cleaning crew had just finished work. There was a growing buzz of excitement among the Daikini who followed her, a thankful realization that at last they had reached safety—but a surprisingly bittersweet one as well, because they also recognized that it would mean parting from newfound friends. Once Elora closed this World Gate, Tyrrel and his people would once again have no easy access to Sandeni. That caused a measure of apprehension among Tyrrel's folk, Elora noted. Shoes were switching feet; this time it was the Veil Folk who found themselves marching into a new and unknown country, swept along by the realization that great changes were in the wind, that might leave the Veil Folk as uprooted as these Daikini.

That last instant, when Elora alone remained beyond the Veil, when she and Tyrrel embraced and exchanged farewells, she saw that their land for all its beauty could also be taken for a kind of prison. That once closed, the World Gates might never again be reopened.

"Rool," she said hurriedly, "Franjean." And she told them to stay behind, with their own kind, their families, their loved ones. She told them to stay safe.

They refused.

"How many times do we have to say this, Elora Danan?" Franjean didn't bother to hide his asperity. "Our place is by your side."

"You think you're the only one can fight for our freedom, hey?" added Rool. "You want to play glory hog, find some other fight. This one, you got to share. And if we lose, can't say we didn't try our damnedest."

In one and the same moment, she'd never felt more proud nor more humbled.

The evacuees were in shadow, and mystery, up to the moment they stepped up to the silver chain on the causeway. Then, of a sudden, they reached the blinding light of midday, crisp and clear, bright with promise.

Couriers had raced ahead of the refugees, bringing word of their arrival, and the plaza was thick with troops and support personnel. The war—first with the Maizan and now with Cheng-wei—had set whole populations to desperate flight. Most had made their way to Sandeni, as the outland settlers along the southern Frontier had fled to Fort Tregare. The city had grown far too practiced in handling the steady influx of people, for which Elora was grateful as her followers were welcomed and fed and put into an orientation process that would assign them lodgings and, where applicable, work.

The afternoon shadows painted streets and buildings in stark contrasts of black and white when at last she clambered out to open air. The plaza before her was in a state of moderate chaos. People filled her vision, reminding her of just how many she'd brought from Tregare, raising a din that put the thunder of the falls themselves to shame as representatives of the city took a census of the refugees, and tried to debrief them as comprehensively as possible about the situation on the frontier, while the refugees attempted to establish themselves with lodging and food and perhaps the possibility of employment. It wasn't easy and harsh words could here and there be heard as newcomers chafed under the municipality's rules and restrictions.

As Elora crossed the bridge, a discernible itch between her shoulder blades told her the sentry chimera had their obsidian eyes on her. She didn't look back; in fact, she did nothing to acknowledge their attention. The first day she'd seen this island, and nearly crossed the bridge, the brownies had warned her away in terms that would not be denied. She trusted their judgment. If the chimera scared them, they were equally worthy of her respect.

Just before she stepped onto the plaza, she heard a familiar and welcome voice, rich and melodious, and caught sight of him in conversation with Khory. In height and build, Renny Garedo was a match for Elora, although she might be a tad broader in the shoulders. Clothes and manner were wholly unassuming, making him the kind of person who could stand alone in the center of the plaza and yet remain so utterly unnoticed he might as well be invisible. Chestnut hair, thick and lustrous, was swept straight back from a sharp widow's peak on his forehead and gathered in a clasp at the nape of his neck to form a ponytail that fell to his shoulders. She recognized the clasp, since he had his back to the bridge and her. It was one she'd made at Torquil's Forge and presented to him at solstice.

His eyes were the one incongruous element in his otherwise inconspicuous persona, which was why he generally held his head low. That stance created an attitude of perpetual deference, which made it quite natural for those he encountered to ignore him, or at least underestimate his abilities. That was a fatal mistake, for those eyes missed nothing and the abilities of the Chief Constable of Sandeni were in fact quite considerable.

He was mixed blood, as were many of the city's citizens, counting the elves of Greater Faery among his ancestors. She called out a greeting, her brow furrowing slightly when her salutation was ignored. It could have been swallowed by the background tumult but she knew Renny's ears were as keen and well trained as his sight. Could be carelessness, or something of more interest in the crowd beyond. Whatever the reason, Elora decided to take advantage of it and see how close she could come to him without being spotted. There was nowhere to hide, she stood in plain sight, so she took a leaf from Renny's book and gathered her personality close in about herself. She let her shoulders slump a wee tad, snugging her cloak about her to hide her distinctive costume. Stance and manner gradually began to match that of Renny's so that anyone who actually noticed them would assume they were together and conclude he was some minor functionary or other and she, his assistant.

His conversation with Khory confirmed her worst fears, and Colonel DeGuerin's strategic analysis. The southern army wasn't the only one the Republic had to deal with out of Chengwei. A force of equivalent size had been making its relentless way west from the Tascara Sea for weeks now, the apparent goal to catch republican forces between a pair of giant pincers and thereby crush them. Even in the face of two such crushing bodies of men, the Sandeni were still confident of victory—it was the Maizan threatening from the Great Plains that tipped the scales. They couldn't fight three invasions simultaneously. There was growing doubt they could do so sequentially, although they had no choice but to try. Given the nature of their enemies, surrender wasn't an option.

"There's been talk in Council," Renny continued.

"Isn't that what they do best?" commented Khory, which provoked a small chuckle of agreement.

"Were Thorn Drumheller here, considering the regard in which he's held, things might be different."

Elora's attention sharpened. This didn't sound good.

"A lot of change in so little time, Constable," Khory said.

"They're frightened. In the city's whole history, there's no record of an elf attack. Some blame Elora Danan for that."

Elora shuddered at the recollection of that bloody night. The Maizan Warlord had come to Sandeni under a flag of truce, to propose a peaceful resolution to any and all disputes between the two states. In reality, what the Maizan offered was surrender as an alternative to being overwhelmed by force of arms. Elora had rallied the people of Sandeni in defiance of the Maizan—and in her mind's eye she once more beheld a vision of the Wall, lit with torches it seemed from horizon to horizon by what must have been the entire population of the city.

That fateful night, she sang of lovers, with the refrain *"We will be free."*

She sang of dreams, with the refrain *"We will be free."*

She sang of dragons, with the refrain *"We will be free."*

She sang of hope, with the refrain *"We will be free."*

With each repetition, more voices joined her chorus, until she was accompanied by every voice in the crowded room that wasn't Maizan.

"We will be free," she sang with full voice and all her heart, as her song built to its crescendo, *"and we shall!"*

That moment had been glorious. The next, the elves came, a raiding party from Greater Faery, determined to slaughter the Maizan Warlord as well as Elora herself.

They failed, but the battle still gave the young woman nightmares.

"Didn't help matters," Renny was saying, "she vanished that night, with you an' Drumheller. It was weeks before you reappeared at Tregare. Politics abhors a vacuum as much as nature does. Into that vacuum went a lot of fears."

"So you mean to accept the Maizan terms?"

"Hells, no. Freedom is our birthright, paid with the blood and sacrifice of too many generations to cast it aside. Resistance isn't the issue, it's whether we're better served with Elora Danan by our side or without her."

"And?"

"Minds aren't made up. The only consensus is that nobody's comfortable with her running loose, as a free agent. My men are searching for her as we speak, through that crowd yonder. They find her, there's a suite waiting inside the Citadel."

"Do they truly believe they can take her, much less hold her?"

"My secret hope is, it won't come to that. I see her ever, I'll have to do my duty. Otherwise . . ." He let his voice trail off.

Khory hitched her sword belt, shuffled her feet, sighed. As far as she was concerned, the conversation was done.

"For the record, Constable," she said truthfully, "I've not seen her since I came through the Gate."

"Nor I" was his reply. "And I pray to keep it so."

He looked around them, raking his eyes along the shore of the island, examining the bridge. He and Khory stood quite alone.

It was near to day's end, and the city's workers were on their way home, adding exponentially to the crowd in the plaza. Elora joined that throng, moving with weary confidence, just like those around her. She caught a trolley and rode it along one of the broad avenues that radiated outward from the plaza like the spokes of a wheel, past Ministry Row (wherein much of the essential bureaucracy of national government did its much-maligned but altogether essential work) to University. From that stop, she proceeded on foot over a half-dozen bridges (of the hundreds) that connected the many patches of rock and earth that dotted the floodplain formed by the upland rivers that spilled over the Wall.

Her original destination was a modest islet called Madaket, whose teahouses and coffee bars, cabarets and taverns, provided entertainment for both students and government employees. One of those taverns was an establishment named Black-Eyed Susan's, so named for its proprietor, where Elora had earned her keep as a troubadour. But when she reached the Street of Lost Dragons, she kept on going. She had too many friends here, she was too well known, this had to be one of the first places Renny Garedo's Constabulary would look for her.

Instead, she turned her steps back toward University, and the home of another friend.

His living quarters were a moderate disaster. Giles Horvath was one of those academics who cared little for his person but lived instead for his work. So while it was only through the stalwart efforts of his housekeeper that his house wasn't condemned for a myriad of health reasons, his study and library—where he did his research and the bulk of his teaching tutorials—were comparatively spotless, the contents of his library meticulously cataloged and filed.

For all his personal carelessness, Giles was a gregarious soul, who enjoyed social interaction and tried his best to be good at it.

Thusly, when Elora appeared quite unexpectedly at his door his initial reaction was to offer tea. He made the usual apologies about the state of his kitchen and ushered her instead into his study while he busied himself with boiling water and gathering appropriate fixings and crockery. Elora couldn't help a grin of recognition as she noted his dishes were as mismatched as ever, with no two pieces of the same set and most of it looking like he'd collected it from a low-rent jumble sale. While she waited, she set out her own gifts for him, the rich dark fruitcake he loved and a selection of buns and cakes, which she'd charmed to stay fresh until he chose to enjoy them, no matter how long that took.

"Oh my" was what he said in delight when he beheld her modest bounty. "Oh my," he said again as he plopped into the chair opposite.

"Have you the slightest notion how hard these treats are to come by?" he inquired, his expression half wondering if this was some trick of the eye, or even a dream.

"Some folks are worth the effort" was her reply, in an equivalent humor. In fact, the difficulty had been a revelation to her and had brought home how much difference even a comparative few weeks had made in Sandeni's situation, and by extension the world's.

By history and nature, the Maizan were nomads. Their horses and herds took sustenance from the vast grasslands of the plains, and the Maizan kept themselves fed by hunting the swarms of bison and deer and elk that shared the land with them. With the change in the weather over the past three years, however, those animals had made their way south to gentler climes. Normally, the Maizan would have followed. But now, unknown to them, their Castellan was no more than a puppet, animated by the soul of the Deceiver, whose goal was to forge this wandering tribe into a ruthless and irresistible instrument of her will. Their first conquest had been Angwyn, the preeminent Daikini monarchy of the west; their latest was to be Sandeni.

The Deceiver was responsible for the change in the seasons, but Elora knew her foe had no magic to spare to protect the troops who fought and died for her. They had to conquer Sandeni before the snows came or in all likelihood they would perish. That in part was why their warlord had opened negotiations with the Council, to spare both sides the cost of a protracted and no doubt brutal conflict.

"I trust the information I helped provide proved of some value," the Professor inquired, though a casual observer might conclude he was far more interested in the hot cross bun he savored.

Elora knew better. For all his cluttered demeanor, very little escaped Giles's notice. In that regard, he was very much like Thorn Drumheller, and Khory.

"Giles Horvath," she mentioned quietly, enjoying his reaction. He looked almost embarrassed at first before a relaxed and lazy smile crept across his face to open a small window onto the man he once had been.

"I was younger."

"Ah."

"The government is being very circumspect about Tregare."

"From their perspective, with good reason."

He understood immediately. "Cyril's library," he asked, meaning the fort's Master Scribe.

"Some we placed in storage on-site," Elora told him. "The rest we brought. Once he's finished making his reports to the Council, you'll likely find him at the Athenæum, sorting and cataloging his collection. Price of admission, y'see. Everyone who passed through the Tregare Gate had to carry a book."

"Cyril left his tower?" Giles sounded a mite incredulous.

"Kicking and screaming, until Colonel DeGuerin had a word with him."

"I know Ranulf. He can be quite . . . persuasive when the need arises. Still, for a master to leave his tower . . ."

"He had no choice, really."

"That's an apprentice's duty, to leave when danger threatens. Our credo is to save the younger generation."

"Luc-Jon"—and Elora forced herself to take a breath so she could finish the sentence—"chose to stay, in obedience to what he felt was a higher obligation."

"I applaud your young man's courage, Elora Danan, but he was wrong."

"I pray you get the chance to tell him so."

"How much of this collection did you gather, Giles," she asked him, taking refuge in a change of subject, "on your own quests?"

"In number, not so many." His sudden grin took years off his appearance. "But some of them are choice. Sadly, the most important isn't here. It was considered too dangerous to try to move. We couldn't craft wards strong enough to mask its presence and had too much experience with the kind of horrors that it attracted. Too long a journey, too great a risk."

She finished her mug of tea and held it out for seconds, buying herself a smidgen more time to collect her thoughts and memories by stirring in some sugar and munching on the last of her own piece of fruitcake.

Then she reached with both hands into her pouch and drew forth the Malevoiy text. It was a marvel to her, that whatever she required from the pouch of what she'd stored within always came immediately to hand. Food she'd stashed away so long ago she'd forgotten it, emerged as fresh and tasty as when it was stored. Weapons, clothes, tools, souvenirs—the capacity of the pouches had no limit nor did the contents add any weight to the bags. No matter what they held, the two pouches sat comfortably on her hips. The only constraint appeared to be the width of the opening. Whatever wouldn't fit, Elora would have to carry the old-fashioned way.

She'd carried magical objects before, without any trouble. Whatever power held sway inside enforced a kind of order among the contents, but the dragon's egg was too precious and the Malevoiy book too fearful to risk them riding together. She'd decided to carry them in separate pouches.

"Oh my," Giles said again, though he made no move to take the massive book from Elora's hands. "Oh my," he repeated, but there was a wholly different quality to the expression than when he'd used it to acknowledge the gift of cakes. The sense she had was of an old campaigner once more coming face-to-face with an ancient and fearsome foe. The battle between them might have been fought long ago but the memory was still fresh, the victory worth savoring.

He withdrew to another room, returned with a pair of ironcloth gloves in hand. They were marked on palm and back with sigils. The fingers were armored and the gauntlets themselves reached to his elbow. They reminded Elora of the gloves she used when working in Torquil's forge but these were designed for combat. He had donned a surcoat of the same well-worn material, split to the crotch for riding, padded to provide protection from the elements and blows.

"As Sacred Princess, you may be immune to magic, good and ill," he told her with a grim flicker across the lips that passed for a smile, the kind you'd see on the face of a hunter before he descended into the woods after a wounded boar. "I have no such natural defense. As I teach my students, regardless of how safe and secure a circumstance may seem, it's always wise to take precautions."

Together, they proceeded into his library and up flights of stairs to the topmost gallery. He had a place already prepared for the book, that until tonight he'd assumed would never be filled. He let Elora handle it, on the presumption that she'd made it this far unscathed. He was confident of his own abilities but it had been a lifetime since he'd last handled this manuscript. He preferred to take no chances.

"Shouldn't there be—?" Elora began as Giles ushered her back toward the stairs.

"Wards?" he suggested and when she nodded, said, "This is Sandeni, child. They have no power here. Neither, thank the Maker, does that foul excrescence, not in the way it was originally intended. It's just a book."

"Is that why you let me do all the work?"

"We have a history, it and I."

"I have others," she told him as she settled once more into the comfy chair in his study. "The ones Cyril and Luc-Jon felt were most important, that should go directly to you. There's one that Luc-Jon found, I call it a diary . . ."

"I know the one you mean. Your warrior companion's in it."

"Khory?" And Elora nodded. "In her original incarnation, yes." She could see a whole host of questions in the Professor's eyes and was thankful that he kept tight rein on them. For all his nigh-insatiable curiosity, he was content to trust her judgment. If this was a story she wanted to tell, he'd let her do so in her own time. If not—he had stories aplenty to take its place.

Try as she might, Elora couldn't stop fidgeting. The chair was a wonder yet her body refused to allow her to enjoy it. More than once, she choked off the impulse to spring to her feet and start pacing. She knew she was exhausted, she knew she needed sleep, she couldn't rest.

She told the Professor everything. Of her birth in the deepest dungeons of cursed Nockmaar on a wild and stormy night, of the midwife who'd smuggled her from those bloody walls and paid for that act of courage and defiance with her own life. Of how she'd been found by a Nelwyn farmer and how that discovery had led to that farmer's becoming one of the greatest sorcerers of the age. How the witch-queen Bavmorda had sought Elora's death but found her own instead, in part at the Nelwyn's hands.

For a year afterward there was peace in the Daikini Realm.

Then, on the eve of her first birthday, disaster. A cataclysm rent the whole of the Twelve Great Realms. It destroyed the fortress that had been Elora's home and all within, save her. Instead, she found herself cast to the farthest end of the world, to Angwyn, where she was raised in accordance with her rank and station as the Sacred Princess of Prophecy, putative Savior of the Great Realms.

What that meant was that she was spoiled rotten.

The problem was, while the prophecy was common to virtually every sentient race throughout the Realms, that Elora Danan was the chosen one, the living divinity who would usher in an era of peace and good fellowship, no one was altogether sure how that goal would be achieved. Some weren't even sure it could be. A very few didn't want to try. They liked the worlds as they were, with various peoples on both sides of the Veil at each other's throats. Conflict for them was a path to power, and profit. Peace was anathema.

The presumption was that, since she was a Sacred Princess (accent on *Princess*), the fulfillment of prophecy meant her Ascension to a throne, as overlord of the Great Realms. Consequently, more than a few politicians and Monarchs were eager to set themselves as the power behind that throne, the puppeteers pulling the strings of a girl who'd be little more than a figurehead. Back then, Elora didn't care.

The rulers of every Great Realm, and many of their subordinate Domains, gathered in Angwyn to celebrate her Ascension. On that fateful night, meant to be the crowning glory of Elora's young life, the Deceiver struck.

Using the same awful Spell of Dissolution that Bavmorda had attempted a baker's dozen years before, the Deceiver tried to seize Elora's soul. Now, as then, the Nelwyn sorcerer sprang to Elora's defense. A dragon died to save her, but while Elora escaped, the city of Angwyn—including all the assembled Monarchs—fell under a terrible enchantment. In a space of heartbeats, the whole of the walled city was enshrouded in a crust of glittering ice, as though all life, even the *potential* for life, had been brutally torn from it.

The Deceiver gave chase and ultimately assumed the form of the nomad warrior-king who'd been her primary cat's-paw in this enterprise, the Maizan Castellan Mohdri.

The years passed and for a time Elora remained hidden within the household of a cousin of Thorn's, Torquil Ufgood. But fate and the Deceiver's machinations drove her once more into the fray and brought her into contact with a roving troubadour named Duguay Faralorn. He taught Elora to sing and dance and with his help she discovered within herself a capacity to move and inspire people through her performances.

Duguay turned out to be far more than he seemed, not a mortal Daikini at all but an ancient figure of power known as the Lord of the Dance. His goal was to claim Elora as his partner through eternity; his means, to win her love. Instead, she won his, to such an extent that when the Deceiver confronted her and Drumheller and Khory in the Dragon's Realm, he sacrificed himself to save her.

One thing more happened on that fateful journey to the Heart of Creation.

Elora Danan came at last to the attention of the Malevoiy.

"That's a name one doesn't hear often," the Professor noted as he charged various lamps and lit a brace of candles, the evening twilight having long since yielded to full night. To give herself something to do, Elora spoke gently to the coals in the hearth and stirred them to open flame, whereupon she added a couple of more pieces of wood.

"Have a care, child," Giles cried, "we've none of that to spare."

"Don't worry, Professor. We've had a proper talk, the fire and I. It'll take its time with this fuel. These two logs should sustain you the better part of a month."

"Bless my soul! It's a shame you can't remind the air what it's like to be spring, or the ground to be fertile. Oh dear oh dear—" his hands fluttered in concert with his sudden apology—"forgive me, child, I spoke without thinking."

"It's all right. That's nothing I haven't considered myself, from time to time. I simply haven't the power."

"And yet, through all these travails, the Deceiver remains unable to overmaster you."

"She had that chance when I was a baby."

The Professor shook his grizzled head, worrying the knob of a finger through the finely trimmed beard that covered his chin.

"Perhaps in her own mind," he said, "but that isn't the story I hear you tell."

"Well, I heard it from Drumheller. He's probably biased."

Again he shook his head, more emphatically this time. "Child," he addressed her, as he would one of his students who'd come unprepared to a tutorial, "you're not listening. The bear that Drumheller enchanted embodied the Spell of Protection, but you yourself sustained it, with your own strength of body and will."

"Terrific job I did, considering all the damage."

"Stop this. I'll not have you sit there feeling sorry for yourself, shame on you, girl! True, a little more age, some wisdom to go with, you might have been able to absorb those energies instead of simply deflect them. But considering the level of arcane forces that had to be involved, the miracle is that you were able to deflect them at all. My students and I have been busy since you left us, researching every aspect of the prophecies; there's nothing in any of the chronicles that speaks to the manifestation of such power. The only encounters that even hint of some equivalence are with demons—What did I say, Elora? Was it of some importance?"

"I'm not sure. Demons." She rose to her feet and started pacing, mixing in a flip-hop of a dance step at random intervals as she used her body to keep up with the furious pace of her thoughts. "They exist outside all the known laws. They consider themselves the embodiment of chaos. What was it someone called them? The bastard siblings of the dragons, without any sense of responsibility or care for the consequences of their actions. The dragons are the embodiment of morality, they stand at the pinnacle of order. Demons have none, and couldn't care less."

The Professor nodded. "That's why they're objects of such desire for wizards with more ambition than is good for them. The goal of harnessing that unimaginable power is worth the equally unimaginable risk. Do you think the Deceiver is such a one?"

Elora shrugged. "Would it matter? I'd still be left without the means to stop her."

"You could find a demon of your own and bind its power."

That prompted a laugh, but not of humor. "I'll pass, thanks." Even as she spoke, however, she heard a tempting whisper within her head: *don't speak so quickly, girl, considering a demon often walks within an arm's length of you.*

And we're bound, the two of us—the three *of us,* she amended, including Thorn in her thought—*by ties far more lasting than any sorcerous ward. Those of friendship,* she thought, *and trust.*

Though the Professor practiced no magic—in that regard he was as bereft of ability as she—he was as familiar with the forms and structures of the art as any adept magus. Much of what was known about the Great Realms beyond the Veil—and especially the Malevoiy—could be found within his walls and though his affect was scattered his memory was as keen as the sharpest of blades. No matter how obscure or arcane the reference, Giles Horvath could find its provenance with unerring accuracy, as though the books were there more for the facility of his guests. The actual knowledge was stored quite comprehensively within his own head.

She asked him about the image that had come to her at Tregare, to complement her vision of the Twelve Great Realms as a series of three interlocking circles—that the cosmos itself operated in similar fashion, the world spinning on an axis, but also revolving around the sun as though the two were tied together by a celestial string for force and energy. From Khory's memories she had pictures of the night sky in those long-forgotten times and found they didn't quite match what she herself could view after sunset. The positions of the stars had changed, which meant they moved as well.

"Wheels upon wheels," she mused, nibbling on a thumbnail until the Professor rapped her with a ruler to remind her of her manners. His students—common folk all and proud of it—knew better, he expected no less of their Sacred Princess. In her mind's eye, she stuck out her tongue at him but she took the hint.

"Coincidence," she wondered.

"No such animal" was his dismissive response.

"A reason then?"

"Mariners find their path across the water with the aid of the stars. Each solstice and equinox, the sun shines a certain way at a specific time. At regular intervals, the world casts its shadow across the moon and blocks it from sight. Same happens in reverse when the moon blocks the light of the sun."

Elora stifled a yawn, swallowing it whole lest her host assume it was because she was bored. *Not so,* she told herself sternly but without a full measure of conviction, *I'm just frightfully tired!*

"You should sleep, child," the Professor suggested gently, having seen that look in many a class.

She wanted to protest, but she didn't have the energy.

Giles scooped her up, with an ease that made Elora feel like a baby. She'd hardly ever been carried; such familiarities were simply not permitted with the Sacred Princess. After her arrival in Angwyn there was precious little in the way of human contact. A part of her yearned for it, so desperately she dared not think about it, because it hurt too much. At the same time, though, she wasn't comfortable when it was offered; she couldn't find a way to deal with it.

So when Giles Horvath raised her into the cradle of his arms, Elora's initial reaction was to go stiff as a board. Then her body seized control of the moment and melted at every joint, turning her into deadweight. That made no difference to the scholar. From the way he carried himself and lived, Elora assumed him a classic academic, frail and bookish in form. In the time she'd known him, he'd done nothing to alter that presumption—until tonight. Now that she considered him properly, she recalled that he moved with an ease that bespoke a far more active life. The bulk of him, she'd assumed came from the robes he wore; she was no longer so certain, noting a breadth and solidity to his shoulders that his garments most effectively disguised.

He set Elora upon the bed in his spare room and tucked her in as best he could, improvising a snug little nest with the down comforter, piling it up and over the sleeping Princess before attending to the coals in the modest hearth, giving them a stir to generate some additional warmth.

The first impression that came to Elora, even before she opened her eyes, was the smell of steel and worn leather, sword oil and a fierce mix of cooking spices. She didn't stir for a small while, content to play bunny in a hutch, all roasty-toasty beneath her down quilt.

"If I didn't feel so good," she said, her voice still dull with sleep, "I'd feel terribly guilty and maybe a wee bit ashamed."

Giles Horvath chuckled. "There's no need for either, Elora Danan. You needed the rest." He carried a tray loaded with cheese and savories, the remains of an egg-and-bacon pie, some bread, and a pot of steaming tea. As Elora wiggled herself upright, keeping the comforter gathered close about her, she noted that the room's easy chair had likewise been slept in and that a scabbarded broadsword leaned against one arm. Giles wore his University robes but underneath he'd donned boots and trousers and a thigh-length, military-style tunic, held at the waist by a belt of sturdy leather.

"Playin' sentry, he was," groused Franjean, from the depths of the pile of pillows that supported Elora.

"Didn't trust us to know our business," grumbled Rool from the other side of her, where he perched on the headboard.

"We all try to do our parts," Giles said companionably, as he set the tray on a nearby table and handed a laden plate across to Elora. She noted at once that he'd apportioned the food for three and she made sure to serve her diminutive defenders first, even though the sight and smell of the meal made her ravenous. "And besides," the Professor finished, "I've never heard of any warrior worth the name refusing the offer of an extra sword."

"You were expecting visitors," Elora wondered aloud.

"I expect nothing," Giles said, relating a catechism Elora had often heard from Khory. "I try to prepare for everything."

There was too much light in the room and the shadows were too small by half; the day, Elora realized, was far closer to noon than sunrise. She wanted to protest against being allowed to sleep so late but kept her peace. Giles was right, she had needed the rest, as much as on the fairy trail from Tregare.

Unexpectedly, at that thought, a pang caught her heart as a vision of Luc-Jon passed before her, followed by a sharp intake of breath as cruel imagination twisted the sight to her worst nightmare. All the dead she'd ever seen, from all the battles witnessed, presented themselves—slaughtered by sword, or pike, or bludgeon, by arrow, by fire, dead in an instant, or after long and drawn-out agony—all of them now transformed before her mind's eye into Luc-Jon.

She heard Puppy howl at the loss of his beloved master and to her horror saw the hound slaughtered as well.

"Stop it," she told herself, "stop it stop it *stop it*!"

"What happened, Elora? What did you see?" Giles asked her, sitting on the edge of the bed and taking Elora's hands in his.

She told him.

"They're not dead," Rool said simply, hopping down from the headboard to take a stand on her shoulder, where he could look her in the eye.

"So you say."

"So I *know,* child." She'd rarely seen the brownie so serious. "We're bound, the lot of us—by ties of fate and enchantment, of friendship."

"Of honor," Franjean interjected. He was staying hidden. Even now, in what had to be a secure location, they took no chances.

"When any one of us," Rool went on, "an' that includes your young lad, cuts their string, you'll know. There won't be a question."

"I've been thinking," Elora began, realizing too late the irresistible opportunity she'd just provided her guardians.

"Ah *ha!*" cried Franjean.

"There's the trouble," agreed Rool.

"You'd think, after all these years . . ."

". . . she'd have learned at least *that* lesson."

"Stop making fun!" she protested, which was futility itself since her plea only inspired the brownies to even more imaginative heights of mockery and derision. "This is important!"

"Finish your food first, lass," suggested the Professor. "You'll feel better. Then we'll talk."

The fare was simple but delicious. However, finishing the meal only served to remind Elora how long it had been since she'd had a proper wash. Refreshed and sated on the inside, she felt a similar yearning to scrub herself clean. Yet again, the Professor had anticipated her desire. A tub awaited her, its water hot enough to fog the bathroom with steam.

When she emerged, wearing clean clothes to complement her clean body, Elora felt reborn. There was no sign of Giles so she followed her ears and searched out the sounds of bustling activity she soon discovered were coming from his library. It looked like he'd drafted a fair portion of the University's students, as men and women Elora's age and older scurried through the stacks, collecting titles, rushing them upstairs to the top-floor loft, replacing them when they were no longer needed, seeking out arcane references in even more obscure tomes, collecting and collating data, running errands.

"Where's Franjean?" she asked of Rool before uttering a yelp of startlement as her sidestep of one student placed her right in the path of another. If that one even noticed their near collision as he clattered up the steps, calling out to his fellows on the landing above, Elora felt sure he'd lay the blame on her.

"With Bannefin."

That told her a lot, as in next to nothing, and she used the peremptory arch of her eyebrows to demand more.

"Constable figures, or so he's been tellin' folks, that since Khory's your minder, an' us with her, find the warrior, find the brownies, find Elora. All eyes on her, why think about lookin' anywhere else, hey? She leads a merry chase, we go our merry way."

"Before you do," Giles said, with a little more emphasis, as he stepped off the stairs to join them, "we need to talk.

"Yesternight, Elora Danan, you told me of the Realms," Giles began, as he ushered her up to the loft. It was as much a hubbub of activity as the floors below, but far more concentrated. Only a few students were allowed up this final flight of stairs and their actions were as purposeful as a duelist's. They were all scribes, wearing robes to denote the various stages of their apprenticeship and standing within the guild. Unlike the students below, these few were dressed more for the road than the peaceful confines of University and their weapons hung from a number of racks around the room. There were books on every table and the floor as well, where she and Khory had fought a practice bout with swords during her last visit.

"It's hard to square the image of a scribe with all this steel," she noted, aiming for a jest and missing her mark by a wide margin.

Giles grinned anyway. "Stodgy and hidebound talk for one who's journeyed to the Realm of the Dragons."

"What's happening here, Professor?"

"We're scholars, you present us with a conundrum. On whose correct solution just happens to rest the fate of the world and its peoples, which includes us. Suffice to say, we thrive on challenge."

He sat her down at the big table and perched himself on it facing her and as he spoke he assumed to himself more and more the manner of a teacher, synthesizing learning and passing it on. He began by holding his hands before her with fingers broadly splayed, as if he were balancing a bowl in each.

"You spoke last evening of the Great Realms," he said, "existing within a network of three interlocking wheels. Twelve Realms, three wheels, four each: the Circle of the World, the Circle of the Flesh, the Circle of the Spirit. Each Realm marks a stage on an ascending spiral from the purely physical to the purely spiritual.

"Evidently," he continued, "you represent a fourth circle that overlies the other three. You touch them all, you link them all. In some respects, they much resemble gears in a celestial machine. The action of one affects the others.

"But if Thorn Drumheller's right, if what you say the dragons told him years past is true, then this world isn't the only world, just as our sun isn't the only light in the sky. We know there are lines of magical power running through the globe."

"The Major and Minor Arcana," Elora spoke up, giving the grid its proper name.

"Precisely. The Magus Points, where those lines intersect, are where we find the World Gates that give instant access to both sides of the Veil, from the Realms of the purely physical—like the Daikini—to those more closely bound to this power we call magic, the Realms of Faery and the Malevoiy. They're also where you'll tend to find the residences of most sorcerers and, regrettably, the most serious infestations of magical creatures such as ogres and trolls. Magic calls to its own.

"But we must never forget, Elora Danan, that the entire world is as much alive as we. Our bodies change over the course of our lives, so does the world itself. As a consequence, over the course of ages, those nexuses, the Magus Points, move. Tregare and Sandeni itself were places where tremendous power once manifested itself. Now that power is but a memory. Other locales now possess it. What can you deduce from that?"

"If we are alive," Elora said excitedly, catching no small measure of the Professor's enthusiasm, "and the world is alive, why not the cosmos? Why do we assume the Arcana exist only in the world?"

"Consider the cosmos as a great machine," he suggested. "Wheels upon wheels upon wheels, all turning in concert like clockwork gears. At the same time, think of a spiderweb, with lines of energy radiating outward from some central hub. What does that tell you?"

She considered the Professor's question no small while before replying and this time her words were hesitant, carefully chosen.

"Everything—turns? The world on its axis, giving us day and night. And further it revolves around the sun, to give us seasons. I've seen the sun through the 'eyes' of firedrakes, and it spins, too, same as the world, casting off huge streamers of fire that curl back on themselves in arcs so huge this entire globe would be lost within them. When hurricanes come, and tornadoes, the winds blow in great circles; that same natural effect applies to solar winds."

"And for everything that spins," Giles said, "there is a center. An 'eye' of the storm. The pattern replicates through the entirety of nature, from the great to the very small. Look at the hair on a baby's head, spiraling outward from the back of the skull to cover the entire scalp. As for the spiderweb, that's my own little conceit. If such is the structure of the world, and if the world has so much in common with the cosmos, we should find ley lines through the stars, just as through the earth.

"Each star is a source of energy," he continued, words and gestures becoming more animated as he warmed to his subject, swept away by the joy of discovery, "as is every world, every component of that world, every living thing, every person. To a great or little degree, we all generate what we call magic, and we serve as receptors for it as well. What makes a sorcerer is the ability to perceive and manipulate those forces.

"You mustn't think of things solely in two dimensions, that's the error in your 'wheel' hypothesis. Consider the elements—the three Circles and the Great Realms that compose them—rather as spheres. The Realms may travel along a flat plane, as the world seems to about the sun, but the prominences of energy they cast forth erupt in every direction. There is power innate to our own world, demarked by the Major and Minor Arcana and their consequent Magus Points. But there is also the arcane energy generated by our own star, that interacts with the world at definable points on the celestial calendar. From that, we speculate that further ley lines of energy exist, generated by the other stars in the sky, some radiating from a central point too distant to be perceived, of a degree that beggars the imagination.

"Remember what I said about the spiderweb, Elora. Each strand in and of itself is quite fragile. Possibly able to support the spider but wholly inadequate to the task of catching prey. But the finished web is a masterpiece of engineering. Each segment in the latticework builds upon the other, anchors one another, providing mutual integrity and support. So it is, I believe, with the ley lines. Individually, their strength is limited. In aggregate, as a network, the possibilities become transcendent.

"If that's true for the world, might it not apply as well to the cosmos? Draw for yourself a schematic of the world, based solely on the network of the Arcana. Now expand that perception to include the stars as well. The same principle has to hold—that points of intersection exist where the force we call magic becomes stronger. The degree of that strength varies in proportion to the capacity of the ley lines that cross. But instead of channeling the energy of a single world, imagine the potential inherent in a multitude?

"We've been cross-referencing all our records, especially the calendars, and we've established the bare bones of a working hypothesis that suggests that the generations of dragons' lives are not random, as so many of us have believed. Neither are they arbitrary. They have a shape, as do our own, defined by this celestial pattern. The passage of our world through one of these celestial Magus Points is what marks the boundaries of their existence, and by so doing forms a window of opportunity when everything for us can change. When perhaps even our relationship to existence itself can be altered."

"Big window," Elora muttered, "to last from my birth till today."

"That's Tall Folk thinkin'," Rool told her, "that your lives are all that matter. What's sixteen years compared to a Nelwyn's span, or a brownie's for that matter, hey?"

"The next question," Giles posited, "is, do you believe the Deceiver is aware of this?"

"Her whole plan's based on it," Elora said. "Khory Bannefin hails from the last point of change, when the Malevoiy were driven from the Realms they'd conquered. The Deceiver must have traveled from the next."

"Is that possible," the Professor wondered, awe mingling with disbelief, "to travel so in time?"

"Not for us," Elora said, her voice growing more hollow as she considered the ramifications. "Not for anything whose existence is defined within the Twelve Great Realms, no. But demons don't acknowledge the Realms, or any form of structure or order. Everything has its balance, you see: good and evil, light and shadow, life and death, order . . . and chaos. Consider demons the rebel ghosts in the great machine of Creation. That's what she is, the Deceiver, that's what she has to be—a ghost. A rebel. A demon."

" 'She,' Elora Danan," Giles Horvath told her. "Not you."

"Not yet. These charts you've been making, the calendars and so forth, can you project dates forward, look to the future as well as the past?"

"How do you mean?" There was a growing measure of approval in the old scholar's eyes as he listened to the young woman skip from concept to concept like she was hopping across stones to ford a stream. She was learning the craft of strategy, and leadership, and putting those lessons to good use.

"We have three key dates already," she said. "My birth, or rather the day Bavmorda chose to sacrifice me; the day the Deceiver first came for me, when Tir Asleen was destroyed; the day of my Ascension, when the Deceiver tried again. If we can determine whether or not there are any more such moments of vulnerability, and when, we can be prepared for her attack. For once, we'll have the advantage."

"If she's truly from the future, won't she know all that to begin with? Our plans and such?"

"If that were so, she'd have won at the start. The fact we're still free means we still have hope."

Books Giles had aplenty, from every quarter of the Daikini Realm and the whole breadth of recorded history, plus a daunting number from beyond the Veil. It was more raw information than

Elora could digest, simply looking at the tremendous wealth of knowledge made her poor head ache (though she told herself it was more likely the musty smell of the ancient tomes). The Professor, by stark contrast, was wholly in his element, as rapturous as a firedrake in a roaring furnace.

"Giles," she asked, as she roamed among his collection.

"Elora Danan?" he replied.

"What do you know of the Caliban?" She stopped abruptly as he raised his palm to shush her.

"Forgive me, child," he apologized, "but certain names should never be spoken." He looked around, as if to make certain they were alone. "One never knows who might be listening."

"You know something then."

He led her around some corners, up another flight of stairs to the loft once more, gathering a title or two along the way, adding them to the considerable piles already in place on the long worktables.

"It is a creature," he began, as if addressing a lecture class, "whose existence was first reported"—and he shuffled through a set of pages in one book, cross-checked it with another, scribbled some notes—"roughly a generation after the banishment of the Malevoiy."

"You'll say their name but not its?"

"They were banished, Elora. It still walks the world."

"Only the one?"

"Thankfully."

"What is it?"

"The most fearsome slayer imaginable, so these chronicles state. In some references, its appearance is as cruel and arbitrary as a storm of nature. In others, there are indications of purpose, that it served some lord or other. Those it opposed were vanquished. But invariably, its employers likewise suffered an ill fate. No good came of any association with this monster."

"It has sorcerous powers, then?"

"It *kills* sorcerers, Elora. Their power, it claims for itself, and their souls become trophies on its hatbrim."

"The bells I heard!"

"So I would assume. If it was this . . . creature you encountered, you and Master Drumheller have no idea how fortunate you were to escape at all, much less unharmed."

"Can it use the powers it's absorbed, Giles?"

"If you mean in the sense of casting spells, enchantments, and the like . . ." More shuffling of pages, for a fair while as the Professor rooted through a half-dozen various tomes to be sure of his answer. Elora passed the time by poking about this end of the room, which seemed to be rarely used by Horvath's apprentices and students.

"No," he said at last. "Apparently not, at least on no occasion that was ever recorded." He shrugged. "These histories are of course far from comprehensive, but the indications are that the stolen power is exclusively defensive, to make the creature functionally immune from magical attacks of any kind. And likely, magical beings as well. By way of example, I don't believe even a firedrake's flame could do it harm. Or a demon's claws. It possesses extraordinary strength, that's how it deals with most of its foes, using brute force. But don't let that mislead you, Elora, for this creature's life span rivals that of dragons themselves. Think of what it has seen, consider who it has fought, and how it has fought. As much as your Deceiver, and perhaps more so, this is a foe you dare not underestimate."

"Wonderful. Any clues as to how it might be beaten?"

The Professor wasn't sure if she was serious, so he hazarded a rueful chuckle, which she took as answer enough. In a rare few cases, the Caliban's prey had escaped—but only for a time. No one had ever found a way even to do it harm, much less end its existence.

As Elora tried to make sense of this latest complication to her life, she found her interest snagged by a corner cupboard close by where she and Giles had stored the Malevoiy text; on it were piled a number of books that resembled that book in size and general appearance. It was disconcerting to find them lying in plain sight, without even the most cursory of locks to guard them. Evidently, such traditional measures of security weren't required; these books seemed well able to look after themselves. None of the other scribes went near that corner of the loft; indeed, for the most part they behaved as if the corner didn't exist. Moreover, despite the effective combination of daylight and candles to illuminate the Professor's library, this particular corner remained stubbornly in shadow.

Elora found herself drawn to these books and as she departed from the light with steps that were strong and confident, she wondered to herself if her role was as predator or prey. They were bound in a heavy leather, each manuscript clearly unique though similar in general style. The covers were plain, lacking completely in title or decorative ornamentation but the bosses and buckles were massive constructs of the same disturbing bone lacquer the Malevoiy used in their armor.

She began to touch one, then drew back her hand, fingers curling reflexively into a fist, as though she'd approached an open flame. Parchment was cured hide, hide was skin—and there was a resonance off these books that made her face twist with disgust and horror at the realization of the raw materials used in their construction. It wasn't only Daikini skin that formed the pages of these grimoires, but elf and fairy as well. Every race that lived was represented and Elora bit back an outcry of protest at the realization that among them was a dragon.

Even more awful, the sure and certain sense that those skins had been stripped from the flesh of their owners while they still lived.

How could they? she screamed silently, undone by such casual cruelty. *How could* you, she wanted to shriek to the Professor, *how could you bear to have such monstrous obscenities within your household?* Small wonder his guests gave this cupboard a wide berth.

Elora looked wildly around, flashing the whites of her eyes much as a panicked horse will before it bolts. She thrust herself blindly from that awful corner, from shadow to light though she took no comfort in it, missed her footing at the landing, tripped and stumbled partway down the stairs before recovering and landing hard at the bottom, jarring ankle, knee, and coccyx all in sequence, hard enough to give her a limp as she bulled her way toward the door.

Giles Horvath's voice brought her to a stop before she crossed the threshold.

"I believe I have your date," he said, from deep within the house.

He made no move to follow, nor any other attempt to dissuade Elora from her headlong flight. This choice had to be hers. She couldn't stop trembling for the longest time, not so much because of what she'd found but because the Malevoiy offered her the opportunity to make such a book of her own, a catalog, a keepsake of her own kills. And she was tempted.

He didn't return her to the loft—that was a test of courage she could leave for another time—but instead led her back to his study, offering the time it took to boil water and prepare tea for her to regain a semblance of composure.

"Do you know what they are," she said, her voice a husk of normal, "those books?" She couldn't help but make the last word a curse.

"Yes" was all he said.

"How can you"—she searched for the most innocuous of phrasing, hoping to use the banality of language to strip the texts of their power—"bear to have them so close?"

"If we hide from evil, if we flee from it, we give it that much more power over us."

"How many of them are yours, Giles?" Meaning, *how many did you find?*

"All."

He shrugged and for the first time allowed Elora to behold how haunted his eyes were. Here was a man whose love of scholarship had led him to the ends of his world, a quest for knowledge to rival Drumheller's, and who had paid a commensurate price.

"When I found the first book," he told her, as stark a confession as hers to him earlier, of the story of her life, "it opened an awareness in me of the others. One led to the next."

"You could have turned away, Giles." Impulsively, she reached out to clasp his hand. It was like ice in hers.

"I couldn't bear the thought of someone else finding them. Of what they could do to an innocent soul. Of what they could do in concert with a corrupt one. Since I survived the initial brush of that poison, I presumed to myself a kind of immunity. You have reason for your terror of the Malevoiy, Elora Danan, and for your attraction to them, for I have felt both. Feel both. All the more reason they must be confronted."

There was silence for a while, while the hearth cast forth its proper measure of warmth as Elora had requested.

"The winter solstice of this year," Giles said at last. "That appears to signify the greatest confluence of these celestial ley lines of energy. It's the closest match I've found to what little remains from the last such encounter. There won't be another such conjunction for farther ahead than we've been able to determine."

"That gives us a time, what of a place?"

The Professor would not meet her gaze.

"Let me guess," she said, to make it easy for him. "A saw-toothed range of mountains, arranged in tiers like the teeth of a great shark, surrounding a valley cast in the shape of a dagger. A long-extinct volcano forms the pommel of the knife and from its flanks grows a fortress, the oldest on the world, and the most accursed."

He nodded, and spoke that dread name: "Nockmaar."

"Stronghold of the Malevoiy on earth, where the *ard-righ* Eamon Asana, for what he told himself were the best of reasons, betrayed the best of friends. Where my story began. Oh joy," she finished bitterly. "Oh rapture," she said, making that innocent word an expletive.

"There's more, I'm afraid."

"Tell me."

"Your circle binds the others. By all accounts, you've made your inroads on the Circles of the World and the Flesh. That leaves the Spirit."

The one secret she'd kept from the Professor when she told her story was that she held the future of the dragons, and their Realm, in her safekeeping. She said nothing of it now.

"Go on."

"The nearest approximation I can determine to describe those Realms are: hope and despair, life and death. Elora, hard enough to face the Malevoiy; easy to see, I suppose, where such an encounter might lead to the Realm of Despair. But what of Death? How can you be the Savior, if you die?"

"I suppose I'll find out when I get there."

"You have an alternative—you can do nothing."

"I beg your pardon?"

"Let the deadline pass. Let this be the era when change is not embraced. Let this torch pass you by and things proceed as they are. Hide. The Deceiver needs to kill you to survive, so I understand from what you've told us. Deny her that opportunity, let her perish, and save the world for the next turning of those wheels you spoke of."

She took a deep breath and drew her knees to her chin, suddenly looking every one of her sixteen years, hardly old enough for a first love, much less to bear the responsibility of Twelve Great Realms and all their people.

"That's a temptation I hadn't considered."

"The Daikini impulse is to rush headlong to disaster and celebrate it as a ride to glory. Nelwyns prefer to hunker in their burrows and wait for better days. This once, perhaps it's best to follow their example."

"Had Thorn Drumheller done so, our world would be a far darker place, Giles. Bavmorda would have possessed the power to shape this point of change."

"If you confront the Deceiver, can you win?"

"On the basis of sheer magical might?" Elora shook her head. "She knows spells I doubt you or Drumheller have ever heard of and my immunity to sorcery apparently doesn't include hers."

"So steer clear of her. Let her own power and ambition consume her."

"I can't."

"Elora Danan, don't be a fool."

"If she's evil, Giles, how can I not confront her?" Elora asked, tossing the Professor's own words back at him. "If what you posit about the Deceiver is true, my friend," Elora told him, "I suspect she should have perished a decade or more ago, when her first attempt to claim me failed. But she didn't. Can you imagine the force of will, the strength of purpose, it took to hold Death itself at bay while she gathered her strength for a second attempt? The courage—yes, the *courage*—to leap headlong into such an abyss. She won't fail, she won't give up, because the consequences of such a betrayal of self won't allow her to.

"Suppose I do as you say. She needs my body to make herself whole but that doesn't mean she can't resort to lesser anchors in the meanwhile. Think of her over all those countless years, stealing body after body, evicting soul after innocent soul, waiting for the chance to try once more for me. Who knows, over such a time, if she'll even remember why she began. The slaughter may well become the end unto itself, rather than the means to a greater goal. That's the Malevoiy way, to kill for the sheer pleasure, to corrupt for the joy of the act, simply because they can. Can we condemn the Deceiver to the same? And that assumes we share the same life span. What happens to the world if its hope and savior dies?"

"You speak like you're in sympathy with her, child."

"I'm coming to know her, Professor. I used to think my own death might be the answer, but all that will probably do is open the floodgates for the Deceiver."

"Presume you're right. Suppose the Deceiver dies. What then? Think of all she's set in motion. Her death won't make the Cheng-wei fall back from the gates of Sandeni, or the Maizan for that matter. Angwyn will remain accursed, the world gripped by the winter that spell has brought upon us."

"Change has already begun, chaos is in the wind. The choice that remains before us is who gets to define that change. The horror is that both she and I believe each of us is acting for the best. The difference is, she's certain, I just have hope. Do nothing, my friend, we're all damned."

"Take action and lose, the same result. I say leave well enough alone. Better the devil you know. We can endure this winter."

Elora placed her fists on the table and levered herself to her feet, leaning forward for emphasis.

"Giles, the dragons are dead. At their own behest, to keep them from being enslaved by the Deceiver, I slew them all. Unless they are reborn, all the Realms lose their capacity to dream, to create, to grow in the best sense of that word, in their spirit. You marveled at the story of how a Princess of Greater Faery could transcend herself and dance with a Daikini, of how they could both set aside the ancient enmity of their races. It happened because I carry the fate and future of the dragons with me. Imagine now, while you can—dream now, while you're able—this room, these people, and their worlds, *without* that capability. As we are, so shall we remain—forever! Nothing changes. We merely wear the ruts of our behavior deeper beneath our feet. Is that what you want?"

"And if you lose, will we be any better off, with the Deceiver shaping our future?"

"To me, what you ask is by far the greater loss." Her lips quirked in ironic amusement. "I can't—I *won't*—embrace despair, Giles Horvath, not when I see in my foe's eyes the soul of someone who's already walked that road." She sank back to her chair, face revealing her astonishment at how unexpectedly she'd tripped over this revelation.

"That's why she's here," Elora marveled. "Not out of hope but from its opposite. Despair. She's lost everything, she's said as much herself. That's the core of her determination, to prevent us, but most of all to prevent herself, from enduring that horror again."

"But is she you? Do you walk the same path? Taking action, Elora, may be the mistake that brought her to this pass."

She nodded. "Could very well be. So all I can do, my friend, is ask you to trust me. Too many have suffered and died in my defense already. Right or wrong, I have to try." She gave the Professor a rueful grin that made her look even younger than her years. "The Hope of the World," she told him, "can do no less."

CHAPTER

7

LATE THE NEXT DAY, NEWSBOYS WERE IN FULL CRY WITH
the news from Tregare. The fort had fallen.

Comments over supper that evening in Giles Horvath's loft
were grim and the assessments bleak. There was speculation
about the Council coming to some rapprochement with the
Maizan. The rationale was persuasive. True, the Maizan were
the most formidable of military foes, with little tendency to
mercy on the battlefield, but the word from the territories
they'd conquered over the past few years had been surprisingly
good. Their rule was strict but the laws were enforced fairly;
their administration could almost be described as "enlight-
ened." By contrast, the history of the Republic was thick with
tales of the various Chengwei incursions, and the depredations
that accompanied them. They were the stuff of nightmares.

In their hearts, the people still yearned to follow Elora's banner, but this was a time when many felt the need to close the casket around their hearts and trust to their heads instead. To do what was practicable rather than what they hoped was right. They had faith, it just wasn't enough to sustain them.

"You could rally them," Giles suggested.

"I rallied the soldiers at Tregare."

"And that battle may prove the stuff of legend. They stopped the Chengwei advance dead in its tracks for nigh a fortnight."

"And how many of them escaped to tell the tale, Giles? I don't want my legacy to be a fable celebrating how bravely and nobly my people died. Haven't you heard the stories being told out on the street?"

"That lot respects nobody and nothing, ignore them."

"The peace offered by the Prophecy of Elora is the eternal peace of the grave, that's what they're saying—and I haven't much of an argument against them! I was just thinking earlier today, if I manage to find a way to victory over the Deceiver and restore the proper order of nature and the seasons, I'll only make things worse. A normal winter won't be much of a hindrance to the Chengwei onslaught and even if it was, all they need do is wait till spring and start again. Oh damn," she cried, pacing like a caged cat back and forth across the nearly empty loft, Horvath having given most of his students liberty for the evening, "oh *damn,* this is so hard. Wheels within bloody wheels, every action interlinked, interacting with another. I can't just deal with the Deceiver without finding a way to counter the other forces she's set in motion."

"So you've said."

"I'm open to suggestions."

"Bless my soul," a woman said, her familiar voice a surprise to Elora, as Khory Bannefin escorted her up the stairs to the loft. "The Sacred Princess Elora Danan actually asking advice, will wonders never cease."

Elora drew herself to her full height, and allowed a thin-lipped smile as she noted she'd gained a couple of inches on the other woman.

"Anakerie," she said, greeting the Princess Royal of Angwyn and the current Warlord of the Maizan as an equal.

There was one other title that Anakerie possessed, but did not use, that of Consort to the Castellan. She had known him since childhood and for a time had been wildly in love with him, in that special way unique to adolescent girls of a certain age and a rebellious nature. The regard she felt for his nomadic people was deeper, more akin to the love she felt for her own nation. Left to their wandering ways they could not help but become a lasting threat to Angwyn as the western kingdom consolidated its borders and inevitably expanded inland. Her goal had been to find a way to integrate them into the Realm. Thanks to the Deceiver that objective had been achieved, but in a way she never anticipated. Now it was the Maizan who held sway in her land and she fought, not for their future, but for the survival of her own people.

She was a woman of character, which is to say she was not pretty. Paradoxically, hers were the kind of features that would mark her in any crowd and make her the natural center of attention. She possessed an allure that was the hallmark of a leader and needed no enhancements to proclaim the fact. Her clothes were plain and serviceable, remarkable only in the quality of material and workmanship, so fine in both cases the work had probably been done by fairy tailors. Her hair was gathered in a thick mane and, save for an insubordinate forelock, held in place by her only ornament, a narrow circlet of silver. She appeared to be unarmed; no sword hung from the empty frogs on her belt, but Elora knew that was a deceit. In a fight, Anakerie could be trusted to be as prickly with steel as a porcupine with quills and far deadlier with their use.

"How's Ryn?" Elora asked of Anakerie's brother, grievously wounded weeks ago when a band of High Elves had attacked Sandeni during a parlay between Anakerie and the government of the Republic.

"I returned him to the sea." That had been a hard decision for her. "My medicines could do nothing for him, he felt he had a better chance among our mother's people, the Wyrrn." She liked admitting that even less.

Giles coughed uncomfortably. Though no official state of war existed between Sandeni and the Maizan, that was considered only a formality. Both states currently stood on the brink of open hostility because the Deceiver's goal was to subdue the entire continent and that could not be done while Sandeni remained free. He knew Anakerie by reputation, which was fierce, and wasn't at all thrilled to have her in his library. Neither were the few remaining apprentices, who very quietly drifted close beside their weapons as Anakerie climbed the stairway.

In its way, their reaction was a gesture of considerable respect and Anakerie responded with a smile of appreciation, a regal nod of the head. The odds against her were considerable but save for the presence of Khory and possibly Elora herself, she had little doubt of the outcome of any fight. Then, after a second, far more assessing glance toward Giles himself, she amended that assessment to include him as a foe worthy of the name.

"Forgive me, ma'am," Giles said with the courtesy he felt was due even an uninvited guest, "but my understanding was that discussions between you and our Chancellor were broken off after the attack."

"It seemed prudent since our safety in Sandeni could not be guaranteed. What a difference a few weeks makes, eh? An accommodation that was anathema then is suddenly quite feasible. And at the invitation of the Sacred Princess, an elven Princess dances with a Daikini, only a wee while after a Wild Hunt of those selfsame elves butchered my escort, my brother, and damn' near me in the bargain? Your timing could be improved, girl. And your wisdom."

"Some moments have to be seized. They dictate their own timing. For myself, I'd rather have Greater Faery as an ally. I'd rather have the Maizan there as well."

"We are sworn to our Castellan. We are obedient to his will."

"Then why have you come, Keri? You know your precious Castellan is dead—!"

"Yes! And what monster wears his face and form like a cloak. I don't need you to tell me that. But Mohdri is Maizan born and I am of Angwyn. Yes, I've proved myself in battle. Yes, the Maizan will follow me. But only to a point. I'm taking my heart in my hands by simply being here. I need to know your intentions."

"The better to defeat them?" Elora challenged.

Anakerie made no reply but kept her eyes locked on Elora.

"Do you ask this for yourself, milady?" Elora demanded.

"Am I the Castellan's cat's-paw, do you mean?" Anakerie was genuinely amused by the accusation. She had to concede, though, that the girl was growing into her role far faster and more effectively than any had expected. "If so, then there's nothing left of me."

"You could stand with us."

"If I were as free an agent as Bannefin, that's a call worth consideration and I thank you for it. But I'm as bound by obligations as you and Drumheller, Elora—to Angwyn by birth and rank, to the Maizan by a pledge of honor. I've shed my blood for both and sent warriors to die at my command. I'll not abandon them. I look to you, girl, for a hope of saving them. Until then, I do my duty— and if that means taking Sandeni by diplomacy and negotiation instead of by storm, I'll weep no tears."

"One of us or the other will greet the new year," Elora said, meaning herself and the Deceiver, as if she'd only just come to that decision. "Not both."

Anakerie returned her proclamation with a curt nod, all business once more.

"Then I wish you well, Highness," she said.

"And I, you, Royal Highness."

"May fortune favor us both."

The Princess Royal spun on her heel and with crisp, military cadence returned to the stairs. She paused before descending and without looking back, almost as an afterthought, tossed a last few words over her shoulder to Elora. "When next you chance upon Thorn Drumheller," she said casually, "tell him he is in my thoughts."

For Elora, there was nothing of either warlord or Princess in Anakerie's tone, only the ache of a woman who misses the one she loves and can never have.

"As you are in his, lady."

"Would that were so." And Anakerie was gone.

"Where'd you find her?" Elora asked Khory.

"She found me, looking for you."

"Everyone's favorite pastime these days. I suppose we ought to inform Renny Garedo of how porous city security is. The next Maizan visit may not be so peaceful."

"Actually, Elora Danan, it was the Constable who brought her to me. He's waiting out front." With that, the warrior hurried after the Maizan Warlord, to see her safely back the way she came.

"Discreet as ever." Elora chuckled. "If he doesn't come inside, he doesn't see me. If he doesn't see me, he can't place me in custody. Very neat."

"What was that all about?" Giles asked. Despite Anakerie's departure, there was no lessening of the tension in the room. She had that effect on people, as did Khory. They were both so tangibly dangerous a presence it was impossible to relax until a fair while after they'd gone. No one wanted to be caught short if they came back. With those two, there was no such thing as a second chance.

"Just reminding me of the lay of the land between us, is all," she told him.

"She cares for the Nelwyn, I caught that at the end."

Elora said nothing, making plain that that was none of Giles's business. He caught the message and let the subject drop as Elora leaned against the huge skylight and tried for a view of the street below. The angle of the roof made that impossible. A low mist made visibility worse, restricting her sight to less than half a block.

"I should have gone back, Giles."

"To Tregare? Don't be daft, child."

"Everyone keeps calling me that," she snapped with a flare of asperity. "I'm not, you know!"

"That point conceded. Doesn't make the other any less daft." He took her by the shoulders. "Tregare was a battle, Elora. This is a war."

"I know the difference, Professor. Drumheller thought it right to stay—!"

"And as right to send you away. Was he wrong?"

"I understand his decision, all right? The people we evacuated needed me, and me alone, to bring them to safety. But I could have gone back, maybe gotten the others out."

"Instead you stayed and availed yourself of a resource—myself, my students, my library—that might help you achieve ultimate victory. Those are the trade-offs required of a leader."

"I'd feel better if those resources provided me with an answer or three."

Giles smiled. "Have faith, as you're so fond of telling others."

She started to make him a rude face, and then stiffened, hushing the room with a peremptory wave of the hand as she turned in a slow pivot, head canted to catch a repeat of that wayward wisp of sound. On her shoulder, Rool checked his weapons, making sure they were loose in their various sheaths and scabbards, while Elora reached into her traveling pouch and drew forth the sword she'd brought back from the Dragon's Realm. In a single, smooth motion, she tucked the scabbard through her belt and settled it over her left hip.

"Rool," she hissed, "did you hear?"

"Not sure" was his reply. "Don't want to be."

"There's trouble," she told Giles as she bolted for the stairs.

"How do you know?"

"I just do! Trust me! And be ready."

"For the Maizan?"

"We should be so lucky! I'll be back, quick as I can!"

As she feared, the mist was murderously thick, making this a night for knife-fighting, up close and frighteningly personal.

She heard the faint tinkling of bells and she gasped with recognition, stifling a fear and a desire to run and hide.

"How can that monster be here?" she demanded, mostly of herself.

"Monsters generally go where they please," Rool replied acerbically, to mask a fear of his own to match Elora's. "Most folks believe in ignorance and bolted shutters to keep them out."

"The mist diffuses the damn bells; I can't tell where he is." Despite herself, Elora sounded frantic, her voice jumping to the breathy upper register of a girl.

"Take some breaths, Elora Danan," Rool cautioned. "Calm yourself. Then you can decide."

"Decide what?"

"Whether to be hunter or prey."

"You call that a choice, brownie?"

"It's one brownies never have to make. Since all you Tall Folk consider us prey, we turn the tables by acting as hunters. Beats you near every time."

"No sign of Khory or Renny or Anakerie," Elora muttered as she moved along the center of the street, her sword drawn and held at the ready. "Franjean?" she asked of him, hoping he might have some contact with him.

"Masked," the brownie told her. "All I know for sure is that he's still alive."

"That's a start."

Despite the dampness to the air, Elora's mouth grew drier with every step. Her feet were silent on the cobblestones but she didn't think that mattered, since her heart was pounding louder than a drum.

They reached the nearest river, the Paschal, and crossed the bridge that led from University to the isle of Madaket, and a new apprehension gripped Elora, a fear for her friends at Black-Eyed Susan's, the tavern where she made her home in Sandeni. Her eagles were in residence there as well, Bastian and Anele, together with their brood of hatchlings.

She thought she heard those damnable bells again, almost cried out in relief as their chiming was suddenly overthrown by the grunt of colliding bodies, the sound of feet scuffling for purchase, the wailing ululation of a man feeling the burning stroke of a blade through his belly.

That brawl nearly proved a fatal distraction for her as another body hurtled from the darkness to ram full-tilt into her. Down they went, limbs atangle, the analytical part of Elora dutifully recording that her assailant seemed as surprised by the collision as she, since both of them lost their main weapons, swords skibbling out of easy reach. Worse for Elora, her tumble landed Rool beneath her, unharmed but prevented from bringing any of his own weapons to bear. Her assailant kneed her, hoping for something soft and yielding in her anatomy and cursing when he struck her hip, which actually hurt him more. Next came a short jab to her skull that splashed stars across her vision and filled her mouth with the metallic taste of blood. He had weight on her and was gaining position; she didn't want to consider her fate if he got wholly on top.

There was a dagger tucked in her belt, the smaller sibling of her sword, with a blade the length of her upper arm. In the same movement, she yanked it free of its scabbard and across the front of her foe, feeling it skitter uselessly across mail. Realizing she had a weapon, he flailed for her wrist but she was too quick for him, reversing her grip on the haft and plunging it into his thigh.

He shrieked, she kicked, and just that easily found herself free. There was nothing graceful about her own escape as she bellied herself over to her sword and tucked into a combat roll that brought her to her feet in a crouch, ready for battle. Off to the side, Rool had alighted on a cobblestone. He stood with bow drawn, arrow nocked, ready to charge the shaft with a portion of his life force and unleash it into the heart of their foe.

The man, recognized now by his uniform as a Barontës, lay still. That glance was all Elora needed to tell that he was dead, his hands still clutching his upper leg in a futile attempt to stem the geyser of blood from the severed femoral artery. The vessel was thick as a finger. Cut it and death would come in seconds.

A banshee sounded from the darkness, the ghastly cry the elves of Greater Faery used to announce their Wild Hunt, and Khory charged into the fray, flanged mace in one hand, short ax in the other. A half-dozen of the Barontës rose to meet her and fell before her almost as quickly as she laid about herself to lethal effect. There was no elegance to her attack and nothing in the way of rules or mercy.

Elora caught sight of a brace of figures engaged in the deadliest of measures, many against one, the one immediately recognized.

"Anakerie," she bellowed, to let the Angwyn Princess know relief was at hand. The other woman paid her gesture not the slightest heed. It nearly cost Elora everything.

A shape rose before her like a mountain, all crags and shadows with a broad, flat-brimmed hat trimmed with bells, each one representing the soul of a victim. Facing the Caliban, Elora didn't stop to think; she swung her sword across the creature's midsection and used the momentum of that attack to spin herself out of his reach. In that same sequence of moves, she slipped her knife back into its scabbard and took her sword hilt in both hands, ready to parry or attack as circumstances demanded.

The Caliban didn't seem to notice.

Then, so quickly she didn't even register the blow, an open-handed slap connected with the side of her head where the Barontës had struck her. Beyond that coincidence of location, there was no comparison between the two blows. The first had been a punch, this was a pile driver, so terrible a shock Elora was sure her skull had been split open as she cartwheeled to a landing like a boneless rag doll. She still had tight hold of her sword but she hadn't a clue what to do with it as her vision splintered, stubbornly refusing to focus.

The street trembled at the Caliban's approach, or was it Elora herself who was trembling, she wasn't sure. She struggled to raise her sword only to discover that it was a hopeless effort. Her only comfort was the rude thought that since she hurt so much already how could death be anything worse?

That blow never fell.

Elora heard a second banshee wail and the feather tread of a pair of boots straddling her body. Mace and ax clattered to the street and the next sound was the hiss of Khory's broadsword being drawn from its scabbard. There was a rumble from the Caliban that might have been recognition, a tension to Khory's legs (which was all of her that Elora could coherently see) that surely was.

Elora waited for the clash of steel, held her breath against the moment when she'd see her companion fall. Instead, there was only the sound of the Caliban's bells, fading in the distance.

Then, blessed silence.

Elora levered herself to hands and knees, then almost found herself pitching forward onto her face as the street went all topsy-turvy beneath her. She couldn't tell if any of her senses were working, the only thing she was aware of was a great mass of pain that wrapped itself around her skull like a corset, pressing in hard on every side. She panted like a spent dog, but it was so hard to draw a decent breath she feared her tongue had swollen into a gag; then, another phantom flip of the ground ignited a rebellion in her gut. She convulsed and was wretchedly, noisily sick.

She coughed the last of the filth from her mouth and heaved herself to the side, so she wouldn't collapse into her own vomit. Spasms wracked her midsection and from there it turned out to be the shortest of steps to sobs of mingled shame and hurt and a terror that struck deeper than any tangible weapon. She hated the moans she made, and the way her body curled in on itself like a child's, because she didn't understand its cause. She'd faced her share of battles and, she thought, of evil. She didn't think of herself as particularly brave—although she was, to the point of being too headstrong for her own good—but she also knew she was no coward.

She dimly felt Khory start to lift and turn her, but that proved a mistake as it set off another seizure. Fortunately for the warrior there was nothing left in Elora's stomach to be expelled; the heaves this time were dry, producing only a bit of bile and spittle. Unfortunately for Elora, that didn't make the experience hurt any the less. If anything, the shame she felt was greater than before.

Elora sprawled on her back, possessing the aspect of a broken and boneless rag doll. She clutched both hands to her head as though they were the jaws of a vise. Her face turned ugly with effort, and the cost of that effort, as she extended planes of energy from her palms, following through on the vise image by pressing inward with all her might. She had an image of herself in the peak of health, that was the template she used to remind her injured body of what was required.

Her skin flushed rose and grew hot to the touch as the healing energies she summoned in turn tapped into the element she was bound most closely to, that of fire. She drew on the molten heart of the earth to sustain her and in a growing circle around where the two women lay the street began to hiss and an occasional cobblestone popped into the air like a cork from a boiling bottle, leaving behind a modest geyser of blistering steam. Pops and cracks sounded through the midnight air as the heat Elora generated spread outward to the nearer canals and river channels, attacking the ice that lay thickly on the water's surface. A great boom was heard as a floe broke loose and crashed into the supports of a bridge.

As suddenly as it had begun the roar of venting steam faded and a measure of stillness returned to the evening.

"I'm sorry," Elora said over and over and over, almost as a kind of incantation.

"Naught needs forgiving, girl," Rool told her matter-of-factly. "How d'you feel?"

"Ready for another fight."

Franjean snorted with disgust from the other side of her.

"Fine," she conceded. "Physically, I'm fine. All healed. Good as new. Please now, may I make like a bear and hibernate away the rest of my life?"

"With our blessing."

"That isn't funny, Rool." She rolled to a sitting position, back to the rail of the bridge where it humped over the canal, fixed her eyes on Franjean. "What are you doing here, why aren't you with Khory? Where *is* Khory?"

"Saw you were healing," Rool told her.

"Left you in our charge," Franjean said, picking up the cue.

"First sensible decision she ever made."

"Probably never be so smart again."

"Told us to wait till you're good an' rested, then wake you."

"She never did! In the middle of a damn fight?"

"Said you'd be grumpy as hell, and looking for someone to take it out on—the perfect mood to face the Deceiver."

"That's vicious."

"She's a demon."

"Bollocks." Thought and action were surprisingly one as Elora rolled easily to her feet and took inventory of her condition. Her flip remark to the brownies had been right on the money: she felt as fit as ever. The ground stayed obediently beneath her feet and the shocks to her skull had been banished, along with any possibility of a concussion. No aches to speak of and she sensed without looking that her skin was perfect, without a scrape or laceration to be found.

Pity the same couldn't be said for the street.

"What a mess," she said as she surveyed the damage, with cobblestones scattered about like chunks of leftover hail.

"Wasn't a moment for subtlety."

"I've never been so afraid, Franjean."

"That's why it's called the Caliban."

"It's the living incarnation of all the ugliness, the foulness, in the living soul," Rool said with uncharacteristic seriousness.

"Look into its eyes," Franjean followed. "You see the worst that can be imagined behind your own."

"I don't feel that way about the Deceiver."

"That's because she follows the oldest road to hell."

"Paved with good intentions. Am I following in her footsteps?"

"We have no gift of prophecy, Elora," said Rool.

"Best we can offer is faith," said Franjean.

"In me?" Elora was astounded. The young woman felt chastened, at a loss for words in the face of such an absolute declaration.

"My wits," she exclaimed, followed by a snarled "Hellsteeth! My body may be fine, I've simply mislaid my entire brain! Where's Khory?"

"Told you," said Franjean.

"Left us to mind you," said Rool.

"Where'd she go? Where's Anakerie? Where's the Caliban?"

Elora stretched to her full height and beyond, seeking the slightest scrap of sight or sound that would tell which way to follow. She cursed the night and the weather. This kind of fog had a malicious streak to it, playing artfully and arbitrarily with sounds so that distant ones might be heard clearly while those close by went wholly unnoticed.

"Think, Elora, think," she told herself. "Work this through. But take your time," she cautioned. "Stay calm and in control. Speed is of the essence, not panic."

First question, she asked herself, *who benefits from the Caliban's attack?*

Easy answer: its masters, presumably the Chengwei.

She looked around and realized that Anakerie and Khory had been busy. Near a double handful of bodies lay scattered about the approach to the bridge, where they must have set their ambush. A dozen wore the livery of the Constabulary or the ebony leather of the Maizan but thankfully Renny Garedo wasn't among them. The rest were Barontës, the Caliban's servants. The bells on the creature's hat represented the souls of his victims. The Barontës were those he had corrupted. Facing death at his hands, they had surrendered all morality, broken every faith, betrayed every ideal and trust.

The Caliban had existed since almost the beginning of recorded history, the first mention in ballads came roughly a long generation after the fall of the Malevoiy. In a parody of the structure of the Great Realms, there were always twelve Barontës, with the Caliban himself as the yoke that bound them all.

There'd only been time for the most fleeting glimpse of the scene before the Caliban's fist connected with Elora's skull. She recollected the bodies of the Daikini slain. Constables and Maizan, they had fallen quickly and to a man, most before they'd managed to draw their blades. Only Anakerie had bare steel and as Elora had called out, she'd slain the first of her foes. Khory helped finish the job.

There were only five Barontës bodies, Elora realized with a start, because there were only five foes.

"Where are the others?" she asked aloud. And the thought came to her, *things of value.*

Before she made the conscious connection, her feet were on the move. She scooped up both brownies, trusting them to scramble safely to their seat on her shoulders as she raced through the silent, fearfully deserted streets, back toward University.

She found the first bodies just inside the gate to the close where Giles lived: a pair of the University nightwatch, a pair of Barontës. She saw another watchman in the gutter, head and body separate, his life splashed liberally across the stone frontage of the house.

Shouts and outcries made themselves heard from the surrounding courtyards and at last a distant cadence heralded the approach of a squad of constables. She heard hoofbeats as well, the mounted cavalry of the Civic Guard.

Swords crossed high above, followed by a terrific crash as something smashed the skylight. Elora cast caution and common sense aside and hurled herself into the parlor. She didn't waste time with the rooms as she passed quickly through them; she trusted the brownies to watch her flanks and back. They could either warn her of a threat or deal with it themselves. Her goal was the library and the top-floor loft, as quickly as she could reach it.

More bodies, and she choked back a snarl as she passed a clutch of students whose sole fault was being in the wrong place at the wrong time. The house was silent, save for her harsh breathing, caused by a stench of brimstone twisting through the air.

Elora went quickly up the stairs, keeping her back always to the wall, her sword in front and angled across her body. Whatever the prize, the Caliban had paid dearly for it. On every landing she found more of the Barontës, most she assumed slain by Khory's hand, or Anakerie's. But a couple had fallen to Giles's apprentices, who'd lived to tell the tale. They said nothing as she slipped by. What they'd faced tonight was the kind of thing they'd spend their lifetimes trying to forget.

The floor below the loft had been the site of a last stand. Bookcases close by had been upended and reduced to kindling, under the impact of weapons and bodies both. Many of the titles themselves had been damaged, crushed, and torn, their spines and bindings broken under the impact of hobnailed boots, their pages sodden with blood and worse. There wasn't room for maneuvering in these close confines; the stairs were as natural a choke point in their way as Fort Tregare and the battle here had much in common with what happened out on the Frontier. The only applicable tactic was brute force, the only way to the top was through the bodies of the defenders. The same held true in reverse. Neither side could afford to retreat a single step and the room bore eloquent witness to the brutality of the combat.

The last of the Barontës spent their lives on this stairway and a broken sword told Elora who was responsible. Its blade was curved in the style favored by the Maizan, but the hilt had come from Angwyn.

Elora found the point of the sword embedded in the wall, which looked like it had taken a stout blow from a battering ram, plaster and wood shattered to bits, revealing the curtain-wall masonry of the house itself.

Only one creature could have caused that kind of damage, and Elora's hand went reflexively to her head in sympathetic remembrance of being on the receiving end of such a blow. There was no body, no sign of blood, and she took comfort in the hope that Anakerie had managed to duck.

Even so, that meant the Caliban had reached the top of the stairs.

Giles was alive, she saw, as she lifted her head above the floor of the loft, and the books were safe. For both, she breathed a sigh of relief. Khory stood framed by the broken skylight, shoulders bent, clenched hands resting on the sill, oblivious to the threat of the broken glass or the fact that she was a perfect target for any sniper.

Of the Caliban, there was no sign. Nor any of Anakerie.

"How is it below?" Giles asked wearily.

"A butcher's boneyard," Rool answered before Elora could find her own voice.

"Be needing new slaveys, though," Franjean announced with some satisfaction. "More bodies belong to his than yours."

"It was Anakerie, held them back," Giles told them, as he levered himself shakily to his feet, Elora offering her shoulder for support as she levered him into a chair and sought for something he could drink. He held his left arm close to his side and her own hand came away scarlet from their embrace. He'd taken a nasty wound early in the fight, facing the Barontës on the main floor. He'd have fallen right there had not some of his students and apprentices hustled him up to the loft. Elora busied herself unfastening his gown and tunic, to examine the wound and begin its healing.

"She and Khory came through the skylight," he went on,

impressed by their foolhardy daring, "up the walls of University itself and over the rooftops."

"Your school only looks like a fortress," Khory told him quietly, without moving from the window. "Child's play compared to the real thing."

"I'm still grateful. Anakerie was first to the stairway," he said to Elora, determined to finish his story despite her repeated injunctions that he hush and allow her to work. "There wasn't room for the both of them. She didn't need the help"—here, Giles took as deep a breath as he could manage, welcoming the stab of pain from his injury, as though these purely physical sensations could somehow lessen the anguish of memory—"until the Caliban came.

"When he swung at her that first time, and struck the wall, the whole house shook. It was like we'd been hit by a wrecking ball from a siege engine. I thought the stone itself would crumble. He dragged her after him by the scruff of the neck. She was alive, of that I'm sure, but her fight was done. She was what he wanted—until he saw the Malevoiy books. He made to take them as well—he seemed almost ready to abandon Anakerie to do so.

"But Khory Bannefin stopped him."

Elora rolled back on her heels where she knelt beside him and looked Giles full in the face, aware of the brownies turning their attention to the warrior, who still had not moved.

"How?" she asked the Professor.

"She blocked his path and he turned away." Even as Giles spoke it was clear to him and Elora both that he still didn't believe what he'd seen. "Not a word passed between them, not a crossed sword, nothing. She stood her ground and the Caliban turned away." He jutted his chin toward the skylight. "Out there, taking Anakerie with him."

"You didn't follow?" Elora asked of Khory.

"Nothing *to* follow," the warrior said simply. "He walked to the edge of the roof and vanished. No sign, not a ghost of a trail, there isn't even a scent of him."

"Magic? In Sandeni?"

Khory sighed. "There are martial disciplines that have nothing to do with sorcery, they just appear so. We follow, we put ourselves on his ground."

"When the Caliban struck me down, Khory, it wouldn't fight you then, either."

"No."

Agitated voices rose from the courtyard, a growing clatter from the surrounding lanes as constables and cavalry converged on Giles's house.

"Someone had better tell them the crisis is past," Elora noted, as she straightened up to do precisely that.

Though brownies and Khory together turned to object, it was Giles who caught her by the arm, and told her, "No."

"What?" she stammered.

"You've closed my wound, cleansed it of any infection, I'll be fine now. There's no more need to stay."

"Why should I go?"

"Think, Elora. The Maizan Warlord is attacked on a visit to you. Slain, perhaps. But of a certes, she's been abducted. There are more stories of ill will between you and her than of friendship. Given all that's happened, some will blame you for this."

"I didn't call the Caliban, Giles. He attacked me, too."

"Yet you live. And against Khory Bannefin, he wouldn't even raise a hand." Giles levered himself upright to face her and there was little left in him of the doddering academic. What Elora beheld was the adventurer who had braved nigh-insurmountable odds to gather his library of arcana. "The library is safe. I am safe. Now our task is to make sure the same can be said of you. This was another battle, Elora. Think of the war."

He gave her a slight shove, sending her stumbling a step or two in Khory's direction. The warrior didn't reach out to her; this was a decision for Elora herself to make.

They followed the Caliban's route, out across the rooftops, Khory leading the way unerringly to an exterior wall far removed from Giles's lane, where they could both slip unnoticed to the street and out of University.

"The fat's in the fire for sure," Khory said, as they took refuge in an alcove to allow a mounted squad to race by.

"How do you mean?"

"No possibility any longer for Renny to turn a blind eye. Given what's happened to Anakerie, the last thing they'll want here is you running loose."

"Good move," Elora said suddenly, as pieces of strategy clicked into place.

"Eh?"

"If I allow myself to be taken into custody, how much access d'you think I'll be given to Giles and his library?"

Khory's snort was pure disdain.

"Precisely," Elora agreed. "The Caliban works with Chengwei, this we know from our encounters at Tregare. What brought it here?"

"You're a key element of Sandeni's resistance, they learned that at the fort as well. Now you're discredited. Advantage to them. As for how they found us, the Khanate has spies aplenty to tell 'em that."

"But they possess a weapon that renders my efforts moot. Be simpler just to kill me."

"You have an alternative?"

"The other person it fought tonight but didn't kill." They both understood that Khory wasn't included in that analysis.

"Anakerie?"

"Why else take her? If you want a man to do your will, what better way to persuade him than with the fate of someone dear to him. Especially if, in the process, you deprive the Deceiver of his premier commander and his consort. They probably aren't even aware they're getting two for one."

"Aye. A bolt aimed at Castellan Mohdri, to cripple the Maizan, strikes Drumheller as well. One benefit for us in this, however."

"What's that?"

"Even the Caliban can't be in two places at once, especially with his acolytes slain. He's limited until he can raise another such circle."

"Be helpful to know why the Caliban chose to work for the Khanate in the first place, but at least while he returns his prize to his masters in the east, we've time to investigate what happened at Tregare."

Khory quirked an eyebrow and Elora found her gaze looking everywhere suddenly but at her companion.

"We need to know what happened," she repeated. "We need to know what that infernal device Thorn and the brownies saw is capable of."

Khory nodded assent but both of them knew that wasn't the true reason for Elora's determination. She needed to count and name the dead, in search of one in particular.

"If you've a way to get us there quickly," Khory told her. "It'll take too long to retrace our journey from Sandeni's World Gate to Tregare's, even assuming the other is still open."

"I can do that."

Row houses lined the Street of Lost Dragons, stout and formidable structures all. They were originally built for the burghers of the town, upper-middle-class merchants and professionals, with a sprinkling of senior academics from University. But fashions in real estate change as often as in clothes and the solid citizenry of the isle of Madaket gave way over time to a younger and more volatile population. Single-family homes were adapted into hostelries and from there into taverns and coffeehouses.

Black-Eyed Susan's wasn't the biggest or the most ostentatious. Quite the opposite, in fact. The dominant impression, without as within, was of comfort. Here was a place where a body could spend some time, where good food and drink combined with good conversation and good entertainment to sate body and spirit both.

The ground floor was divided into a series of three rooms, the smallest being the reception foyer, which led guests upstairs to the rooms that were for rent. Immediately off that was the small restaurant that formed a fair measure of the establishment's reputation. Through another set of doors opposite was the tavern, combining a good-sized bar with table service. There was the obligatory hearth, big enough to qualify as a room unto itself, and a dais that served as the performance stage. In addition, a couple of alcoves afforded special patrons a modicum of privacy. The ceiling was unusually high, prompting comments that the original builder must have possessed a measure of giant's blood to justify such formidable dimensions. The beams that supported the building's upper floors were of a piece, solid lengths of oak and mahogany that looked like they'd been in place for an age and were likely to withstand many, many more. The brownies loved it up there, for the open beams afforded them a spectacular view of the room below, where they could pick their targets with relative impunity. The eagles, Bastian and Anele, also made their home in those rafters and the sound of their hatchlings made an interesting counterpoint to the bustle of nightly conversation.

There was a stir among the patrons as Elora made her entrance, at the sight of the great golden male eagle swooping from the ceiling shadows to a landing on her upraised arm. She wore no guard on her sleeve, neither gauntlet nor vambrace of any kind, with only the leather of her tunic between her skin and claws that could score plate armor. The eagle's wingspread matched her height and more and Bastian's strength could lift her from the floor, and if necessary break her bones. Most disconcerting of all, for any who met the eagle's gaze, was the intelligence that danced behind his amber eyes. Here was a mind that was a match for many Daikini, mated to a noble spirit that put those many to shame.

He balanced easily on her shoulder, turning his head back upon itself in that boneless way birds do, to nibble behind Elora's ears. He knew where she was most ticklish, the fiend, and she couldn't help a bubble of laughter that was answered in him by an equivalent *chrrup* of delight. They'd been too long apart, these eagles and she, and they had no qualms about letting her know how much they'd missed her, especially since they realized she had returned only to take her leave.

As she and Khory gathered their gear and made their final preparations, Elora took the proprietress aside and told her what had transpired. Susan was a handsome woman of middle years whose calm and generous nature made her a good friend as well as a host and she took the message in stride. Elora ended with an injunction for Renny Garedo to take care with the slain Barontës. Being servants of a magical creature, special precautions and procedures would be needed for the safe disposition of their remains.

Susan assured her the missive would be delivered promptly and then, characteristically, turned her concern to Elora herself. Her worry was plain and Elora found no easy words to assuage it.

"Whenever you're ready, Elora Danan," Khory prompted, as they stood before the tavern hearth. The room itself had been cleared, the front door locked. Save for Susan herself, they were alone.

Susan brought over food for their journey, which Elora speedily transferred to her traveling pouch.

"Someday," the older woman commented with a chuckle, "you'll have to make one of those for me."

"Someday," Elora assured her, "Drumheller and I will."

Susan took Elora in her arms, enclosing her in a mother's embrace.

"Come back soon," she said, with the force of a commandment. "Come back safe. I want to hear you sing again."

"Do my best," Elora replied, but the lightness of her tone sounded too forced. She rubbed her palms down the thighs of her trousers to exorcise a sudden attack of nerves.

"Problem?" Khory inquired.

"This is safe, yes?" asked Franjean, feeling quite exposed on Elora's shoulder.

She assured the brownie that it was quite safe but that spoken affirmation lacked a measure of confidence.

"This is safe, *yes*?" repeated Rool.

"There's a risk," she confessed.

"You tell us so, now?" both brownies squawked in tandem and Elora's imagination filled in a rush with the vision of the inconceivable heat of the World's core flashing them all to ash.

"I've done this before," she told herself sternly. "Why am I so anxious tonight?"

"Thinking too much," said Khory. She took Elora by the shoulders, looked her straight in the eye in a manner that few were able to; Elora found herself meeting that level, assessing gaze, which was even more rare. "Time's wasting, girl. You spoke bravely of taking action. Now's the time to start."

All Elora could manage in return was a curt nod as she took

both Khory's hands in her own, noting as she did that each woman bore her share of calluses. They were strong hands, these two pairs, shaped and defined by years of honest toil.

"It's a hard thing," she said, emotion turning her voice even deeper and huskier than normal, "being worthy of respect. Being worthy, period. Until Thorn rescued me from Angwyn, I never knew what that meant."

"Had Drumheller not come to Anwgyn in search of you, I'd never have lived at all. We each have our debts, girl, and our obligations. I've come to learn it's how we shoulder them that matters."

"I just want to say that nothing means more to me. It's an honor I will treasure always, more than any title, more than any victory."

Just like that, a thought struck her, more piercing than a spearpoint, and she couldn't tell if the voice was hers or Khory's: *if you want a soul to do your will, what better way to persuade him than with the fate of someone dear to him? What better price to demand, than what he treasures most?*

Worse than that was a faint and distant chittering, the mocking, knowing laughter of the Malevoiy, as if some monstrous comedy was being performed and they alone knew the punch lines.

To silence them, to burn the fear from her awareness, Elora pitched herself backward, carrying Khory and the brownies with her.

They never touched the floor, they passed right through it. Down they plunged, as if riding the funicular from the crest of the Wall to the plains below, only without controls or brakes. Through flagstone floors and open cellars, then floors of heavier stone, past structural foundations of quarried granite until they reached the substance of the Wall itself. Here were layer upon layer of primordial rock, composed of the same basic fabric as the mountains that formed the Stairs to Heaven and the Shados.

Deep into darkness they descended as Elora's call to the Realm of Earth was answered by safe conduct and a comparatively easy passage. For Elora, thrill danced arm in arm with stark terror, as she beheld the inner body of the world in a way no Daikini had ever done. The farther they went, first through the surface crust—itself the thickness of a score of miles—and then into the semisolid mantle, the greater the pressure grew around them, and the heat as well, quickly reaching white-hot intensity, a temperature where most metals would have long since melted. Strangely, again because of the density of the environment, the rock wasn't liquid but more like a thick mud. At the point where crust and mantle met was where magma formed, the raging lifeblood of the world that burst free from time to time out of the mouths of volcanoes and deep ocean vents.

One way for Elora to travel was how she and Drumheller had escaped from the Caliban, by remaining at rest and letting the world spin around them. That was wonderful for moving from east to west, something of a misery if your destination was toward the sunrise. Moving north or south could likewise be a chore. In this case, she faced the worst of both situations, since Tregare was located south and east of Sandeni.

That's why she called for help.

It was quick in coming.

They presented themselves as quicksilver flashes against a backdrop of absolute darkness, generating a radiance so bright it left fierce afterimages on the eyes, even when closed. Covering the face with an arm was little help, for their light turned flesh so transparent the skeleton (itself translucent in that infernal glare) could be seen. To behold firedrakes in a Realm closely akin to their native element was to come face-to-face with the legendary gorgon and by so doing, be struck instantly and forever blind. Elora's advantage was her ability to heal, in this case herself by constantly reminding her eyes of what it was like to see; her physical contact with Khory and the brownies allowed her to do the same with them.

In form, firedrakes closely resembled eels, but their boneless sinuosity put those creatures of flesh and blood to shame. They gamboled through the molten heart of the world as easily as if rock were no more hindrance to them than open air, twisting their bodies through an incredible series of gyrations as they recognized and welcomed her.

For mages, as for the common folk, there were few creatures more feared. They were considered kin to demons, but only because no one could decide how better to describe them. Their origins were as unknown as their purpose, for the simple reason that almost every attempt to contact them, and by extension control them, had met with disaster. Thorn had shown her such a spot, during the early days of their flight from Angwyn, where a sorcerer had opened a doorway to allow the firedrakes access to the Daikini Realm. A castle had stood there, as proud and magnificent as any in recorded history, its massive walls proof against the force of arms as the spells that were laced through its stone and steel construction protected it from magical attack.

Nothing remained.

In its place was a shallow bowl, roughly a half mile across, where the ground had been fused by such incredible heat it had turned to glass, a mirror finish that the passage of countless epochs had not dulled in the slightest. For a hundred leagues in every direction, so the stories went of that terrible day, whatever could burn, did. Lakes, ponds, rivers, streams, they all boiled dry, and the land close by the stronghold was left cracked and broken, as if by the cruelest of droughts. What was fertile became a desert, and the people who called that country home, no more than a memory.

Elora had seen firsthand what firedrakes could do, again during their flight from Angwyn. She and her companions had crossed to the peninsula north of the city, dominated by the ancient seat of the mountain kings, Doumhall. The forest there was consecrated to the fairy queen, Cherlindrea, who for Elora had acted as a kind of guardian angel. The Deceiver had loosed a school of firedrakes on that sacred grove, and though it was supposedly impossible, they had gleefully set it to the torch. The fire swept on Elora's party like a wave, consuming everything before it with a casual ease that Elora still found hard to believe. Thorn had cast magical wards to protect them. Elora believed they would have, but also that the effort would have cost the Nelwyn mage his life. That had been the Deceiver's intent, to strip her of every champion.

The Deceiver forgot what Elora herself had for so long, that she had within herself the strength, the will, to be her own champion. In that frightful conflagration, she began to prove it—not by conquering the firedrakes, or imposing her will on them, but by making friends.

Now, as friends, they came to her aid and the rock around her and Khory rang with the delightful passion of their greeting.

Hello, they cried, rolling around the pair of them and even through Elora herself, in a ticking caress that made her laugh aloud. **Hello hello hello hello.**

Her own greeting to them was the opening phrase of the Nelwyn catechism: *The First Realm is Fire.*

It burns, the firedrakes responded in a rollicking chorus. **We burn. All things burn.**

And from that eternal, infernal fire, she thought, *are all things reborn.*

She didn't need to voice her desire, they knew that when they came. The school grouped around her and Khory and from them Elora gathered the ability to move as they did through the substance of material things. It was as if, when the 'drakes coursed through her body, they consumed her bones, allowing her to twist and flow with the same natural sinuosity. The sensation was wonderful and as she glided through the earth she had to remind herself constantly not to leave wayward pieces of herself behind. It was so tempting to lose herself in the wild physicality, the raw and untamed passion—and above all, the simplicity—of the firedrakes' lives. No thought of past or future, what existed for them was an eternal "now," without conflict or complication. For them, existence was pleasure; their purpose was to burn a reality whose purpose was to be burned. And when nothing was left, their own immolation might well be the spark to ignite a whole new volume in the saga of Creation. They had no comprehension of the lives consumed along that road; to the firedrakes, all was fuel. It had no other reason for being.

There was no awareness of any passage of time. Night in Sandeni gave way to night in the ridges overlooking Tregare. Elora took care to emerge through rock, at a fair remove from the nearest stand of anything combustible, preferring the lack of cover to the possibility that the heat she carried with her from the mantle might accidentally ignite a blaze.

"Well," Khory said in a battlefield voice that carried her words to Elora's ear and no farther.

"Are you all right?"

Elora heard wry humor in the reply. "Ask me in a thousand years, I doubt I'll have an answer. I will say, Elora Danan, you make the damnedest friends."

"It's a gift, so I'm told. My first friend in Angwyn was your sire, a demon."

"I remember. And a rookery of Night Herons." They carried the name and general shape of birds but in fact they were a foul amalgam of flesh and sorcery, as were Death Dogs, and were as feared by decent folk on both sides of the Veil.

The brownies had no comment. They simply breathed the fresh, clean nighttime air and beheld the world of growing things about them, and were thankful for the chance to see all that again.

There was no moon and a tracery of high clouds cast a film over the heavens, hiding from view all but the brightest stars, which made the night as dark as it could be. That was of no consequence to either Elora or Khory, since both possessed Mage-Sight, which allowed them to see as easily as daylight in far worse conditions than these.

A brisk wind skirled along the ridgeline and carried away much of their excess heat. Khory took the point and they hurried to the tree line, staying below the crest of the escarpment until they gained an unobstructed view of the fort.

Bad as Elora had feared it would be, the reality was far worse.

The fort itself appeared little changed. The walls hadn't been breached nor any of the interior structures torched or scored by the impact of solid shot and thunderstones fired by catapult. No sign either of the fabled Chengwei rockets. There was a garrison in residence but Elora didn't need a spyglass to reveal that they wore Chengwei colors and that the flag of the eastern emperor flew in place of the Republican standard. The surface appeared so normal . . .

. . . until you spared a glance at the highway leading downriver toward distant Sandeni.

At even intervals on both sides of the road, posts had been

erected. On each, roughly ten feet above the ground, was impaled a body. Not all were Daikini, the fairies who'd fought beside them had suffered the same brutal fate.

Elora's only prayer, with all her heart, was that they'd all been dead before suffering this final desecration.

"This obscenity must stretch for miles," she said, a little shocked at how calm her voice sounded. Her mouth was dry, but a swallow of water gave no relief.

"And you can bet the Chengwei will make sure word of this races ahead of their column."

"The price of resistance, you mean?"

Khory nodded.

"It could have the opposite effect. People who fear they've nothing to lose may well fight all the harder."

"Certainly a possibility. Either way, it gives the defenders a hard choice."

Elora turned away from the road, sank into a huddle with her back to rock.

"If I walk that road—!"

"Don't go there, child, don't even think it."

"Khory—!" There was no bravado in her voice. It was the yearning cry of someone still more girl than woman, struggling to comprehend the cruelty of the world.

"Yes," Khory told her, "you will find people you know upon those posts, is that what you want to hear?" She ignored the tears on Elora's face. "But their story's done, the book of their days closed forever. What they deserve, especially now, is to be remembered as they were in life, with all the richness and texture we can muster. Not like that."

Still silently crying, Elora looked up at her companion. "Inside the fort, how many Chengwei?" she asked.

From Khory, a thoughtful huff. "From all I read of them in the Colonel's library, the standard garrison would be a reinforced company, minimum. Say two hundred men. Considering the location and the circumstances, most likely more. You're planning something foolish, I can tell."

"Supremely. The Chengwei aren't the only ones who can deal

in gestures. And object lessons. But first, we have to pay them a visit."

"The two of us? They're sure to be impressed."

"I can ghost walk. They'll never see us."

"Normal ground. Normal foes. Normal odds. I'd say, why the hell not. None of that applies here. That fort wasn't razed by storm, it wasn't bloody scratched. Something skunked DeGuerin. I'm not about to find out what by letting you walk into its mouth."

"Then stay behind."

"Elora Danan!" Khory's tone was dangerous; she wasn't used to being crossed.

Elora's was a match.

"I'm going."

There was no apparent trail down the steep ridgeline so Elora made one of her own, picking her path with the unerring ease of a mountain goat and prompting Khory to raise an eyebrow in acknowledgment of her skill. There were plenty of opportunities for disaster yet the young woman avoided them all, as did Khory, who made sure to follow precisely in Elora's footsteps. It was a good route, bringing them to the flat as close as possible to the fort while keeping them masked from sight throughout the entire descent. The marvel of it, Khory noted when they reached the bottom and Elora picked her wary way to the edge of the cleared land, was that Elora hadn't even realized what she'd accomplished—she simply went ahead and did it.

"You *have* been paying attention," she complimented the young woman as she slipped into a crouch beside her.

"I beg your pardon?"

"Later. What do you see, Pathfinder?" Phrase and question were a deliberate choice, what a patrol commander would ask her scout. Elora responded in kind.

"The road's beat all to hell. It was never designed for such traffic. Take a look at those ruts, Khory—hundreds of wagons, at least, probably more came through here." She thought furiously. "I wonder how much that limits their mobility?"

"Meaning?"

"On the flat, they'd have room to maneuver. Until they break through the Shados, they're confined to this single road. It must be giving their commander fits. He may have one of the great armies of the world at his disposal but he can only bring a fraction of it into action at any one time. Meanwhile, he's vulnerable all along his line of march."

"Pity his opposite number among the Sandeni faces the same challenge. The terrain hinders the defenders as much as these invaders. The Sandeni can harass from the flanks but there's no way to mount an assault in sufficient numbers to do serious damage. The best they can hope for is to block the road, as DeGuerin did here. Hence, the Chengwei object lesson."

Bodies were mounted on either side, leading off into the distance on the left, to the main gate of the fort on the right. Elora had deliberately tried not to look at them from the moment they'd come into view. The chances were fair of finding someone she knew and she didn't trust her reactions.

As always in such moments, Khory seemed to read her thoughts.

"Turn away, Elora," she said gently, laying a hand on the young woman's shoulder. "You don't have to do this."

That solicitous touch galvanized Elora to action. She rose lithely to her feet, leaving bow and arrows and knapsack in the underbrush. Khory set aside her own haversack, but kept her bow in hand, nocking an arrow as she followed Elora onto the road. A picket stirred atop one of the corner towers, but the glamour Elora wove about them held fast. She'd originally composed this song as a practical joke to confound Drumheller—when she'd first learned she could do such things, *persuade* the elements and forces of nature to her will where sorcerers and mages commanded them—inveigling the very air to twist and bend around herself and any companion she chose so they couldn't be seen. It was a simple cloaking spell for any sorcerer worth the name, one of the most basic taught to apprentices, along with healing incantations. But for Elora, it wasn't sorcery. She did nothing; it was the natural forces of the world which acted, of their own volition. As a consequence, her "conjurations" couldn't be detected by any sentry spells. She was likewise unaffected by most wards.

That made Elora functionally undetectable when she chose to be, by any save the Deceiver. And Khory had yet to see a ward cast that could keep her at bay. Thorn had tried. Khory was a warrior, though, which meant that she was also fundamentally a skeptic. She had died and been reborn; she was demon, she was Daikini; for her, nothing was absolute. Eventually, she knew, Elora would discover her limits, but only when they hit her in the face.

Now, like any sixteen-year-old—despite all she'd seen and endured—Elora still considered herself immortal.

As they approached the gate, Khory couldn't help but wonder in that context how Elora Danan, so much the personification of Life and Hope, would cope with the Realm of Death. And worse, that of Despair.

Close up, the signs of battle were far more evident. Nightfall had cast a charm of its own over the fort, masking much of the damage done during the siege. Vicious scars marked the wood palisade and its massive stone foundation, where pots of boiling oil had been poured on the invaders and then set alight. There were cracks in the massive timbers from the impact of huge stones hurled from mangonels. Many of those projectiles had been broken by the shock and still remained along the base of the ramparts, in pieces that were themselves of a size with the two women. Surprisingly, to Khory's eye, there was no evidence that the Chengwei had employed explosive thunderstones.

This time, it was Elora who apparently kept pace with Khory's thoughts.

"They just threw rocks at the walls. I'd have thought a volley of thunderstones would have done the trick a lot more effectively."

"There are spells to inhibit their combustion. They may be saving them for later, the defenses at the passes through the Shados maybe."

Elora turned suddenly to face her. "Or maybe their infernal machine affects their own weapons as much as ours?"

"It's a possibility. Do you feel anything?"

"Strange, you mean? Not yet—!"

Her voice broke off, and Khory feared something had happened to her. Then she saw where Elora was looking and followed her gaze upward to find the brutalized visage of First Sergeant Shando spitted on a post, arms and legs akimbo. He hadn't died easily and the Chengwei hadn't been kind to him afterward; add to that the ravages of carrion birds and vermin, it didn't make for a pleasant sight.

The main gates had borne the brunt of the Chengwei assault. The flanking turrets of the barbican were scored by fire, one stood almost wholly gutted, the collapse of roof and battlements taking with it a fair portion of exterior wall, exposing a couple of interior levels to view. The gates themselves were likewise gone, looking as if they had somehow been exploded. The blast pattern could be seen in an irregular fan shape over the ground, the force of the concussion such that splinters had been driven deep into solid earth and stone. For anyone standing unprotected in the waryard beyond, there would have been no mercy.

A makeshift barrier had been erected and through the opening both Elora and Khory could see that construction was well under way on proper replacements. In the meanwhile, security was the province of a guard detail.

Elora stalked toward them stiff-legged, the one glance she spared Khory before she began her approach giving fair warning that the warrior was not to interfere. Elora's hands were empty, she hadn't yet drawn her sword, but that would change with terrible ferocity once she came in reach. Khory took her own measure of the dozen soldiers on duty, and offered a silent orison for their souls, such as they were, for they were as good as dead. She also assumed a shooting stance. The Chengwei wore armor, a comprehensive array of layered leather and mail and tough horn only slightly less sturdy than steel plate. The arrows Khory chose had bodkin tips, with stiletto points of fearsome sharpness designed to punch straight through even a reinforced breastplate.

For the sentries, there was no warning. The night was quiet, the region totally subjugated, they had little to fear from enemies on either side of the Veil. Despite that, they were professionals, well trained and experienced. Their manner might have appeared casual to the untrained eye but they were ready for trouble. Anything less would have guaranteed them either a session at the company whipping post or a final kiss of the headsman's block.

One moment, the approach to the gate was clear. The next, the air shimmered the way it does in high summer under the midday sun and the figure of a young woman strode into view, silver-skinned, her clothes the color of dark wine. She wore one sword, on her left hip, and at the very moment that fact registered on the awareness of the soldiers, she drew it from her scabbard. Without breaking stride she slashed first to the right and then to the left, that gleaming length of steel leaving a burning trail in its wake the same colors as herself—blinding silver, splashed through with scarlet, as the blade cut through armor like it was rice paper. Each cut was fatal, for Khory *had* taught her well, and the men dropped to their knees, to their faces, without a sound, without time or opportunity to comprehend what Elora Danan had taken from them.

Their fellows were less fortunate. They had moments to see Death come for them and to try to forestall it, though their frantic efforts proved to no avail. One tried to bring his halberd to bear, to cut Elora down from beyond the reach of her sword, but Khory's arrow pinned him through his heart to the wall. Two more died just as quickly. One soul, more sensible than the rest, tried to cry out an alarm but Khory switched to a broadhead point and took him in the neck, right across the throat, nearly decapitating the man.

A couple of the detail tried to mark Khory as a target, but she stood beyond the circles of light cast by their torches. The plain fact of the matter was that the sentries couldn't spare the attention to worry about the archer; in the swordswoman, they faced murder incarnate.

Elora had never fought like this. The analytical part of her accepted that when this fight was done she would howl her anguish and horror to the stars. It would leave a scar more permanent for Elora than any physical wound because those at least her healing power could erase. She would recall all the faces that fell before her blade and they would be a part of her forever, their hopes, their dreams, their fears, what they loved and what they hated, the totality of their existence. Brought to an end by her.

She didn't care.

A blade flashed before her, she parried the attack, and steel sounded a clear, clarion note amidst the shuffle of feet and the grunts of blows given and taken. She ducked beneath his counter, lashing out with her leg while he was off-balance to trip him up. Down he crashed onto his back, the shock of landing nothing compared to the blunt realization on his square and unremarkable features that he would never draw another breath. Elora rose above him and drove her sword through his heart.

Another came for her from behind with an ax and she dived over the body of the man she'd just slain, abandoning her sword for one of her enemy's. She was ready but her foe was too strong, the backswing slapped the scimitar from her grasp with such force that her hand was numbed. He drove forward to catch her, but Khory's arrows caught him first, three in a space not larger than a Sandeni shilling.

Start to finish, the slaughter took hardly more than a minute.

Without a word or a gesture of thanks to her companion, Elora wrenched her blade from its final victim and continued on her way with that same stalking gait, toward the center of the waryard. Khory began to follow but a peremptory slash of the hand bid her hold her place amidst the slain. Before Elora had taken a couple of more steps, she understood why.

The ground around Elora began to glow, streaking lengths of pure radiance sliding and wriggling beneath the surface as if the earth had no more solidity to it than water.

At last came a hoarse shout from above and along the battlements that alerted the Chengwei to their danger. A drum sounded, its cadence picked up by a shallow-voiced horn. An archer with more initiative than sense loosed a shaft aimed for Elora's back, right between the shoulder blades, the perfect killing shot.

It never came close. A firedrake leaped from the earth in a perfect arc to catch the arrow and incinerate it before the creature vanished once more beneath the surface.

She marched to the center of the waryard where the flagpole stood, from which now hung the standard of the Khagan, as the Chengwei Emperor was called. She faced what had been Colonel

DeGuerin's quarters and called out in a voice that would have done the Colonel proud.

"Who commands here?" she demanded, first in Sandeni and then in Court Chengwei, thankful that she had an ear for language and that Drumheller had taken the time during their travels to give her modest knowledge of the continent's major tongues.

The barracks emptied so quickly she might have sounded reveille or the call to arms. Soldiers appeared in a hodgepodge of clothes but all carried their full complement of weapons as they raced to take position on the ramparts. A couple of squads were diverted to the waryard, to form a killing circle around Elora. They all carried spears and halberds; bows were the province of their comrades on the wall. Notice was taken of the carnage at the gate, and the second woman who stood with her own bow at the ready, but the primary focus was on Elora.

When the troops were in place, their commander made his entrance, having taken the time to don uniform and armor. He was an imposing man, radiating strength of purpose and body, and no doubt possessed of courage to match. He gave the impression of someone who wrestled bears for sport. Physically, there was a resemblance to Colonel DeGuerin but that was where their similarities ended. DeGuerin needed no tests to prove his mettle, it was evident from every aspect of his being.

"I have that honor," the commander replied, in Chengwei. He wanted to view Elora with the proper contempt accorded a western barbarian and a woman at that but the flashes of light and color from beneath her feet undermined his arrogant posture.

"I am Elora Danan," she said simply. "Leave this place."

Laughter erupted from among the commander's subordinate officers, harsh and full of derision. He kept silent and watched the lights beneath the ground.

"My orders command me to hold this stronghold for my Emperor in the face of an army," he told Elora and nearly wept at the faint but telltale tremor of fear in his voice. "I will not yield to a lone slip of a girl."

"I am the Sacred Princess of Prophecy. I stand over *all* the Great Realms, on both sides of the Veil. If you have prisoners, deliver them to me, unharmed and unbound, and depart. I will not ask again."

Before the commander could stop him, one of his lieutenants shouted an order and from every wall, arrows flew toward Elora. Had they struck, she would have resembled a pincushion. Instead, firedrakes erupted from the earth and burned each and every shaft. Behind her, the flagpole flared incandescent, so brightly the closest soldiers had to cover their eyes and cower. When the glow faded, nothing remained. These were brave men, hardened campaigners, and it was a mark of their valiance that they stood their ground as a brace of gleaming shapes swam from earth to air and wound themselves around Elora's body. She reached out a hand and stroked one, the firedrake responding as sensuously as any cat. The creature smiled, pulling gasps of shock from those Chengwei who could see as its face flowed from serpentine to human, assuming a guise that was a twin for Elora's own. The soldiers stood a good ten paces from Elora and the raw heat emanating from the 'drakes struck them like the blast from the open door of a foundry furnace.

"I offer safe conduct," she said. "Do no further harm, and none shall be done you in return."

The commander had no illusions about his fate. Even if the general believed this tale of madness, the best he could hope for was a cup of poison or the headsman's ax. Better that, than disembowelment or being drawn and quartered. The Chengwei were not tolerant of surrender. And yet, these men had served him and the Khanate well. Against mortal foes, he would spend their lives like the sky casts forth rain. There was nothing in his arsenal that would serve against one who befriended demons.

He snapped a series of brusque directives and a half-dozen scarecrow figures were cast forth from the stockade. They hobbled because they'd been chained so cruelly their bones and joints had nearly broken. They were in rags and tatters because they'd been stripped of clothes as well as dignity. They were battered, bruised, bloodied, but they were also alive—because the Chengwei had intended to return them to the Empire and parade them through the cities, so the populace could see how their old enemy had at long last been humbled.

At the same time, the Chengwei garrison formed ranks in the waryard. Wisely, their commander ordered them to march out as they were. Allowing his men to gather their proper uniforms and possessions seemed to him to be pushing luck that was already stretched beyond endurance.

As he took position at the head of his troops, her voice stopped him.

"You won't need to tell your general what happened here," she said. "He'll receive a message of his own."

"A declaration of war?" the commander asked of her, amazed at his own temerity when what he really wanted to do most was run.

She smiled and he thought of the stories of the legendary basilisk, who could savage a man's soul with a look and do far worse to his flesh before he was allowed to die.

"Don't tempt me," she told him.

"Come against the Empire," he said, "and you will suffer for it. Even your magic cannot prevail against our might, as these fools learned to their sorrow. Enjoy this victory, girl, we will not allow another."

A snap of her fingers brought the entire school of firedrakes into view and the whole complement of Chengwei reeled as if struck. The commander ordered them to the gate and discipline held for the first few steps, although there were too many anxious glances over the shoulder, from officers as well as common soldiers. It was a shameful display but the commander couldn't find it in his heart to condemn any of them as cowards.

Then Elora Danan spoke a single word, and the withdrawal became a rout.

She took a firedrake in hand and told it, *"Burn!"*

Death Dogs wouldn't have responded with more alacrity and delight. The firedrakes uttered a cry which no man present could have repeated yet which all recognized, on some primal ancient level passed down through the countless generations since the dawn of their race. And as with Death Dogs the reaction was as uncontrollable as it was instinctive. Some firedrakes leaped through the air in graceful arcs of eye-searing brilliance, casting afterimages so intense they would remain imprinted on watching eyes for days to come. Others dived back into the ground, making soldiers holler with alarm as the 'drakes streaked beneath their feet with lightning speed. Men placed their weapons at the ready, though all knew that would do no good.

The first of the firedrakes landed on one of the corner towers.

The bastion didn't burn, it didn't explode, it . . . *changed*. The structure began to glow from within, in the same way hands do when cupped around a light. Like charcoal on a hearth, the stone and wood began to radiate first heat then light, generating such a fearful incandescence that the surrounding air immediately began to shimmer. Another tower ignited in the same way, and another, until all but those flanking the main gate were ablaze. With the effervescence of children playing tag, firedrakes raced from tower to tower and through all the connecting buildings, setting them alight in the same manner.

It happened so quickly. By the time the Chengwei realized what was happening, there was fire on every side but one. They didn't understand why they weren't dead, although the heat was such that nothing living could long survive where they stood.

No training, no experience of battle, prepared them for this. No threat of punishment could prevent their altogether human reaction.

They ran for their lives.

None thought truly that they would reach the gate, they assumed this was some dreadful trick, but it was their only hope. Weapons were cast aside in panic, and armor as well, to allow them to run faster. Any who fell were trampled for their clumsiness, as were the foolish few who tried to help their comrades.

They ran until legs and lungs gave out, which turned out to be a messy scattering of bodies that began a few hundred yards beyond the gate and extended to the tree line. They collapsed, panting, spent prey run at last to ground, and begged and pleaded and prayed for mercy, though they'd never shown the least of it themselves.

Strangest of all, there was no sound of fire. The entire fort glowed with that awful radiance, save for the barbican, which remained impossibly untouched. It was being consumed to ash before their eyes, in near-total silence. The only exceptions were the gasps and sobs of the fleeing soldiery, the noises made by their bodies staggering through the grassy field and collapsing. And there was laughter, inhuman yet recognizable, from the firedrakes, exultant in being allowed to do what they loved best.

Thunder sounded from within the fort and with it came the shocked realization that the garrison's entire complement of live-stock remained within the walls. Horses led the way in a flat-out panic, ears flat to their skull, the whites showing around their eyes. Right behind them came the very few cattle and sheep and barnyard fowl left behind by the army, which had confiscated the rest for its own use. None of the Chengwei made a move to stop their headlong flight.

Figures appeared amidst the heat haze, as Khory Bannefin led the survivors from the conflagration. The commander thought his eyes were playing tricks on him—the number of former prisoners appeared to have doubled and then some. Then, as Ranulf DeGuerin approached more clearly into view, the Chengwei offi-cer howled silently within himself like one demented, though he fought to keep his features cast in their professional, stoic mask.

The Sandeni had brought with them every man who'd fallen within the fort, showing their enemies far more kindness and gen-erosity—and honor—than they had received in return. A mortal blow could not have done the Chengwei commander more harm. This was shame a lifetime's penance would not expiate.

Without a word, but with a gruff gentleness, DeGuerin laid his burden at the commander's feet. His companions did the same. The commander mustered what remained of his dignity and accepted their gift with a deep bow, the kind he would offer a Khan. DeGuerin turned his back and it dawned on the comman-der that Elora Danan was nowhere to be seen.

That was because she'd climbed the barbican. A flagpole stood there as well, from which generally flew the regimental colors of the garrison. The standard she raised was a cobalt so dark it appeared black in the night, decorated with twelve silver stars, arrayed in three interlocking circles of four. In the center of that design was a greater star, which managed to be superior to the others yet also as one with them. In the heart of that final star, the image could be seen of two intertwined dragons, one rampant, the other clearly its consort.

At the sight of that flag, DeGuerin let loose a cheer. He called her name as his men had in the waryard.

"Elora!" he cried, so hard it broke his voice, and raised in salute the sword she'd given him. *"Elora Danan!"*

None of his comrades took up the cry. That wasn't necessary. He'd spoken for them, and for all their valiant dead.

Atop the barbican, the Sacred Princess opened wide her arms, and the firedrakes rushed to answer her embrace. To the watchers—mixing wonder with horror—the creatures not only wriggled and slithered around the young woman, joining their merry laughter with her own, but actually passed right *through* her, as if she were no more substantial than a ghost.

If Elora noted the distant reaction she paid it no mind. She had more important concerns.

"One more favor," she told the 'drakes. "One more treat."

Play play play,

they cried joyfully, beside themselves with excitement.

Burn burn burn.

"Do you see those posts that line the road?" she asked them, filling her thoughts—and what passed for theirs—with the images of those awful spikes, stretching along the highway. "Find them all," she said. "Burn them *all,* as you did the fort." But then, to their dismay, she added some restrictions.

"Burn *only* the posts. Consume only the dead. Nothing more. Not a blade of grass beside the road, not a speck of dirt that lies on it. And especially not the soldiers who may guard them. Dance with them if you like. By all means let them see your power. But do no harm."

The 'drakes didn't like that. They pouted. They fumed. They protested.

They made Elora repeat her commands, and she did so in tones and terms that brooked neither argument nor disobedience.

"These were my friends," she told them at the end. "They died for my cause, as much as for their own. All I ask of you is to do them the honor they have earned."

As one, every firedrake's face became a match for hers, their way of signaling assent.

In a flash, they were gone.

Shando's post was the first to flame, glowing from within as the structures of the fort had under the firedrake's onslaught. His body turned to ash, to physical nothingness, in a trice. The wood of the pole shouldn't have lasted any longer. Yet in the same unreal manner that the fort maintained its form long after the point when it should have been consumed, so, too, did each and every post along the road.

In lightning succession, the one after the other, the firedrakes set them alight. From her vantage point, even looking across the hellpit furnace that was the waryard, hotter now by far than the open crater of an active volcano, Elora could see the line of torches disappearing off into the distance.

Unless they were blind, the main body of the army would see the fire coming, snaking relentlessly after them over the ridges and through the gorges. She hoped they'd be scared.

Her body was the next best thing to cast lead as she trudged down the stairs, so she took a deliberate pause before exiting the barbican, to center herself and gather what remained of strength and wits. The Chengwei had to see her as supremely confident in her power. She'd played a fair hand against them; she couldn't let them realize what followed was mainly bluff.

She'd entered the fort with a military stride, a predator bounding to the attack. She appeared utterly relaxed now, as she ambled clear of the conflagration she'd ignited. She looked comfortable. No less dangerous, simply—sated.

"You're still here?" she asked the commander, offhandedly taking notice of his presence. He reacted as if she'd struck him with a quirt.

"I told you to go," she continued in that same disdainful manner, not giving him a chance to speak. "Whether to your homes or to your army, I don't care. But here, you will not stay. You profane this honored ground with your presence. Do I make myself clear?"

She finished with a charming smile, the kind the tiger gives the goat when discussing dinner.

The commander dropped to his knees and to his face, prostrating himself before her as he would before his Khagan.

"I crave pardon, Sacred Princess."

"You live, do you not? As I told you, Commander, do no harm and none will come to you. That is my pledge. That holds for your army as well. There's room enough, and wealth enough, for all in the Great Realms. There's no need for such greed, and such a waste of life. Tell that to your general. If I have to tell him myself, our conversation won't be anywhere near so pleasant."

They were a formidable body of men, that was made evident when the commander marshaled them into formation and, with a farewell salute to Elora Danan, led them onto the road, between the double line of burning posts. This time, discipline held as he led them at a deliberately sober pace.

When the last of them was well beyond the bend in the road, Ranulf DeGuerin lowered himself to one knee before Elora and bowed his head in mingled fealty and thanks. Then he had to catch her as her knees lost all tension and her body collapsed in on itself, dropping her sharply on her bottom.

Luc-Jon immediately slipped in behind her, to give her something solid and comforting to lean on, and was rewarded with a purr.

"Bless you, child," the Colonel told her, taking one of her hands in both of his. And then rank and responsibility reasserted themselves. A quick sweep of the smoldering ruins told him there was nothing left aboveground worth salvaging but the fort, which contained hidden caches of emergency stores that both the Chengwei and the firedrakes might have missed. With a word of caution to his officers, he sent them back for whatever could be found. He'd have gone himself, but Elora had returned his handclasp with one that couldn't be broken.

Her eyelids fluttered. "I should have been here sooner," she murmured.

"And what then, Elora Danan?" Khory asked from above and

behind, where she remained on alert. "What would you have done in the face of the whole Chengwei army?"

"Why are you so harsh with her, warrior?" DeGuerin demanded. "She saved our lives!"

"It was a splendid bluff, I'll grant you. Let us all give thanks there were none among the Chengwei with wit enough to realize it."

"How so?"

"Were any touched by the firedrakes? Were any harmed?"

"You didn't do so badly at the gate," Luc-Jon noted.

"Her steel, mine and the brownies' arrows. To let them know we meant business. That we were prepared to be bloody."

"They love to *burn,* you see," Elora said in a soft voice, meaning the firedrakes. "Anything and everything. They make no distinction between hero and villain, Daikini and elf. Given leave, they'd gleefully turn this world into a cauldron. This probably won't stop the Chengwei, they've too much invested in victory to withdraw now. But they'll know the firedrakes came when I called and did as I bid them. Might make 'em think twice about how to proceed. And how they treat their captives."

"The sorcerers . . ." Luc-Jon began hesitantly.

"Took Drumheller east?"

He nodded, which she felt more than saw since she was still snuggled against him. To make herself an easier burden to bear, because she felt so damned comfortable in his arms, she slipped a portion of her own strength into him, seeking out those hurts easiest to deal with and charmed them back to health.

"Figured as much," she said, "when I saw he wasn't amongst you."

"It has to do with their infernal machine."

"Damnedest thing," muttered DeGuerin.

"How so?"

"We'd made a decent fight of it, even when they brought up mangonels that hurled rocks big as houses." The Colonel chuckled ruefully. "Or so they seemed when they bounced off the walls. So long as those ramparts held, we had a fair chance. And bound as they were by magic as well as mortar, the walls should have held till doomsday.

"Not sure myself what happened, the mechanics of it, I mean. They came in the night, dark of the moon, the Chengwei wizards. First I knew of trouble is Drumheller screaming."

"They hurt him?" Elora levered herself to her knees, all ease banished from her body, replaced by the same predatory tension she'd manifested during her approach to the barbican.

"From his actions, they must've. He was rolling and twisting on the ground like a man with a seizure, foam at the mouth, his body bouncing so hard I feared he'd break his bones. Shando tried to hold him fast but he got pitched aside as if he was nothing. The whole room, this was in my office, we were planning strategy for the next day's assault, it went mad along with him. Things came alive, they changed shape, I saw . . . creatures I never want to meet again, even in my worst nightmares. He spoke words that took tangible form before my eyes. He changed himself, into a score of different animals, monsters I'd only read about in legend, as though his body was candlewax in the hands of some demented sculptor. And bad as it was for him, it was far more terrible for those fairies who'd remained to help us.

"The walls," the Colonel continued, "were shot with lightning, like WitchFire, bolts tear-assing every which way. There was no saving those on the ramparts. The flames the Chengwei conjured did less damage than yours, Elora, but they weren't anywhere near so merciful with my men. We assumed it was the precursor to an attack, which indeed it was, and the call to arms brought most everyone else in the fort to the waryard."

"Which is precisely what the Chengwei were waiting for."

"Aye, that's the truth of it. The gates went next. I'll never forget that sound, not the blast itself, that was like the detonation of a thunderstone, but a metallic whistling pitched so high it was almost a shriek. Didn't know better, I'd say they unleashed a banshee on us. Splinters punched straight through the planks of my walls, doors, smashed through windows, turned my waryard into a charnel house.

"They hit us in two waves, right after. Heavy cavalry, then heavy infantry. With the gate breached and most of my command wounded, if not outright slaughtered, we were done by sunrise."

"What happened to the scribe's house?" As she strode across the waryard, surrounded by ashes and devastation, Elora saw what she'd missed from the heights during her initial inspection of the fort, that the ancient stone house and its tower were no more, erased as though they'd never been.

"Damnedest thing, in a night of 'em. Nastiest collection of WitchFires was concentrated around the tower, where the World Gate was."

"The whole building just seemed to collapse in on itself," Luc-Jon broke in. "As if it was being folded over and over again until it reduced down to nothingness. There isn't a trace of it left, not the house, the tower, the Gate, everything's gone. The ground there's like polished glass, glazed over like a piece of fine lacquered porcelain."

"Think of it as a scab," Elora said. "The Veil's way of protecting itself."

"Whatever the device," DeGuerin reported, "while it took thirteen wizards to activate it, only a few were needed to actually carry the thing."

"But they needed Drumheller," Elora mused. "So urgently they rushed him back to Chengwei and left the rest of you behind."

"Another day or more would have seen the last of us in this place," DeGuerin told her, after confirming her supposition. "Transport and escort east were just about ready. In the meanwhile, they wanted what information we possessed—especially from the lad." He indicated Luc-Jon.

"He's a scribe," the Colonel explained further. "They assumed, since he was the only one they found, the house and tower were his."

"They hadn't expected what happened with the tower," Luc-Jon said. "I think it scared them, the sorcerers, I mean. When they realized who Drumheller was, that's when they got so eager to rush him home."

"For what it's worth," DeGuerin said, "I've seen that look before, the one we saw among the sorcerers. Usually on the face of a new recruit taking his first ride. Nothing so unnerves a body as the realization the creature you're riding has a mind of its own. Strikes me they have a weapon they've never used before in the field and they've just discovered there's a difference between what they expected—what it's *supposed* to do—and its actual performance."

"They want Drumheller to help them fix it? But he wouldn't—!" Even as she spoke, Elora made another set of connections and turned toward Khory. "Could the Caliban have wanted us both? Me and Anakerie together?"

"Worth considering."

"What do you mean?" the Colonel asked, and Elora quickly told him of the pitched battle in Sandeni.

"They use their device, Tregare falls," Elora said, "they spirit Drumheller off to Chengwei—and within a day the Caliban's hunting. It makes too much sense to be coincidence: grab Anakerie for the effect it'll have on Castellan Mohdri, grab me for the same regarding Drumheller." And she thought, *but in Anakerie, because of the feelings she and Drumheller have for each other, they achieve both objectives.*

"You're going after them," DeGuerin said.

"It's why I'm here, Colonel, yes."

"Then we'll come with—!"

Elora shook her head and assumed once more to herself the mantle of leadership, gaining a gravitas of mien that was disconcertingly the equal of his.

"Khory and I will go. You take these others, use the Chengwei horses, make your way to Sandeni. Scout the enemy en route if you can, the Council will need the fullest possible report on their capabilities and intentions, especially this device."

"You'll need me," Luc-Jon told her, and to forestall her certain objections: "You speak a little Court Chengwei, hooray for you. Do you know the culture? The lay of the land? The cities?"

"Do you?"

"It's part o' my job. A scribe needs t' know everything, especially on the Frontier. Case in point: two women traveling alone, y're doomed b'fore you start. Chengwei women ha' no rights outside the home. They're defined as either daughters or spouses. Anything else, you're a slave. An' there's no travel at all between cities without a *paiza,* an inscribed passport-medallion."

"Why do I suspect you have access to one?" Elora wondered with an appreciative grin.

"On me, no. But I can forge one wi' the best."

"Are you that eager to lose your head, Luc-Jon?"

"I've already lost my heart. And I'm done wi' being left behind."

Her own heart leaped at both statements, and from the way DeGuerin and Khory were looking at her, Elora assumed that response was as plain on her face as a firedrake's inferno.

DeGuerin held out his hand, but when she reached out to take it he gathered her into a strong and enfolding embrace, hugging her as he would his own daughter before sending her off to battle.

"Fortune attend you, Elora Danan," he said, and there were tears in both their eyes as she returned the gesture in kind, accepting that she was standing surrogate for his firstborn child, whom he feared he'd never see again. In turn, she used him as proxy for the father she'd never known but would always desperately adore.

They watched DeGuerin and his companions strike out for the highlands, then shared a meal on the field while Luc-Jon told them of the land and dangers ahead, while Luc-Jon sampled what clothes they'd recovered to find what fit him best.

"Now what?" he asked, as they finished the last of their meal. "How do we follow the Chengwei?"

Elora stabbed her thumb toward the remnants of the fort.

"By swimming through the fire at the heart of the world," she told him. "If you're game."

To Elora's surprise, and delight, Luc-Jon cupped her face in both his hands and gave her a gentle kiss on the lips. So light a touch, so fleeting a caress, yet it shot a charge of energy all the way to her toes.

"Lead on," he said. "My life is yours."

CHAPTER
8

To the Chengwei, theirs was the greatest nation in the world, the oldest and richest civilization. Its wealth, in history and resources, was beyond counting, just as they considered their power beyond true comprehension. While other lands might claim one city or perhaps two worth the name, the Chengwei boasted a score, with populations numbering in the millions, greater than many countries. In the south, the Stairs to Heaven formed a nigh-impassable natural barrier, both to invaders and expansion. To call it a mountain range was akin to labeling a steel forge hot. These were peaks where the winter snows never melted, whose summits thrust themselves higher than there was air for climbers to breathe, that didn't so much form the backbone of the continent as the armadillo's spiny shell, a knobby shield, roughly oval in shape, stretching from near the midpoint of the mainland to the Sunrise Sea. There, the range came to an abrupt end, forming a rank of serried cliffs that ran along the shore for near a thousand miles, as much a wall as the one that rose at Sandeni. Beyond the coast, extending better than a week's sail, was a magnificent archipelago composed of the straggling remnants of the Stairs to Heaven, spectacular seamounts that reared skyward from the stygian depths of the ocean floor, achieving heights so extreme that if they'd been set on land they would easily have topped the highest summits of the Stairs themselves.

Aside from mountains, the other defining topographical characteristic of Chengwei was its rivers, and again reality dwarfed the meaning of the term. Chief among them was the Quangzhua, believed by the Chengwei without hyperbole to be the greatest in the world. In length it was matched by the westward-flowing Cascadel but that was where all comparisons ceased, for in places the Quangzhua was so wide one bank couldn't be seen from the other, and while the Cascadel fed the occasional lake along its route, the Quangzhua nursed a trio of outright seas, beginning with the Tascara.

It was an old land, with the arrogance that comes of might unchecked by any foe worth the name. Like a champion gladiator just a hair past his prime, Chengwei strutted on the world's stage and expected applause as a matter of right, not to mention triumph. Innovation had long since ossified into tradition, tradition into dogma. Things were done, not because they were right or even made sense (though once they might well have had that purpose), but because that was the way things were done. The bureaucracy and civil service, still a marvel of efficiency, were superb at maintaining the established order. Far less so at adapting to new threats and changing realities.

The world to the Chengwei was a delicacy beyond price, a feast set solely for them. They saw no reason to share.

At the southern end of the Quangzhua delta, where that majestic river reached the Sunrise Sea, was the city of Ch'ang-ja, itself considered one of the wonders of the world. Partly built on the mainland in the comparative shadow of the Stairs to Heaven, its populace had spread over time to a dozen islands that rose like stalagmites from the floor of the continental shelf. These best resembled a thicket of spires or a grove of nursery saplings planted too close together, grouped in a sprawling arc no more than a league from land and ranging for a couple along the shore; they conspired with a significant dogleg notch in the coastline itself to form a deep-water harbor that like so many other elements of this ancient land defied superlatives.

Bridges connected the seamounts to the mainland and flying causeways—suspended at varying levels up the slopes of the near-vertical peaks—connected some of the islands with the others. Within the sprawling harbor itself was a kind of floating city, called Freemantle, composed of boats of every size and description, permanently moored together to provide housing for those who couldn't afford to live on land or wished a minimum of interference from the local authorities. This was the roughest district of the city, where even the prefecture of police ventured only rarely. As a result it was also one of the centers of business and commerce.

Ch'ang-ja was a trading port, its anchorage serving as the Empire's official point of entry for foreign traders. As such, it had much in common with both Sandeni and Angwyn. The shoreline was thick with warehouses and the mercantile exchanges that operated them, as well as the myriad of peripheral companies and establishments that serviced their needs, professional and personal. It was a city of banks and credit institutions, of light industry, of shops and markets offering goods from every corner of the Empire and the wide world beyond. Winding alleys so narrow folks had to twist themselves aside to pass by each other vied with esplanades that ran straight as an arrow for miles, wide enough to accommodate a triple score of men marching abreast. Buildings were jumbled one atop the other, without regard for any need but to house a population that grew daily, yet parks could also be found, of such a size and tranquillity that one might wander for hours without a hint of the hustling, bustling municipality that lay beyond their boundaries. There was wealth to beggar the imagination and the mansions and palaces to show for it, this being that rare metropolis in Chengwei where a merchant prince could dare live in greater ostentation than the local Khan.

Yet it could never be forgotten that while the merchant lords had power almost beyond measure, it was the Khan who ruled both city and province, in the name of his Khagan, for on the headland overlooking the entrance to the harbor stood the fortress aptly named Gate of Peace. From its topmost battlements the whole of Ch'ang-ja could easily be viewed. Look the other way and the same could be said for the seaward approaches. It was stacked in terraces, from sea level to better than three hundred feet above the crest of the bluff and was of such a size, the Sandeni stronghold of Fort Tregare would have been lost within its confines. Its construction was stone, its foundation walls three times as thick as most men were tall. On the various levels, arrayed against land and sea, were a multitude of huge mangonels, ballistas, catapults, bombards, and siege crossbows. Across the harbor entrance, slung well below the surface, was a massive wood-and-chain boom that reached from the Gate of Peace to the nearest island, Bayan, named for the first Khagan (the official title of the Chengwei Emperor). The other islands were named for Bayan's eleven successors. In case of attack, the boom could be raised to trap any invading naval force. As well, a tremendous network of pipes and runnels honeycombed the outer curtain wall, allowing for cauldrons of hot oil and flaming pitch to be deployed against any direct assault on the fortress.

From its earliest construction, the Gate of Peace was considered impregnable. It was a measure of its reputation that for generations past no one had even made the attempt.

The only more imposing structure in the city was a lighthouse, planted atop the summit of Bayan, a beacon fire that, thanks to its intricate arrangement of lenses, could be seen brighter than any star at a distance of a hundred miles.

In nearly all the ways that mattered, Ch'ang-ja considered itself the preeminent city of the Empire. Surprisingly, though it was the self-evident seat of the nation's wealth and commerce, there was no significant interest in making it the seat of government as well. The people valued their relative independence from the central bureaucracy, the opportunity to do as they pleased with a minimum of official interference. So long as they supported the Khagan, happily ensconced in the Imperial Capital of Daido some five hundred miles inland and to the north in the Sagamar Highlands, and paid their appropriate share of taxes, they gained the privilege of being left alone.

There was one other reason for the Gate of Peace and the fact that its fearsome weaponry could reach virtually every quarter of the city, and why the Khagan preferred to keep a fair amount of distance between his Imperial Court and the source of much of its economic might: Ch'ang-ja was a city of sorcerers.

Ch'ang-ja was one of those rare points on the globe where a Magus Point was found, though it lacked sufficient power to sustain a World Gate. As with the material fortunes of the merchant princes, magic, too, had its hand in defining the shape and nature of the city. The location and positioning of any building of importance was determined by priests, to place it in harmony with the local fields of power. At every entrance could be found stone *fu* dogs, to guard against any disruption of that harmony. Magic allowed for designs that stretched the laws of nature to their limits and building materials whose beauty was as unearthly as their origins. A Jade Palace composed entirely of that precious stone, surpassed by one of crystal. Where the towers of Sandeni appeared as solid and unshakable as the rock on which they stood, and the primordial stone of which they were composed, their counterparts in Ch'ang-ja—on the whole much taller and far more dramatic—presented themselves more as confections of gossamer.

Sandeni was a city of industry and invention, Ch'ang-ja one of art. There was no doubt in the minds of its millions of citizens which was by far superior.

Elora and Luc-Jon entered on horseback, Puppy trotting at their side. He'd joined them at Tregare as they made their preparations to depart, having taken refuge in the forest when the stronghold fell, and made it plain that, like Luc-Jon, he would not be left behind. Elora had brought them only part of the way through the bowels of the earth. She'd never encountered so thick a fog of magic as lay about Ch'ang-ja and didn't want to take a chance of unwittingly triggering an alarm by using arcane means to enter the city. There were preparations to be made as well.

Elora's first decision was that the three of them go separate ways, she and Luc-Jon to follow Drumheller while Khory sought for Anakerie in the Imperial Capital of Daido, which is where royal hostages such as she would be held. That was also to have been the destination of Colonel DeGuerin and the other prisoners from Fort Tregare. Drumheller, however, had been transported to Ch'ang-ja. She sent the brownies ahead on reconnaissance, accepting their assurances that they could reach Ch'ang-ja much more quickly through secret trails known only to their kind and roam the city undetected far more easily than Elora could, on horseback or riding fire. They all accepted Elora's rationale, that leaving Anakerie in Chengwei hands would create a lasting window of vulnerability in Drumheller. He cared too deeply for the Angwyn Princess and would blame himself for whatever harm came to her. None were comfortable with the notion of splitting up; by the same token they could see no other way to rescue Drumheller and Anakerie both.

The Empire was linked by a vast web of trunk routes, paved highways that allowed for the speedy movement of goods and people and—when necessary—troops. Courier stations were established at regular intervals, allowing both for regular coach service and the swift transit of Imperial Heralds. In a hurry, sparing neither horses nor riders, a message could reach Daido from the most distant province in a minimum of three weeks. Coaches generally took double the time. Travel required a *paiza,* an internal passport, plus secondary documentation relating to city of birth, point of departure, rank, occupation, and the like. There was a whole host of regulations and the smallest violation carried a punishment of fine and imprisonment. If the bureaucracy wanted an excuse to place someone in custody, it rarely had to be manufactured; the slightest legitimate pretext could easily be found.

Luc-Jon was as good as his word regarding the *paizas.* Lacking both his full complement of tools and his reference books, and short of time in the bargain, the results he presented Elora were nothing short of remarkable. It turned out he had a gift for intrigue. The roles he chose for them played to their strengths— he and Elora would be a pair of traveling players, bards as she and

Duguay Faralorn had been, the kind who generally tour the smaller cities and towns of the outer provinces, performing for coppers or an occasional sliver of something more precious in addition to a meal and a place to sleep. At festival time, which this was, the greater cities were full to bursting with such folk, all angling for a position with some house or tavern that could afford full-time entertainment. Khory would stay as she was, a warrior, although in this land she would present herself as a man.

In Chengwei, gender mattered. Even in the hinterlands, where women were essential to the survival of a household or village, they had no legal standing or rights. They could not own or inherit property. They had no identity beyond their father's house, or their husband's. Education was denied them, as was an apprenticeship in any of the multitude of craft guilds. They didn't even have the escape of religion, though the occasional convent could be found; neither order nor community had official standing. They existed at the sufferance and whim of the local lord and could be wiped away just as easily.

As a consequence, theatrical roles regardless of sex were played by men. The great paradox in Chengwei society was that an actor could win for himself a tremendous reputation and acclaim for his ability to masquerade as a woman, whereas a woman in the same role would be considered the functional equivalent of a street-walking whore, and be treated as such. To the audience, and the public at large, Elora would present herself as a man pretending to be a woman; no one would think to look beneath the surface of that deception to discover that she was really a *woman* pretending to be a man, pretending to be a woman.

In Khory's case, since her figure was comparatively lean to begin with, and her carriage wholly that of a warrior, disguising her was mainly a matter of hiding the distinctive raptor tattoo that covered the left side of her face. That turned out to be Elora's responsibility, as she drew on the skills learned during her own apprenticeship in the forges and foundries of the Rock Nelwyns to craft a steel mask to hide them. It was wafer thin, molded to match the precise contours of Khory's features and so artfully constructed that it fit quite comfortably, accommodating any gesture or expression. When he saw it in place, Luc-Jon laughed aloud in appreciation, predicting that it would most likely become the season's fashion accessory of choice for those of the nobility who wished to emulate the style of the warrior castes. A shame, he mused, they couldn't go into business for themselves; this line of adornments would probably make their fortune.

Elora hit him before Khory could, but she had to concede his point.

"When I'm done saving the world," she commented wryly, "it's nice to know I have a profession to fall back on."

"Saving the world's just the first step," Luc-Jon said gaily. "When that's done, you've still got to run it."

Elora stared at him, aghast, as if he'd just transformed into the most venomous of serpents. She had no riposte for him; just the contemplation of his words left her speechless and shaken.

"No," she said at last, and mainly to herself. *"Never!"*

The night before they parted, as Elora helped Khory make some final adjustments to her disguise, a uniform appropriated from one of the Chengwei officers at Tregare, she told them what she'd learned from Giles Horvath.

"The timing of events is no accident," she said. "We're on a clock, approaching a significant confluence in the patterns of energy and force that comprise the cosmos. For want of a better term, think of it as a celestial Magus Point. That's the moment of change, when the Circles of existence realign themselves."

"Suppose we let it pass?" Luc-Jon mused, which made Elora smile a little ruefully as she recalled how passionately Giles had argued the same position.

"Then the world as you see it is the one we're stuck with, for an Age to come. The Deceiver won't go away, Luc-Jon. Existence will continue as she defined it, a place of unending chaos and warfare between the peoples of each Realm, between the Realms themselves. Nothing will change, because without a new generation of dragons to bring life to the Realm of Dreams, no one will imagine a life that's any different. Things may not get better, ever. This could be our future, till the end of time.

"Giles and the others, their conclusion was that the crucial moment would come at solstice," Elora continued. "But the more I think about it, the less sense it makes. Solstice is the turning of the year, and the longest night—but only for us in the northern hemisphere. In the southlands, it's the longest day. Regardless, it doesn't matter.

"What we're talking about is a *balance*. That's the equinox, the moment when a day throughout the globe is neither short nor long. It doesn't matter where you are, the moment applies equally throughout the Realms."

"If you're right—!" Luc-Jon began.

"Time is at a premium," Khory finished, nodding in agreement. "Not months to act, but barely weeks."

"If that's so," Elora hurried on, "if the Deceiver truly is some future incarnation of me, then she's already lived through a version of this moment. That's the whole reason for her being here, to make the outcome different. The thing is, if the Chengwei follow Horvath's analysis, they're aiming for solstice. If the Deceiver strikes at equinox, three months early, they won't be ready."

"Strikes at whom?" Luc-Jon asked. "I dinna ken what part the Chengwei play in this, how great a threat that device of theirs truly represents—but from all I've heard, Elora Danan, *you're* the one she absolutely has to have. Strikes me, lass, she'll move heaven an' earth t' lay her claim once an' f'r all."

Elora nodded, turtling her head between her shoulders and poking idly at the embers of their campfire with a stick. It was a realization that stalked her every hour, awake or asleep, alongside the fear that when the confrontation came between them it would be Elora who was found wanting.

"Can you be in Ch'ang-ja by the dark of the moon?" she asked Khory.

"A fortnight hence," the warrior said. "I'll be there."

At the very last, as they said their good nights and so suddenly it seemed she acted on a whim, Elora unclipped one of her traveling pouches from her belt and handed it across to Khory. The warrior made no obvious outward reaction but their horses noticed the dramatic rise in tension and began to skibble on their toes, registering their own distress and anxiety by flaring their nostrils and flicking their ears back and forth in a frantic, futile attempt to pinpoint any possible threat. Khory started to rise from the fire to the picket line, but Elora beat her to it, waving back the others as she took it upon herself alone to gentle the animals. A few calming words, a stroke of the hand along their muzzle, a treat of some carrots from a farm they'd passed, and the horses gradually relaxed. Elora wished she could do the same.

When she turned back to the fire, Khory was waiting. The warrior said nothing but searched Elora's eyes with her own, to satisfy her own concerns about this unexpected decision. All Elora could offer in return was the shallowest of nods, as she stepped around her companion and snuggled into her bedroll. Surrendering even one of her pouches proved among the hardest things Elora had ever done. Her whole life, past and future, could be found within the enchanted confines of that bag. She felt like she'd just given away a piece of herself, she felt unbalanced without a bag settled on each hip, she felt strangely . . . naked. Vulnerable.

She thought better of it come morning, but Khory had removed that option. Only two horses remained on the tether; the warrior and all her gear were long gone. Elora did nothing at first; she sat wrapped in cloak and blanket, staring at the space where Khory's horse had been, debating whether or not to give chase. She was tempted, but that was all.

She had a mission of her own to accomplish.

As she had in Sandeni, Elora applied her own makeup as if her naturally silver skin were but a base coat, painting her face in broad bands of contrasting colors, scarlet and black with cadmium yellow for highlights. The effect was vaguely feline, suggesting the patterning of a Highland snow tiger, but definitely predatory. This was a face that bespoke danger.

Their production built on that initial image, presenting a hero tale involving the conquest and subjugation of a demon queen. Luc-Jon played the hero, of course, stalwart and brave and seemingly doomed from the start, like all his predecessors. Elora was the personification of the wicked seductress and it made her laugh aloud to first behold and then don the appliances designed to present her as the ultimate female body. She utilized that sense of humor in her performance, creating a villainess who seduced the audience as much as her foe. She gave them much to admire about her, and to desire, so that when the depth of her evil was ultimately revealed, the audience was truly shaken. When the hero at last triumphed, over seemingly unbeatable odds, the spectators shared that cathartic moment of victory with him.

It was a good little piece and it got better with each telling.

They started down by the harbor in Freemantle and spent their first days in Ch'ang-ja wandering through that lowlife district. The boat city was even more rowdy and independent than the metropolis itself; the language of choice there, among more different sizes and colors of Daikini than Elora thought possible, was the Cascani trading tongue, in deliberate defiance of the local language laws, which refused to officially acknowledge any other speech but Chengwei.

Before they parted, Khory had provided the lead that brought them to the port, though logic would also have sent them in this direction. Interrogation of the Chengwei prisoners, and information developed during Drumheller's and the brownies' reconnaissance of the Chengwei camp, indicated that the sorcerers accompanying the invading army all hailed from the Ch'ang-ja Chapter House of their orders.

On the face of it, that wasn't so unusual. Magic was woven inextricably through the heart and soul of Imperial life. Every city of significance was patron to an order of wizards. However, during the decade and more since the Cataclysm, the finest occult minds in the Empire had been gathering in Ch'ang-ja. Magical sects that had been at each other's throats for generations set aside those differences and began pooling knowledge and resources toward a common goal so secret that it was death to mention it aloud. Even in Freemantle, where thumbing noses at authority was second nature, references were circumspect. The work had intensified tremendously over the years since Elora's abortive Ascension; that expansion was the primary cause of the weakening of the security strictures. Too many people knew something was going on, and the more forbidden the topic, the greater the tendency to talk about it, even if only to repeat the most recent and outrageous rumor.

"A baker's dozen chapter houses, thirteen in all, monasteries, abbeys, call 'em what'cha will," grunted Baghwan Saltai, the rogue who was their patron for the evening. He guzzled another mug of grog, a rough-and-ready rum that he preferred topped off with a mix of heady island spices. Elora was in awe of the retired pirate's capacity; one sip left the young woman gasping, the entire glassful turned her brain to mist. She believed she was in control of her wits but virtually everything he said, and she said in response, was accompanied by a bout of laughter, as if their conversation were a running succession of brilliantly funny jokes. He didn't seem to mind. She prayed she wouldn't be sick.

"That's what's been built here lately. Couple of 'em, belike to sprung up overnight an' that's no error."

Hailing from the sea as he did, he was more comfortable speaking Cascani than his native tongue. That was one of the reasons Elora focused her attention on him, as opposed to the other Freemantle ganglords, since that trader's language was the first she'd learned after leaving Angwyn. He controlled a fair stretch of territory along the waterfront, but she also noticed that his vessels appeared surprisingly seaworthy, compared with most of the other boats that comprised the floating city. To the casual glance, the untrained eye, Saltai's ships were as derelict as the rest but they rode too well at anchor and their slovenly appearance didn't seem to extend beneath the waterline. It made her wonder, in a pinch, how quickly they could clear the harbor. And also why Saltai felt the need to be ready to do so.

"Like attracts like," Luc-Jon observed. He held his liquor much better than Elora but sounded far worse.

"Phauggh! Got two tigers, they look alike. Might even be related. You don't bunk 'em in trees right next to one another. Each to their own range, that's the way of things. Trespass at'cher own risk, fight to the death to protect it. Damnable wizards ain't no different. Most cities, towns, whatever, they're home to one house, pledged to one sect. Don't tolerate rivals an' interlopers, no way, nohow. Ch'ang-ja, it's got the University, an' the Gate of Peace t' keep folks polite, got by with as I recall now three, it was. An' they guarded this turf more fiercely than any tiger, I'll tell you that straight! Twenty years back, maybe twenty-five, fourth house tried to open. Had the Khagan's blessing an' all, an' our Khan's tacit support in the bargain. Built themselves a lovely temple, they did. Dint even last the night. Come the sunrise, no sign of the building, no sign of the priests."

"Now everybody's friends," Luc-Jon toasted with a hiccup that rolled into a basso burp.

"Wonders, they'll never cease."

Much later, after Saltai finally collapsed amidst the detritus of a truly sumptuous feast—for all his rough-and-tumble ways he served a most excellent table, again reminding Elora of the difference between perception and reality, in others as much as herself—Elora made her way to the forepeak of his ship. She'd taken time to make the chieftain more comfortable on his pillows, avoiding a beery embrace in the process, and then tidy up the remains of dinner.

Most of the bigger ships in Freemantle were built for cargo, favoring capacity over speed. Saltai's craft was much sleeker. It could carry a decent load but its strengths were in its swiftness and maneuverability. *Ideal,* she thought, *for a pirate.* Moreover, the others were mainly coastal cruisers, who in their working lives would never venture out of sight of land. Saltai's ship was designed to only visit harbors; her home was the deep blue of the open ocean, and there was a roguish solidity in the vessel that would likely see her safely through any storm.

The view from the bow was dominated by the nearest of the twelve barrier islands, Sagat, rising like a pillar straight up from the water, with only a modest leeward beach to provide access. There were structures visible on the island, perched on ledges with the daring tenacity of mountain goats and just as little means of obvious support. It had been home to a merchant of the city, until he and his family were summarily evicted some months back by the latest of the sorcerer sects to come to town. To hear Saltai tell it, in the time since, buildings grew on those impossible slopes like warts and were about as attractive to his eye. The merchant appealed his case to the Khan and was imprisoned for his trouble. The fortunate members of his family disappeared into Freemantle, given refuge by the merchant's customers and business partners. The rest found themselves on the auction block, sold into slavery to pay off debts and fines that popped up out of nowhere. It was a clear and unmistakable message. The wizards had the full support of the Khan, and beyond him the Khagan; what they wanted, they got.

"Another object lesson," Elora muttered when the story was done.

"Might makes right," agreed Luc-Jon. "There is a rule of law in Chengwei, but the law that ultimately rules is the Khagan's will. Not so bad a thing, I'll wager most folks argue, when the Emperor knows his business. Mercy save them from one that doesn't."

A flash of emerald light rolled along the base of a mass of clouds that had stalled a little ways inland. A minute later, a similar flash lit them again, only this time the light was golden. This was the Bayan beacon, its lenses making a complete revolution every two stately minutes, with unvarying precision. Green, then gold; green, then gold, so mariners and travelers could tell it from a purely natural phenomenon.

"You have to admire their skill with machines," Luc-Jon noted.

"Coming from a citizen of Sandeni, that's rare praise."

"We're pretty good ourselves, in our way, dinna get me wrong. But no one in the world—I'd say no one in the Great Realms entire, on either side of the Veil—can match their ability with clockwork gears. Haven't you ever heard the phrase *true as a Chengwei timepiece?*"

"As trusted as the word of a Cascani trader," she concurred, for the latter was considered coin of the realm throughout the Daikini Realm and in many Domains beyond the Veil as well.

"It's a big city."

"Can't argue that. I've never seen the like."

"We've been here nearly a week, Elora, we've barely scratched the surface. We c'd be forever tryin' to find Drumheller. I mean, it's no' as if we can walk up to the wee doors of the various chapter houses and ask if they're the ones holding him prisoner."

"Won't have to."

"You're sure o' that."

"Actually, yes."

"You can track him?"

"I could use my InSight, yes. I've considered it, melding my awareness with some bird or animal or insect or other and go scouting. Or reach out to Thorn himself." She drew up her legs and hugged them close, wedging herself into the fork of the bow as if she suddenly didn't trust the solidity of the deck beneath her or the calm anchorage that supported the boat.

"But there's something about this place, this city. I know you see wonders, Luc-Jon, but to me . . . it's like claws scraping down a chalkboard. It's all fragments, held together by I don't know what, as if the very fabric of the buildings—the stones and mortar themselves—actively hate the structures they composed. How is it Thorn described me? As a beacon? Magically, I shine more brightly than the Bayan lighthouse; that's partly why the fire-drakes come when I call. I'm the only mortal form they've ever encountered they can perceive on a par with themselves. My energy's a match for theirs. Worse, I'm unique. If I use any of my talents, if I call on any of the powers I've befriended, every adept in the city will know it."

"So how do we find him then?"

She smiled, very slightly and full of mischief.

"*We* don't."

"Elora Danan," Franjean demanded in the most aggrieved of tones, "did you have to send the damned *dog* to fetch us!"

"Hi!" Elora greeted them brightly, thankful to see the brownies hale and hearty. She'd cut them loose to go exploring the day they'd all arrived and had heard nothing since. That was why she'd asked Puppy to seek them out.

"Of all the inconsiderate, unfair, unconscionable—!" Franjean was building to one of his trademark rants. Rool's response was a sigh of weary resignation, he'd heard it all before, broken by a laconic comment to Elora.

"Nice face," he told her.

"Put it on just for you," she retorted in kind.

Franjean struck a courtier's pose and examined her as he would some ragamuffin dumped on his doorstep.

"We must do something about the way you take care of yourself. Or rather, neglect to."

"I'm in disguise, remember?"

"We'll never tell," Rool said.

"Because that would mean admitting we knew you in the first place, heaven forfend," added Franjean.

"You put up with this?" Luc-Jon sounded amazed, and Elora realized belatedly that he'd yet to encounter the brownies in full cry, when they verbally took no prisoners. *Well,* she thought, *I had to learn the hard way.*

"Is it any of your concern?" demanded Franjean.

"Boyfriend," answered Rool.

"Rool!" squawked Elora, at this complication she did not need right now.

The catalyst of this reunion allowed himself a yawn, baring his fangs and then snapping them closed with an audible *clack* before lowering himself to the deck and resting head on paws. Puppy looked very pleased with himself.

"Well, isn't he?" Franjean asked Elora, in all mock innocence, picking up his friend's cue. Inside, he was bursting with laughter at her discomfiture.

"Never you mind, the pair of you! It's a private matter, between Luc-Jon and me, and none of your damn' business!"

"Wouldn't be so testy if it weren't so."

"You want to see 'testy,' keep this up." She sounded dangerous and they knew they'd pushed the limits of raillery.

"Smart play," Rool conceded, "sending the hound."

"Thought his nose might find your scents, even in this rats' warren. And who'd give a second look to a dog?"

"No worries on that score, Elora Danan," Luc-Jon assured her. "You'd be astonished at how hard Puppy is to spot when he doesn't want to be found."

"Second that, I will," Rool said.

"So talk to me, the pair of you. We need to find Thorn and win him free."

"You'd best gather an army then, because that's what you'll need."

"Consider this a challenge. The greatest of tests for the greatest of thieves."

Both brownies gave her a gimlet pair of eyes. They appreciated compliments but they also knew when they were being fed a line of hogwash.

"Had a chance t' cut him loose the night we arrived," Rool said.

"That easily? Why didn't you tell me? What happened?"— since obviously, they'd failed.

"Wouldn't come, curse him," Franjean said, as if Elora hadn't spoken.

"Whyever not?"

"Blessed if we know. He's in the Crystal Palace, working with the Chengwei."

"Because they're threatening him with Anakerie, correct? Her survival depends on his cooperation."

"If you say so," Franjean said, but Rool shook his head vehemently.

"She's frost on snow," he told Elora. "He was helping before they grabbed her."

"This makes no sense. He must be under a spell—!"

"Elora Danan, stop grasping at straws," Rool said, tossing his hands in exasperation. "Drumheller is in what passes for him as his right mind. No drugs, no sorcery, no coercion of any kind that we could see."

"Obviously you missed something. Or he's playing a double game."

Rook shrugged, but Franjean spoke.

"We were there," he said flatly.

"He dines with them," Rool said.

"Thorn? With the Chengwei?" And he nodded.

"Not with the acolytes or journeymen sorcerers, y'understand. Nor even the adepts. It's him and the Vicars-General, the Lords and Masters of the Sects, the Magi."

"And they have no idea you're here?"

"Take a moment to listen, an' you'll need no more'n a moment, you'll hear no tread of brownie feet. No elves nor fairies nor any of the Veil Folk of any shape or kind in this benighted hole."

She thought of the silence that accompanied the presence of the Caliban.

"They've all been driven out?" she asked, adding a silent, *or worse?*

"Left of their own accord," Rool said. "So long back the locals, they've forgot we ever existed. The likes of Lesser Faery, we're nothing to them. We could strip this town bare, they wouldn't have a clue."

"Makes me nervous."

"Why, Franjean?"

"No balance to the magic. Take a cup, Elora Danan. You can fill it past the brim, if you're very careful an' use a steady hand, trusting to the surface tension of the water to keep it from overflowing. That's Ch'ang-ja, filled past its brim with magic. But there's more. Suppose that cup were paper. Sure it'll hold that water a wee while, mayhap even through the length of a proper meal. But the longer it sits full, the more saturated the substance of the cup becomes. What happens then when you try to pick it up to drink?"

"It collapses."

Rool clapped his hands once, to indicate the disintegration of Franjean's cup. "Welcome to Ch'ang-ja," he said.

"And nobody suspects?" She found that hard to believe, in this city chockablock with magicians.

"Warnings a'plenty," said Rool. "None wi' wit enough to pay 'em heed."

"Hubris, thy name is Daikini," suggested Franjean.

Elora had a better idea, but she stated it gently and without sting. "And here I thought it was *brownie.*"

Then she went on to state the obvious: "We have to get him out."

"From an impregnable fortress," Luc-Jon noted, "and a palace of magic. You don't demand much. Do you have any ideas?"

"The way to get to Thorn is the way he got to me in Angwyn.

We'll reverse the old adage: what's good for the gander should be good for the goose."

"Chances are, you'll both get cooked."

"Oh ye of little faith."

"Aphorisms aside, Elora," Luc-Jon inquired, "what are you talking about? How did Thorn get to you?"

"Who's the one kind of person who can go anywhere in a palace and never be noticed?" To make the point, Elora rose lithely to her feet, then crooked her back ever so slightly, assuming an air of abject subservience. She kept her head bowed, so that she was always looking up at those around her and never met their gaze. She withdrew all aspects of personality deep within herself, becoming as featureless a character as the bulwark against which she stood. She didn't say a word, because her sort didn't speak unless spoken to but her body language made clear her readiness to serve, quickly and well.

"Servant?" Luc-Jon hazarded.

"The more menial, the better."

"Why you?"

"I'm the better actor. Thorn knows me. If I have to run, or fight, I have more options open to me than you do. Their magic shouldn't be able to touch me. And one thing more." She paused, and turned to take stock of the Crystal Palace, on its knoll, as imposing an edifice in its way, with as bald a statement of power and purpose, as the Gate of Peace.

"Which is?"

"He came for me, Luc-Jon. Can I do less in return?"

"Suppose it's a trap?"

Her reply made them all roll their eyes.

"Actually," she said, with a hint of mischief and an utter disregard for the risks, "I'm kind of counting on it. Look," she continued, ready for their objections and determined to press on regardless, "if Drumheller wants to stay, I have to hear that from his own lips—and even then I may not accept it. In the meanwhile, what I require from you lot is a way out of the city."

"No more swimming in fire?" Rool asked innocently. Neither

brownie had much enjoyed those journeys. Their reluctance was shared by Luc-Jon.

"Only as a last resort," Elora assured them all. "And there's Anakerie."

"Thought that was Bannefin's lookout," Franjean said.

"So it is," Elora agreed. "I just wish I had some news, is all."

"Be patient," Rool assured her. "It'll come."

The comforting constant about wizards was that they loved the perks of their profession. Perhaps because of the rigors of their various disciplines, perhaps because they spent so much time in "other" worlds they forgot what it was like to strive in their own, many of them felt society owed them a living. They accepted the best of amenities as a matter of right and too often within the confines of their palaces were a law unto themselves.

That was Elora's greatest risk. If she was caught, she would have no one to turn to for aid. Unlike in Angwyn, there'd be little likelihood of finding a companionable demon imprisoned within the foundation stones of the catacombs.

After a couple of precious days of intense observation, she concluded the risk was justifiable. Like any grand household, the Crystal Palace ran on a strict schedule. The wizards had to be provided for, their needs catered to. Beds had to be changed, chamber pots emptied, clothes and linens washed; food had to be procured, both staples and fresh produce for the daily meals. The more exotic raw materials required for their work were the province of journeymen sorcerers and acolytes. Elora gave them a wide berth. Her interest was in the slaveys, who scattered to the four corners of the city markets every morning before dawn.

Imposing as the Crystal Palace was from afar, closer inspection proved it even more dazzling. It rose straight and slim as a spike, as though trying to combine the design aesthetic of the High Elves of Greater Faery with the natural grandeur of a mountain. Any other building rising to such a height would require a broad and solid foundation, with stone laid artfully and with precision upon stone to properly balance and sustain its mass and volume. This tower took all those rules and presumptions and threw them aside, presenting the illusion of being in harmony with the world when in fact it stood in rank defiance of every natural order.

"What d'you think?" wondered Luc-Jon as they made a slow circuit of the Palace. They were still better than a quarter mile clear of the tower, in a neighborhood that was undergoing a forced relocation. The sorcerers highly valued their privacy and had informed the Khan that the local buildings crowded too close about their temple; too many people, too much ugliness, wouldn't it be nice if someone made all that unpleasantness simply go away? It didn't matter that the neighborhood had been here first, that it was only in the past few years that the Crystal Palace had grown so in size and especially arrogance. The Khan had his directives from the Khagan, added to his own reluctance to force any kind of confrontation; the citizens thus affected could deploy no equivalent force in opposition. So, they were evicted and their houses and businesses—some of which had stood for generations in a society that revered its ancestors—leveled.

"As without, so within," Elora commented. "I don't like 'em."

"Can't fathom how they got that built."

"It wasn't built," she told him. "It's growing."

"Alive?"

She shrugged. "Depending on who you talk with, that term has a meaning too broad to be useful. Everything's alive, each to its own way. You see a palace, I see a mountain. Only the sorcerers have refined it to its essence, stripped it of anything dross, of the slightest impurity."

"It *is* beautiful, Elora."

She grunted. "Spend some time at a forge, scribe," she told him. "Purity has its uses, but a lot more liabilities."

"It isn't very big," Luc-Jon mentioned, after they'd meandered through another circuit, taking care to wander somewhat afield, into the surrounding byways and alleys to avoid arousing any undue notice. "Around, I mean. At its base."

"Yah. Certainly not big enough to fit all the traffic we've been watching roll in and out."

"You have an explanation?" he presumed aloud, which she did.

"There are spells that fold space. Larger versions of the enchantment Thorn cast over my traveling pouches. Most wizards use 'em to camouflage their worth, to give a hovel floor space grander than a royal palace. But the spells needed to sustain that kind of scale—!"

"The other orders, the sects, they're all following suit."

A dozen similar but unmistakably subordinate spires rose above the city, grouped in a rough circle about the Crystal Palace, echoing the design of the Palace as the various orders attempted to evoke the structure of the Great Realms themselves.

"Y'know what's interesting," Luc-Jon told her. "Ch'ang-ja now has a mountain range of magic to go with the range of stone that defines the harbor." Meaning the Twelve Kings, as those islands were called.

"They're mad," Elora said. "There are only two, maybe three, places in the world that I know of could possibly sustain such a concentration of arcane forces: Tir Asleen, Nockmaar, and, perhaps in its heyday, Sandeni."

"This Magus Point isn't strong enough?"

"Not even close. Luc-Jon, it can't even support a World Gate, what does that tell you?"

"Perhaps they know what they're doing?"

"They're mad," she repeated. "Luc-Jon, it's like using a stewpot as a cauldron in a blast furnace. Sure, the iron may withstand the heat and the pressure of the molten steel a wee while but that isn't what it was designed to do. And these nimwits keep increasing the stress on the vessel. It can't hold, it won't." She spoke with flat certainty, as if relating an article of absolute faith. "The sooner we're quits of this place, the happier I'll be."

A different time, a different place, a different occasion, Elora would have been transfixed with delight. Everywhere she turned was a new scent to intrigue the palate, shaved ginger to use as spice or ointment, tarragon, cardamom, pepper, chilies so hot the merest sniff set her eyes to watering. There were planks of raw teak and sandalwood, each with their own delicious fragrance, to be transformed into articles of furniture oiled and polished to so lustrous a sheen they rivaled mirrors and whose texture surpassed silk. Fishmongers offered delicacies she'd never seen before (and

some she'd rather not see again) and most stalls offered the opportunity to choose from still-living catch. She counted sweets in
abundance, candies and cakes, fruits and vegetables of all types
and description. Weavers offered cloth of every imaginable quality, in a riot of color and design, and just along the market could be
found tailors who'd turn those purchases into garments. Jewelers
hammered out their wares, from the very crude to pieces so
exquisite Elora couldn't understand why they were being sold
from a stall.

In Angwyn and Sandeni, the goal of a merchant was to open a
permanent establishment, to possess a shop, to become a man of
property. In Ch'ang-ja, the goods themselves were paramount. In
this most structured of Daikini societies, Elora found a market that
was truly egalitarian, where a tyro plied his trade right beside a
master artisan and it was up to the customer to tell the difference.

Yet even as part of her was dazzled by the abundance of choice,
almost irresistibly tempted to partake of the market's wares, Elora
recognized the flaw that ran through every stratum of this community. Every stall, every artisan, every retailer, to some degree or
other employed magic. Each of the wealthiest of these merchants
had a minor wizard on retainer, while the less affluent banded
together to engage one, either by vendor (such as an association of
butchers or greengrocers, to keep their produce from spoiling) or
by the street. The enchanters made it easier to do business. Their
spells allowed Daikini seamstresses to equal the otherwise match-
less skill of a brownie tailor, they cast impurities from metal and
erased the blemishes from precious stones. They cast wards of
protection against thieves.

If Sandeni was a city wholly bereft of magic, whose hallmark
was the ascendance of technology and mechanical invention,
Ch'ang-ja was grounded just as extremely on the opposite shore.
Nothing existed here—not the people, not the city itself—that was
not shaped and defined and sustained by magic, to an extent Elora
wouldn't have imagined possible even in the Realms beyond the
Veil.

She couldn't say which disturbed her more, that the situation
existed, or how blithely the people took it for granted. The more

she saw, the more it strengthened her determination to be quits of both the city and the Empire it represented.

They found a purveyor who was the main supplier of commodities to the Palace and quietly joined his gang of laborers. The work was brutal, manhandling hundredweight sacks of corn and millet, rice and grain from pallet to shipping cart, and it made Elora thankful for her years in Torquil Ufgood's forge. She would never match a Nelwyn in raw strength but she could hold her own with any Daikini man.

When the carts rolled off to the Palace, she made sure she was aboard. Luc-Jon she told to return to Saltai's schooner with the brownies, in case she ran into trouble. It was a caravan of decent size. The Palace larder must have been fairly depleted, and Elora positioned herself about midway down the line. That would give any guards enough time to be bored by the procession of drones trudging back and forth beneath burdens almost as large as they were.

The carts weren't allowed in the Palace itself and for a terrible moment Elora feared that its own servants would carry the supplies the rest of the way. It turned out that horses and mules couldn't be driven across the moat, their steel shoes and the steel bands around the cart wheels evidently set up unacceptable resonance patterns in the crystal matrices of the drawbridge. Also, it was said the nature of the moat itself had a tendency to drive dumb animals, and the occasional Daikini, quite mad.

It was a disconcerting walk, that Elora readily confessed. The bridge was translucent, presenting a vague and distorted view of the moat below. Worse, though it appeared to be a kind of liquid, the substance that filled the moat was in no way water. Even so, something appeared to live down there. Elora saw ripples on the surface when there wasn't a breath of moving air and from the distortion patterns concluded that it was a creature of size. More than that, she preferred to do without.

The interior of the Palace was dark, at least down where the menials plied their various trades. The surfaces were all crystal and should have been as clear as the bridge outside, yet some property had rendered them opaque, which made sense on a purely practical basis, allowing the staff to move about more easily. Elsewhere in the Palace, Elora was sure this consideration was not applied. The sorcerers would depend on their own MageSight to guide them and the servants would have been touched by a minor spell to grant them a facsimile of the same talent, so they could go about their own tasks. Anyone else would be dazzled by the prismatic effects of light passing through the myriad layers and facets and weights and colors of crystal that comprised the Palace, and if they had any sensitivity to magic at all be equally disoriented by all the energies it generated. There was little need, she realized, for defensive wards or even an abundance of guards; the building itself was its own ideal champion.

She quickly found the domestic quarters and from there pilfered the robes of a scullery maid. In an ordinary household, these would be the most ragged and plain of apparel, as befit someone whose duties required her to spend most of her workday on hands and knees, scrubbing floors. Those, however, were in buildings of stone and wood. In the Crystal Palace, the job was more akin to polishing fine jewelry, from the inside. Though the cut of the garments was serviceable, the material was silk, of a quality that would have brought a fair price in Sandeni. Trousers with padded knees, soft-soled slippers. A short tunic that fell to her hips, with a stand-up collar that enclosed her entire neck. It buttoned at the throat and then along the line of her right collarbone and on down the seam beneath her right arm. Elora grabbed a scarf as well, wrapping it about her head and face in the fashion she'd seen among a number of the servant classes. That was primarily to hide her outrageously short hair; the color of her skin was covered by a coat of makeup. Nothing about her disguise would withstand intense scrutiny; her gamble was it wouldn't come to that.

Equipment in hand, as though she were late for work, Elora scurried through a labyrinth of service passages, letting instinct guide her footsteps. She emerged into an upper gallery and immediately unlimbered her wash gear, dampening her chamois cloths and beginning to polish the gleaming floor. Her first goal was to establish herself as an innocuous part of the landscape, as transparent in her way as the crystal she so diligently cleaned.

She'd guessed right at the market. The sudden inrush of goods was in preparation for a formal celebration of some kind that very evening. The lords of this palace wanted it shown to best advantage, so the scrubwomen had been marshaled during daylight hours, when they normally plied their trade, after most of the other residents had gone to bed.

The gallery overlooked a spectacular atrium, a fan-shaped box five floors in height, short walls parallel, the long ones opening out from the entrance toward a shimmering curtain that closed off the head of the room, to hide from view whatever was contained there.

Elora dearly yearned to play the tourist. The images she snared with her occasional sideward glances were as enticing as chocolate. She was enfolded in an ever-changing riot of light and color, the radiance of the sun twisting and bending again and again through an infinite series of refractions as it passed through all the crystal shapes and surfaces that comprised the Palace. She saw rainbows dance beneath her hands, prismed into hues of such subtlety and life they would make a painter weep because while his palette might replicate the tone, paint was too tangible a medium even to hint at the texture.

There were sounds as well; the crystal fabric of the Palace played with the aural spectrum as well as the visual. It was clear to her now why the air about the Palace remained supernally still, regardless of the weather over the city as a whole. The slightest breeze, even the faint in- and outrush of breath from those within its wall, struck a chord in the crystal, so that a faint background hum was ever present. Elora supposed the sorcerers in this particular order got used to it over time but it made her edgy.

It reminded her of the Malevoiy.

Thunderstruck, she forgot her role, dropping onto her heels and resting too long in that shocked huddle, fortunate when the moment passed that no one had taken notice. There was too much independence in that stance for a slavey.

She withdrew a step into herself and cast a look into the vault of memories she'd gained from Khory, of that last series of battles with the Malevoiy. They were the oldest of the elven races, it was they who pioneered the use of crystal as a raw material in construction. The gemstones they preferred were dark, possessing the power to imprison the light that shone on it. That was why their world was one of Shadow, an echo of their own nature. All the beauty of life, all its potential, the Malevoiy reserved unto themselves. What Elora had seen in their Realm were the few pitiful remnants of those extraordinary constructions, their fearsome luster dulled by the passage of an inconceivable amount of time.

She shook her head and enjoyed the latest dance of color through the floor, appreciating how the film of her washwater created another layer of refraction. Then her eyes narrowed, concentration focused, and she stepped farther back into memory, returning herself almost physically to Giles Horvath's library and hoping as she did that her recollections remained true. In her mind's eye she rolled a ladder down a line of shelves, not even sure of what she sought until, of their own volition, her hands plucked a modest volume into view. As expected, it was a grimoire, a book of spells and incantations. Nothing of great power or notoriety; it was essentially a primer.

It taught sorcerers how to manipulate the world's spectrum of radiant energy, primarily light. And how to trap it.

Each time a beam passed through crystal, a few candelas of energy remained behind. Hardly enough to notice, but in a structure of such size and complexity, the cumulative effect had to be staggering. She didn't bother considering what such tremendous power might be used for; where sorcerers were concerned the answer could be anything.

A trill of sensation through the fabric of the crystal broke Elora from her reverie. It was a gossamer feeling, the analogy that came to her was of the faintest possible pebbling of grit marring an otherwise immaculate surface. Yet when she stroked her fingertips across the crystal, all felt normal.

Hackles rose on the back of her neck. Every alarm she was born with, or which she'd learned over time, was poised to sound, so much so that it was an actual physical effort to force herself to move at a scrubwoman's deliberate, soul-weary pace and meticulous precision.

She left the gallery, following the directions imparted to her by the brownies, wondering now if they'd truly been as cunning as they thought. Or as undetected. Perhaps someone decided to let them go, in hopes of snaring a bigger catch later on? Or maybe, from Elora's standpoint, it was just bad timing?

She threaded her way through a maze of subordinate corridors, up some flights of stairs, across a final gallery to a sumptuous suite of apartments of the kind generally reserved for Princes. En route, she passed some members of the order but none took any notice.

Getting in is always *easier,* she reminded herself. *Be it trouble or the villain's stronghold.*

This, of course, she knew, was both.

It was here that she found Thorn Drumheller.

His greeting was precisely what she'd expected.

"Elora Danan," he squawked as she stepped across the threshold, "are you bloody *insane?*"

"Glad to see you, too, old duffer."

"You must leave, at once!"

"To what point, after all the trouble the order's gone through to make me so welcome?" She stretched another set of kinks out of her back, feeling a sudden rush of sympathy for the women who had to spend their working lives on hands and knees. "Thorn, I felt the Caliban. It tried its best to hide but its signature is as distinctive as my own."

On impulse, she turned to the doorway and peered deep into the structure of the Palace. Pellucid though the crystal was, the overlapping layers combined with the energies coursing through its structure tended to blur perceptions, casting a form of mist over anything more than a couple of walls or floors away. Elora couldn't properly see the Caliban, she had no real sense of his presence. However, she found a point close to the central gallery, at the junction of a number of main and secondary hallways where the fog grew exceptionally thick. It was a fair distance removed from Thorn's apartment; a fugitive would easily be misled into believing she had a clear run to freedom. Thing was, every possible route intersected one of the corridors leading out of that junction, and there were convenient stairs for the Caliban as well, if she chose to descend to the cellars.

"I'm all for a game of hare and hounds, Drumheller," she told him, raising her hand to the distant Caliban in a chirpy wave, "but I do require at least halfway-decent odds."

"Why did you come?" He still sounded exasperated.

She didn't dignify the question with anything more than a pitying glance. There were no windows to the apartment, hardly necessary when the walls themselves were transparent. Thorn could see the world outside while that same fog effect that hid the Caliban also served to mask him from exterior view. There was no hearth but according to Thorn no need for one. As Elora herself could feel, the climate within the Palace was quite comfortable, and altogether independent of the weather outside. The structure was as hermetically sealed as a greenhouse.

Without a knock, the door opened. No one of significance, Elora spotted that right off, little more in fact than a messenger conveying the Vicar-General's invitation to dinner. She gave him the kind of look she'd perfected throughout her childhood, that had made her the bane and terror of servants and nobility alike in Angwyn. It was the purest distillation of royal hauteur and it stopped the poor man dead in his tracks as though he'd unwittingly taken a turn into the den of a basilisk.

With offhand grace, Elora accepted, and thanked him as well for the gown servants presented on the Vicar-General's behalf. The herald began to explain that the servants would remain to care for Elora's needs and prepare her for the evening, but she demurred, informing him that while the offer was greatly appreciated she would see to her own requirements.

When she and Thorn were once more alone, Elora suggested a bath. Thorn had long since yielded her the field; sometimes she could prove as unstoppable as an avalanche, and just about as devastating to those unfortunate enough to be in her vicinity.

The tub was deluxe, big enough for her to share.

"You used this?" she asked of Thorn and when he nodded of course, said, "Next best thing to swimming in a pond."

"Fine for a float," he conceded. "Not really for exercise."

"I got everyone safely to Sandeni," she told him.

"I know."

"Want to tell me of the device they're building downstairs?"

"You'll see it soon enough. It's finished, that's the reason for tonight's gala. The Vicar-General wants to show it off."

"What does it do?"

"What every despot worth the name seems to want most these days, conquer the world."

"Cute."

"This weapon may do the trick."

Elora dunked herself, staying underwater till her lungs burned. But she didn't resurface. Instead, she extended her awareness to the medium that surrounded her, and by extension to the ocean far beyond. There was little character to the bath; the water had been washed through so many filters, both physical and magical, in an attempt to remove every conceivable impurity, that almost nothing remained of its essential arcane energies. It could sustain life, but possessed virtually none of its own. She drew on that first aspect, taking what oxygen she needed through the pores of her skin, allowing herself to become as porous as a sieve for as long as she remained submerged. It was a relaxing interlude.

She resurfaced finally with a shake of the head and a spout of water from nostrils and mouth to ask of Drumheller, "What happened at Tregare, Thorn? What did the Chengwei do?"

"More to the point, child, what did *you* do?"

"You heard?"

"By courier, by scrying pool, by every means of communication possible through methods both temporal and arcane."

"I wanted to send a message."

"That, you did."

"They were my friends, Thorn!" She held up a hand before he could speak. "I know about war, I'm not that great a child any longer, I've seen my share of slaughter. And"—her voice caught just a little—"been a part of it. Death I accept, but the defenders at Tregare didn't deserve to be planted like scarecrows."

"The Chengwei don't understand your restraint."

"From all I've seen, they don't much understand restraint of any kind. Or acknowledge it."

"True. The fact still remains."

"You've seen what firedrakes can do. *I* know how they *feel,* right to the essence of their being. I could only trust them on a tight leash, with specific and absolute limits. Believe me, with them, there are lines you don't want crossed. Taking a life is one of them. It's a lesson the Chengwei could profit from."

"You called, and cousins to demons answered. You spoke, they obeyed. The Chengwei are impressed."

"As well they should be."

"What's so funny?"

The biggest of grins split her face, stripping her mien of every scrap of maturity and presenting Elora once more at her true age, radiating an innocence she felt was constantly slipping through her fingers no matter how tightly she tried to hold fast to it.

"After Tregare, if I showed up at your front door and strolled in as if I owned the place, what would you assume?"

"Another object lesson?"

She smiled like a predator.

"A fair analysis, I'll grant you," Drumheller conceded. "The Vicar-General probably sent runners to the other orders, to bring in reinforcements."

"Should I be flattered?"

"Have a care, girl. You're sounding too dangerously cocky by half. These are serious people, and this, very serious business."

She dunked herself again, and surfaced like a dolphin, flooding the room with her splash. The sole exception, hardly a surprise, was Drumheller, who remained dry as old toast.

When she spoke, though, resting her chin on crossed arms on the side of the tub, levity had been banished from voice and manner.

"What's your part in it?" she asked and while on the surface her voice sounded quite companionable, in keeping with the established mood, there was an undertone to it that reminded Thorn of Anakerie.

"They don't know what they're dealing with," he told her. "They have a demon by the tail and they think they are its masters."

"So your goal is to stop them?"

There was a silence before he replied, with a single word, "No."

Elora didn't look at him. She heard his answer, she refused to see it in his eyes.

"Can we beat the Deceiver?" she asked suddenly.

"In battle, you mean? You and I?"

"Yes."

"No."

"If we asked for help?"

"Elora, I'm sorry. This whole city of sorcerers is no match for her. She ensorcelled the Monarchs of the Twelve Great Realms. In mortal combat, she slew a dragon!"

"I slew them all," Elora said, in barely a whisper. "I slew them *all.*" Then, at last, she faced him. "So. Magic can't defeat the Deceiver. We know she possesses attributes of demons, she has no corporeal existence of her own, she needs a host to live and function in our world. That's why she claimed Mohdri, that's why she wants me. For all intents and purposes, she may well be composed of magic. And here are the Chengwei with a device that destabilizes magic. And here are you, helping them perfect it."

"The Deceiver is the enemy, Elora. This weapon may make the difference against her."

"How can that be? You just said this whole city of sorcerers is no match for her."

"They are Daikini. That fact, and the arrogance that walks with it, may prove their undoing. They work only with Daikini tools, see only with Daikini eyes; the magic they wield is that which comes most easily and naturally to Daikini. Even Bavmorda understood there was more to the world than that. If we can take the foundation they have laid and expand it to include the forces and powers of the other Great Realms, then we may have something."

"You've seen, you've *felt,* what it can do. Yet you would make this device even more deadly?"

"I've also seen, and felt, what the Deceiver can do, Elora."

"Consider this well, Drumheller. You know the truth of who she is. The Deceiver is me."

"Not so." His voice was still as hers, but the vehemence in it made her blink. "She is someone who bears the name Elora Danan. She is not *you*."

"Semantics, Drumheller. Mixed with a little sophistry. She claims to hail from a future consumed by Shadow. A world so bereft of all that we value and treasure she felt she had no choice but to destroy it in order to save it. Is hers the path we should follow?"

"If you were a common soul instead of the Sacred Princess, would you follow her?"

She climbed from the tub and padded warily into the next room for a towel. She took care with every step. Crystal might be lovely to look at but it was slicker than ice when wet and she had no desire to take a tumble, tempting as it was to yield to the oblivion of violent unconsciousness.

"So what then?" she asked as the light caught her, flashing off her glistening skin as off a polished surface. "We eat the stones that are set before us?"

"If you follow the Nelwyn proverb, when offered a banquet of stones you crush them to powder and use them to season your fields for the next crop. Also, as we've discussed before, if the Deceiver knows everything, by rights we should have been beaten at the start."

"From year to year, generation to generation, the Quangzhua changes its course. New twists and turns, new sandbars, it's been known to wander for miles off an established route. But the destination never changes. Always, it flows to the sea. Could time be the same? The details can alter, but the thrust of history remains intact."

"I don't know. I pray not."

"Drumheller, should I surrender?"

"Is that why you came, to ask me that?"

"I came to rescue you."

"By walking into a trap you knew was there?"

"I came to stop you."

"That's better."

"You still owe me an answer."

"Surrender, Elora Danan? Ask yourself first, would you trust the fate of the world—of that future you spoke of—in her hands?"

Elora had no answer for him then, nor when they were escorted down to dinner.

The gown provided for her was silk but that was the only thing it had in common with her scullery costume. It came in layers and it was obvious at a glance that it couldn't be donned without considerable assistance. In addition, a wooden mannequin head had been provided, made up to demonstrate how her face was to be painted; atop it was set the wig she was likewise expected to wear. It was composed of real Daikini hair, arranged in the most artful and elaborate of styles, anchored in place by a set of enamel pins. The bulk of the coiffure, however, fell in a waterfall mane that was half as long as Elora stood tall. Supporting the weight alone would give Elora's neck a wicked strain.

She cast a jaundiced eye toward her companion, who'd been presented with a suit of robes so layered and complex he'd be lucky to be able to breathe, much less move.

"It is the most formal culture in our Realm," he explained.

"In *any* Realm," she countered.

The makeup was equally ornate. A base coat of chalk white would cover her face, her neck, the front of her shoulders to the upper curve of her breasts and down her back to her shoulder blades. As well, her forearms and hands. Every part of her that would be on public view. Compared to this, and at its most statuesque, even her normal silver hue appeared more alive and animated.

Once Elora's features had been stripped of their defining characteristics—no hollows for her cheeks, no indication of lines about the eyes or nose—a brush of black ink would stroke the shape of an eyebrow with slightly arched deliberation. Her eyes were to be outlined in kohl, the border extended slightly beyond the orbit and upward to a small point, creating the impression that they were slanted, and then that space colored a striking shade of maroon. The hue chosen for her mouth tended more toward scarlet, defining its overall shape so as to make it appear much smaller and delicate, with sharply delineated points on the upper lip and a deep bow on the lower.

As for the clothes themselves, the first item was an underslip of gossamer magnificence, to be followed by layer upon layer of robes fastened as tightly as possible by sashes that reached from breasts to hips. Worse, the gown was so restrictive that her walk would be hobbled. She'd only be able to manage mincing little steps, like the modish women of the city, in their stacked heels and platform soles.

Elora scooped up the entire costume and the effort made her grunt. Fully arrayed, she'd be carrying the load equivalent of a knight in full armor but with virtually no freedom to maneuver.

Her face was set as she confronted the majordomo and she dismissed him with a single word.

"No," she said.

The man had sense enough not to argue. He turned visibly pale, but from outrage, and the barely veiled sneer was a masterpiece of restrained, refined, and absolute contempt. As he bowed and withdrew, he made no attempt to hide thoughts that were as transparent as the walls: *what else should one expect from a barbarian? And a girl!*

From her traveling pouch Elora drew a pair of trousers that fit as snugly as hose and which she tucked into soft-soled knee-high boots. Next came a long gown of wool so fine it was fair competition for Chengwei silk. Worn over a blouse of pristine samite, the gown's pagoda sleeves fell just past her elbows; it was likewise slit to the waist up both legs where it hugged her torso with becoming enthusiasm. Its stand-up collar fastened at the neck with ornate brocade frogs. The base fabric was a blue as dark as her eyes, embroidered with a pair of magnificent dragons in scarlet and silver. The threads glittered as she moved in the dress, creating the illusion that the dragons themselves were hiding in shadows; indeed, that they themselves were moving. Their eyes were appliquéd precious stones, with an additional dusting of gems to highlight their sinuous bodies. To finish, she buckled her belt once more about her waist, snugging it beneath the bodice of the gown, arranging the pouch so that it hung through the slit that exposed her left hip.

The ensemble was undeniably royal and bespoke a culture that valued practicality as much as ceremony. A formal occasion was no excuse for lowering your guard, or forgetting your warrior origins. Dressed so, a Princess could easily lead her consort onto the dance floor, or her men into pitched battle.

She gasped when she saw Drumheller, who'd forsaken his usual dark earth tones and ruggedly serviceable cloth for a suit of pristine samite, a white so pure and unsullied it hurt the eyes, with a minor enchantment woven into the threads themselves to repel dust and any and all stains. Interlaced with the basic fabric was a pattern worked in gold, accented in precious stones, making it a gown fit more for a Prince than a sorcerer. Yet the cut and workmanship was of such quality that every element managed to complement the wearer. Thorn's lack of stature didn't matter, nor his barrel chest, nor the fact that he wasn't the most beautiful of men. He looked like what he was, a figure of uncommon strength and courage, character and valor, a match and more for those two and three times his height whose rank came to them as an inheritance.

She saw he was nervous and that moment, that purely human reaction, made her heart ache with relief. For her first thought when he stepped into view was a memory of Angwyn, the night of her Ascension, when the Nelwyn she believed was her protector tried his best to steal her soul. Somehow, that fateful night, the Deceiver had managed to craft herself a semblance of Thorn's features. That version of Drumheller had worn white and gold, and Elora herself had been wrapped in gowns so tight they might have been the swaddling clothes that bound her as an infant.

She could barely move that night. She was a lamb well trussed for the slaughter.

If not for the real Thorn, the Nelwyn walking by her side, this War of Shadows would have been over before it began.

Together, the Sacred Princess and her Sorcerer strode down to confront their captors.

Elora found herself thinking of the lives taken in the years since. Not just those who fell on the battlefield but people far afield, who knew nothing of the combatants of the conflict yet whose fate hung just as much in the balance. Who would be blessed or cursed by an outcome over which they had no control.

"It always comes down to killing," she muttered aloud by accident, giving voice to thoughts she meant to keep to herself.

There was no escort, beyond the majordomo. There was no need. An itch burning up and down Elora's spine told her the Caliban was close.

"I beg your pardon?" said Thorn.

"We consider this a war. That means someone has to win, someone lose. You win by defeating the enemy. The surest way to defeat that enemy is to kill him."

"That is the usual way of it, yes."

"What a way to bind the Great Realms together, Thorn, by slaughtering whoever disagrees with you."

"The Deceiver has no such qualms."

"And isn't that supposed to be why we're against her?"

"And sometimes a fire must be started to stop a greater conflagration."

"I've never heard you talk like this."

"Perhaps I've never had reason."

"You never answered me before, about Tregare. What happened there, Drumheller?"

A pair of double doors blocked their way. Without preamble, once more dodging her question, Thorn pushed them open and ushered Elora into the atrium hall. Impressive as the space had looked from high above, beheld as it was meant to be seen it stole her breath away.

The floor was the most intricate mosaic, a multitude of jeweled tiles, none larger than a fingernail, as carefully cut as they were delicately colored. There was a quality to the air that made all her physical senses register things far more intensely. She perceived more shades to every hue than she had names for, yet viewed each with a clarity that was almost painful. From the floor rose fluted columns that might have been carved, but might as easily have been naturally occurring pillars of crystal that were shaped and pruned as an arborist might do a tree.

There was no distinct light source that Elora could discern, nothing to cast the slightest shadow; radiance appeared to burst forth from the core of every gem, as though the world itself were a star and they, visitors in its solid heart.

Everywhere Elora turned, she noted beauty, of a quality and perfection to make her head swim—not so hard a thing, regrettably, when the best she could manage was a hollow gasp—yet the more she saw the more disquiet she felt.

"Your friends didn't come up with this on their own, Drumheller." Her voice didn't go with the setting or the ceremony. It was too deep, too resonant, too much of the earth. "They had help."

"Inspiration."

"Whatever."

"Power always calls to power, Elora. So does ambition. It's a combustible mix."

A scattering of sorcerers from the Palace was already present. As if Elora's entrance were a cue, each succeeding minute brought new arrivals until the hall was thick with learned scholars. Though they clearly knew one another, they congregated among their own kind, each order wrapping itself in its own sense of superiority. They might be cooperating on this project, pooling resources and knowledge on an unprecedented scale, but none of them were happy about it. It forced them to look upon one another as equals, when each in his own heart knew himself to be greater by far.

The sole fanfare announced the arrival of the delegation from the Gate of Peace, led by the Khan himself. Elora, as the only woman present, as much as by her attire, had drawn her share of stares and sneers throughout the gathering. Now it was Anakerie's turn to bear the brunt of such attention.

She felt Thorn Drumheller stiffen beside her, as shocked by Anakerie's presence as Elora was, since the Princess Royal was supposed to be a "guest" of the Khagan in Daido.

"Must have taken some inducement to cut her loose," Elora muttered.

"She should not be here," Thorn breathed.

"The night's still young, my friend."

Unlike Elora, Anakerie hadn't been given the luxury of refusal. Her costume was similar to the one the young woman had been presented. It made her look like a doll, a toy brought along for the amusement of the host and other guests. He'd brought a retinue, and a detail of guards. The courtiers were allowed within the atrium, but only one officer. The guards remained beyond the moat. That made them the happiest of men.

The officer's armor gleamed and beneath his ornate helm he regarded the room as he would a potential battlefield. His height made him distinctive, yet he had the knack of fading from view every now and then. It wasn't that he actually disappeared. He seemed to withdraw from the awareness of those around him, and thereby blend with the background. The eye saw, but the mind ignored his presence.

Thorn had noted the officer's arrival, and recognized who it was as instantly as Elora had. It was Khory Bannefin.

On impulse, Elora pivoted on the ball of one foot, sweeping her gaze over the galleries that rose from the atrium. They were gone from sight, masked by the same translucent fog that hid the object at the broad end of the room.

"They're taking their privacy seriously, Drumheller," she muttered to the Nelwyn beside her.

"With good reason."

"So damn' mysterious."

"Telling you won't help you understand, Elora. This, you have to see for yourself."

To a scattering of applause, the Vicar-General of the Crystal Palace stepped before the assemblage. He made a speech of welcome and then, proudly, unveiled his marvel.

The device was roughly twelve feet square and twice that in height, topped by a roofed platform that was reached from the ground via a steep stepladder. Its corners were framed in foot-square panels, each bearing the sigil of one of the Great Realms. Otherwise the interior workings of the mechanism were open to view. Elora made out a rotating drum, twelve levels high, with twelve figures mounted on each plate like horses on a carousel. Each figure was a representation of the dominant element or race of the various Realms: a firedrake for the Realm of Fire, a golem (a creature made of stone) for that of Earth, a zephyr for Air, Wyrrn for Water. But the plates themselves were the real marvel. Thanks to multiple sets of interlocking gears and wheels, not only did the main plate spin but so also did three subordinate ones built into it, representing the Three Prime Circles, the World, the Flesh, the Spirit. Move any one of those four plates and you set the other three in motion, thereby altering the relationship of all the various components.

The drum as a whole was linked by clockwork gears to a series of waterwheels, which could allow the plates on the drum to turn independently of each other and at different rates of speed. At the heart of the apparatus was another wheel, on which were mounted a dozen intricately faceted crystals. The hub of that wheel enclosed yet another gem, which Elora took to be a diamond since it was as clear as the Palace itself, and bigger than Khory's clenched fist. Directly above that crystal-spoked wheel, on a floor level with the topmost plate of the rotating drum, was mounted a globe of the same jeweled substance, better than a foot in diameter, far too big to occur in nature.

During her apprenticeship with Thorn's cousin, Torquil, Elora had mainly worked with metal. But the Rock Nelwyns were as renowned for their artistry with gems as their facility with ore. She knew the effort and skill that went into cutting and polishing those precious stones, she couldn't imagine what it must have taken to produce this monster. The slightest flaw, the most minute imperfection, at any point in the process, would ruin everything. The sorcerers would have to start again from the beginning. Judging from the expressions she saw around her that must have happened, more than once.

To her amazement, she saw something in this convocation of sorcerers on the order of a miracle. On these faces, by turns and degrees aged, dissolute, degenerate, corrupt—on these men who had sacrificed everything for their art and the ambition that drove them—she saw a flash of wonder. Of an innocence that hearkened back to the first sublime moment each of them had accomplished a feat of magic.

It was a moment that she would never forget, but that she prayed they would. For to be reminded so starkly of all they might have been, of the potential they had squandered, the gift they had dishonored, and then be confronted with the inescapable reality of what they were and likely would remain, that was a punishment too cruel to be endured.

Thorn spoke quietly, as if he'd read her thoughts.

"Some might say it's no less than they deserve."

"No argument. I'd just prefer this once to err on the side of mercy." Elora couldn't stay still. She was like a racehorse champing at the bit, wanting to charge, forced to remain at rest. The raw tension in her bones and muscles tested her more than a full-scale workout.

"What's wrong?" Thorn asked.

"Too much magic," she said. "Too much power concentrated in a single place. Did people not learn *anything* from what happened in Angwyn?"

"An attack?"

"It's what I'd do, given this tempting a target."

"You counted on this being a trap. They're counting on the Deceiver being that predictable."

"You said they were no match for her."

"They aren't. They know it. They're also Daikini. They're used to being overmatched by every other race in the Realms. How is it that Daikini tend to resolve that riddle?"

"They build a machine."

"And here you have it. The device they hope will prove their great equalizer."

"Forgive me, Thorn, but it's far more than that."

The Vicar-General had begun to speak.

"For the glory of the Khagan," he proclaimed in a dry and serene tone, his voice so bland it took considerable effort to pay attention to it, "recognizing both the peril of these days and the opportunity, we rival orders set aside our ancient differences." Elora understood at once the reason for the Vicar-General's obviously artificial composure; the more extreme the noise, of any kind, the greater the danger of introducing a flaw into the body of the Palace. That also explained the mist that rendered the walls either translucent or outright opaque. It probably possessed some sound-dampening qualities as well, to protect the crystal.

"This is the moment"—the Vicar-General waved an arm to encompass the device behind him—"and this the means, to be not the subjects of prophecy, and mayhap its victims, but the masters of our fate.

"The Great Realms stand poised on the brink of a transcendence that occurs once every epoch. When it passes, nothing that we know may remain the same. The opportunity will not come again until long after the brightest lights of our own era have burned out, and our greatest works fallen to dust. If ever there was a day to be seized, this is it!

"The primal arcane energies of the cosmos itself will be harnessed by our Clockwork Resonator, focused and amplified to a degree unattainable in nature alone. Then, through a meticulously crafted magical formula, those forces will be applied to each of the Great Realms in turn, reordering them—even restructuring them—according to our requirements."

Klik-klak Klik-klak

The Vicar-General paused, brow furrowing, features twisting with evident discomfort, as though he'd been wickedly pinched.

Elora meanwhile was aghast, and she gave full voice to her horror and her disbelief with Thorn's own words.

"Are you all bloody *insane?*" she cried.

Klik-klak Klik-klak

The Vicar-General worked his mouth, but no words came forth. One arm flailed to the side and behind him, fingers scrabbling for purchase on the carved and polished surface of the device, the only object in the Palace save for various rare bits of furniture not cast from crystal.

"This—*toy?*" Elora shouted. "This building? The conjurations of finite, *mortal* beings against the whole of Creation?"

"It can be done, Elora," Thorn said quietly. "In theory."

She rounded on him, more in shock than rage.

"And you should know better than anyone why it must not. Have you forgotten Tir Asleen, Drumheller? Have you forgotten the Cataclysm? You've felt the power of this device, how can you stand by and watch it used?"

"Have you considered the alternative?"

Klik-klak Klik-klak

The Vicar-General's other hand pressed against his chest, in a futile attempt to force out the piercing ache that was tormenting him. His body hunched over itself, its language speaking eloquently of confusion and disarray.

"What's the old engineer's saying," Thorn said, " 'Provide me the proper lever, I can topple the world'?"

"The operative word being *topple*. And when this device brings all the Realms crashing down to ruins, what then?"

"At the very least the Deceiver will be neutralized."

"That's too neat a choice of words, Drumheller. How very Chengwei of you. Better to say she'll be dead."

"I would consider that a fair price for all she's done."

"*I* would consider you wrong."

"Elora Danan, how can you say that?"

"This can't be about killing, Thorn. Killing's where it all started, with my mother, remember, butchered in a Nockmaar dungeon. No," she realized with a blinding flash, "it started long before that, don't you see? Our Epoch began with a war, maybe the cruelest ever known. And that war ended with a betrayal. Those are the defining keystones of our world: blood and treachery. Yes, the cause was noble. Yes, it was a fight for freedom against the most tyrannical of oppression. But it could also be the reason why the Realms have been at each other's throats ever since.

"The *ard-righ* Eamon Asana betrayed his warlord, the woman who loved him, for what he thought was the greater good. The ends justified the means. After that, who could dare trust again? And if the Malevoiy could be cast out by blood and fire, why not the Daikini, or the Realms of Faery?

"The Malevoiy should have been at my Ascension. Every other Great Realm was represented, why not them?"

"They're evil, Elora."

"You can't pick and choose, Thorn. They're a Great Realm for a reason."

"I'd call it a mistake."

Klik-klak Klik-klak

The Vicar-General brought his hand away and found it soaked, as was his robe, with his own blood. He cried out, but no one heard. No one noticed. In a room full of the most powerful sorcerers in a nation constructed upon the bedrock of magic, he had been fully enshrouded in a glamour and none around him was the wiser.

Too late, Elora made the connection between the man and the distant sounds that had been gradually, but ever more emphatically, impinging on her consciousness. Sharp, staccato taps, striking like spikes but with the unwavering constancy of a metronome, so regular a cadence she almost mistook it for the ticking of a clock and wondered if the Vicar-General had set his infernal device in motion without telling anyone.

They were footfalls.

With that realization, the very air before her appeared to shred, the way a piece of cloth will if left too long at the mercy of the elements. The Vicar-General seemed to sense Elora's awareness of him, he turned a little toward the young woman, tried to reach out a pair of imploring arms, her own eyes going round as marbles at the sight of him.

Klik-klak Klik-klak

The old man's body spasmed, as though he'd been struck from behind by some monstrous edged weapon. He arched like a drawn bow and blood sprayed from him in an awful fountain, to strike the floor and Elora together. His own cry was matched by hers and though she knew he was dead, she dived forward to catch him as he fell, in the vain hope that there might be something she could do.

As he toppled into Elora's arms, the glamour vanished, allowing all present to behold what was transpiring.

In the background, a susurrus of agitation and alarm rose from the crowd, accusations flying every which way, accompanied by demands that the Khan summon his troops, that the sorcerers repair to their own palaces for safety. The chaos and panic was reflexive. It would last but a minute before some more rational soul—possibly the Khan, who had seen his share of battles and bloody murder, or Khory or even one of the sorcerers—applied common sense to the situation and calmed everyone's fears.

Elora knew they wouldn't have that minute, and figured rightly that even if they did, it wouldn't save them.

Her eyes sought Khory's, meaning to coordinate some defense and possibly an escape, but when their gazes locked Elora found herself staggered by an image thrown forth from the collective memory they shared. The force of the vision was so emphatic that she lost her footing, tumbling almost all the way to the floor before she managed to catch herself, though one leg was twisted from the hip at an angle it didn't much appreciate, enough to make Elora wince.

The pain didn't register. Nor did any aspect of the atrium. She was in another room, worn stone, dank air, as badly lit as heated by a reluctant hearth. She saw the scene through the eyes of Khory Bannefin and beheld her friend, her comrade in arms, her monarch, the *ard-righ* Eamon Asana hand up a golden goblet to toast the impending battle with the Malevoiy and the hope of triumph. She drained it dry, for the wine was delicious. The next she knew, her captains were slain by those selfsame Malevoiy and she had been delivered to them as their captive. Her King, her friend, had betrayed her, for what he firmly believed was the good of his Realm, and all the others.

Now Elora Danan was being given leave by Khory to do the same.

"No!" she cried, in her fullest battlefield voice, but nobody heard her.

Because that was when the doors shattered.

Being crystal, the sound should have resembled shattering glass, but it was nothing of the sort. It began with a note of music, so extreme in pitch and intensity that it hurt, yet also projecting a wondrous beauty. The note splintered, as though it could be parsed like a sentence into all its constituent elements, each vibration a match for the hairline fractures that erupted across the face of the doors.

The explosion, when it came, was marked by the abrupt cessation of that melody. In silence, shards of gleaming, dagger-point crystal burst through the air, as murderous a fusillade as any barrage of arrows. The quiet was short-lived, hardly more than a heartbeat, before the air filled with shrieks of pain and alarm as the projectiles struck their targets. Sorcerers clutched at themselves, twisted desperately to and fro in an attempt to find cover, dropped in terror, in agony, in death while those shards which missed ended their flight against walls or floor with a succession of elegant chimes.

Khory was bloodied by the attack but her armor saved her and Anakerie from any grievous harm, as she shielded the Princess Royal with her own body. Elora did much the same with Thorn, dropping over him on all fours and crushing him beneath her.

"Did you think I wouldn't notice?" said the Deceiver from the doorway, in that mocking good humor reserved by executioners for the condemned.

Elora levered herself around for a view of her foe. The Deceiver was as she'd appeared in Tyrrel's Realm, though perhaps more beautiful than ever. Gold of hair, fair of skin, this was the Elora Danan that should have been if you ignored the cruel twist that accented even the most overtly generous of expressions and the fact that the eyes were flat inside, the soul so well hidden it was like looking into the doll's eyes of a shark. Her armor was the same as before, making the Deceiver appear as though she'd been dipped in gleaming onyx chitin. The boots looked better made for posing than for any sort of activity, be it walking, riding, or battle, with a heel like a spike.

But then, Elora thought, *what better way to strike at the magicians than through the Palace that was both home and the repository of their power?* With every step, those heels struck the crystal floor of the Palace like chisels, and the constant, inflexible pace had set up a resonance pattern whose cumulative power was deadly beyond words. The simple act of striding from the building's entrance to this chamber had not only fractured the surfaces the Deceiver walked on but the Vicar-General's body as well.

"Did you think I wouldn't know what you planned?" There was genuine bemusement in the Deceiver's tone, that she could still be so underestimated. "Poor, pitiful, benighted wretches, you've been mine from the start."

A new sound intruded, that of tiny bells chiming in concert to the tread of feet like pile drivers. Huge though the doorway was, the Caliban seemed to fill it, to make it and the atrium itself appear somehow smaller than life-size, thereby diminishing those within as well.

The Vicars-General of the other orders took heart from the creature's entrance, even as the Deceiver moved into the room, clearing a space between her and the new arrival, and Elora saw an echo of herself in the way the woman cocked her head, set her body, assumed a wary thoughtfulness as she assessed what had to be a potential threat.

From one voice, cracked and shaken by what had happened so that what was meant as a martial command emerged more as a querulous plea: "Kill her!" From another: "Destroy the abomination!" They weren't afraid, not really, not yet. They respected the Deceiver's power, but they assumed the Caliban would prove its checkmate, especially in concert with their own.

Right or wrong, Elora wasn't interested in staying to find out. She looked for Thorn, to discover that the Nelwyn had crossed to the dais and, after a glance at the remains of the Vicar-General, was staring intently at the Resonator, the way Elora herself did when she was trying to fix a picture indelibly in her mind.

She called to Khory, in time to see the warrior draw her sword. It was a Chengwei blade, shorter and thicker than her own broadsword, but she handled it just as well. Khory yanked Anakerie clear of the crowd, at the same time putting as much distance as possible between the pair of them and the villains at the door. Then, in a maneuver executed so quickly and superbly that it registered on Elora's senses as only a blur, she slashed her weapon straight down the length of Anakerie's back.

With that weight of steel, and the force of a roundhouse strike like Khory employed, it was the kind of blow that easily broke bones. The slightest error would have crippled Anakerie for certain, and more likely left her dead. What happened instead was that Khory slashed through nearly all the gowns impeding the other woman's movements. The pair of them scuttled about the edge of the crowd, Anakerie engaging in a series of awkward hops and skips as she wrenched herself loose of her ensemble, leaving herself just a silk shift.

While this was occurring, the sorcerers took the initiative in their own defense. In the blink of an eye, the air became supersaturated with the hollow smell of ozone as bolts of lightning ripped forth from scores of hands, the prelude to combat spells of incredible lethality.

For all the good they did, the sorcerers might as well have been fighting the Deceiver with wood swords in a training yard. Infuriated more than afraid, still confident in their ultimate triumph, the Chengwei wizards redoubled their efforts.

It was a magician's kind of fight; Elora had no qualms about leaving them to it.

"We have to find another exit," she bellowed over the steadily increasing din, many of the spells generating a threnody response from the Palace, like the wailing of lost souls.

"From this room," Thorn told them, "there isn't one!"

"Can we climb or levitate to the next level and use the gallery to escape?"

That must have been the right idea, because it galvanized the Caliban into purposeful action. To that point, the creature had simply held its position. Now, to the sorcerers' alarm it charged, bulling its way through their ranks toward the Deceiver with the force of a battering ram.

The consequences for the Chengwei were devastating. These were sorcerers, whose greatest weapon was their knowledge. They could summon forces capable of reducing fortresses of stone and steel to dust, and laying waste to whole cities, but they had as little experience as liking for a brutal, old-fashioned, knock-down-drag-out fistfight. Bodies went flying, some so broken by the confrontation that they didn't move again. Others scrambled for their lives, while a mad few attempted to stop both the Caliban's onslaught, and the Deceiver's as well, as she took advantage of the sudden confusion.

Wizards discorporated the fundamental order of matter and thereby transmuted collective physical reality into a collapsing house of cards. Spells were unleashed of such malevolence and ferocity that even Drumheller blanched at the sight, for he knew the terrible cost exacted by such foul conjurations.

Specters of ice were conjured, and of fire. The Deceiver was assaulted with spells that slowed time to a crawl, and accelerated it to such a rate that decades passed in the space of heartbeats. The Chengwei transformed air to acid so corrosive that metal armor was eaten away to nothing at the merest contact; its effect on flesh was even more dreadful. All of this horror was hurled at the Deceiver and was as deftly parried, so that this fearsome attempt by the assembled sorcerers to destroy their foe served only to decimate their own ranks instead.

Those exposed chose to end their lives with a single breath of that toxic cloud, considering it a merciful release from the unpardonable agony of an entire body being eaten alive. And that was far from the most terrible effects of those increasingly loathsome spells. Bodies were seen to sweat blood, they went blind, flesh melted from bones which then remained animated and deadly until smashed to bits.

Throughout, the Deceiver and the Caliban maintained a delicate and deadly balance that reminded Elora of stories she'd heard of bull dancers, where folk her own age would go into a ring with a full-grown longhorn. It was part performance, part ritual, as they tempted the bull into a charge again and again, trusting to their own speed and agility to spare them from harm. Honor was won through the closeness of the miss, and the grace of the evasion. But this was a game with little margin for error against a foe with no concept of mercy.

So it was here between the Deceiver and the Caliban. She dared him to the attack, and used each charge to lay waste to more of the Chengwei sorcerers unfortunate enough to be caught in his path. He may have been an unstoppable force but she was an object who never stopped moving; regardless of how hard the Caliban tried to reach her, the Deceiver always managed to be somewhere else. She used none of her power against him. That she left to the Chengwei, preferring to take the fullest possible measure of her new foe.

As the battle progressed, she didn't seem pleased by what she saw.

Thorn added nothing to the carnage. His sole focus quickly became the safeguarding of his companions, mainly Khory and Anakerie as they made their way around the edge of the killing ground to join him. Some of the threats could be dealt with by a basic, all-encompassing mystical shield. That was what he used to protect them from the acid air. Most, unfortunately, required specific counterspells and they had to be blocked with the same skill and care a warrior would use against an oncoming blade or arrow. Worse, this had to be done at breakneck speed, without hesitation or margin for error since these attacks came at them from virtually every quarter, either directly or as ricochets. At the same time, Thorn had to keep himself alive, and Elora as well—though in his heart of hearts he gambled that, since this was a magical battle, her innate immunity would afford her a significant measure of protection.

In truth, Elora thought much the same.

They both forgot the maxim that Drumheller had repeated so often: immune she might be to spells, but she was still a living woman, existing in corporeal form in a physical world. The pure spell might do no harm, but the collateral damage—its tangible consequences—could be fatal.

A knot of sorcerers, from at least three separate disciplines, all of them magi in their own right, at the peak of both craft and art, conjured a melding spell, sacrificing their own individuality in favor of a gestalt that would increase the raw power and lethality of their abilities tenfold. They tore a ragged gash in space before them and a frightful howling was heard; a hurricane wind suddenly sprang into being within the atrium, as though this other place they'd contacted was utterly empty of *everything,* and all the sum and substance of this reality was flooding through the hole to fill it. At the same time, as the poor souls closest to the opening were plucked off their feet and hurled into what was hopefully oblivion and even the Caliban's massive feet began to slip ever so slightly across the polished floor, the edges of the melded wizards began to blur and crumble themselves. This last-ditch attempt to destroy their foes was consuming them as well. The race was to see who would perish first.

Amidst the chaos, with lesser but still fearful spells flying thick and fast, only Elora noticed a wall bow ever so slightly. Only Elora heard a jangling tone that was the closest the Crystal Palace could come to an outright shriek. She beheld how the patterns of force and energy were being twisted by the gestalt and, far more alarming, that once the life energies of the melded sorcerers were bound into the portal they had opened, the spell would become self-perpetuating. This gateway could never be closed. To save the world, they had set in motion the means of its total destruction.

She cried to them to stop but even if they heard her over the unholy din she knew they were beyond hearing, or caring.

She lunged for them, although she had no idea what to do to shut them down. Too late, she realized someone else had been pacing her thoughts, step for step. Only when the Deceiver acted it was with characteristic ruthlessness. Elora was searching for an answer that might somehow save the men involved. The Deceiver preferred them dead.

They were so focused on their purpose, they had neither wit nor assets to spare in their own defense. The Deceiver merely gathered up the cell of acid air and puffed it straight for them.

The cloud and Elora arrived together.

For the three sorcerers in the meld, it was like touching a match to a grand illustration outlined in Chengwei thunderpowder. There was a cascading rush of sound and light and color that filled the atrium with a brilliant succession of rainbows, a series of escalating explosions that taken as individual events were no more than a sequence of *pop* sounds. Yet as an aggregate, the force of their annihilation flattened every figure remaining in the room, save for the Caliban and the Deceiver, who too late saw that her stratagem had claimed one unintended victim.

At the moment of contact, Elora lost all capacity for thought and thankfully for sensation. This experience was too far beyond her mind's capacity to comprehend. As if she were someone else, watching from a safe remove, she saw her gown shrivel, its threads instantly burned to cinders by the caustic atmosphere. Her skin didn't fare much better and for the first time, she saw that argent perfection—which had withstood every insult since her initial transformation without a flaw or scar—utterly ruined. Raw welts appeared along the length of her body as animal reflex wound her into a tight little ball. The flesh was being seared like meat on a roasting spit, right down to the bone.

She wanted to turn away. She wanted more than anything to sever the link binding this spirit form of hers to its physical host. The alternative, returning to her body, was unthinkable. She didn't know if she possessed the power to heal such frightful wounds, she feared suddenly more than anything that she did—because to do so would mean having to experience the agony that the paralyzed pain receptors in her nerve endings had thus far spared her. Better to embrace death.

Sacred childe, she heard from a familiar voice, there is an alternative.

A new figure revealed itself to her bruised perceptions.

It stood alone yet was the embodiment of its entire race. Daikini in basic form, though no Daikini was ever so tall nor so lean, and precious few of the High Elves of Greater Faery, either. Here was something that relished the delights of the flesh and saw no purpose in denying any of them. There was an overlying air of softness and corruption about him, like looking at something dead before its time, but Elora recognized it as a deception. It moved too easily, its strength well masked but unmistakable, its fundamental nature that of a predator too long absent from the hunt and eager to pick up where it left off. It was a presentation in chiaroscuro, stark contrasts in black and white: alabaster skin, ebon hair, jet nails sharpened to dagger points, lips and eyes defined by dramatic sweeps of paint. In presentation, it was a disconcerting mix of genders. Both form and ensemble created an androgynous combination that proved irresistibly enticing to either sex of any living race, from either side of the Veil.

Its clothes created the sense that it was cloaked, gathering portions of darkest night, allowing only the barest, tantalizing glimpses of the form within. Watching, Elora felt a disturbing mix of sensations, the enticement of gazing upon something utterly forbidden vying with the certain knowledge that it was wrong. However, those many, intricate folds couldn't disguise the flash of sigils and mail, the shimmer of personal defensive wards, the outline of hidden weapons. It was extraordinarily well protected against attacks both temporal and magical. Despite its languid manner, it looked eager to join the battle, sad that such was still impossible.

Still, if it could raise a champion to stand in its place.

"What do you want from me?" Elora demanded of the Malevoiy, hating the tingle the sight of this ancient creature inspired in her. It had presented himself in the form and manner that would prove most attractive to Elora, reaching out on levels she didn't even know existed within her. The terror she felt at her own response was as unbearable as it was delicious.

Thy destiny was its infuriatingly amused reply.

Two howls came to her dimly, as if from the greatest imaginable distance. Elora turned her phantom head, saw twin masks of shock and horror stamped across the features of both Thorn and the Deceiver, as if they were twisted reflections in some macabre funhouse mirror. Wholly different beings manifesting an identical emotion, torn without warning or mercy from each of their souls. They reacted as one, casting forth waves of energy that wiped the contagion clean from around where Elora's body lay. Powerful though the Chengwei sorcerers might have been, this casual display of strength put them in their place—and at the same time cruelly humbled both practitioners, for that was the extent of what they could offer in Elora's aid. She was immune to magic, and for all their good intentions—in this one, unique moment where circumstance demanded they work in concert—they could do nothing to reverse the terrible effects of the acid mist. Those wounds were purely physical; Elora would have to manifest any healing herself.

Their attention was focused on Elora's body, and the young woman realized neither was aware of the Malevoiy's presence.

Thorn reached her body first but could not bring himself to touch it, on his knees before the utter ruin of her flesh, his own hands trembled with a helplessness he'd never felt before, not even when he beheld the scarred landscape where once had stood the fortress of Tir Asleen. His eyes were wide with shock and the kind of madness that comes to those who've tempted the Abyss for too much of their lives. The only difference between his gaze and the Deceiver's was that she had long ago embraced this madness, clutching it to her more passionately and completely than any lover. It was what had allowed her to survive all those bleak and bloody years, and to do the things she felt were required of her to save her world.

The melded wizards mistook this instant of stillness as the perfect opportunity for a final attack, but they'd reckoned without the Caliban. It struck with hands so massive they could enclose a man's entire head, backed by the strength to crush bone like eggshells. Which it did, with ruthless, implacable efficiency and afterward breathed in the heady essence of the slain men's souls, as if it were the most intoxicating of fragrances, adding them to its trophy collection of chimes.

"No more," moaned the phantom Elora.

The power to end this conflict can be thine, Sacred Princess.

"What do you mean?" she demanded, reacting to the Malevoiy's mild words as though they were a burning lash across skin already tormented beyond endurance. She knew it spoke of far more than just this battle. It offered her victory.

Wouldst dissemble, at this juncture? Thou know'st full well what is required of thee and what thou wouldst gain in return.

"They don't have to fight, Thorn and the Deceiver."

But they shall. They know no other path.

Anakerie leaped forward in a mad dash, rolling under the Caliban's sweeping left arm to bring herself right up against Thorn. She grabbed him by the arms and tried to pull him clear, only to learn the utter futility of trying to move a Nelwyn who wasn't in the mood. Easier by far to shift a mountain bare-handed. Sadly, that left both of them at the mercy of the Caliban, who of course had none.

"Stop this," Elora commanded of the Malevoiy. "Save them!"

The creature opposite her merely laughed, that dry, malevolent chuckle that carried with it the sense of bones cracking between predatory teeth.

To claim thy birthright, Sacred Princess, it said at last, thou must accept *all* the Great Realms within the circle of thy dominion. Shall We who are the greatest Realm of the Circle of the Flesh, who stand sentinel at the gateway to the Circle of the Spirit, be denied Our true and rightful place because of what once was?

And do it quickly, Elora told herself, *before these lives you hold dear pay the forfeit.* It wasn't just Anakerie and Thorn who were at risk. She sensed without looking—for some instinct of primal self-preservation mandated she not take her awareness away from the Malevoiy—that Khory was moving forward to confront the Caliban, sword at the ready, futile though the warrior knew her gesture would be.

Elora's thought of Khory transmitted itself to the Malevoiy, for the creature drew itself up and away, mouth curling in a sneering rictus that was the embodiment of hatred and disgust.

It didn't need to state the terms of this alliance, they were utterly clear as could be in the inhuman gaze that met Elora's, and the young woman had to marvel at how it could so closely mimic the Daikini form and yet retain an essence that was wholly alien to it, and inimical.

The world is in thy charge, Elora Danan. And the future.

It said no more. It didn't have to.

She had no choice. There'd been none from the start. As the Malevoiy said, there were twelve Great Realms. They were one of them. They had to be embraced. By her.

Whatever the cost.

It smiled, as radiant an expression as Elora Danan could remember seeing, and she felt a thrill of horror at how naturally that word could be applied to a creature so quintessentially baneful.

Then she smiled back, matching its welcome with one of her own, and felt a warm explosion of excitement deep within her belly. Something new and fearsome reared up, swelling like a riptide to fill the casement of her spirit.

On the floor of the atrium, her left hand spasmed closed. A small movement, that should have gone unnoticed beneath the looming bulk of the Caliban as it closed on Thorn and Anakerie and Khory. Except that as her fingertips scraped across the gleaming crystal on which Elora lay, her nails suddenly elongated into claws and they made an awful, keening noise as they gouged deep runnels in a surface that had thus far remained pristine and unmarred, even by the acid.

Those wizards who still survived, who called the Crystal Palace home, shrieked in concert with that sound, adding to the general bedlam. They reacted as if they'd been stabbed by ice picks and the more powerful among them clutched at themselves as great wounds opened in their bodies and blood and life fled from them as from their Vicar-General.

With a lurch, Elora Danan shoved herself to all fours, revealing that her front had suffered from the acid as badly as what could already be seen. Even Anakerie, the most hardened of campaigners, choked back a wail at the sight. Thorn had no words to offer, not comfort, not rage, not grief; all that came from him were tears, representing a sorrow that had no truer expression.

She answered both with a grin, revealing fangs that stood out with supernal purity against her charred skin.

The Deceiver released the greatest cry of fury any of them had ever heard, as if she'd somehow tapped into all the rage of all the beings who had ever walked this world since time itself began and given it full voice. That outburst brought her to the attention of the Caliban, which had ignored her before now. It seemed somehow to recognize her as prey that had once escaped, and appreciated the opportunity to finally claim her.

The blow it struck at her never landed.

As she had in Sandeni, Khory straddled Elora's hunched and blistered form, and by doing so placed herself between the Caliban and the Deceiver. Her Chengwei blade burned the air with the speed and force of her attack. She struck true, with all her extraordinary skill and strength—and the blade snapped cleanly in two.

Still, the impact was sufficient to stagger the Caliban. That was all the opening Khory needed as she reached down and scooped Elora into her arms. Her intent was to pick up where they'd all left off a few minutes before, and find a way out of this charnel pit.

She never got the chance.

Elora used a move that Khory herself had taught, to tangle the taller woman's legs and shift the balance of their weight in Elora's favor. Revealing a power that easily eclipsed both Khory's and Elora's herself, she pitched the warrior over a hip, allowing the momentum of that throw to carry them both across the sleek crystal floor away from the others until they dropped beyond sight over the edge of the dais.

Darkness flared, a shadow so intense it hurt the eyes to behold it, so that even the Deceiver was forced to squint. It refracted crazily from every facet of the wall and floor and ceiling, from pillars and decorative arches, from each piece of crystal that had been scored or chipped or broken during the battle, as though lines of blackest paint, composed of such fierce energy that their merest touch raised burns, were being drawn in the very air.

In the heart of this maelstrom, Elora and Khory reared up together into view. Elora's hand speared upward; it was impossible to tell whether or not it held a weapon until Khory's reaction made the answer plain. The warrior spasmed forward, her face twisting into a fearful rictus of pain, and she filled the room with such a scream that all the others who still survived paused a moment, shocked to stillness even in this slaughterhouse by such primal agony.

Elora scooped up her companion and held her aloft, the young woman illuminated by such sable glory that her very silhouette appeared to melt. Savaged flesh desiccated to ash and flaked off her body, as though the darkness itself carried with it the force of a wind, revealing underneath the sleek, seamless perfection of obsidian.

She held that pose for a moment that seemed to last forever, and then cast Khory Bannefin to her feet, into the heart of the darkness that had claimed her.

As before, Elora Danan best resembled a sculptor's casting brought to life—only the nature of the material had undergone a fundamental change. Where before she was silver, of a glistening argent purity, now she was a being of absolute ebon darkness. Nothing about her was comforting or even remotely kind, her every aspect bespoke the power and nature of a huntress.

She offered the room a lazy, inviting smile and took the measure of every being before her, lingering longest on the Deceiver, then the Caliban, then Drumheller.

"Elora Danan," Thorn managed to say, amazed that he still retained the power of speech, "is that you?"

There was pity in her eyes but not from gentleness. It was the look seen by prey at the outcry of a last, futile plea for mercy.

"I am Elora Danan," she said, sucking hope from the hearts before her as she might soon the marrow from their shattered bones. "I am Malevoiy."

CHAPTER
9

FOR A TIMELESS MOMENT, NOBODY MOVED. NOBODY dared. Thorn's hand was in his pocket; at his fingertips, a set of acorns that he always managed to carry with him. They were his ultimate defense, charged with ancient enchantments so virulent they could transform any living being into stone. They'd saved his life on more than one occasion but in his most miserable fantasy, he never dreamed that the day would dawn when he'd even consider using them against Elora Danan. Yet the moment she sprang for him, he knew he would hurl them without hesitation and pray for their success.

Elora ran her tongue over her teeth, savoring the sensation of her fangs, adding to an expression that made everyone present wonder how eagerly she anticipated the crunch of flesh and bone between her jaws and the taste of hot, fresh blood. Her fingers ended in claws and a line of equally wicked spurs flared up the leading edge of her forearm to the elbow, creating the indelible image of a creature who was all spikes and edges, who could not be touched without the risk of harm. The shape of her body, the way she moved and carried herself, bespoke a grace that transcended description, yet the purposes to which that grace and movement were dedicated could not be more deadly. Nothing that walked the world, on either side of the Veil—nothing ever created, or even conceived of, in those myriad Realms—came close to matching the elegant perfection of her form. She was beauty, in the fullest sense of the word. At the same time, though, nothing in reality, nothing in imagination, appeared more terrible.

The Hope of the World had become destruction incarnate. She needed no weapons, she *was* one herself, as well forged and keenly honed as any blade plucked from a swordsmith's foundry.

The Deceiver was the first to break the tableau, surprising the onlookers who knew her by striking directly instead of through a surrogate. And attacking physically, when all expected her to use magic. With a speed and suddenness that took them all by surprise, the Deceiver crossed to Elora in two giant steps and swung at her with both clenched fists, a blow that likely would have made a significant dent in the main walls of the Gate to Peace.

They never touched their target. Elora laughed aloud, a liquid trill underscored by the sound of grinding bones, and seemed to melt away from the Deceiver's attack. Many of those watching, who lacked the skill in sorcery to perceive the truth of what was happening, assumed she'd altered her shape. Thorn, among a very few, knew better, that Elora had simply moved away from her foe and then back again with such quickness and grace that the mind was fooled. She ducked in behind the Deceiver, adding her own strength to the momentum of the other's charge and heaving the woman away from her. She'd executed a textbook parry and was rewarded by the solid crash of the Deceiver's body into the nearest wall. The Deceiver opened a hole right through, sending a spiderweb of cracks and fissures off to either side and upward well past the first gallery.

With a banshee yowl that made the strongest of hearts seize up with terror, Elora leaped for her, only to find herself slapped down with the same casual brutality she'd employed herself. Her ebon form did its share of damage to the floor, but the woman herself wasn't harmed in the slightest. She regained her feet in an instant but that was as far as she got before the Deceiver hit her again, with a roundhouse sideswipe of energy that hammered her the length of the atrium. When Elora arose once more, without the slightest hesitation or any sign whatsoever to show that she'd suffered from blows that would have smashed any lesser being to a pulp, she was struck yet again.

For all the Deceiver's efforts, and they were considerable, Thorn saw at once that she was doing no damage to her foe. They were too evenly matched, the contest had become a stalemate, and would remain so until one or the other tired.

The scales of that balance could be tipped either way, by someone with the power to act, and the will. The Chengwei were of no use; those still capable of resistance were busily engaged with their turncoat Caliban. That left him.

But to aid the Deceiver, or this avatar of the world's most ancient enemies, that was his torment.

Either way, he knew the choice would doom him, as he knew it had to be made.

That was when one of the Chengwei took matters into his own hands—by starting the clock.

The mechanism had been primed for a brief demonstration, mostly a show-and-tell light show that would leave impressive memories in the audience without generating substantial tangible effects. Those had been determined beyond all doubt by the miniature prototype that had been used against Fort Tregare.

The only warning any of them had was a rippling fanfare of chimes and tympana, courtesy of a rotating drum added solely for that purpose. The sphere began to spin, casting off bursts of sparkling radiance that flashed through the air like meteors, leaving trails of multicolored fire before quickly fading to nothingness. That would change, Thorn recollected from discussions he'd had with the Vicar-General, as the flywheels built up speed. The pulses would soon become strong enough to reach the surrounding walls of the Palace itself, where they would catalyze the energies already stored within its near-bottomless reservoirs and rebound to the Resonator a quantum level more powerfully than before. From that point on each succeeding pulse would double its force—two to four to eight to sixteen to thirty-two and so on. The initial increases were deceptively small, which in turn allowed the operators the greatest measure of control, so they could fine-tune and adjust the focus and scope of the beams in relative safety. The principle that went into the power curve was derived from the old story about the philosopher and the King: in return for service provided the throne, the philosopher was granted any boon. He asked for rice, the staple food of the kingdom, one grain to be doubled over each of the sixty-four squares of a chessboard. The King, who wasn't good at mathematics, that was why he employed philosophers, laughingly agreed—until the numbers to be doubled rose into the millions, the tens and hundreds and thousands of millions. Well before the final square, the philosopher held title to all the rice in the land.

He'd meant this as an object lesson for his sovereign, to inspire the Monarch to think a little more carefully before making decisions.

In a sense, he got his wish. The King gave his next decree more than ample consideration—and then he signed the warrant for the philosopher's execution. Sometimes, royalty has no sense of humor whatsoever.

Neither does fate.

Thorn was among the first to recognize the danger. The operation of the Resonator had been based on a seamless interaction between the globe and the surrounding structure of the Palace. In effect, the Palace acted as both power source and governor for the device, providing limitless reserves and at the same time a receptacle for dumping excess energy should the operators decide to scale back the Resonator's operation. It was a brilliantly engineered system, a breathtaking fusion of magic and technology, but it was also constructed on a foundation as delicately balanced as the underpinnings of the city itself. It presupposed that the Resonator's function would be constantly and properly monitored and that likewise the structure of the Palace would remain fundamentally sound.

Nelwyns at heart were engineers. They were one with the earth, they built things. By nature, therefore, they were conservative. They embraced the concept of margin of safety, crafting the already generous tolerances of their structures with a little bit extra to spare. To allow for the unexpected.

The Chengwei sorcerers considered themselves artists. Their goal was precision and efficiency, wrapped in an aesthetic that would be pleasing to behold. At no point in design or construction did they skimp on materials or on the care of workmanship; the finished product was one the finest Nelwyn or elven artisan would be proud to call their own. It just never occurred to them that something would go wrong.

The Palace had been struck a series of increasingly severe blows. The patterns of its internal matrices had been badly warped, if not outright broken, along with more than a few walls. Anyone possessing a smidgen of a wizard's InSight—their ability to perceive realities beyond the purely tangible—could feel the jangling toll the battle was taking, generating a background dissonance more disruptive than claws screeching down a blackboard. For Thorn, it was akin to being spiked repeatedly through the skull. Even Anakerie, whose sensitivity was far less than his, reeled from the onslaught.

He tried to cry a warning, but couldn't make himself heard over the din.

He tried to reach the dais, only to be blocked by the lumbering return of the Caliban to the fray.

"What can we do?" she demanded of him, as he hurriedly explained the situation, then flipped him to his back, sprawling herself on top of him—using her far larger form to best advantage—as a shower of broken crystal cascaded down from one of the galleries overhead.

Thorn saw that Elora was paying them no heed whatsoever, as if they were beneath her notice, prey that was hers for the taking whenever she pleased. Her focus was wholly on the Deceiver and she stalked her foe with a sideways crab scuttle that always managed to keep the other between herself and the Caliban. Watching, both Thorn and Anakerie realized that Elora and the Caliban were working in tandem. It was like a staged hunt, where the game is gradually driven into a fenced enclosure where they can be slaughtered at the hunter's convenience. He was the fence, patiently waiting for the Deceiver to come within reach.

Elora's gleaming sable skin proved as impervious as armor to the assaults of both the Deceiver and surviving Chengwei wizards, for whom survival had taken over as the order of the day. She paid them less notice than she did Thorn and for all the effect their spells had on her that was about what they deserved.

The strangest and most disturbing aspect of her transformation was her smile. It was cruel and utterly without mercy yet it was also wholly genuine. There was a fearsome joy to her in this duel, as though at long last, after years of perceiving herself as being somehow less than her foe, she could now confront the Deceiver as an equal. To Elora, this was fun.

The Deceiver appeared ready to make her choke on that delight.

That was when the first charge from the Resonator made actual contact with the Palace.

Thorn had experienced the effect in small when the Chengwei made their final assault on Fort Tregare, but that was scant preparation for what pounded him now.

It was as if a bell the size of the whole world had been struck, with him standing at its heart. He assumed there was a sound but if so it was beyond the power of his ears to register, much less his mind to comprehend. It pummeled him like a wild surf, a wave of blunt, brute force, overrunning with contemptuous ease his best attempts to stand against it. He staggered, he fell, he cast about in desperation until his flailing hands caught hold of Anakerie's shift and then he gathered her close, his tremendous Nelwyn strength making a mockery of the difference in their sizes. He pressed her head to his chest, while her own longer arm looped around his head and squeezed him just as close. Against such a monumental tempest, they could offer each other only sparse protection, so they settled for a measure of comfort instead, pulling their bodies together into a tight little huddle.

For a moment the room vanished about them and Thorn thought they had all been destroyed. In another fraction of a moment, death would claim them.

Then, as thought continued, and shapes made their presence known amidst the landscape of his dazzled vision, he realized that what he'd seen was some gigantic lightning flash, a radiance so powerful and pure it had been purged of all color. He reacted immediately, allowing his unconscious mind to dictate his response as it wrapped himself and Anakerie in a swaddling blanket of interlaced energies, the strongest wards he could manage given the situation.

These were spells he'd long ago learned to always carry with him primed for release, so that a single word or gesture would be sufficient to activate them. It was a strain to maintain such powerful enchantments on such a hair-trigger basis but there wasn't always time to start from scratch.

This was one such occasion.

The defensive cocoon was hardly in place when thunder followed the lightning. The two elements were of a pair and this explosion of noise dwarfed the bell clap that preceded it. If that resembled the shock of storm-driven waves on a beach, this was finding yourself on the anvil of Creation beneath the hammer of God.

Thorn's wards flexed, making him grunt, then bellow in agony and defiance, at the effort demanded to sustain them. Tears burst from his eyes, and every sinew of his body stretched taut; he gave up trying to draw breath and concentrated instead on forcing his heart to beat, the pressure on him so extreme that the muscle couldn't pump. He squeezed his own and then Anakerie's, then his own, then hers, establishing and maintaining a steady rhythm even though it felt like they were being crushed beneath the weight of the entire Stairs to Heaven.

He couldn't spare an iota of concentration or awareness to see what was happening elsewhere in the room as the energies unleashed by the Resonator grew increasingly demented. For that, he was grateful.

A monstrous tearing impinged on his faculties, followed by

thuds of varying weights crashing all about him. His head was at the wrong angle; he couldn't see. There wasn't time to be gentle, he'd have to apologize later and take whatever thumps and lumps Anakerie chose to deliver, as he forced her eyelids open and used his wizard's InSight to claim her vision briefly for his own.

One entire wall of the atrium was buckling, becoming more liquid than solid as a series of waves rolled up its surface. That was the cause of the impacts. The swells were separating the galleries from their mountings. The balconies in turn, deprived not only of physical support but of magical as well, were collapsing under their own weight.

He tried to move, to no avail. Worse, the attempt diverted precious concentration from the maintenance of his heartbeat, and Anakerie's. Didn't much matter. They'd neither of them drawn a breath since this chaos claimed the room and without fresh air to recharge the blood with oxygen the strongest and most dependable of heartbeats wouldn't matter a damn.

He wanted to kiss her. He wanted to reveal all the longing in his heart, for the world that was, for the one he'd fought so hard to bring about.

He stopped his heart, and then he stopped hers.

In his head, a sandglass turned, its grains racing through the funnel measuring the moments left to them both. He ignored it and turned every ounce of concentration he possessed toward his right hand in his pocket.

Try as he might, he couldn't shift his arm. He'd have to make do with the extension of his fingers. Here the curious paradox of Nelwyn physiology worked wholly in his favor. For all his lack of stature—at least in Daikini eyes—his fingers hearkened to the High Elves who were the Nelwyn's most distant and far-removed cousins. They were long and nimble, and blessed as well with the strength that was a Nelwyn hallmark. He snagged one acorn, then a second, the barest contact with each. He allowed himself a smile; that should do the trick.

He dropped both.

Had he the energy to spare, he would have launched into a tirade of curses foul enough to make a sailor blush. There wasn't time. Already his chest was beginning to ache, the fringes of his vision to blur. Lacking Nelwyn stamina, it would be worse for Anakerie and since he needed her eyes to see with he couldn't afford another slip.

Thorn wanted to rush, which required a dollop of extra effort to force himself to relax. No deadline, no pressure, that was essential.

The tips of his fingers stroked the polished curve of the acorns and all his pains nearly went to waste with the slashing fear that he might have pushed them out of reach. He stretched his fingers until the joints threatened to pop, spreading them wide as well, then gently closed them around where he estimated the acorns lay.

The solid contact made him want to weep. He shelved the impulse for later.

He closed his fingers, rolling the acorns into his palm. The situation around him had deteriorated markedly while he'd been busy. His wards acted now as a lightning rod, drawing down the rampaging energies generated by the Resonator the way innocence attracted Death Dogs. All along the line of contact was a flashing curtain of fire, displaying colors and patterns so antagonistic to his eyes that the merest glance set his stomach to churning. Anakerie, thankfully, was beyond any such response. She had tumbled into unconsciousness, from which she'd never awaken unless he acted at once and with unerring precision.

Her eyes kept wanting to roll up in their sockets, as the muscles of her body lost all tension and allowed them to drift out of alignment and focus. With a ruthless ferocity he'd learned during his travels, Thorn broadened his control over her body, risking his own in the process.

The acorns, too, were one of those spells he kept on a hair trigger. He completed the enchantment and flicked first one, then the other, from his grasp as if they were marbles. Only these he shot, not across the floor, but through the air.

One struck the lip of the dais and plopped onto the single step. The other struck an upright panel of the Resonator and came to rest on one of the revolving platters.

As Thorn watched through Anakerie's eyes, the step of the dais where the acorn landed turned from crystal to granite, the effect spreading outward on either side, following the path of least resistance all the way around the platform. At the same time, the gears within the Resonator slowed, the mechanism itself groaning with almost human weariness and pain as it, too, underwent this transformation.

For Thorn, it was as though the world had been lifted from him. With a great gulp of air he took a breath. A bellow of agony came next, his torso doubling over with such force that Anakerie was cast aside like she weighed nothing, accompanied by a thunderous pounding in his chest as his heart resumed to beat.

He had no time to waste. Ignoring the protests of his battered body, Thorn dragged himself atop his companion, straddling her and placing both hands over her own heart.

"Breathe," he commanded her, his own voice sounding so hoarse to his ears he must have shrieked until it broke, as Elora's had done years ago.

"Damn you, Anakerie. I haven't come this far to watch you die! You mind me, woman, you prove to me you're a warrior worth the name. You fight for your life! Princess Royal of Angywn, Warlord of the Maizan though you are, you do as I tell you—*breathe!*"

He felt her stir beneath him but he was more transfixed by her face. Her features had faded to a shade of alabaster, so drained of life they might have been a porcelain casting. As his words beat upon her, though, a flush returned to her cheeks, skin growing faintly warm to his touch. Eyes flickered beneath closed lids and she managed a tiny cough, a collapsing sigh to flush the last scraps of air from her exhausted lungs.

Then, for Thorn, the miracle occurred, as she responded immediately by drawing in a proper breath.

He fumbled for a pulse and found it strong and steady beneath his fingers.

He wanted to hug her, to cheer like a schoolboy given leave from class, but the tremendous crash of another block of falling crystal reminded him of their ongoing peril. Shielding her with his body as best he could and fighting back coughs from the pumice that filled the air, as impact after impact threw forth clouds of glittering dust, he cast about for a sight of the others.

Of the Chengwei sorcerers, the less said the better. His eyes regarded images of their fate but his mind refused to record them—though he feared the scene would return to haunt him in nightmares. The clarity of the crystal had originally given the atrium a vaguely aquamarine quality; now that sapphire was liberally splashed with scarlet, and the screams of men had been replaced by those of the Palace itself. The lifeblood and agony of the slaughter were soaking into the body of the stone, altering not simply its color but the very nature of the building.

Blessedly, Anakerie regained her senses with a warrior's alacrity, her eyes clearing almost as soon as they were opened, brow immediately furrowing with concern as she realized their predicament.

"This is not good," she said, dryly making light of her statement of the obvious.

"I've noticed" was his response in kind. Thorn had never felt so outright scared, he was overflowing with the awareness that at any moment his life might come to a violent and murderous end, yet he felt filled as well with a wild excitement. A heady acceptance of whatever fate came for him, coupled with the equal sureness that he would find some way for himself and Anakerie to survive. It was an altogether Daikini sentiment, one that would have sent the most madcap of Nelwyns reeling from him in horror.

"What can we do?" Anakerie asked, pulling her body close to herself in preparation for making a move.

"Only the obvious, I'm afraid—run for our lives!"

"But Elora Danan—!"

"She is lost to us."

It was as if saying those words finally made it so, bringing home her metamorphosis in a way that could not be denied. Thorn thought he would howl, would feel the kind of grief that accompanied the loss of a child—for that was what Elora had become for him, as much as his own offspring—but nothing happened.

He heard a crackling that reminded him of the sound of thick slices of bacon frying in a pan, and felt a chill skirl about his heart as he realized what that meant. Even as his enchanted acorn transformed it into solid granite, the Resonator continued to draw power from the Palace around it, the two forces battling each other like a pair of sorcerers. Thorn had hoped for the best but understood the outcome was never in doubt. Powerful though it was, his own spell was finite. It had limits, where the Resonator had none. As he and Anakerie watched, solid granite became little more than a stony shell, which proceeded to flake off the device in sheets and chunks. Set free, the Resonator's components came once more to life, the gears began to turn, the platters to spin.

Thorn cast about wildly for something he could use to jam the gears, a pry bar of cold-cast iron would be best, the kind of tool that could be found in almost any Nelwyn household, whether forge or farm. Of course, in this place, there was nothing remotely resembling one. Not a bar of any kind, and especially not a piece of iron. Far too disruptive of any magical patterns and too aesthetically displeasing in the bargain. These sorcerers dealt in only the most noble of metals; they spared scant concern for something as base as common iron.

That, Thorn thought uncharitably, *is partly why they died.* They designed and built the Resonator to function solely on their terms, forgetting that the world isn't always so accommodating.

Unfortunately, that revelation, however apt, wasn't going to be Thorn's salvation, either.

That role, surprisingly, went to Elora Danan.

He didn't think so at the time. He thought she'd come at last to finish him as she spun lithely and lazily through the air, in utter and contemptuous defiance of the ongoing chaos, to a landing on the dais opposite him. He'd lost track of her with the first outburst of energy from the Resonator, part of him hoping she'd escaped its onslaught, a larger part wishing she'd fallen before them. A quick glance around the room revealed that the Deceiver and the Caliban had taken their own leave.

"Elora Danan," he demanded of her, because he had to have that answer above all, "what have you *done?*"

"What I must, Peck" was her reply, with that same hateful smile, as if those four words would solve every riddle.

Then, as lightly as she would a goblet of finest crystal to draw forth a chime, she extended a single claw and tapped it on the dais.

Immediately, the floor beneath Thorn and Anakerie tilted, the pair of them buffeted by a savage riptide of raw sound that marked stone tearing from stone. They scrambled frantically to push themselves clear of the dais as the floor first groaned, then collapsed utterly under the terrible weight of the transformed step and the Resonator. This was a greater shock than the surrounding crystal could withstand and the end came with astonishing suddenness. The atrium was defined by a series of lancet arches around its perimeter, better than twenty feet tall, meant to help support the first gallery. The stress placed on the dais was uneven, the greater mass of stone concentrated on the side closest to Thorn and Anakerie. That in turn created a severe torque so that when the platform collapsed it did so in a vicious twisting motion, much like a crude screw, which opened great fissures across the floor itself to undermine the arches. To Thorn, it was painfully reminiscent of being on a frozen river when the ice decided to break. Where once had been solid and dependable footing, there was a whirling madhouse that bounced up and down upon the water in addition to spinning round in circles. This was much the same, as the foundation structure of the Palace shook from an increasingly powerful succession of hammerblows.

By themselves, neither he nor Anakerie would have escaped. He lacked her rangy height and she, his strength. He managed to hook fingers over the edge of a tilting floe of crystal and with a heave no Daikini could have matched, pitch her to a ledge that remained secure amidst the chaos. Anakerie then used the length of her own body, treble and more the height of the tallest Nelwyn Thorn had ever seen, to lean back, catch hold, and yank him after.

There was an opening in the wall. Without question or hesitation, they scrambled through just as the dais finally and completely gave way, plunging to the catacombs with the force of a mangonel stone. The impact couldn't have been more devastating, shaking the entire Palace with such force that its towering spires visibly swayed against the skyline, and one actually snapped. Shock waves rippled past them on every side through the fabric of the building—floors, walls, ceilings, plus all the pillars and beams that supported them—in serried bands of color and intensity, deceptively beautiful until they struck the boundaries of the wall. Then they reacted just like water in a pool after striking an obstacle: the wavelets bounced back upon themselves, interacting quickly with reflections off other contacts, creating a vortex of increasingly antagonistic crosscurrents and countercurrents, complete with undertows and riptides.

In the confined space of the Palace, limited by the size and form of the structure itself, these conflicting pulses of arcane energy quickly built to a frenzy. Had the building remained substantially intact, it could have absorbed the overload without significant stress; that was what it was designed to do. But many of those pathways had been blocked, adding to the chaos they were intended to relieve. The oscillations became corrosive, displacing first the delicately woven patterns that comprised the magical matrix of the Palace and then the physical bond of the crystal, setting in motion a cascading sequence of failures as inexorable as a line of falling dominoes.

"Did I ever tell you, Drumheller," Anakerie bellowed as they found themselves bounced along a corridor that twisted head over heels around them in rude defiance of the laws of common sense and nature together, "how much I hate magic!"

By rights they should have been sent flying when the hallway upended itself. Yet their feet remained firmly fixed to the floor beneath them, even when every other sense told them they were running at right angles to the ground, and then upside down.

"At the moment," he had no trouble saying in reply, "I'm inclined to agree with you!"

Lightning glanced off their bodies but ripped gaping scars in the crystal, forcing them to take care in how they went since neither of their clothes offered more than scant protection from the broken shards. Colors were mashed and mangled, then cast forth in hues and formations neither had ever seen. Some were wondrous to behold, others struck at their senses harder than a ruffian's cudgel. Thorn had no resources to spare for any kind of counterspell, and was glad of it, because in this pandemonium he had no idea what form those enchantments might take.

They reached a final doorway, which needed the combined efforts of both of them to force it open from its warped and waxen frame. There, Anakerie put her legs to good use, scooping the Nelwyn into her arms and muscling through the gap to emerge from the victualers' gate which Elora had used to enter the Palace. Anakerie stayed to the exact center of the bridge as she crossed the moat in record time, refusing to spare the slightest glance at the columns of spray erupting from below. If nothing was in them, why take the look? If something was, she preferred not to see. She heard a splash close behind her and trusted the hackles on the back of her neck as they suddenly rose stiff as spikes. That was all the goading she needed.

Just before the end, with relative safety at hand, she was almost undone. The surface of the bridge was slick enough to begin with, creating one of those circumstances where bare feet weren't that much of an improvement over shoes. Whatever came from the moat coated it like grease and as a surge of the sludge washed past, Anakerie's legs went out from under her.

She landed in a mess, for there wasn't time to recover or properly brace for the impact, but decided that wasn't so bad a thing as a set of nasty jaws closed with the steel snap of a beartrap right where her shoulder had been. Her own speed served her well at this point, for she kept on sliding, toward a mess of broken and abandoned carts at the far end of the bridge. Without losing her grip on Drumheller, Anakerie pulled her legs tight to her body and pivoted herself around so that she was approaching the land broadside. She didn't know what was chasing them, or how close it was; from that sole glimpse when she fell she assumed it was big and nasty and far too close for comfort. In truth, she didn't think they'd make it and was determined to shove Thorn clear the instant those terrible fangs closed about her.

To her surprise, she felt dry land before the creature's bite, and she didn't waste the gift. Denying the protests of brutally overtaxed muscles, she dug her toes into the first line of cobblestones and, using the momentum of her slide as a springboard, thrust herself forward in a dive underneath the nearest wagon. She didn't stop there, she hardly slowed, clasping Thorn to her with one hand and using the other plus both feet to propel her through the maze of smashed vehicles in a three-limbed lope.

She didn't emerge unscathed, the price she paid for bulling her way along a path better suited for Nelwyns than Daikini. A cracked singletree had torn a ragged scratch between her shoulder blades, adding to the ruination of her slip, and she was bleeding as well from her scalp. There were also bruises and scrapes aplenty. She didn't care a whit. What mattered was reaching the far side of the barrier alive.

To Anakerie, it was the sweetest triumph she'd won in years.

They both laughed, though a little tentatively, exultant over their escape yet not quite ready to tempt fate any further with a dose of hubris. They were a mess, Anakerie so far beyond the local standards of decency she might as well be naked, while Thorn's ceremonial robes had been reduced to a patchwork of rags. He shucked them, reducing his attire to waistcoat and tunic, trousers and boots, still too elegant an ensemble for Thorn's tastes but it wasn't as if there were an alternative handy. He was panting, as was she, and that realization prompted a fit of phlegmy coughs as the pumice he'd inhaled continued to irritate his bronchial passages and lungs.

"I don't believe it," Anakerie said.

"What?"

"Look about you, Drumheller. Listen."

"I don't hear anything."

"That's just the point. There's hardly a sense of anything wrong."

He clambered to his feet, staring up at the layered spires and minarets of the Palace, proud and beautiful as always as they soared into the sky. A crowd was gathering at the edges of the plaza that surrounded the Palace, attracted by the sense of danger but also by the increasingly spectacular display of hues and textures flickering within the substance of those transparent walls. Some even applauded an especially violent collage, thinking this performance was being staged for their entertainment.

They paid no attention when Thorn rounded on them.

"You can't stay," he cried, furious at how hoarse his voice sounded. "This isn't a show! Everyone within the Palace is dead, and that monstrosity with them! There's no time left you! Take your loved ones and flee to safety! Get away from here, while you still can! *Run!*"

He was cursed for his trouble, and mocked, but mostly ignored. He redoubled his efforts and succeeded only in drawing the attention of the guards who'd accompanied the Khan and been refused entry to the sacred precincts of the Palace. They immediately recognized both him and Anakerie—after all, how many Nelwyns could there be in Ch'ang-ja, not to mention round-eyed Princesses of Angwyn—and stepped forth to arrest them both.

Once more, it was Anakerie who took the initiative, and, Thorn in her arms, she ducked down the nearest alleyway. That initial burst of speed gave them a decent head start. She continued on at a breakneck pace that made no concession to route or terrain and allowed not the slightest margin for error. When an obstacle threatened to block her path, Anakerie rounded it with a quick battlefield pivot, or scampered beneath it, or cleared it like a hurdle. They plunged into the midst of a troll's warren of streets and houses, so haphazardly arranged that there was no way to make objective sense of the neighborhood. It seemed like each block had a different name, changing at every corner. Clearly, the residents knew how to get around for the lanes were crowded, but Thorn despaired of any outsider making sense of this mess. The buildings themselves were arranged as row houses, butted snug against one another with common walls but rarely with shared ones. Each building was separate, architecturally and structurally dissimilar to the ones on either side, sharing only a general sameness in height and width. The only element that was repeated were the magical *fu* dogs who guarded every doorway, carved and dramatically painted beasts whose fearsome aspect was intended to frighten away malevolent spirits and forces. The clutter of housing combined with the narrow and twisting layout of the streets to give the district a claustrophobic air and leave ground level almost perpetually in shadow. Thorn knew Anakerie possessed no MageSight—which allowed sorcerers such as he to see clearly in pitch-darkness—so he melded their perceptions slightly to allow her access to his. After all they'd been through, he didn't want their saga to end in some rank back alley because of a pair of broken necks.

He'd forgotten that blending abilities allowed them to share a modicum of thoughts as well, until her chuckling comment reminded him.

"You don't trust me, Drumheller? To find my way even in the dark?"

"Why oh why," he despaired, "is it my fate always to fall into the hands of Daikini who are patently and incurably mad?"

"Opposites attract. You're simply too blessed sane for words. You need a touch of madness to loosen you up!"

"I like sanity. I like calm. I like peace—*watch out for that clothesline!*"

She ducked, reflexively gathering him tight against her body, avoiding the obstruction with room to spare. Unfortunately, there was also a matron present who was busy filling it with the morning washing. That collision couldn't be avoided, and the poor woman uttered a squawk of righteous alarm and indignation when this nearly naked outlander spun her twice around in a circle before resuming her flight without a missed step.

Both Thorn and Anakerie spoke at once, and said the same thing.

"I assume you know which way to go."

"The harbor," Thorn said with a laugh, which Anakerie echoed.

"Downhill, then."

"You won't get lost?"

"That I cannot promise. The only layout I know of this town is from maps and none of them were ferociously detailed. Think we lost the guards?"

"They're not important. Even without them we can't delay."

"What are you afraid of, Drumheller?"

"That Palace is a volcano building its own lava dome." In a rush, he told her the parable of the philosopher and the rice. Being the daughter of a King, Anakerie of course had heard it herself.

"I thought your acorns and Elora's claws took care of the Resonator," she said.

"That doesn't matter; the pattern has already been established. The pulses will continue, and continue their geometric progression, regardless. The only thing the Resonator might have done was exert a measure of control."

"Not so good then, your destroying it, eh?"

"I wondered about that myself before I threw the acorn. But the entire magical system of the Palace had already destabilized. And the wizards who knew best how to operate the device were dead."

"I assume that's bad."

"The tremendous capacity of the Palace makes the situation all the more deadly, guaranteeing a monumental explosion of arcane energy."

"Whatever."

"You've seen volcanoes erupt, haven't you, Keri?"

"In Angwyn, more often than I care to remember. The other name for the Rampart Range that lines our coast is the Wall of Fire."

"Instead of lava, imagine a flash flood of raw, untamed magic, sweeping over a city whose very foundations are grounded in the stuff. Imagine what happens when that blast wave hits the chapter houses of the other magical orders—except that their mages, the ones folks will count on to save them from this disaster, they're mostly dead already."

"Just like in Angwyn," Anakerie muttered, "when the Deceiver disrupted the Ascension of Elora Danan. That bitch has a lot to answer for."

As it turned out, the Guard hadn't followed them into the maze of streets and alleys—but they also hadn't given up the chase. An alarm had been sounded and word passed to every district station, so that when the pair of them emerged into the mercantile department they found patrols searching for them on foot and horseback.

"What now, Peck?" she asked of him, making that insult a tender endearment.

"Elora told me of a man over in Freemantle, who she suspected had ties with the Cascani traders. If we can reach him . . ."

"Freemantle's halfway around the bay from here. What's wrong?"

Thorn was staring at his hands. He held them up before her, and Anakerie watched flickers of saffron lightning roil about his splayed fingers, gathering intensity as they swarmed past his wrists, around and through the weave of his shirt—making her wonder if his flesh would prove any barrier to them—plunging down his chest and diving headlong into his heart. Thorn went on tiptoe, back hunching as if from a blow, his arms flying wide to full extension. Anakerie reflexively reached to catch hold only to find herself slapped away from him and off a convenient wall by a backsurge of energy that packed a more than respectable punch. His eyes and mouth opened and the lightning poured from one and into the other, out his nostrils and into his ears. His back arched the other way, to so extreme an arc that Anakerie feared it would snap, and then as suddenly as it had appeared the lightning vanished.

She heard a thunderclap, a report as impressive as any that ever sounded over the Great Western Plains, and Thorn dropped like a castaway puppet, to knees, to face, without making the slightest attempt to break his landing.

There was a sharp stench of ozone to the air, the kind of atmosphere that heralds the worst kind of storm, and if she'd been with the Maizan on the open prairie they'd be looking for shelter against an oncoming tornado. Her first attempt to touch Thorn was a quick stab of the finger against his breast; concerned though she was, she didn't want to risk another such shock. She was bruised enough from the first.

Whatever force had possessed him, however, was gone, and she gathered his limp form onto her lap, swiftly seeking his neck for signs of a pulse. To her relief, it was regular and gaining strength with every beat.

"Too late," he breathed when he found strength and wit to speak.

"Maybe it's better this way," he said further.

"Why?"

"You saw," he told her. "The Deceiver."

"Looks like the Elora who grew up in my father's palace, so what? These past three years, I've seen that monster wear the body of Castellan Mohdri. And before that, it took a fair stab at impersonating you. That's why you call it the Deceiver, is it not?"

"So I once thought. Did you not see Elora as well?"

"Aye," she replied with a terse nod. "Wish to Goddess I'd been blind for that one, I'll grant you. The way she looked at us"—she shuddered at the recollection, with a sudden and disturbing empathy for how the bug must feel impaled on the pin of the collector—"the way she laughed."

She looked down and her brow furrowed, as if she were seeing something for the first time. Clutched tight in her left hand, where it had been all along, was a leather traveling pouch, plain of decoration but of quite respectable workmanship.

"She gave me this," she said, a thread of wonder and mystery to her voice. "Why didn't it register before now? As she got up, just before she attacked Khory Bannefin, Elora thrust this bag of hers into my hands. The belt it hung from was useless, rotted away to nothing by the acid, but the bag was untouched."

"The protective spells are mine," Drumheller said. "The power to sustain them came from her."

"Why would she give me her traveling pouch?"

Thorn shook his head. He had no answers. He was tired of seeking them out. He wanted to sob, to yield to such misery as he'd never known.

"Probably," he said, "because she had no further use for it."

"But why attack Khory?"

"She had bound herself to the Malevoiy. Our companion wore the face of their greatest foe. Perhaps they wished to avenge that ancient defeat? Perhaps it was the price demanded of Elora for their aid, that she betray one who trusted her—just as Eamon Asana did. Pick any answer you like, Highness. What matters is that she is lost to us. Whatever the reason, this is a crime that cannot be forgiven."

He fixed bleary, beaten eyes on the Angwyn Princess, and Anakerie saw in them the hollow stare of men who'd been too long in combat, who'd fought so hard, in conditions of such unspeakable brutality, that they could conceive of no other existence. Men for whom life had become just another unbearable burden. "So tell me, Anakerie, renowned as you are as a strate-gist—when your greatest foe and your greatest champion may well be one and the same, and that selfsame champion willingly embraces the most fearful race in the Twelve Realms, what are we to do?"

There was no mercy in her eyes as she returned his stare, nor tenderness. She had seen her share of death, taken her share of lives; she knew that awful look because she'd seen it in her own mirror. She spoke to him not as a friend, nor as a woman who in another time and place would have embraced him as her lover, but as a commander. There was steel in her voice to match what she usually carried in her sword hand.

"Whatever, dear friend, this isn't the time or place for such a decision. Any warrior worth the name should know when's the time to fight, when to yield, and when to run. This, Drumheller, is the last."

"First by damn sensible comment I've heard from *any* of you Tall Folk lot!" New voice, new arrival, comment capped by a gruff basso bark of major irritation from the hound the brownies were riding.

"Where in all the hells," Rool fumed, mood and manner match-ing his companion's, "have you bloody *been*?"

"Have you any notion, the pair of you," cried Franjean distract-edly, with anxious looks past the shoulders of the fugitives, and he wasn't worried about any pursuit, "of how *doomed* this accursed city is?"

"How did you find us?" Thorn asked of them as they huddled close.

"The old-fashioned way," Rool replied, scratching the base of the hound's ear. "We followed Puppy's nose." Normally, such attentions would be a pleasure, but the great hound was as trou-bled as his riders. He kept dancing on his toes, claws making quick castanet taps on the cobblestones, the stark tension of his body making plain how much he wanted to be far away from here. His breed wasn't good at whining, so he conveyed his growing con-cern with a series of staccato subvocalized growls from deep in his throat. In their own way, these sent as primal a message as the laughter of the Malevoiy, reminding Nelwyn and Daikini both of an earlier and more primal Age, where the order of the world was considerably different from today. When those races who now considered themselves Lords of the Earth weren't even certain of their own survival.

"If you've been searching," Anakerie said, taking charge of the situation, "then I assume you've somewhere safe to lead us to?"

"That would make sense," agreed Franjean, never one to acknowledge anyone as his superior, even when she was both Princess Royal, heir to an Imperial throne, and a warlord.

"We've a boat in Freemantle," explained Rool.

"I told you," said Thorn, staring once more at his hands, which were crackling again, though not quite as fiercely as before. He suspected that would soon change, and not for the better. "There's no time."

Anakerie didn't bother with a reply; she simply embarked on a course of action.

Crouched as they were in the shadows of a service alleyway, they'd thus far escaped the notice of roving mounted patrols. She spotted a quartet of horsemen approaching along the street and strode out to meet them.

The brownies were master dissemblers and had few equals at the art of the ambush but even they were impressed by her ploy. Anakerie's reaction was picture-perfect, that of a fugitive who'd unwittingly stumbled into her pursuers. Of course, she bolted. Of course, they spurred after her. Her every action bespoke panic; theirs, an obvious and overweening contempt. After all, she was alone, a foreigner, and a woman. How difficult could her capture be?

They soon learned.

She let them catch up to her and then she dropped flat, right beneath the hooves of the charging horses. The animals perceived her as a hurdle, as she knew they would, which they proceeded to jump. The moment they thundered past, she was up and scrambling for the rearmost rider. He meanwhile was too busy reining in his mount, who wasn't at all happy being jerked from a full gallop to a dead stop. For those few critical moments, the trooper was too busy staying in his saddle and trying to calm his frenzied and furious animal to realize his predicament. By that point, too late, he realized he wasn't alone on the horse's back. Anakerie jumped up behind him, using the momentum of that leap to propel the man to the ground. He dropped with an impressive crash of armor.

She wasn't in the saddle herself yet, and there wasn't time to seat herself properly as the other three troopers belatedly responded to the rapidly changing situation. Anakerie grabbed the reins and slapped a palm sharply against her mount's flanks to spur him into motion. Off he went, straight for the others.

Despite what had just happened to their companion, the others still exuded confidence. They were armed, she wasn't. They figured she was charging to her death.

One slashed at her, but his blade sliced through empty air as Anakerie pitched herself from the horse's back, using its speed as a springboard to bounce herself off the street, her powerful arms and shoulder muscles adding thrust to her leap as she rose up and over her mount. Normally, this was a racing remount, which would end with her astride the animal. However, Anakerie kept both legs together and turned the maneuver into a wicked kick that caught the rider on the opposite side full in the chest.

He reacted as if he'd run straight into a pole and hit the street somewhat harder than the first man. Anakerie executed another racing remount, this time into the saddle, and looked for fresh targets.

In fairly short order, with sword now in hand, she rejoined Thorn and the brownies.

"Which way," she demanded of the brownies as she lifted the Nelwyn into the saddle in front of her.

"Can you keep up?" Rool challenged.

"Just make sure to lead me somewhere this beast can follow. As for you"—this was directed at Thorn—"your job's to keep those damnable cracklings to a minimum. That last shock was hard enough on the ground, I don't want to be on the receiving end at a gallop."

He was thin-lipped and sweating already from the effort, unwilling to trust himself to more than a curt nod.

The hound launched himself into the street to the wild yells of his brownie riders, standing astride his withers and holding fast to makeshift reins they'd hooked to his massive collar. Anakerie was right behind them.

If they needed encouragement, it was provided within minutes as they thundered along the waterfront, gathering their share of attention and pursuit. Thorn was leaning forward, as though to embrace their mount around the neck; the easy presumption was that the Nelwyn was holding on for dear life. Considering that his stature made it difficult just to sit astride such an animal, that wasn't an unreasonable conclusion. It was also wholly wrong. Instead, he was generating as strong an energy field as he could around the horse, to keep it calm and focused in the face of whatever might come.

It was a prescient act.

A high-pitched shrieking suddenly pierced the relative peace of the afternoon. It might have been a steam whistle, if such a device had been constructed for the use of giants. It was heard in every district of Ch'ang-ja, and for quite a ways beyond. All along the waterfront, glass shattered as every window touched by that awful noise instantly exploded. People screamed as well, clutching hands to heads, dropping to the ground in agony, deafened for the little life that was now left them.

Thanks to Thorn, Anakerie perceived it as no more than an ache. The horse, with far more sensitive ears, was similarly protected, as were brownies and hound. Anakerie wanted to see what was happening behind her but she dared not spare even so much as a quick glance over her shoulders; all her attention was required to keep her mount on track and the hound—whose speed was truly magnificent—in sight.

Thorn provided an answer, via the link they still shared. Without loosening his grasp on the horse, he twisted around until the Crystal Palace came into view, allowing Anakerie to behold the world through his eyes.

"Am I wrong, Drumheller," she gasped, "or has that damnable Palace grown?"

She wasn't wrong, it had doubled in size and more as the

increasing levels of energy stretched its glittering substance to its limit and well beyond. It had dominated this end of the city, as the Gate of Peace did the harbor; now it loomed like an opalescent mountain, its spires topping even the Sagat beacon. There was no trouble making out the swirling ropes of lightning that erupted ever more vehemently from the Palace, as their lesser counterparts had from Thorn's hands. Anakerie was reminded of an accident she'd seen as a child, during one of the few occasions someone at the Angwyn court attempted a display of Chengwei fireworks. There'd been a bit of carelessness with the strikers, and considerable sloppiness with the layout of the fuses. Detonation of the first wave of explosives ended up igniting the entire presentation. While the audience scrambled and fled for cover, Anakerie—with the arrogance of one yet to reach her teens—stood her ground to watch, and marvel at the spectacular display. The blasts, she remembered, had occurred in sequence, as one level of munitions ignited the next, albeit in lightning succession.

The same was happening to the Crystal Palace, although on an apocalyptic scale.

Lightning raced up the tower, as it had Thorn's arms, and stabbed through to the center of the structure, toward what Anakerie guessed was whatever remained of the atrium. From that spot grew a light that was unlike any she'd ever seen. It cast forth nothing she could describe as radiance. Indeed, if looking at the sun was akin to gazing at the Heart of Creation, this was a view into the essence of chaos itself. Every aspect of it was antagonistic to her being as a Daikini and she knew that if she were beholding it with her own eyes, she'd feel like she was being turned inside out.

Thorn understood immediately what was happening. This was a manifestation of the energies sorcerers encountered when trolling for demons. Such a materialization was considered the acid test of a mage, the ultimate challenge to training and skill and talent. It could take years to bring such spells into being and he'd read and heard of those who'd slaved a lifetime without ever coming close. None but the most powerful of adepts—and precious few of those over the countless generations—were able to produce such a conjuration, much less survive it. For the rest, the kind-est fate was death. The most frequent consequence was a terrible living madness, as the hapless sorcerers came away from the expe-rience possessed by the essential chaos that was the fabric of the demons' existence.

Thorn could look on it in safety because the work he had done to bring Khory into being had touched his soul with a demon's. He shuddered at the thought of its effect on a city of ordinary folk.

Then it was as if a monstrous invisible ax descended from the heavens to split the Palace in twain. The two great pieces of crys-tal calved apart, that act of separation creating a backwash that sucked the chaos light back within the body of the Palace. For a heartbeat, Thorn prayed that would be the end of it, that he'd seen the worst.

The explosion proved him wrong.

There was no smooth progression of events. The blast regis-tered on Thorn's eyes as a sequence of still images, pieces of frozen time. Air took on the properties of water and a great swelling wave of force rippled outward from the Palace, even as the core crys-talline matrices that composed the structure discorporated, trans-lating in a heartbeat from tangible reality to energy. In its wake, all the manifestations of magic were taken in hand and savagely twisted. Nothing remained fixed. Buildings lost cohesion, the col-lapse of those whose construction was abetted by spells dragging down those around them that used none. Thorn didn't want to consider the fate of those within those rooms when the structural boundaries failed. The most prosaic examples of the arcane arts flashed to their extremes: a spell designed to regulate the environ-ment of a house instantly made it as hot as a dragon's flame, as cold and lifeless as Bavmorda's soul. The states of physical objects changed capriciously—solid to gas, liquid to solid—and once they reduced themselves to essentials, the elements themselves took on lives of their own. *Fu* dogs turned on their masters, or each other, or they became precisely what they appeared to be, gaily painted statues, with no more life to them than a rock. Every natural law was perverted into a mockery of itself: walls that appeared solid turned out to be liquid suspended vertically from the street. That street, in turn, was now partially air. The air, solid as stone. What went up didn't necessarily come down.

Everything happened with such suddenness, there was no time for panic. Many were consumed before becoming aware of their danger. The rest were overwhelmed by the enormity of the disaster. Their minds couldn't cope with what their senses reported, it was too far beyond human ken. The city was already supersaturated with magic, as it would be with humidity in the midst of monsoon season. The Resonator was the catalyst that made it rain. It didn't matter anymore whether one was born with the talent to be a mage; the power came to everyone, whether they wanted it or not, whether they could handle it or not.

When Thorn was very young, *long* before the thought of becoming a mage entered his head, magic for him was everything the word implied. Strange, mysterious, wonderful in the way a sunrise was, or the blooming of a flower, or the raw, marginally tamed passion of a naked flame in his hearth. It was the stuff of dreams, and, he believed, the means of making those dreams reality; a way, he believed, of making them reality. He'd thought the High Aldwyn, the wizard of his village, the most blessed of Nelwyns and though he came to yearn to follow the old man's path, he never truly accepted that day would ever dawn.

Even now, he found it hard to credit that the Aldwyn had watched over him from birth, that the gift of his power and his destiny had marked him as inexorably as it had Elora Danan.

It was while saving the baby Elora that Thorn came to behold the other side of magic. The baneful arts. He saw, and felt the lash of, sorcery that had no other purpose than to do harm and discovered in himself the capacity to do the same.

But he had chosen this path. Yes, he may have been marked by fate but at every crossroads in his life he'd faced the opportunity to turn away from it. That he was here, that he was the man and mage he'd become, those were conscious decisions, of his own free will, and he accepted responsibility for them.

This was different. The fault of the people around him was solely that they chose to live in Ch'ang-ja. The horror for him was that there was nothing he could do to save them.

What was inanimate erupted to life around him. Cobblestones grew teeth and snapped hungrily at the feet treading upon them. The wood of joists and beams, of floors, of furniture, of utensils, all regained a portion of the life it once possessed, and a twisted shrieking filled the air, adding to the already unholy din, as dryads found themselves reconstituted in tortured pieces, gripped by a terrible rage at the violence done them and determined to relay it in kind. Like the skins they once had been, hides and leather wrapped themselves tight around the people wearing them, bending and breaking the offending body until it assumed a crippled semblance of the original beast. From every thread of silk, a thousand worms bloomed, to spin new webs from strands of flesh.

Shapes changed at whim, as beasts assumed human semblance while men and women took their place. With each outburst of energy, the transformations became more extreme, and Thorn saw figures with scales for skin, with wings, with claws and fangs, small as church mice while others could shatter a whole house with their fist. The earth itself came to life, and people were reduced to clay. Others became fire, became ice. The fire attacked the ice and melted it to water, which threatened to drown the fire, which boiled it away to air, which extinguished the blaze with a puff, save for the stray sparks which ignited some combustible tinder nearby and began the cycle all over again.

Beyond the circle of Thorn's power, no one was safe, no one was spared.

"Can this be stopped?" Anakerie demanded, her voice ragged.

He wanted with all his might and heart to cry yes. To find within himself the enchantment which would set things right.

Instead, he told the truth: "I don't know."

And then, "The Palace is like any other machine. Eventually, it has to run out of fuel, of magical energy."

"Eventually means how long, precisely?"

Again, he didn't know, but took heart from the fact that the city around them was increasingly less chaotic as they neared Freemantle.

"Praise all the Makers that ever were and ever shall be," he breathed in a rush. "It's finite, the effects have a limited range."

The whole of Freemantle was on the move, that was apparent well before they reached their destination, the berth of Saltai's schooner, and that panic swept disaster over the sprawling anchorage as surely as the Palace's magic had ravaged the land. Hawsers were cut without regard to the ability of one ship or another to stay afloat, much less get under way, or of those aboard to function as any kind of crew. There were thumps and groans and screeches as hulls came together, and sharper outcries followed by splashes as people went into the water. Once that happened, the swimmer's fate was sealed. The huge assemblage of vessels functioned much the same as a field of pack ice; holes that might reveal open water one instant slammed closed the next as a movement forty hulls away triggered a ripple reaction in the surrounding boats. Few there were mariners but had instead grown up viewing their wooden homes as an extension of the land. They never conceived of having to put these ships to use.

Lathered, foam dripping from muzzle and soaked chest—as much from terror as exertion—the horse Anakerie and Thorn rode staggered to a stop on the dock. Anakerie swung herself off the saddle with Thorn tucked under her arm and handed him up to the deck without letting his feet touch the planks. The hound boarded with a single leap that cleared the gunwale with room to spare, to the demented, delighted shrieks of his brownie passengers, who considered this a ride to tell their great-grandchildren about.

Anakerie was about to follow when Thorn called back to her, in a battlefield voice reminiscent of her own.

"You can't leave the horse!" he told her.

"I'll turn him loose."

"To go where? He's done us good service, Anakerie; he deserves better. We'll need him later, trust me. And his friends."

Thorn didn't have to point. The clatter of hooves was already sounding drumbeats on the planks as a half dozen more animals, cavalry mounts by the insignia on their saddle blankets, clattered riderless down the wharf.

"No," bellowed Baghwan Saltai, over and over as he thrust his way forward to the gangplank. "No no no no no no *no*! I'll not have it, you'll not bring one of those mangy hides aboard my ship. Free those lines," he told the anchor watch. "Warp us into the stream so we can be free of this hellpit! We've got to go *now*," he pleaded with Thorn. "We've waited too long for you, maybe, as it is; there'll be too many other hulls ahead of us, blocking access to the main channel. Mount your sweeps," he called to his crew, meaning the great oars laid out on a rack between the main and foremast, for use when the ship was becalmed or for maneuvering in port. "We'll row clear if we must!"

"You heard Lord Drumheller," said another voice softly, with the thinness of tone that comes from severe sickness but also with a strength of will and purpose that refused to be denied. "Load the horses," he said. "I'll get you clear."

In his heart, Thorn welcomed Ryn Taksemanyin with the greatest grin possible, but too much was happening right now for any of that to show on the Nelwyn's craggy face. He trundled as best he could down the gangway, reaching out with his InSight to touch the thoughts of each horse in turn, to gentle and calm them so that they would allow themselves to be led aboard and behave themselves during the madness surely to follow. He didn't command, though once he might have for that was the way of sorcerers; he took a leaf from Elora's copybook and asked the animals' help. Limited though their intelligence might seem to Daikini, these horses were nobody's fools; they wanted out as badly as anyone and quickly allowed Anakerie and Luc-Jon to lead them aboard. There was no time to put them below, and no space rigged to accommodate them, so they were tethered on deck, and the boom of the foresail raised above their heads.

As the final set of hooves clattered on deck, the gangway and the remaining hawsers were cut loose. There was sufficient breeze to establish steerage way and with agonizing slowness the schooner began to open the distance to the land.

All the while, Baghwan exhorted boat and seamen. "Hurry," he said, with the force of an incantation, never taking his eyes off the city across the harbor, "hurry hurry hurry hurry hurry."

Anakerie was thunderstruck to find her brother awaiting her, and she felt no shame in the outburst of scalding tears as they embraced. There was salt to his scent and to the taste of his fur, telling her he'd just come from the deep ocean that was his home.

Their father had been Daikini, their mother of the seafaring Wyrrn. In the manner of such things, in the defiance of all custom and the wishes of their parents (who were certain no good would come of the union) they had met and fallen passionately in love. He was heir to the throne of Angwyn, she was firstborn of a sept of some note. For love of him, she left the sea and assumed the form of the Daikini. She never regretted that choice, for while she never lost her love for the sea she also discovered a deep and abiding affection for the wild coastal domain that became her new home. As a warrior, the King had few peers and while her own martial skills were considerable, the Queen's true vocation lay in governance. He defended the kingdom and she ran it. She bore him twins, girl and boy, and when the children were barely a dozen years old, she died, in the same fearful cataclysm that brought Elora Danan to Angwyn.

That night, so the world was told, the young Prince perished as well, but that wasn't what happened. With her dying breath, the Queen committed her son into the care of her own people, in hopes he would find more safety there than on land. As she had taken on the form of the Daikini, so did Ryn assume that of the Wyrrn. His height was his own, regardless of race, but as a Wyr he was covered top to toe in a pelt of luxurious mahogany fur. The arrangement of the limbs was the same as the Daikini but the proportions were skewed, with webbing between fingers far longer than any had a right to be and a broader shape to the foot. He was impossibly limber and while he could move with ease in the air his grace underwater beggared description. He smiled more easily than his sister and his nature was more generous. She had the better laugh, but his had more practice.

Another surprise awaited Thorn at the rudder wheel. Steering the boat was Maulroon, Master Trader of the Cascani and one of his oldest, dearest friends.

"What," he managed to gabble, his confusion amusing the other man tremendously. Maulroon was built like a barrel—Nelwyn proportions actually, but in his case mated to legs that

matched the size of his torso—his head ringed by a thicket of curls
that had once been the color of midnight but which now showed
a hefty scattering of snow. The mistake most people made meeting him was to assume that he was fat. Watching Maulroon
aboard ship soon disabused them of that notion.

"Yon Ryn, he called in a marker," the Cascani said, but his attention never wavered from the sea ahead, the sails aloft as he sought
to squeeze every possible speed advantage out of the schooner.
"Said come, I came."

"Soon as we heard you'd been taken, Drumheller," Ryn established, "I sent out the word, to be of help if needed."

"Ryn," demanded his sister, "I left you on the west coast of this
continent. Ch'ang-ja is on the *east*! What, you swam near the
whole of the way around the world?"

"You think the only secret ways in the world are on land?" he
countered good-humoredly.

"If you've one o' those handy, lad," Maulroon interjected, "I'd
be grateful. Elsewise, we've a problem."

He stabbed a thumb forward, at the jumble of hulls and masts
that was slowly but inexorably sliding across their intended
course.

"Shards," breathed Drumheller, who was looking the other
way. "Maulroon, you speak better than you imagine."

Anakerie turned to follow Thorn's gaze, back to the Crystal
Palace, which for all the height it had assumed was still a refresh-
ing distance removed from their side of the harbor.

The flash from the peak of the tower would have blinded all
present, had Thorn not had a shield spell primed; as it was, the
intensity of the blast was like a spike through the eyeballs. But
compared with the sound that followed, this was nothing.

Thunder comes in as many different varieties as the lightning
that spawns it. One example is low-pitched, rolling, sonorous, like
rumbling a thunderstone over a wooden floor. It's broad and heavy
and ponderous. Another stands in stark opposition, sharp and furious, taking all the strength of its counterpart and expelling it in a
single, incredible report.

Imagine a whipcrack of sound, only from a lash that could etch a scar deep into the face of the world itself. A hard hammerblow impact to the body, meant to break it to bits where the more resonant thunder acts to crush it to dust.

As all aboard Saltai's schooner reeled from the shock, Thorn beheld what they did not, a bolt of energy leaping from the Crystal Palace to one of Jade.

"Talk t' me, Drumheller," said Maulroon calmly from the wheel. He'd deliberately turned away from the railing and put his back to the city and had thus endured the flash relatively unimpaired. "Where away now?"

A silence descended on the harbor, as though the tremendous clap of thunder had stolen away all other sounds. Then Drumheller heard a distant wail, from one of the other boats, of such misery and despair it squeezed his heart like a vise, forcing him to bend near double at the waist and clutch at a gunwale for support. It was a cry of someone who had lost all hope, whose only prayer now was that the end come quickly and with no pain.

He wanted to add his own to the rapidly rising chorus but he was Nelwyn and that meant he could be more stubborn than any Daikini. He also had pride in abundance, which refused to allow him to be beaten.

"We can make it," yelled Saltai, pointing to the leading edge of the boat city. There was still a fair gap between it and shore. Given the schooner's lines and a decent breeze, they had a reasonable chance of beating to freedom.

That would be a false victory, Thorn knew. They needed a better way, a quicker path.

"Maulroon," he called, indicating the strait between the mainland and the closest of the Twelve Kings, Sagat.

"Can't be done," Saltai said, following Thorn's gaze. "There's no proper channel," he explained. "Shallows t' ground ye, rocks t' tear out 'cher keel. An' worst of all, out yonder, right past the island proper, the shelf drops deep straightaway. Wi' the turnin' o' the tide, there'll be a wicked whirlpool forming where harbor water meets open ocean."

"It's that or nothing," Thorn said simply. "And even then, it'll be a close run."

Maulroon shook his head. "We've a fair breeze f'r this course, Drumheller. T' cut the way you ask, we'll be forced t' tack. E'en without the rocks an' shallows an' such, we've no room in that wee passage for those maneuvers."

"Ryn," Thorn called, casting aside Maulroon's caution, "can you be our pilot and lead us through there?"

The young Wyr didn't bother replying with words, he simply dived over the side, breaking the surface with hardly a splash.

"You steer your boat, Maulroon," Thorn told the Cascani trader. "Leave the wind to me."

Reflexively, Thorn reached for his coat pocket only to discover to his chagrin that the state finery provided by the sorcerers of the Crystal Palace had none. Anakerie held forward the traveling pouch she had from Elora and asked if it would serve.

Gratefully, he thrust his hand inside, came up with precisely what he needed, a square of paper, which he began folding with meticulous precision into the shape of a boat. With each bend and crease, he mouthed the words of a spell, imbuing it with the essence of the larger vessel.

Another whipcrack across the sky announced that lightning had struck a second tower, beyond the Jade Palace.

Anakerie intuited what was happening and spoke for Thorn to inform the others. "Thorn thought the powers running wild in the Crystal Palace would eventually burn themselves out," she explained, "like a fire exhausting its fuel. Those incredible idiots, how could they have not seen the danger?"

"They saw," Thorn told her, as he finished his folds. "They believed themselves equal to the task. And the prize worth the risk."

"See how the other palaces all echo the design and structure of the Crystal Palace. Like a pure breed of plant or animal. In return for a kind of perfection, you make yourself uniquely vulnerable— because whatever disease affects one, affects all. As the runaway spells consume the Crystal Palace, they jump to the nearest available source of fuel. The more such links it establishes, the more powerful it grows. Drumheller, what happens when it links all twelve?"

"Do we want to be here to find out?" Franjean inquired.

Rool shook his head vehemently, echoing Saltai's earlier chorus of *no's*.

"What happens to any vessel when you apply more pressure than it can possibly endure?" Thorn asked in return. "Ch'ang-ja sits atop a Magus Point, that's always been the source of its wealth and power. It's a city built on magic. But this isn't a major point, there's a limit to the amount of enchanting energy it can handle. I'm not sure *any* Point can handle what's building over there."

"Can you stop it, Thorn?" Anakerie asked. "Can you do anything?"

"I can try and win the war, Anakerie" was his somber reply. "So that this may never happen again. Will that suffice?"

He took a deep and calming breath to center and focus his will, then spoke quietly to Maulroon. "Set your sails, Master Trader," he said, "and follow Ryn's lead. Here comes your wind."

Thorn formed his mouth into the shape of an *O,* compressed the circle of his lips ever so slightly with the paper boat held just before him in his cupped palms. It hardly qualified as an exhalation of any kind, the little model didn't even stir.

But overhead the great sails rattled their mast hoops as they belled full of air. Creaks and groans made themselves plain as masts and spars, the entire fabric of the ship, adjusted to the new strains. Those on deck could hear the slap and gurgle of water rushing ever faster along the hull as they gained headway.

"Not too fast, Drumheller," warned Maulroon. "Steady as we go."

"Understood." It was the most delicate of balancing acts. They required speed to get through the passage as quickly as possible, yet too much would deny Maulroon the accuracy he needed to weave his vessel between the many obstacles before them. Despite the cool of the day and the breeze that covered the deck, both men were soon sodden with sweat, all of it from tension. Baghwan Saltai took his post in the bow, watching Ryn ply the water ahead, using hands to wave instructions back to Maulroon at the wheel. Maulroon kept a light grip on the spokes, for the adjustments to their course were measured in fractions of degrees.

They couldn't afford gross deviations from their path; Maulroon's plan was to skate as closely as possible to every obstacle and thereby maintain as straight and true a track as possible. Meanwhile, Thorn kept the sails filled and the schooner moving at a steady pace.

A rustling in the water ahead made one of the crew call out about giant sea snakes or some other kind of monster. Perhaps he meant it as a jest, to relieve the increasingly unbearable tension; if so, it was a wretched failure and the ripple of anxiety and distress that resulted communicated itself to the horses, who began to whicker and stomp their feet. They were already upset enough at the normal movement of the deck beneath them; it wouldn't take much to trigger a frenzy.

Anakerie stepped into this breach, with a sharp command to Luc-Jon to help. Without being asked, the brownies pitched in as well, while Maulroon offered a scathing assessment of the crew and what passed in them for courage. The noise was the whirlpool, in the first stages of its generation, as the outflowing ocean tide reached through the channel to pull the harbor water after it. This made Maulroon's and Thorn's jobs both easier and significantly harder. Less wind was required to move the schooner, the water itself was assuming more and more of that work. At the same time, though, that ever-swifter current limited Maulroon's overall control over their progress. There was less warning of any obstacle and less opportunity to pivot around it. To compensate, he ordered men to the sides, manning both bumpers and sweeps, to fend off any obstruction he couldn't avoid.

The sky behind them was lowering fast, the way it does in advance of a monster storm when in a matter of minutes bright sun can give way completely to a darkness to rival night. The shadows were shot full of weird lights and colors, purples and vermilion and a ghastly green that made the healthiest of faces look like an animate corpse. The cannonade of thunder beat constantly upon them, as though they were being pummeled by spiked hailstones, and not a few mouthed prayers of thanks at their distance from the city. None wanted to consider what it must be like directly beneath such a display.

"Past the whirlpool," Maulroon bellowed, to make himself heard over the din, "the lad signals clear water."

He twitched the wheel, taking them onto the outer edge of the vortex, letting them join with the current itself in adding to their speed. He'd timed the maneuver perfectly; the schooner accelerated with a surge that was noticeable on deck.

"Hands to braces," he yelled. "Gimme all the canvas she can fly!"

Lines whistled through blocks and great sheets of cloth unleashed some snap and thunder of their own as they were opened to the sky. Topsails and staysails were added to the mains, booms winched tight to present their best aspect to the breeze.

Thorn spared a quick, flashing glance at the city and then at the Palace built out of the substance of Sagat. Its spire might well be mistaken as an extension of the peak itself; of all the chapter houses, it was the only one constructed of what appeared to be stone rather than the more stylish and elegant gem crystals and precious metals favored by the other sects, and he wondered how that might affect the original spells.

As for the city itself, he could no longer bear to look at it; nor could any of the others aboard. It seemed from the glances he spared that it had stolen a measure of its aspect from Elora Danan and the Malevoiy. It was defined now wholly by darkness, in negative imagery, the buildings standing out as filigreed etchings of gray against a sable background. He was reminded of the Void that the melded sorcerers had created to consume the Deceiver and feared suddenly that the rift was still open.

The schooner reached the far end of the whirlpool, but fast as she was going through the water she lacked sufficient speed to break free of the maelstrom's clutches. In less than a heartbeat, her bow would be turned toward shore and Thorn knew with absolute certainty that there wouldn't be time for a second attempt. Even a single revolution around the circle would doom them.

Once more he held his little model boat before pursed lips, but this time he offered up a puff of breath.

Instantly, ropes snapped taut and the whole structure of the ship groaned at the effort demanded of her. Her bow attacked the waves ahead like a charging lancer, dousing the foredeck under a shower of foam and spray. The deck as a whole tilted alarmingly to the side and a number of sailors rushed to the aid of Anakerie and Luc-Jon as all their efforts with the horses were nearly undone.

Maulroon offered a roar of defiance, his face alight with the passion of the moment as he sent his ship into the teeth of the ocean. Saltai, looking half-drowned, his finery ruined, had the presence of mind on his perch forward to pitch a grappling line over the side, wrapping it around himself and a cleat to provide sufficient anchor for Ryn to clamber back aboard.

They were racing free of the shore now, faster than any sailor aboard could remember, even the oldest, most experienced salts among them keeping wary eyes on the masts as they flexed under the press of the wind.

"Y' did well, lad," Maulroon congratulated Ryn as the Wyr made his way aft, but Ryn had no eyes for the trader, no ears to hear his praise.

Thorn followed his look, as did Anakerie and the brownies. Saltai looked for Maulroon, who kept his own gaze on the task at hand, the sea ahead, the ship below, the sails that drove them. It was his responsibility to make sure this was enough to save them. If it wasn't, he had no interest in seeing whatever was to claim their lives.

Anakerie uttered a small sound, the kind some make when pierced by a mortal blow. She dropped to her knees because she needed to be held and while she loved her brother dearly, that wasn't the emotion she required. Thorn held her close and let her tears stand surrogate for his own. His own eyes burned with grief and rage but he could no longer find within himself the tears to ease that pain. Like the Magus Point in Ch'ang-ja, overflowing with more magic than it could bear, he had endured too much sorrow. He was done with weeping.

Ch'ang-ja was done with magic.

The lightning was continuous. Likewise the thunder. And as the schooner ran for the horizon, as the range opened, as their perspective broadened and more of the Twelve Kings came into view it seemed to those watching that the seamounts stood like a last barrier against that onrushing chaos. The bars of a cage.

Except the lightning was picking relentlessly at Sagat, whittling it away, and Thorn wondered suddenly if like called to like. He had been a guest of the Crystal Palace, his own magic had been incorporated however slightly into its substance. Once it clawed and scratched its way through Sagat, would the lightning seek him out?

He forgot how well Anakerie could intuit his thoughts.

"Plenty of opportunity for that when we were ashore, Peck," she told him softly.

"We'll know soon enough, I'll wager."

"No," said Ryn in a voice as strange as Anakerie's had been before she knelt.

By contrast, he stood a little straighter, determined to face this test the only way he knew, on his feet and full of defiance and courage.

Something shimmered against the landward horizon, as though a curtain had been raised right across that back wall of the world. It made no sense at first to those on the schooner, because they had nothing in their experience to compare it with, not even Thorn, who could draw on the collective history of his people. As they watched, it kept rising, quickly dwarfing the highest towers of Ch'ang-ja, and the peaks of the Twelve Kings as well. The scale confused them; for objects to be so tall, they had to be comparatively close to the city, yet through Saltai's and Maulroon's spyglasses—and to Drumheller's MageSight—the city appeared unaffected by this approaching onslaught.

It was Luc-Jon, of them all the only one of them possessing not a whit of magic, who made the connection.

"Mountains," he said, in a whisper as bare as the puffs of breath Thorn used to push them past Sagat.

"Those are mountains," he repeated, not believing his words himself.

"Ahhh," he cried at last, as if struck. *"Those are the Stairs to Heaven!"*

The spine of the world ran straight past Ch'ang-ja, and for nearly a thousand miles farther on. But the land here had collapsed beneath the waves in ancient days, creating an undersea version of the Wall to rival the one that bisected the continent, so that only the tallest of these peaks thrust their summits above the surface. That meant, to the south and west of the port, there was little in the way of foothills; the land reared straight up into the middle reaches of the range itself, plains yielding at once to mountains five and ten thousand feet tall.

Compared to what was advancing now upon the coast, those were nothing.

For Luc-Jon and Anakerie, it was like watching an avalanche. For the seafarers, a tidal wave. For Thorn, the superheated flow of mud and molten rock down the slope of a volcano, racing at incredible speeds even the fastest animal couldn't outrun. It was as though all the Great Realms of the Circle of the World—Earth, Air, Fire, and Water—had gathered together to cauterize this gaping wound before its infection could spread.

Of them all, only Thorn had ever beheld the active power of those Realms; at one and the same time, that experience saved his life and very nearly destroyed it. Though he was a mage, he felt very small and insignificant and humbled—he felt very Nelwyn— and compared to what transpired before him, that was nothing.

The heartland peaks of the Stairs to Heaven reared better than eight miles above sea level; that might well have been the height of the wall of rock sweeping down on Ch'ang-ja. Not only did the wave fill the horizon, it filled the sky, to such an extent that the schooner—far out to sea as it was—was cast into freezing shadow. That much mass and volume, at any speed, casts before it a battering ram of air and Thorn was thankful the city itself was hidden behind the Twelve Kings so that none of the schooner could see the results when it struck.

Of the Twelve Kings themselves, Sagat—weakened by the infernal lightning drawn to its chapter house—was the one that broke. It shattered from within, almost in slow motion, fissures splitting its substance into countless pieces that somehow held themselves in place, separate but motionless, for a discernible moment before being wiped indelibly from existence. The air ram swept the ocean flat and Thorn had barely a moment to cast a shield about the schooner before it caught up to them. As it was he had to suffer a measure of the shock, which shoved him brutally back against a capstan and threatened to squash him flat. Anakerie never let him go, even though that meant taking some of that fearful ordeal unto herself—which was, of course, her intent.

The wave of rock crested so high above Ch'ang-ja it might well be touching the lowest vaults of the stars themselves, and then it fell.

Once more, there was desperate need for Thorn's magic; once more, he knew there would be no margin for error or for weakness.

Stone fell like water from a cataract, straight into what must have been a bottomless maw, because nothing whatsoever came past the boundary line represented by the Twelve Kings. Over the days to come—over the months, the years, the lifetime—each recollection of this day would bring forth a new memory. Something seen, or smelled, or heard, to bear witness to the event and give it richer and more lasting texture. They would never grasp the enormity of the moment, just as they could only marginally comprehend the forces that were involved, but the passage of time allowed for a more complete perspective.

For a score of leagues in every direction, up the coast and down and inland, the world reordered itself. What had been part of the Realm of Earth yielded its dominion to that of the Realms of Water and Air and Fire, creating a new seabed as deep on one side of the still-standing Kings as on the other. Now that tremendous basin had to be filled and a new sound filled the air, a different quality of thunder, as the ocean swept over its latest conquest. Suddenly, the distance from land the schooner had come seemed like nothing at all as this monstrous tidal surge tugged them back the way they came, either to smash them on the rocky shores of the Kings or pitch them over the cataract beyond. No wind the schooner could handle could counter such a primal current.

Thorn made sure it didn't have to. He kept his place on the afterdeck, the space between the wheel and the taffrail, seated with Anakerie by his side. He traced signs in the air and on the wood beneath him that blazed with a kind of colored fire, one color seeping into the fabric of the ship while the other leaped aloft to enshroud it in what most described as a giant soap bubble. Thorn had bound the ship to him, made its life force one with his own, and created a field of energy that lowered its resistance to almost nothing. As far as the water around them was concerned, the schooner had no physical substance.

Just to make sure, Thorn etched a third sigil and cast it from him as powerfully as any arrow shot from a longbow. Into the ocean it went, straight to the bottom, through the accumulated silt and soil of ages until it struck bedrock, where it took hold as firmly as any harpoon.

The enchantments were all in place. All he had to do now was sustain them until the danger passed. He guessed that would be tomorrow dawn, because that was about as long as he believed his strength would last, even augmented by Anakerie.

It was a terrible night. The shock of their flight, the narrowness of their escape—the fact that they still weren't free—wove a tapestry of gloom about the crew. There was too much time to reflect on what had happened, what might yet happen, too little to do to keep minds and hands occupied. Fear knuckled about the deck because most Daikini were comfortable with the world as it was; those who bothered to learn the catechism of the Twelve Realms rarely took it seriously, even those who had truck with the other Realms. Storms and earthquakes they understood and accepted as part of the natural order. But the world turning itself inside out to obliterate a city of millions, that left them wondering when it might happen again and who might be the cause. Eyes turned to the afterdeck and sought out the brownies and talk turned to retribution.

Thanks to Thorn's InSight, Anakerie sensed the shifting currents in the crew's emotions, because they struck small resonances in her own heart and soul. Once before, when they first met in the dungeons of the Palace Royal in Angwyn, she and Drumheller had shared minds. The experience had been hard for both of them, because it was an interrogation. The aftermath was harder still, because they had fallen in love.

The problem was, Thorn was pledged to another, whom he loved as dearly, though he hadn't seen her since the Cataclysm. And Anakerie was pledged as strongly to her kingdom.

Through the night, they strolled the byways of each other's dreams. They shared an intimacy most couples cannot imagine and found a fulfillment that would last them to the ends of their days.

Anakerie stirred first, a soldier's habit, sight returning to her eyes to reveal the stillness that heralds sunrise. The horizon aft was like ink, with no line of demarcation to separate sea from sky. As she rose from her seat, surprised to feel no protest from muscles and joints that hadn't moved in the better part of a day, she made out a pale lightening ahead. Maulroon sat on a folding captain's chair by his wheel, which had been lashed in place; a folding table was set before him and he was finishing his transcription of the day's events in his log.

There was a carafe of coffee, steaming from the galley, but only the one cup. He was generous enough to share.

"You'd best hoard this blend, Master Trader," Anakerie mentioned after savoring both the scent of the rich and aromatic brew and its taste. "This is the last we'll see of Chengwei Spice."

He chuckled. "I'd forgotten, the fields were terraced just below the city. Casks in the hold should allow us to turn a tidy profit on this voyage then, even assuming we all drink our fill."

"The sea seems calmer. We're not moving as much."

Another chuckle. "Moving more, actually, but it's the natural rhythm of the sea. Light breeze, moderate swell, fair start to the morning."

"It's so still," she said suddenly, looking toward the darkness.

"Aye," he agreed. "The noise's been droppin' steady-like since midnight."

"I half expected trouble overnight."

Maulroon shook his head. "Stands t' reason, there'd be mutterin', with all that's happened. But Saltai's as good a judge o' sailors as I am. It's a decent crew, his. Y've nowt t' fear from the likes o' them."

"Even with the world crashing down about our heads?"

"Especially so, Royal Highness. That's the mark o' true Cascani, not just blood but strength o' heart an' soul."

"I pray so. I've a feeling we'll need all you have to offer and more—*what's that?*" she cried with alarm as the darkness was suddenly speared by a flash of golden light that raked down on their position from north to south before disappearing, to be replaced almost at once by a similar spark of emerald.

"The Bayan beacon," Maulroon said with admiration and thankfulness, both at the quality of the workmanship that had allowed it to survive this catastrophe and the fact that the fates had been merciful enough to allow its survival. It had only reestablished itself over the past few hours, which told him that someone had been in the lighthouse to fix it and start it running again.

With the dawn came the discovery that only one of the Kings had fallen, Sagat. The others reared skyward as proudly as they always had, albeit in a more solitary state than before. Maulroon's spyglass provided one other startling revelation, that the Gate of Peace had likewise survived.

"There's a story t' tell our grandchildren," Maulroon noted as he closed his glass with a *clack*. "Assumin', Drumheller, we'll any of us have any."

Thorn hadn't moved from where he'd sat the night, but had busied himself rooting through the traveling pouch Anakerie had got from Elora Danan, building a small but impressive collection on the deck before him. It was clear, though, that what he sought wasn't to be found.

"East, Maulroon," he told the Master Trader, in a husk of a voice. "Under all the canvas your ship will carry."

"To?"

"Where this all began, my dear friend. To the upper reaches of the river Freen, past Tir Asleen to the Sawtooth Range."

"Damme, you say!"

"We have five days to reach the gates of Nockmaar."

"Then we're done, because that can't *be* done. Not by this ship nor any other. Blessed bones, Nelwyn, y're talkin' about sailin' a fair ways 'round the bloody world! We've a whole *ocean* t' cross, don't 'cha' know."

"As I told you, Maulroon: you tend to your ship, I'll provide the wind."

"Y'll need a gale, Drumheller. The sticks"—meaning the masts—"won't hold."

"They will," Thorn spoke with flat assurance, though Anakerie knew the cost to him in strength and endurance would be murderous. Her twin must have picked up on her apprehension because he spoke next.

"I believe I can be of help," he said. "The Wyrrn have ways through the water, as the brownies and Nelwyns do through the earth."

"Then it's settled," Thorn said, and pulled a shallow ceramic plate from the traveling pouch. He set it on the capstan and tipped some clean water into it, just enough to cover the base entirely. Next, he set his little paper boat right in the middle. A pass with fingers over the plate rendered the surface of the water smooth as glass. Then he blew on the boat.

It didn't move. It wasn't supposed to. But no sooner had the mage finished that exhalation than the sails began to flap under the pressure of a rising breeze. Maulroon barked orders, keeping it simple at the start, to allow the crew to remember what it was like to be sailors. He didn't raise anywhere near the volume of sail Thorn requested, and wouldn't until he'd satisfied himself fully in his assessment of vessel, crew, and especially the weather. He was too good a sailor to take anything for granted, especially when it came gift-wrapped in sorcery.

"A fair wind, Maulroon," Thorn told him, "and a fair sea."

The Master Trader stared at Drumheller, as if seeing him for the first time. Knowing your friend was a mage was one thing; actually watching him wield a significant measure of that power was another altogether, and not entirely comfortable.

"Even with the lad's help," Maulroon said, "we're still talkin' days."

"I know. I'll not fail you."

"Drumheller—!"

"Get me there, Maulroon, that's all I ask." His tone, though, held more of the peremptory command *all I require of you,* and

Maulroon nearly bridled under it. Then Thorn seemed to step back within himself, hands clenching once, twice, as he took a deep and cleansing breath. "Please," he said after a time, in the voice Maulroon knew and trusted, and that made all the difference.

As the Master Trader shouted his commands, the schooner increasing its speed markedly with every new stitch of canvas that was flown, Anakerie knelt beside Thorn to look him in the eye, no matter how determined he was to avoid her.

"You stick to sorcery, Drumheller," she told him in that quiet, implacable way of hers, "leave the leading and motivation of troops to me, yes?"

"There's too much to do, Anakerie," he said, allowing a fraction of his weariness to seep into his voice, "and so very little time."

"Delegate, then. Hallmark of a leader, knowing which responsibility's yours and which can be fobbed off on staff."

"That's not my role."

"Look about, Peck. If not you, then who?" She smiled, mischievously mixing amusement and irony. "Center stage is yours alone, Drumheller, where no Nelwyn's ever been. Might as well make the best of it; who knows when such an opportunity will come again?"

He made a rude face and ruder gesture at the thought, which made the Angwyn Princess laugh outright.

"Tell me what you need, Peck," she told him, her matter-of-fact tone belied by the fleeting caress of her thumb across the knob of his jaw and the way she cupped his head, as though she were about to pull him into a kiss. "I'll do my best for you."

With the voyage properly under way, the first order of business was to set the ship to rights. Gear and passengers had to be properly stowed, which for much of the morning meant rigging stalls for the horses in the hold and then lowering them into place, making sure as this was done that the animals didn't panic. The bulk of that responsibility landed square on the brownies' shoulders, and they were constantly leaping from animal to animal, using cajolery on some, a calming draught for others, muttering all manner of dark imprecations as they levered precious cubes of sugar and a carrot or three into the horses' mouths.

A shelter was constructed for Thorn on the afterdeck, once he made it plain that he wasn't stirring from the spot until landfall. Despite the stiff and constant following wind, the air around his spot remained supernally still, allowing him to work and write in relative ease.

When Anakerie returned from below, bearing the midday meal on a tray for both Thorn and Maulroon, he was once more rooting through Elora's traveling pouch, his expression speaking most eloquently of his frustration and dismay. From a chest in the captain's cabin, Anakerie had scrounged more practical attire to replace the rags she was wearing when she came aboard. Loose trousers of duck canvas hung over soft-soled seaboots whose leather had been treated with oils and a minor enchantment to repel water and keep the feet warm and dry in the most wretched of weather. Above the waist, she wore a layering of shirts that offered ease of movement with protection from the sun and other elements. She'd bound her dark hair into a thick braid but still muttered at how easily it got in the way.

"I'm thinking," she told Maulroon, though her voice was pitched for Thorn to hear, "of taking a leaf from Elora Danan's book."

"What'cha say there?" Maulroon sounded scandalized. "Cutting it? Tha' short?" Precious few men wore their hair so, and no women worth the name.

"Save a lot of trouble."

"Cause a lot more in a different direction, I'm thinkin'."

"I suppose." She ladled some stew into a bowl and held it out to Thorn. He nodded acknowledgment of the dish and indicated that she set it aside.

"Not find what you're looking for?" Anakerie asked politely, refusing to take the hint.

He sighed, accepting that this distraction wouldn't go away until it had its way with him, and plucked the bowl from her hand, almost dropping it that selfsame instant. He set it quickly down and flicked his hand up and down, blowing on singed fingers and trying to recall a quick healing charm.

"It's hot!" he squawked in outrage, belatedly noticing that she was wearing a glove.

"Fresh from the cookpot, yes. Good, too. That Luc-Jon, he's a lad of hidden talents."

"Have to be, out on the Frontier." He took a cautious sip and nodded. "Very good," he said. And then he sighed again, because Anakerie hadn't shifted position or taken her eyes off his and wouldn't until she got her answer. They'd come to know each other so well, so quickly, it was driving him mad.

He told her what transpired in the Realm of the Dragons, of what Elora had done, and of the wards that safeguarded the egg.

"It's not there," she said, and he shook his head.

"She wore two pouches, remember," he replied. "I was just hoping in this instance fate had cast a favorable glance our way."

"She has it, then?"

"So I would assume."

"I only saw the one pouch, Thorn. Her right hip was bare."

"It doesn't matter if she hid it; the pouch and the egg are just as lost to us."

"I wonder how we'd know?"

"Know what?"

"When the dreams went out of the world? I don't feel any different but then, I suppose I wouldn't. That would take imagination. The ability to dream."

"Stop, Anakerie. I hate metaphysics and philosophy, they make my head hurt."

"You're the sorcerer, Peck. Aren't they supposed to be your stock-in-trade, the keystones of power?"

"And stop laughing at me as well. I'm a farmer. I like what I can hold in my hand. Magic is a tool, just like my plow, although it can occasionally be as stubborn as the pig who used to pull it."

"So what're you going to do, Thorn?"

"About the egg, nothing. About Elora and the Deceiver, whatever I have to. Those plans at least, I've set in motion. Now if you'll excuse me, Highness, I'll finish this delicious meal—my compliments to the cook, by the way—and continue with my work."

Now it was Anakerie's turn to feel bedeviled by the insights they shared, because she knew him to be as adamant in this decision as she'd been earlier. He needed his solitude, and from her especially, to complete his task. She didn't like it but she conceded him the field and withdrew.

Their last thought as they parted was the same, it was of Elora Danan and there was longing in them both. Despite all that had happened, they wished her well.

The Sacred Princess Elora Danan, now champion of the Malevoiy, stormed across the face of the world.

She stood at the base of the Stairs to Heaven, on what had once been highlands some twenty-five leagues west of Ch'ang-ja and which were now a fairly spectacular coast, with old-growth forest growing thick as fur right to the edge of a sheer cliff. Powerful combers hammered at the rock, sending up continuous explosions of spray, as if the sacrifice of this portion of Chengwei land had merely made the ocean hungry for more.

Elora perched right on the edge of the precipice, feet apart, a madcap grin splitting her features, daring all the elements to do their worst, the air to sweep her over the brink, the land to give way beneath her, the sea to rear up and wash her away. None of those things happened, and she told herself it was because none of those Realms dared test their strength against hers.

In her argent incarnation, appearances to the contrary, her skin remained flesh. Only its color had changed. Here, the transformation was complete. She gleamed because she was as hard to the touch as a beetle's carapace, a sable so pure and absolute it was the quintessence of darkness; she cast no shadow because she was one. Nothing that lived could do her harm; by contrast, she could deal death with an ease and in a multitude of ways that once would have seemed terrifying to her. She stroked a finger across the surface of a granite boulder and giggled as without the slightest effort her claw gouged a furrow as deep as her knuckle. The hardest steel would cut as easily and as for whatever lay beneath—she hugged herself in anticipation of the blood, of the fear in her victim's eyes, of the taste of the souls she yearned to claim.

One life topped the list, and she could hardly wait.

She thought of ensorcelled Angwyn and couldn't repress her delight at the thought of raising a fountain of raw magma right in the heart of that frozen city, of transforming the whole of what had been *her* Citadel to fire.

She reached out with her thoughts to open the familiar path to the World's core, so that she could ride the flows and currents of its molten substance to her destination . . .

. . . but the earth denied her.

She raged, she snarled, she threatened, she cursed, she struck out with every ounce of strength and power at her command, and did no more than create a modest excavation on the cliff top. Never once did she ask, that thought never occurred to her, which made her that much easier to ignore.

She demanded power from the Malevoiy, only to learn they had precious little to offer beyond what had already been granted. Of all the Great Realms, they stood closest to the Circle of the Spirit, with only the barest corporeal presence on the Daikini side of the Veil. They had been able to grant Elora Danan a measure of their aspect, their physical attributes, and their strength but anything more had to come from her. Since she possessed no magic, she had no power to command.

In short order, she discovered that all the secret ways once open to Elora Danan had been locked tight. She responded with threats of bloody vengeance but they sounded hollow even to her ears.

Her rage and frustration made her so blind she was unaware of the Caliban's presence until it loomed beside her, features perpetually shrouded by the wide brim of its hat, with its decorative ring of chiming bells. This close, it seemed wider to Elora than the tree trunks around them, and some of those when hollowed would make a decent house. Her own height was decent, yet it made her feel small. She didn't like that and thought of testing her claws against him. He caught her fantasy and approved, giving her a distinct sense that it was a struggle he longed for, a victory that was assured, and she found herself taking a reflexive step away at the image of her own soul mounted on that damnable brim.

The Caliban didn't say a word, it merely set off through the trees at its normal, deliberate pace. There was no clear trail that Elora could see, yet the Caliban walked unhindered and she wondered if the forest moved itself aside to offer clear passage. She didn't much like the creature, she'd rather find her own path, yet she found herself drawn after it, quickening her own steps until she walked a body length behind.

Like it or not, she was compelled to trust the creature.

To pass the time, she considered how best to slay her enemies. And made sure to place the Caliban second on her list.

Maulroon and Ryn exchanged glances, then notes as they leaned over the chart table in the captain's day cabin.

"Y're sure," Maulroon challenged.

Ryn shrugged. "You have your instruments, Master Trader. I know what my relatives tell me."

"Is there a problem?" Anakerie asked them both.

"Depends on how y' define the term," Maulroon said. "We both agree, y'r brother an' me, we jus' dinna care for the result." They didn't like it at all.

Maulroon spun the chart to face her, so she could clearly see the line of their course that he'd just marked in place. This was the second full day since leaving Ch'ang-ja. Given a steady wind, the best they might hope for was to have traveled perhaps two hundred leagues, six hundred miles. According to their position, they'd done three times that and more.

"We'll hold to Thorn's schedule, then?"

"Wi' time to spare, an' all stays well." Maulroon made a quick sign to ward off malefic spirits and forces. "What happens after is anyone's guess."

"What's he been doing aft, Keri?" asked her brother.

"Sending messages" was her thoughtful reply. "Drawing schematics."

"Of what?"

"I suspect he's having his relatives build a weapon to use against the Deceiver."

"That isn't good?" Ryn asked, picking up on her tone.

"Ask the sorcerers of Ch'ang-ja; it's their design."

"Bloody hells," exclaimed Maulroon, flailing arms and body and wishing for something to hit. "He canna be tha' daft!"

"Driven," she corrected, before assuring both men, "and determined."

"Can't be done," Maulroon snapped, making a captain's instant decision. "I won't allow it."

"Try to stop him then, Maulroon. I've argued till my voice broke, I might as well be talking to a rock. He believes it may be the only way, and his ultimate dictum is, would you rather see the Deceiver define the world to be?"

"Does winning matter when it leaves y' wi'out a world to enjoy?"

"Is there an alternative, when losing means the transformation of that world into Hell?"

She turned from the table.

"Whereaway, Princess?" Maulroon called after her, and she replied without looking back.

"My voice may be broken, Master Trader, but I can still make myself heard."

"What d'you think happened with the Caliban?" she asked Drumheller on deck. She lay a little outside his bubble of protection, so she could feel the wind across her body as she stretched full length to bask in the sun. They'd be turning north come nightfall, toward the latitudes where the Deceiver's unnatural winter held sway; she wanted to store as many memories of warmth as she could embrace. "From its actions at Tregare and the infiltration of Sandeni, we all assumed it was working for the Chengwei."

"So did they" was his laconic response. "Obviously, they were betrayed."

"That was what Elora said in the atrium, remember: the last such moment of change, when the world threw off the yoke of the Malevoiy, was defined by an act of blood and betrayal."

"Yes?" His patience was exaggerated, which meant he had none at all. Anakerie acted like she didn't notice, but was merely musing to herself.

"That's been the shape of the world ever since, a state of perpetual conflict between the Great Realms themselves, between lesser Domains within the Realms. How often have we been told we are hunters, we are killers, it is merely obedience to our nature? What established that nature, Drumheller? A war that came to a conclusion, but not a proper end. That concluded with a breach of faith and honor.

"We're paying the price, like all the generations before us, for Eamon Asana's arrogance. And," she said, acting on a sudden inspiration, "his weakness."

"How so, weak?" Thorn was properly intrigued, so much so that he set down his pen and looked toward her. "His solution saved countless lives."

"Some wounds can't merely be bound if they're ever to heal, they have to be cauterized. Yes, he guaranteed victory but he also made sure he'd be the only one to claim credit for it. And who's to say how things would have turned out had Khory not fought free of the Malevoiy's chains and spoiled the spells they had prepared for her? Eamon Asana betrayed her, why couldn't they then betray him?"

"You're uncommon knowledgeable all of a sudden."

"Conversation helps pass the hours when you're mucking out stables. You'd be amazed how much scribes and brownies love to talk."

"Hardly."

"And how concerned we all are."

"Your point, Highness?"

"This infernal device failed before."

"The Chengwei were not properly prepared. They didn't comprehend the forces they were wielding, nor truly what they were up against."

"And you do." When he said nothing, she made a noise of regret. "I'd hate like hell for you to be wrong, Peck."

"Or like Eamon Asana, do you fear losing the credit?"

Now she looked at him, her own face set. "I'd be careful whose shoes you try on, Drumheller. Some may take you down a trail you don't want to go."

"If there's a betrayal here, Anakerie, it's Elora's. You were there, you saw! She embraced the Malevoiy." Saying the words was like drawing a blade from an encrusted wound, tearing it open afresh.

"I *was* there. She saved our lives, do you remember that?"

He remembered the dais in the Crystal Palace and the Resonator. His enchantment was shattering before his eyes, the clockwork mechanism gradually erasing its transformation to stone. In moments it would be free to operate once more at peak capacity and he had no clue how to stop it.

That was when Elora appeared before him, to tap a single claw upon the dais.

It had been transformed as well, to a shelf of granite, and with that brief touch the massive stone slab tore free from its mountings and supports of crystal, plunging the Resonator into the Palace's catacombs, buying himself and Anakerie the time they needed to flee the Palace, and then Ch'ang-ja.

"Saved her own, you mean. We were an afterthought. She killed Khory!"

She'd known that one was coming. She had no answer, for him or for herself, beyond a soft and miserable "I know," that emerged in barely a whisper.

"I'm a warrior," she said. "I am my father's daughter. Show me a battle, I'll find a way to win it. Yet I cannot rid myself of the belief that those terms, those attitudes, don't apply here. No, that they *mustn't.* You're the mage, for Goddess's sake, why the hell are you taking my part?"

"Find me another way, Anakerie, I'll gladly take it. I'm sorry but I can't see one for myself. Until that happens, all I can do is prepare as best I can, and if that means they both must die, the Deceiver and Elora Danan, then so be it."

CHAPTER
10

Once again, Thorn Drumheller came to Nock-maar.

The last time, he'd ridden at the head of an army, with the warrior Madmartigan at one side and the Princess Sorsha at the other, and their cause was buttressed by the power of the sorceress Fin Raziel.

No army today, merely a gathering of old companions, though Thorn still found himself riding with a Princess. In addition, there was the young scribe, Luc-Jon, and his warhound. Maulroon and those of his crew willing to follow. Anakerie's brother, Ryn. Franjean and Rool. A motley crew for any purpose, much less to save the world. He might wish for more of them, he couldn't wish for better.

The hooves of their horses, and his pony, made a lonely

succession of *clip-clops* as they progressed through the winding succession of switchback passes that led to the vile heart of this range of mountains. No engineer could have designed better defensive fortifications. The way was narrow, the steep defiles providing ample opportunities for the defending troops to harass any invader with continuous enfilading fire. At the same time, rockfalls could just as easily block the way forward and back, leaving those forces trapped and helpless. This was a natural killing ground and anyone who hoped to survive it would have to spend lives and time clearing the slopes as well to secure safe passage. It could be done, but the cost would be as brutal as the battle itself.

Thorn snorted unpleasantly. *That,* he thought, *was why the common term for casualty lists was butcher's bill.*

That first time, nearly two decades ago, events had happened so quickly that Bavmorda's generals didn't have the opportunity to muster a proper defense. By the time they realized the full extent of the threat, Thorn and his companions had swept up to the walls of Nockmaar itself like a flash flood, to lay siege to that dread stronghold. Then again, when you serve a sorceress of the power of the likes of Bavmorda, who can transform an entire army into swine with the wave of a hand and the utterance of an ancient curse, the fundamentals of tactics hardly seem relevant.

Thorn allowed himself a grim smile, appropriate to the memory and his demeanor. When you're a sorceress of the power of Bavmorda and your foes are a withered crone who might once have had delusions of being your equal and her protégé, a Nelwyn hedge wizard, overconfidence comes easily. The battle hardly seems worth the effort.

That fearful night was when he beheld the best and worst of magic and found within himself the courage, and the skill, to wield it as he and Fin stood fast against all the wickedness of Bavmorda's enchantment to keep themselves from succumbing like their comrades. Afterward came the equally daunting challenge of restoring those poor souls to their true forms, without alerting either Bavmorda or her acolytes to what was happening.

Anakerie leaned over in her saddle and pressed a copper into his hand. It was an Angwyn penny, probably filched from Maulroon's strongbox, which held coinage from every mint in the Realms. There was nothing grim about the smile she flashed him, only the gentle invitation to share his thoughts, and his burdens.

"Nothing of import," he told her.

"Thorn Drumheller, you are *such* a liar."

"So you say, Royal Highness."

"So I know, Peck. You can no more dissemble to me than to Elora Danan, we both know you too well." His face made plain his feeling at the mention of Elora's name. "Don't you glower at me, Nelwyn, or try to bind me with your rules and strictures. I'll speak my mind to you, as I will to any comrade. Or Monarch, for that matter."

"So much, I see, for tact."

"I'm a Princess Royal, and a warlord, my friend. Tact is a weapon like any other, to be wielded or not as circumstances require."

"You still oppose me, then?"

"I think you're wrong, Thorn. There's a difference." As Anakerie spoke, she levered herself upright, standing on her stirrups, and turned right the way around for a look at the surrounding slopes.

"What?" Thorn prompted.

"We had to break ice from the moment we reached that river of yours, all the way inland from the sea. Snow was packed so deep across the countryside most houses couldn't be seen and the wind was so cold and dry we might as well have been crossing a desert."

"It's worse on the plains below Sandeni."

"I can well imagine. What I don't understand is why the landscape here is clear. These mountains are as cold as outside . . ."

"Colder, actually," Thorn muttered, but not loudly enough to interrupt.

". . . but they're dry. There's been no snow here, where I'd have thought the valleys would have been choked with the stuff. Impassable."

"It never snows here," he told her. "And it's always been cold, regardless of the season. There are legends that call this place an open wound on the body of the world, to remind us always of the horrors that once were. Nothing good ever came from Nockmaar."

"Elora Danan came from Nockmaar," Anakerie commented. "As I recall, you told me she was born here."

His silence was his answer, his visage so hawklike and predatory that the Angwyn Princess reined in her horse and swung herself down to the ground. He stayed mounted, her height and his pony's allowing them to face each other eye to eye.

"Do not do this, Drumheller," she told him flatly.

"You oppose me, Anakerie?" His own tone was as dangerous as hers.

"I say you're wrong," she repeated. "What you intend is as much an abomination as this place."

"It's our only hope."

"So *you* say!"

"This is wizard's business, *I'm* the wizard. Why can't you trust me?"

"Because I've seen that device in operation, as close as you."

"It's the only power left with even a prayer of challenging them, don't you understand?"

"That was tried in Ch'ang-ja, remember?"

"The Chengwei made mistakes."

"And you'll do better?"

"I understand what they did not."

"Share y'r insight, laddie-buck," suggested Maulroon, looking like a ridgeline himself as he reined in his animal. He wasn't terribly comfortable on horseback. Here was a man who could keep firm footing amidst a full gale, with his deck tilting every which way, pelted from all the corners of the compass by wind and rain and sleet and hail, complaining from the start about how the beast's movements felt "funny" to him. His mount clearly shared those sentiments, but they both made the best of it.

"What do we find a' the end o' this wee track?"

"A slagheap of a stronghold," the Nelwyn replied, pulling hard on his reins to yank them from Anakerie's grasp and tapping his heels against his pony's flanks to start him walking again. He wasn't trying to escape Anakerie, merely regain a measure of initiative. She didn't remount, but chose to pace him on foot, leading her own mare. "So old," he continued, "so . . . fitting to this abominable place that most mistake the fortress for part of the landscape. The walls are all in grays and blacks, as though once they were hosed with flame the way you or I might water a garden, with a great sweeping spray of fire."

"Dragons did that?" Maulroon asked, and Thorn shrugged.

"I suppose they must have, I'm not sure I want to imagine anything else capable of expressing such power. The heat should have cracked those stones to powder, yet all they did was score the facings, the way a pot will look after being left too long on a stove, so the food burns.

"Nothing will grow in these mountains," Thorn told them. "That's why we have to pack in all our supplies."

"But an invader would control the lines of supply," Anakerie noted, "so that should be no problem. The advantage would go to the besiegers. They could simply starve Nockmaar into submission."

"So you'd assume," agreed Thorn. "Except that according to the chronicles, the larders here were never empty. Be it sustenance or armaments, what was needed was always at hand."

"That's like Elora Danan's traveling pouch," said Luc-Jon, though he knew the mere mention of her name was a lash across the Nelwyn's shoulders.

"Magic," snorted Maulroon.

"Of course," Thorn told him. "This hole fairly chokes with it. There's more potential concentrated among these rocks than at any other point on the globe. Supposedly, this is the Prime Magus Point, the first that ever existed, and the most powerful."

"Yet it was left untouched by the Cataclysm?" Anakerie wondered.

"I've wondered about that myself, in recent years. Tir Asleen, the original seat of Elora's power, was destroyed. Nockmaar, the home of her enemy, was left unscathed. I always suspected it was more than just fate being perverse."

"Why is everyone so scared of it?" Luc-Jon asked.

Thorn pulled his pony to a halt, nudging it around to more easily face the lad, genuinely amazed by the question that had been asked.

"I thought you knew," he said to Luc-Jon, "you of all people, with the access you had to your master's archives."

"Forgive me, Master Drumheller," Luc-Jon suggested with a smile, "but that was half a world removed from here. And while my master's collection may have been eclectic it was far from comprehensive."

"True," the Nelwyn agreed. "For some reason, I keep seeing you in Giles Horvath's library. Most curious, as though that was your destiny."

"It's a dream I've had, sir, to study at the University in Sandeni."

"No no no, not studying, teaching." Thorn fell silent, realizing that his companions were staring at him, none of them having the slightest clue how to deal with this minor revelation. "That's curious," he managed to say at last, hoping to deflect any concern with an attempt at humor.

His hope shriveled in the face of the brownies' withering commentary.

"Bloody daft is more like it," suggested Rool.

"Playing with those damnable spells as we crossed the deep water," agreed Franjean. "Dancing yourself through who knows what kind of wormholes. Y'know, don't'cha, Drumheller, the stench o' demon's about you stronger than ever."

"If that's so," the Nelwyn replied, showing teeth, "be careful you don't earn yourselves a bite!"

"Drumheller," interjected Anakerie, "the young man's question."

"What? Oh, yes, I beg your pardon, Luc-Jon. I always sound more scattered when I'm agitated. I *sound* more scattered, thank you very much." This impassioned declaration went to the brownies, whose comments were no less pithy because they were entirely silent. "In every other respect, I'm quite fine."

He visibly gathered himself, sitting straighter in his saddle and adopting a more commanding mien.

"Perhaps we should camp here for the night, Maulroon," he said, and for all the qualified phrasing this was as much an order as any Anakerie—or Maulroon himself for that matter—had ever uttered.

"There's still a fair piece o' daylight left us, Drumheller."

"I know, and we haven't all that far to go. But I'd rather we reach Nockmaar with the day before us, not the night."

"You expecting trouble?"

"Not the kind you mean. I just don't like the ghosts."

"Bloody *hell*!" snarled the Cascani Master Trader. Gaunts and ghoulies were the last thing he wanted.

"The castle's haunted?" Luc-Jon asked.

"In ways you cannot begin to imagine."

"Is that why people are scared?"

"Not by the haunting itself, but what it represents. Before the last turning of the wheels, when the Great Realms were theirs alone to command, Nockmaar was the greatest stronghold of the Malevoiy. It was said to be the only place in the Realms that existed as much on the Faery side of the Veil as on ours, allowing the Malevoiy to cross back and forth as easily as they pleased.

"My fear, my friends, is that if Elora Danan has her way it will be so again."

Once again, Elora Danan came to Angwyn.

The first time, she came wreathed in fire, cast down from the heavens like some godling hero out of legend. Now she approached on foot, across the icy expanse of Angwyn Bay, which had frozen solid right down to the sea floor. The wind howled and shrieked, assaulting the land in a katabatic storm that generated winds whose velocity put the strongest hurricanes to shame. It was a dry, angry wind, the kind you'd expect to find on a desert, driving a wall of dust before it. This one made do with ice, imbuing the minute slivers with such force and fury that they cut more sharply than a surgeon's scalpel and were capable of stripping the flesh from the bones before the victim had time to realize he was doomed. She'd passed a number of examples on her journey. Some were animals, too old or weak or unlucky to find shelter from this now perpetual tempest. The rest were Daikini who'd been foolish enough, or desperate enough, to make a try for the Deceiver's life. Nothing remained of them save bones so coated in hoarfrost that they gleamed prettily in whatever light touched them, be it sun or moon. She found a sword stabbed into the ice. An attempt to pull it free snapped the blade; a tap of the two broken pieces together shattered them both to shards and powder, which were immediately blown from view by the gale.

This was a tempest so fierce that a deep breath seared the lungs, the intense cold doing the same damage as breathing flame.

On every side was desolation, a stark and barren landscape that had been scoured of even the potential for life. Overhead, the sky roiled, as clouds swept down from the north in a great Coriolis circle centered on the city of Angwyn itself, colliding with one another in a colossal pile that thrust them as high into the sky as there was air to sustain them. Lightning flashed constantly amidst that titanic maelstrom, bolts that seared the eye and did not vanish in an instant but lingered as though summoned. She assumed there was thunder to match but nothing could be heard over the keening howls of the wind, so piercing a threnody she wondered idly if it was being produced by the souls the Deceiver had enslaved.

That prompted a grin, feral and hungry, complete with bared fangs and a flex of both hands to extend her claws.

Amidst this field of limitless whiteness, she was the jarring note. Animation and life, where there should be none. And as the ice pack she strode across had been leached of all color, Elora Danan by contrast was the absolute and total amalgam of it, her body painted a black so intense it seemed to absorb the available light.

There were ships moored at the mercantile docks, with crews on watch and people on the wharves beyond. Though not the equal in size and population to the metropolises of Chengwei, Angwyn was one of the great ports and great cities of the Daikini Realm, capital of a kingdom that laid just claim to a significant portion of this continent. It was modern and cosmopolitan and crowded.

None of that mattered anymore, for Angwyn was a city

sheathed in ice, buildings and people gathered into a frozen hibernation in the space between one breath and the next.

With a grace far beyond even the most elegant of the High Elves, and that could not be comprehended by the Daikini even in their dreams, Elora danced along the magnificent thoroughfares of Angwyn, from the Royal Promenade to the shore-hugging esplanade more popularly known as the Rambles. For the first time in her life, she visited Silver Square, that legendary market a square mile in size where anything imaginable from either side of the Veil could be bought or sold. She had lived in Angwyn nearly her whole life, yet had experienced nothing of this fabled city, for she had spent that entire time sequestered in a tower adjacent to the Palace Royal. She'd been allowed out of her apartments only on rare occasions of state, under the close escort and strict supervision of her guardians, the Vizards, a dozen cloaked and cowled specters culled from the finest families in the kingdom and meant to represent the Twelve Realms over which she was expected to claim dominion.

As she neared the palace, the wind lessened its fury. This was the center of the cyclone, the engine that drove this elemental machine. Here all its forces achieved a measure of balance. There was no wind, no precipitation. For all the fury and madness raging scant yards away, here at least could be found a measure of peace.

Elora wasn't surprised to find the eye of the storm centered on her own tower.

Nor, at long last, to be attacked.

Even the weapons weren't wholly unexpected.

At some point in her youth, a rookery of Night Herons had been established in her tower. They were creatures of the vilest sorcery, as feared in their own way as Death Dogs, and no one at Court was pleased with their arrival. Unfortunately, there were no sorcerers in the kingdom willing to make the attempt to drive them off. By the same token, the King—Anakerie's father—though he was a warlord of well-deserved renown, was reluctant to take any action that failed. This, he concluded, was as clear a case of letting sleeping dogs lie as ever he'd seen and his ministers were equally quick to support him in his decision. So long as the birds did no harm, they would be left alone.

Elora knew nothing of that. She'd actually befriended them and fed them tidbits from her own hand.

Now they repaid her by seeking her life.

They were shadows themselves, coated with the same shade of pitch that had stained Elora's argent body, and their beaks and claws could rend the strongest steel armor. Unlike many of the races that lived beyond the Veil, in Lesser and Greater Faery, Night Herons weren't bothered in the slightest by cold iron. Worse for Daikini, they couldn't be killed by it, either.

Elora, however, was no longer Daikini. She had bonded with the Malevoiy. She *was* Malevoiy. So she merely stood her ground, projecting an attitude of casual unconcern to mask the excitement in her breast. This would be slaughter. This would be fun.

And it was.

She made a mess of the flock and for the briefest of moments was liberally coated with their blood. That moment was all the time required for her chitinous armor to absorb it, filling her with a piercing joy that made her cry out with delight, sensations so intense the distinction blurred for her between pleasure and pain, agony and ecstasy.

And these were but *little* lives, she heard within her head, the desiccated tones of the Malevoiy itself, still bound to their own Realm though their link with her had given them perceptual access to the other Realms they hadn't enjoyed since their exile began. Imagine, childe, how it will feel to claim thy mortal foe?

The thought made her tremble with anticipation. It quickened her pace into the main entrance of her tower and up the winding circle of stairs, around and around and around until she burst through another doorway and into the vestibule of her apartments.

She had no doubts as to where she'd find the Deceiver. A steady stride took her into the amphitheater where her Ascension was to be consummated.

All within was as she remembered it at the moment Thorn jumped with her into the body of the floor. The Monarchs of the Great Realms—save one, conspicuous now by its absence—and their retinues, flash-frozen by the Deceiver's spell. That empty space represented the Malevoiy, still so hated, so feared even after this immeasurable length of time that not even a representation of them was allowed, to mar the celebration.

Fools, she thought, the Realms are of a single whole. Cast aside one, you cast aside all. You should have used the opportunity to try to make your peace with the past. She laughed, and it was a sound far colder than the air outside these walls. Now that chance is gone. There will be peace, but on *my* terms.

She heard chittering in the depths of her soul and knew the Malevoiy approved. In her, they had finally found their true champion, a far better choice for them than Khory Bannefin.

The faces that surrounded her were all smiling, as though they beheld their hearts' fondest desires, without a clue as to what was really happening. Assembled there were some of the most powerful beings in the Realms, yet the Deceiver had wrapped them up in her enchantments without any of them being the wiser.

As Elora passed the Queen Magister of Greater Faery and Her consort—noting with amusement that the Lady of Lesser Faery had come alone, leaving her consort Tyrrel the keys to their kingdom, just in case—her steps faltered. Predator though she'd become, filled with the dark passion and ancient hatreds of the Malevoiy, she could not look upon the body that lay before her and not confront the immutable reality that Kieran Dineer, a dragon, had fought and died for her.

That was supposed to be impossible. Not the fighting part, but the dying. Dragons were the Monarchs of the Realm of Dreams. They were Creation incarnate, beyond such petty concerns as life and death.

Yet Elora had seen it happen. And had done far worse herself.

She knelt on one knee by the dragon's great wedge-shaped head, so huge it alone dwarfed her entire body, the contrast in their sizes offering a glimmering insight into how such as Thorn Drumheller must feel in a world of Daikini. She wanted to reach out and touch Kieran but her hand refused to cross the gap between them. Though he was dead, the Malevoiy in her refused to abide the slightest contact with its most ancient and implacable foe.

"Hurts, doesn't it?" the Deceiver said cheerily. "To discover what you've lost."

When Elora turned toward the other woman, all emotion had been stripped from her face. She had made herself as alien in aspect as the Malevoiy had originally presented itself to her.

"This is your doing, Deceiver," she said softly.

"Like the voice. And the look. And the manner. The silver was too stark a contrast. This makes us more of a piece."

"We are nothing alike."

"Of course we are, that's the point." The Deceiver raised a gauntleted hand and from each fingertip extruded claws identical to the ones manifested from Elora's armor. She mounted the dais with a flirty pirouette, her skin alabaster pale against the shadow of her own armor. Elora might have resembled a statue, the Deceiver was more in the nature of a waxworks doll. As Elora watched, not quite spellbound, the Deceiver conjured a brilliant rainbow and wrapped its spectacularly vibrant colors about her like a sash, across her hips, her breasts, the elegant column of her throat, one end dangling from an outstretched hand while the other circled her leg and trailed off behind her. Then, with a snap of the fingers, all that beauty was drawn into the Deceiver herself.

The results were instantaneous and dramatic. Pale rose dusted cheeks whose flesh glowed with an inner radiance of health and vigor. Her hair became spun gold touched with flame, her eyes cut lapis lazuli, her mouth a generous slash of crimson.

"Most impressive," Elora conceded. "But ultimately, a lie. As are *you!*"

"I'd be careful what I said, if I were you."

"Or what, my life is forfeit? According to you, that judgment is foreordained, it holds no moment as a threat."

"You want to end it then, once and for all? Bless my soul . . ."

"I didn't think you had one in you."

The Deceiver laughed. "A fair retort. You've been taking lessons from the brownies." Her face grew somber, the eyes losing a bit of luster, allowing Elora a glimpse of the wasteland within, as bleak as the growing ice field that surrounded Angwyn. "They remained with me almost to the end, Franjean and Rool. They kept faith far longer than I gave them credit for."

"What have you done?"

"What I've told you from the beginning, weren't you listening, *ever*?" She sounded petulant, as Elora remembered of herself not so long ago. It was an ugly way of speaking but the Deceiver didn't appear to notice or care. "I did what was *necessary*, sacrificing a few for the good of all."

"Your friends? Those who loved you?"

"That's the price demanded by some spells. Those bargains can't be struck over the slaughter of enemies, believe me; I tried enough times! Oh dear, child, have I shocked you? I didn't think that was possible with one who wears the colors of the Malevoiy.

"We have that in common as well." And she gave a small curtsy, to present her own version of the Malevoiy armor.

"You killed the brownies?"

"Tiresome wretch, *yes*, does that satisfy you? And Sorsha, and Madmartigan when the fool tried to come to her rescue. Fin Raziel died naturally, though there were stories aplenty to slander me that it was really a broken heart. Do you know it was said that her dying words were a wish that she hadn't saved me from Bavmorda, that the world would have been better off with both of us dead. The bitch!"

Elora stayed silent through the Deceiver's tirade. Instead, she began closing the gap between herself and her foe, using her grace in such a way that it was impossible to see her move. She was in one place but after the blink of an eye she was somewhere wholly different without having given off the slightest sense of a body in motion.

She didn't anticipate the Deceiver using the same sets of skills against her. Her other self met her halfway, before Elora was ready, with a kick like a hammer to the solar plexus that set the younger woman sprawling. The Deceiver leaped after her, landing astraddle the fallen Elora, plumping her bottom down on Elora's pelvic girdle and jamming her boots down hard on Elora's elbows, effectively pinning her arms.

Her voice when she spoke was chiding and full of disappointment.

"Child child child," she said, idly tracing designs on the body of Elora's armor with a claw and watching blood swell up to fill the runnels, appreciating Elora's shock at how casually her impenetrable armor had been breached, "have you so little regard for me, for all I've accomplished, that you assumed the acquisition of some power, the forging of a new alliance—I grant you at some considerable and lasting personal cost—would be sufficient to make you a match for me?"

She rocked her feet back and forth over Elora's elbows and the young woman bit back an outcry at the shooting pains that filled both arms. The Deceiver worked a tad harder and was rewarded by a grunt.

She flashed fangs of her own and sank both sets of claws through the material of Elora's armor as if it weren't there. Elora's back arched, face twisting with a sudden, vicious rictus of excruciating pain. It felt to her as if the Deceiver had literally grabbed her by the heart.

"Pick whatever road you please, little one," the Deceiver said with an undertone of melancholy and genuine regret, "you'll find my footsteps to blaze your way. There is nothing you can do that I haven't done before you."

"And this is how you seek to set matters aright?"

"I know the full measure of what is to come. I know what you cannot, which are the pathways to damnation and which to a better place."

"Done a terrific job so far!" There was unbridled fury in Elora's voice, which was answered in kind by her foe.

"All that has happened is on your head, not mine. Had you been less willful, this would have been avoided."

"If as you say, we are one and the same, only from different epochs of time, how could you possibly imagine I'd be any less willful than you yourself?"

"It doesn't matter. I have you now. As lamb, as lion, you've still come to the slaughter."

She reached out to Elora's face but to do so had to rise fractionally from her perch. That was all the opening Elora required; it was what she'd been counting on. Recognition and action occurred as one, as she lifted both legs from the hips, bending them out and around to hook her ankles under the Deceiver's jawbone. Next came a flex of Elora's entire body, putting the whole of her strength into a spasm that heaved the Deceiver head over heels off and away from her.

Elora used that same move to roll off her back and into a fighting crouch, regaining her balance as the Deceiver flung herself to her own feet.

The next attack was a scorching blast of arcane energy, from the Deceiver's outstretched hand to Elora's torso. Contact wouldn't have been fun, so Elora made sure to be somewhere else.

There was no more conversation, no more gibes or japes as the battle between them was joined in earnest. For both of them, this was a last chance. Only one could walk away and with her would go the fate of a world. Mercy then was a luxury neither could afford.

They were so intent on their own battle, as the air quickly filled with the snap and sizzle of bolts of magical energy and the residue of powerful spells, neither noticed a stealthy figure slip into the amphitheater. Or the faint gleam of that figure's drawn sword.

Thorn's party beheld Nockmaar at dawn, which like every sunrise in this accursed region was a misery that combined gunmetal sky and a chill, damp wind that carried with it the stench of something rotten that must have just died in some noxious marsh. Dawn was signified by a gradual lightening of the sky, no sign of the sun itself was visible, nor would there be any sight of stars in the night. Nockmaar existed under a perpetual overcast that offered an icy drizzle and threatened worse and somehow managed to soak a body to the skin, regardless of the thickness and efficacy of foul-weather gear, oilskins, and woolen sweaters.

It was a place that made intruders feel like they wanted to be somewhere else, preferably far away.

The main gates hung open, sagging from smashed hinges, but

Thorn and his company took little comfort from the sight. Too much resemblance to the jaws of a trap.

"Pardon my asking, Master Drumheller," said Luc-Jon, as they rode down from the crest of the final escarpment, into the broad valley that led up to the derelict stronghold, "but why'd you leave it?"

"Intact, you mean?"

"If it was no use to you, why not make it the same for everyone?"

"Sound strategy. We spent the better part of a fortnight trying. We used fire, we used magic. We mined saltpeter, sulfur, and charcoal to mix our own batch of Chengwei powder and set about blasting the place to bits. It wouldn't burn, the spells wouldn't take, and our explosives fizzled in the damp. Some of the men even attacked the walls with sledgehammers and chisels. Their steel broke, and their mallets, their muscles, and their will, without them even chipping the surface. Whatever brought Nockmaar into being, my young friend, it's beyond our power to destroy."

As they approached the moat and saw that the drawbridge remained down, the portcullis beyond still raised, they beheld two other parties marching toward an evident rendezvous. Both were as quickly identified as they proved a surprise.

The leader of the Nelwyns spoke first, a bluff plug of a man, a little taller than Drumheller but far broader in the shoulders and body, proclaiming to all the world the strength that Drumheller preferred to keep hidden. There was a similarity of feature that marked them as kin, but they weren't close relations. As well, a tension existed between them.

When they met, after Thorn dismounted, the newcomer didn't extend his hand in greeting.

"Greetings, cousin," Thorn said, ignoring the discourtesy. "I bid you welcome."

"That's no' a word fit for this accursed place, Drumheller," replied Torquil Ufgood. "Any more than decent folk are fit to visit. Nockmaar was built by the damned, I say leave it to 'em."

"I can't, Torquil. I told you why."

"An' you know my mind on the subject."

"Yet you're here."

"We're family. Bound by blood, clan, an' sept. An' you're a Magus."

"Since when did that count for much among the Rock Nelwyn?"

"Old Jaffrey cast his runes, Drumheller. Near worked hisself into a fit tryin' t' puzzle 'em out. What he saw scared him silly."

"What did he see?"

"Dunno. Wouldn't tell me, only Manya." She was Torquil's wife and leader of their clan. "The wife, she tells me, do as y're bid. So here I am, an' here are y'r toys. I'd wish y' the best of 'em, Drumheller, but in this pisshole what's the point?"

In his hand, Torquil held a faceted globe, the most brilliant and perfect diamond ever cut from the earth. Its size was less than half that of the sphere Thorn had seen in Ch'ang-ja but he knew without examination that this was without flaw. Here was a case where Nelwyn care and craft far outstripped the best the Daikini could offer.

He recognized the style of the facets.

"You did the cutting, Tor?"

"Manya," the Rock Nelwyn replied with a shake of his head. "Insisted on it. An' proved by doin' so she's no' lost her touch."

"That's no error."

The globe was once more wrapped in a felt cloth, then packed into its carrying case. Torquil's companions had brought with them the twelve platters, as intricately carved as their Chengwei precursors but scaled more to Nelwyn dimensions.

The High Elves had brought the mechanism itself, perhaps ten feet tall instead of nearly thirty and lacking the ornamental filigree that had decorated the original machine. Elves had no love of machines, but there were none finer in the craft of woodworking. Their artisans had constructed the components, and then delivered them to another clan of Nelwyn to fit those pieces properly together.

Thorn spent the better part of an hour snaking his way through its innards, inspecting every working part with meticulous precision. Perfection in both form and function was the benchmark here; anything less, or the slightest flaw, and there was no point even making the attempt. Ch'ang-ja was a relatively benign environment. Nockmaar was not. Unleashing the power of the Resonator would be risky enough; if its power went wild here . . .

He need not have worried. The Faery artisans had done their work as well as the Nelwyns.

Thorn carried the focusing lens and led the way inside. Maulroon and his crew brought torches for illumination, though they proved unnecessary. Despite the many and oppressive shadows inside the fortress, there was sufficient ambient light to see. The torches in fact proved of little practical help, though carrying them made the crew feel better. As they proceeded, Thorn would stop occasionally, grapple with his notebook—no mean feat considering he was also trying to safeguard the diamond ball—and seek out the relevant passage in his voluminous notes. The farther they went, the more pensive he became, especially as they continued past the throne room and through a doorway which opened onto a rising circular stairway.

"Of course," he muttered as he began the climb. "Could I have expected anything less?"

It was one of those ascents that seemed to go on forever and by the time he reached the top Thorn's legs were spongy, thrust through with acid-tipped and cruelly barbed pins and needles. He managed to achieve a couple of steps into the room before they gave way, which suited him fine, allowing him a little time to strike an armistice with his memories and his emotions.

This was Bavmorda's sanctum, where she had performed her most vile and baneful magics. There was no roof, the entire summit of her tower was open to the sky, yet the elements of nature held not the slightest sway. He felt no breeze, no chill of the outside air—the stones of the tower and the furniture in the room cast off sufficient chill of their own to make a body wonder if he'd wandered into some abattoir by mistake—not the slightest moisture, save for the sweat he'd generated himself with his climb.

Straight ahead, in the exact center of the room, where Thorn knew the ancient ley lines intersected, was Bavmorda's altar, the spot on which she'd called down the most ancient deities to claim the infant Princess's soul and consign it to ultimate oblivion.

That was where the Resonator would stand.

Moving the altar was no picnic, the damn' thing was far heavier than it looked and wasn't too thrilled with the prospect of eviction. The stone became slippery and minute barbs grew from nowhere to tear at the fingers of the men who tried to grapple with it, even though they wore stout seamen's gloves.

They made quick work of their business. None wanted to linger.

With steady hand and inhuman care, Drumheller slipped the globe onto its cradle. Once more, he inspected every component, testing the ease with which the platters revolved around their axis, and the interaction of all the various propulsion wheels and driving gears. This was a thing of beauty, of that there was no mistake. The artisans who'd crafted this had imbued it with a portion of their own essences, as had those who'd built the larger clock in Ch'ang-ja.

Now it was Thorn's turn.

He thought of his wife and children and prayed that they would remain safe and hidden regardless of what transpired here. He also knew that if the Malevoiy regained ascendance, his family would be sought as no others in revenge for his actions.

"Elora Danan," he breathed, "how *could* you?"

It was a heartfelt entreaty, but what shook him was that he wasn't sure which Elora he meant it for—the one he'd help raise or the other who'd crossed centuries to destroy her.

The slide of sword from scabbard disturbed the silence of the sanctum. As he opened his eyes, Thorn heard a companion blade likewise drawn free. Two figures flanked the doorway, both holding bared steel—Anakerie and Luc-Jon. She had no armor and the clothes she wore had been scrounged from various hope and slop chests aboard Maulroon's vessel. They were serviceable, they fit comfortably, they afforded some protection from the weather but they were useless against another blade, or any other weapon. Anakerie didn't mind. She placed her faith in her arm and her blade and was content. Luc-Jon was more formidably attired, but only because he'd found a crewman pretty much his own size.

"Is this for my benefit?" Thorn inquired.

"The others have withdrawn," Anakerie told him. "We four elected to stay."

"Four?" he started to ask, then nodded his head at the sight of the brownies, Rool on Anakerie's shoulder, Franjean on Luc-Jon's.

"We've come this far," Luc-Jon explained. "We want to see it through to the end."

"And if there's trouble," Anakerie finished, "find a way to pull you out of it."

"If this doesn't work," Thorn said, "there's probably nowhere in the Realms left to run."

"Then it had better."

"Aye."

He slipped inside the mechanism and pulled the lever that unlocked the gears. He checked the settings, compared them with the calculations laboriously entered into his notebook, then checked them again.

He ended his inspection with a slight, wry grin, the kind he used to give Elora before trying a new spell. Then he gave the main flywheel a flick of his fingertip and as it began to spin he held both cupped hands over it. He sketched an image of the wheel in his thoughts and imagined it racing up to its rated speed. A heaviness swept over his body, a sense of flesh taking on the characteristic of stone, the sign that he had achieved a measure of rapport with the primal forces of the earth. As fire was Elora's personal sigil, so was the earth his. Breath left his lungs in a sharp but basso *hufhf* and all that solidity started to shift within him, as massively as the tectonic plates that comprised the planetary crust. Up from the balls of his feet, outward from his shoulders, that tremendous power flowed with ponderous deliberation down his arms to his hands. Thorn bared his teeth in a grimace as his body took up the extraordinary strain of sustaining extremities which had assumed the mass of mountains. This wasn't like Ch'ang-ja, where lightning flashed about his body, nor did it resemble what often happened to Elora when she summoned fire to her. Outwardly, there was no visible sign of the forces he had manifested—beyond his stance and the tenor of his breathing, which was somewhat labored by this juncture, a cause of some concern to Anakerie.

With a suddenness that made Thorn stagger, the pressure vanished. His hands regained their correct weight and as he drew them apart for a look at his handiwork, he beheld a blur where the flywheel had been. He had imbued it with power to spare.

He reached for his notebook, then left it in his pocket, giving it a reassuring pat instead. He knew what was required; he needed no more reminders.

He reached for another level, and engaged the first platter.

They fought like starving wolves, neither offering nor accepting quarter. The Deceiver slashed at Elora with spells and enchantments, and the young woman responded with brute force and claws. As the battle between them raged, Elora discovered to her amazement and delight that magic was no longer denied her. The Malevoiy could not reach her when she stood on the cliff in Chengwei; that land was wholly on the corporeal side of the Veil. Here in Angwyn, the seat of the Deceiver's power was even more supersaturated with arcane energy than Ch'ang-ja had been right before the end. The Deceiver needed such awesome levels of power to maintain her very existence in this reality; but because her own nature contradicted and even violated all the structures and laws of nature, because at her core the Deceiver was closer kin to demons than she dared acknowledge even to herself, the barriers between the Realms were consequently weakened. The Malevoiy could reach out with their power and cast it into Elora.

She didn't understand the nature of their sorcery. These were conjurations that dated from the dawning of the world, and the use of them reduced her to little more than a conduit for the Malevoiy themselves. She was their weapon, the hands that directed her. She didn't care. What filled her mind's eye were the images of the friends she'd lost over her lifetime thanks to the Deceiver, what filled her heart was a black, choking, toxic cloud of rage and hatred whose only outlet was the struggle with her other, older self.

For all that might, for all the dark and brutal emotions that fueled it, Elora's efforts came to naught. Every move was parried, every stratagem anticipated. Wherever she turned, the Deceiver was a half step before her. Whatever she tried, the Deceiver cast back in her face. She was an open book that her foe had committed to memory.

The longer they fought, the more Elora began to change, the less that transformation seemed to matter to her. Gradually her limbs elongated, taking on the aspect of the most ancient race of elves. Though the general arrangement of those limbs might be considered human, the overall result became increasingly less so. Elora achieved a beauty beyond the aspirations of mortal beings and yet at the same time seemed more and more a creature actually carved from the obsidian shell that covered her. She gained height on the Deceiver, and reach, and speed. Anticipating her actions became less relevant because Elora was able to react to the changing fortunes and necessities of the duel with an alacrity that made the Deceiver appear clubfooted by comparison.

A sheen of sweat glistened on the Deceiver's features and the gay accents provided by the rainbow had long since faded, leaving her pasty-faced and increasingly desperate. Elora meanwhile was having fun. A flick of one finger scored her opponent's armor without fear of similar retaliation. The same from another opened a slash in the Deceiver's cheek deep enough to draw blood. Only nothing fell from the wound; there was no blood within the other's body. No life, either, save that sustained by what until then had been an indomitable will.

"I hear no boasts, Deceiver," taunted Elora. The Deceiver's response was so profane it made Elora laugh the louder, never noticing that her amusement presented itself with the chittering twitters of the Malevoiy.

"No," the Deceiver snarled. "It won't end like this, I won't allow it!"

"You'd do better trying to stop the stars in their course across the heavens. There is the mark of the Malevoiy upon you. Accept that. Be One with Us again."

Elora had no idea what prompted the offer. Her speech, like her actions in the battle, was increasingly dominated by the Malevoiy, while the essence of Elora steadily shrank within herself almost to nothingness. However, it proved the wrong thing to say, with a vengeance.

The Deceiver lunged forward like a berserker and for the first time in a while Elora found herself seriously on the defensive, being driven back across the central dais of the amphitheater toward the section of the audience that had been set aside for the Malevoiy.

Another breath, another lever to be pulled, another platter to set in motion. This was the eighth, Thorn noted, the one representing the Malevoiy.

As it began to spin, a snap of energy flared up from the platters to strike the crystal. That made Thorn jump, partly from surprise but also from a flash of alarm, because that was how things had started going wrong in Ch'ang-ja.

Again, as in that doomed city, there was a tremendous tearing sound, as though two titanic forces had gripped the crust of the world and ripped a length of it apart as they might a piece of cloth. He reeled from the shock and saw that the remaining platters had started spinning of their own accord.

"No," he cried, clutching at the governing levers. *"No!"*

He might as well have cursed the Cataclysm, or the storm that raged over Angwyn, or his own mortality. The levers had no effect.

He staggered from the interior of the box and was cast to his knees by a basso *thrumm* of such a low frequency it was felt more than heard. The sensations were awful, making his insides feel like they'd been turned to jelly. A look toward the doorway revealed no sign of Anakerie or Luc-Jon and he feared for a moment that they'd suffered the same fate as the Chengwei sorcerers. Then, the young man's hand caught him by the collar and hauled him behind an upturned table, where Anakerie gathered him close into her arms. He returned the embrace, thankful for human contact, grateful that it was with a dear and beloved friend.

"Is there anything to be done, sorcerer?" Luc-Jon demanded, assuming the manner of a Pathfinder officer, casting aside the deference of the scribe for the decisiveness of a warrior, a battle-seasoned leader of men.

"I thought you said you could control this, Peck," Anakerie chided, not unkindly.

"I can. I will." He thrust himself to his feet, going up on tiptoe to peer over the edge of the tabletop. "Just not with gears and levers."

"It's going to open that damned portal again, isn't it?"

"That's the plan."

She faced him, aghast.

"But not quite yet," he explained. "Not without our principals."

He held up a pair of fetishes, superb carvings of both Elora and the Deceiver. Anakerie's mouth twisted in disgust as the Elora model lost cohesion in Thorn's grasp, reshaping itself before her eyes into something that was recognizable both as the Sacred Princess and as one of the Malevoiy.

"And then what?"

"Shove them through and slam the door."

"That's your solution?"

"Have you a better one?"

"What about hope, Drumheller? What about the dragons?"

"That was lost when she slew Khory. I told you, Anakerie, the binding spell was sealed by the *three* of us. It can only be released the same way."

"I refuse to believe that!"

"Then you're a fool!"

"Drumheller, you're not *listening*! I have *hope,* damn your eyes, you silly little peck! I can imagine better days! How can that be if the dragons are extinct?"

He stared at her for what seemed the longest time, as if she'd been speaking gibberish. His eyes were slightly unfocused, a dissociative look she recognized; it meant he was thinking, fast and furiously, processing whole new orders of information.

"I'm an idiot," he said, and just as she replied, "No news to me," he idly tossed the fetishes into the maw of the Clockwork Resonator.

Again they were hammered by that fearful noise, this time

accompanied by that disturbing atmospheric effect that gave the air the properties of water. A pulse of energy rippled from the Resonator, gathering up everything movable in the room—whether debris, furniture, or people—and shunting them along until they collided with the closest wall. Even then, the oscillation was so formidable that the massive walls themselves actually groaned with strain.

Within the space that was cleared, a new scene had superimposed itself on the sanctum. Both Thorn and Anakerie recognized it at once: the dais in Elora's tower in Angwyn. The Deceiver was battling an Elora by now almost completely subsumed within the form and personality of a Malevoiy. The fury of the older woman's assault had driven Elora back until she'd sprawled atop the body of the slain dragon, Kieran Dineer.

As they watched, pulse after pulse erupted from the Resonator, on a regular basis that Thorn only belatedly realized was in tune to his own heartbeat. With each outrush of power, the merged scenes became more tangible. Figures perceivable as outlines became translucent, then opaque, gradually working their way up to solid.

The Deceiver lunged, outlined in a corona of power, but she'd passed the crest of her rage. The fury that sustained her, that enabled her to get the better of her foe, now ebbed from her body as quickly and dramatically as it had manifested itself. Initially the difference was minuscule, no more than the smallest of fractions.

It was enough.

Elora caught her with a sideways sweep of the arm that slammed the Deceiver through the air to a brutal impact against one of the stone worktables. Her body bent in ways that only babies can manage and when she crumpled to the floor, there was blood on the counter and she made no immediate move.

Elora rose shakily to her feet, a trifle disoriented, confused by the double images of place—was she in Angwyn or Nockmaar, the amphitheater or some sorcerer's workshop?—and that bewilderment was her undoing.

From the shadows in Angwyn, strode a tall, angular figure, approaching Elora from her blind side. It seemed like she was crossing a fair distance yet within a couple of steps she was there and Thorn was gasping with amazement once more to behold Khory Bannefin.

For a fateful moment, he didn't register the implacable look on her face, the gravity of her mien. She wore her normal broadsword strapped diagonally across her back; at her belt was the curved blade forged for her by Elora. The moment the pieces fell together for Thorn was when Khory reached for the sword.

So much happened so quickly. To Thorn, although every element remained distinct and sequential in his thoughts, it was all pretty much simultaneous.

He cried, *"No!"* and started forward, breaking from Anakerie's grasp as if her strength were nothing.

Elora turned to confront this new threat, managing a hate-filled curl of the lip as she saw who it was.

Khory pulled Elora's blade clear and raised it overhead, joining one hand with the other.

What was strangest to Thorn was Khory's speed. He'd never seen such quickness, in Daikini or elf, never imagined it was possible. That cry and Elora's snarling reaction were all they were allowed before Khory's sword reached the apex of its draw and descended, propelled by every scrap of strength the warrior possessed.

It entered Elora's body at the collar and proceeded diagonally across the thorax, slicing through the major blood vessels in the shoulder, the heart itself, the lungs, the primary organs below. The blade left her body at the hip with such a spray of blood that Thorn knew Khory had severed the abdominal aorta and the femoral artery as well. Paradoxically, that was the only sign of damage. Elora's chitinous skin didn't split or shatter under the blade's assault, but appeared to flow around the edge and close behind it so that when Elora fell there wasn't a mark on her.

That didn't matter. She was dead.

Thorn uttered no outcry as his child struck the floor. He'd believed her lost to him when she accepted the Malevoiy. If he now told himself this was a mercy, he wondered if he'd believe it. In silence, oblivious to everything else about him, he stumbled to where Elora lay and gathered her head into his lap. From there, his arms folded her up to his shoulder and he began to rock back and forth, uttering a keening lament.

Yet another pulse erupted from the Resonator, putting the final seal on the transition, allowing Khory and the Deceiver and what had once been Elora to remain while the rest faded to insubstantiality, returning whence they came.

"Save your grief, Drumheller," Khory told him calmly. She hadn't relaxed her stance in the slightest. If anything, she was more wary than ever, as if an attack was imminent. By the door, Anakerie hauled Luc-Jon to his feet and shoved his sword into his grasp, taking her cue from the warrior. Luc-Jon, to his credit, after a startled stare at his slain sweetheart, paid her body no more heed. There'd be time enough for that when the fighting was over. Or it wouldn't matter to him anymore because he'd be dead, too.

Thorn, however, wasn't in that kind of mood.

"Go to hell," he snarled.

"This isn't over, mage. It's only just begun."

Anakerie made the connection, remembering what Thorn had told them on the road.

"The Resonator's reenergized the Magus Point," she said.

"So there's magic to this accursed hole once more?" Luc-Jon grumbled.

"Magic and more. This was the Prime Point, scribe. The one place where the Malevoiy could walk freely from their Realm to ours!"

An outcry from Khory was their first warning. Shadows came to life in the hallway and the sharp *tang* of steel was heard, then a heartfelt curse as the blade broke. Luc-Jon thrust himself to the center of the room under his own power, Anakerie came by air, courtesy of a blow powerful enough to crack bones and draw blood. She'd have been in much worse shape had Luc-Jon not broken her landing with his own body, the pair of them going down in a tangle of limbs. The Princess Royal managed to turn that collision to her advantage, using the momentum of the impact to roll herself to her feet in close proximity to Khory and Drumheller.

"The Malevoiy," she bellowed.

They had never seen more than one and that lone representative solely through Elora's eyes, passed on to Thorn through the rapport they shared and from him to the others in their turn. The Malevoiy were incredibly tall, so elongated in every respect they seemed much like stick figures. And while they walked upright, there was an element to their carriage and stance that reminded Thorn uncomfortably of a praying mantis. Like Elora after her transformation, the Malevoiy presented themselves for battle shrouded in a shade of black so intense it tried to swallow the surrounding light and color. They carried no weapons, they needed none; as Elora herself had proved in battle with the Deceiver, they *were* weapons. In a purely temporal duel, their claws could cut more savagely than any sword and their chitinous armor was totally impervious to anything crafted at a Daikini forge. As for magic, in many ways, they defined the term.

Khory wasn't bothered in the slightest. While one hand held her blade at the ready, the other reached into Elora's traveling pouch, which hung from her left hip, to procure a similar blade for Anakerie and one for Luc-Jon.

"No guarantees, I'm afraid," she apologized. "But since mine cut through Elora's armor, they might do the same with the Malevoiy proper."

Luc-Jon wasn't thrilled. "I've never fought with a blade like this," he explained.

"Hang back then," Anakerie told him. "Watch how it's done."

With that, the Princess Royal of Angwyn charged. She couldn't match the Malevoiy for sheer speed but that wasn't crucial. Her blade made all the difference. It had come from a Rock Nelwyn forge and was composed of an alloy that mixed ore from Nelwyn mines with those imported from Greater Faery. It was composed of steel, but also of noble metals such as silver, its cutting edge coated with a ceramic compound to maintain its sharpness indefinitely. Being single-edged, it was primarily a slashing weapon, though its point was good for stabbing as well. Elora had put blood and toil and tears and sweat into their creation. They were far from the ultimate expressions of the swordsmith's art—she would need a lifetime to achieve that pinnacle—but they remained exceptional pieces of work that somehow transcended their origins.

They weren't perfect, but they were very special.

As the Malevoiy quickly learned, to their sorrow.

"Have I gone mad?" Drumheller wondered, perhaps aloud, more probably to himself as the battle raged about him. He had fought too many battles to sit on the sidelines while dear friends shed blood on his behalf, but he couldn't bring himself to leave Elora's corpse or even to let it go. "I saw you die," he said to Khory's back.

"You saw her vanish, duffer. You assumed she died."

He yelped in startlement, then felt instantly foolish, telling himself this was his imagination speaking to him, nothing more. Regardless of Khory's fate, he'd just seen Elora slain, been struck by her life's blood.

That was when he heard the crack, like the breaking of an eggshell. The figure he held had grown stiff. With the end of the wearer's life, the chitinous armor lost all fluidity as well. When he peered more closely, however, he saw a hairline fracture threatening to split the casing along the line left by Khory's swordstroke.

He heard the kind of grunt uttered by someone making a tremendous effort, coming from within the armor, and felt a faint shudder, the tiniest of follow-on cracks that hardly extended the opening by the length of a fingernail.

"Elora?" he called, casting about frantically for either a mallet or a wedge to crack the casement wide. The tools weren't necessary. He saw movement within the shell, heard a faint scrabbling of hands groping for a purchase and then with a tremendous heave and a roar he couldn't imagine coming from Elora's breast, she was free.

Within the shell lay an altogether human, altogether naked, altogether argent—except for her blue eyes and the rudest, most unruly shock of black hair—Elora Danan, beaming up at him like a madwoman, without the slightest respect for setting or situation.

One of the Malevoiy slipped past someone's guard and took a swipe at Elora, who yelped in alarm and sprang clear so that the creature struck only the cocoon she'd just emerged from. It swiveled about for a second strike but got no farther as a pair of brownie arrows, supercharged by the life force of their bowmen, detonated in its back. A split second later, a madcap pivot by Anakerie removed its head at the shoulders.

That death heralded a natural ebb in the fighting, as the Malevoiy withdrew to regroup.

"How?" gabbled Thorn, his confusion split between Khory's escape and Elora's.

Her smile was a wonder, albeit brief, as she filed it away for the duration of the conflict.

"My own variation on your disappearing pig trick."

"Sleight of hand? By all the blessed Fates, child, *why?*"

"The last of the Realms of the Flesh is the Malevoiy. The first two of the Circle of the Spirit are Life and Death. I have to know them all, Drumheller."

"By dying?"

"You said yourself you were considering using the Resonator. I knew how badly the Malevoiy wanted me, I also knew their strength was my best hope for reaching the Deceiver and confronting her directly. It didn't take a genius to figure the price they'd demand for my help, but I couldn't risk telling anyone for fear they'd overhear."

"You improvised—everything?"

"Sort of."

"What about what just happened, your own death?"

"Drumheller, while Khory carries my pouch, she's the caretaker of the dragons, the living embodiment of the Realm of Dreams. That allows her to work miracles. Whatever she does, she can undo, especially in so concentrated a nexus of magic as Angwyn and here."

"You took a fearful risk, girl!"

"You taught me how, mage."

Luc-Jon didn't say a word, he simply crossed to her, dropped to his knees, and enfolded her in an embrace he wished could last forever. She matched him strength for strength, though her own passion was tempered by a hefty dollop of serenity. There was a maturity to her eyes he hadn't seen before, not so much due to her own death and resurrection but her sojourn within the Malevoiy shell.

"They're not done," she told them after she and Luc-Jon finally pulled apart. The young scribe stripped off his shirt and offered it to her for clothing. It was long and full enough to serve as a tunic—and looked quite attractive once she cinched her belt snugly about her waist and settled her traveling pouches on her hips.

"They've been in exile too long," she continued, "they're too hungry. They see this as their sole chance to regain the rank and stature they once possessed."

"By seizing the dragons?" Thorn asked.

"Can you imagine," Elora said, "a world whose dreams are shaped by the Malevoiy?"

"I've seen it," the Deceiver told them, voice turned bleak and hollow by despair. "I've fought my whole life to stop it. In the end, to save my world"—it wasn't pleasant laughter, what emerged then from her bruised and swollen lips, there was too much in it of the Malevoiy—"I had to destroy it."

The Resonator pulsed again, accompanied by a succession of *clicks* and *whirrs* and *thunks* as gears shifted and platters rearranged themselves. No one paid any attention to the device, however. Their eyes were riveted on the Deceiver. She was like a painting from which a layer of detail had just been removed. She stared at herself in horror, then collapsed in upon herself, wrapping her arms about her head in a futile attempt to hide, refusing to comprehend what had happened to her.

"Drumheller," Anakerie said, "it's eating her alive."

"Something's happening," Luc-Jon announced from his sentry post by the entrance, fear and wonder wrangling for dominance.

"Something's coming," Khory agreed, the stillness of her tone telling them all how serious this was.

Elora heard the chimes, felt the reverberations of the Caliban's massive footsteps on the staircase.

"Bavmorda," Drumheller said in hardly more than a whisper.

The sorceress Queen of Nockmaar was younger in these ghostly images than he'd ever seen her, in the full flush of youth, her world chockablock with infinite possibilities. Right here in what was to be her sanctum, she was flirting with a young man whose raiment marked him as royalty, and his fiery hair, as Sorsha's father. He didn't know he was doomed, any more than Bavmorda suspected herself in those early days to be the instrument of his destruction. This was a happy time for them and the inexpressible delight that lit her face when she spoke of wielding her magic struck a strongly resonant chord in Thorn himself.

"What is happening?" Luc-Jon demanded again, torn between his fascination with the scenes presented by the Resonator, drawn forth from the history of this foul place, and his real apprehension about the creature advancing along the corridor.

"The three of us together," Anakerie suggested to Khory. "We can take him!"

"We'll get in each other's way" was the warrior's laconic response. "He'll make mincemeat of us." She shook her head and let a dangerous smile stretch across her face. "This is my fight, Highness."

Anakerie nodded. This, too, was the kind of battlefield decision she'd seen before. She held out her right hand and Khory took it.

A sharp cry from Elora broke them apart, leaving Khory to stand alone before the doorway while Anakerie and Luc-Jon withdrew to where the others huddled together, holding on to one another as the only elements of stability in a space that was rapidly losing all other coherence.

"The Resonator's more under control this time," Elora noted. "There's no fireworks like in Chengwei."

"In a way, this is worse," Thorn told her. "It's creating an active pocket of chaos instead of a portal."

"What does that mean?" demanded Luc-Jon.

"The Resonator creates a field of energy," Thorn explained hurriedly, thoughts racing in a frantic effort to find a solution. "Within that field, the concepts of space and time as we comprehend them no longer have meaning. Past, present, future, here, there, they can all be jumbled together. When the field stabilizes, it's possible to move from one to the other, as you saw when Elora, Khory, and the Deceiver were transported to Nockmaar. There's no danger of that at the moment," he assured them hurriedly. "What we're watching are shades, no more, images of other events, like ghosts in a haunting."

"She's no ghost," said Anakerie, tossing her thumb toward the Deceiver.

"Not yet," Luc-Jon noted. "Not for a while."

The scene changed to a woodland glade, a man and a woman riding. They were both of a height, even for Daikini, though there was something about the man that set him apart from the general run of the breed. The woman had golden hair and a marvelous laugh and only an idiot could fail to see the resemblance between her and the Deceiver. Strangely, Elora's features tended more toward the man. His hair was dark as a raven's wing and altogether unruly, his eyes like chips of cobalt, blue highlights against a magnificent darkness. There was strength to both their faces, but the woman's was softened by a life of privilege, whereas her companion had been pared down to his essence. His coat of arms and gear marked him as a knight errant, a wandering paladin bound to no house, vassal to no lord. It was the sight of his shield that had prompted the outcry from Elora, for it was emblazoned with the same dragon rampant emblem she'd designed for her own battle flag.

Without thinking, Elora stepped forward into the scene, eyes flashing from one rider to the other as they cantered past, reaching out to them both and looking as if she'd been whipped as their horses passed through her. They were ghosts to her in every respect and she was the same to them. Suddenly, though, the man pulled on his reins, twisting in his saddle as though he'd heard or sensed something untoward. He looked Elora in the eye and flashed a grin bright enough to light her heart forever.

All father and daughter had was that moment of recognition, so quick and fleeting she might well have imagined it, for with the next brace of seconds the knight's attention was demanded elsewhere. The woman had pulled a little away during his pause and she waved for him to catch up.

That was when lightning smote the earth. A fat and messy bolt, mere feet from the nose of the knight's animal. It reacted by rearing, intending to flee. The knight hadn't been expecting an attack of any kind and found himself unhorsed, his landing as undignified as it was painful.

Elora heard a kind of thunder, but it had nothing to do with the weather, as a score of burly riders clad in black leather and mail hurtled from the surrounding woods. Their leader was a mountain of a man with spiked pauldrons on his shoulders and a skull-faced helm. Thorn recognized him at once.

"Kael," hissed Drumheller.

"Who?" asked Luc-Jon.

"Bavmorda's general."

A net was hurled and the woman's horse went down, a pair of soldiers leaping to the ground to take her prisoner. The paladin, of course, wasn't about to let anyone abduct the woman he so clearly loved. He drew his own sword and made for them afoot.

The first to try that blade paid for it as dearly as a man can.

Kael wasn't perturbed.

Again from a clear sky came a pair of lightning bolts, each as powerful as the first, to bracket the knight. The concussion alone would have slain the strongest Daikini and the release of such energies seared the knight like meat on a spit. Impossibly, he still lived, still groped for his sword and struggled to his feet. The woman he loved was in mortal danger and he meant to rescue her, regardless of odds or cost. She screamed at the sight of him, not in horror but in sorrow, while Kael laughingly called for a spear. One was tossed to him and he spurred his charger into a gallop.

"You're a fool, General," Elora said with quiet delight, as she watched the knight set himself. Either his burns were mostly show and he'd hardly been scratched by the lightning, or he had the same gift of healing that had saved Elora's life on more than one occasion, because he wasn't moving like one of the living dead, which is what he looked like. It was a decent performance but he was too relaxed in the joints, there was no sign of trauma or even significant pain anywhere on his apparently scorched flesh.

Evidently, Bavmorda noticed as well. As Kael closed on the man, a final bolt struck. It was nowhere near as powerful as its predecessors, this wasn't designed to slay but to bedazzle. All the witch-queen desired was a few fatal seconds for Kael to finish the job and she would be content.

The spear took the knight through the heart, lifting him from his feet and punching him back against the trunk of an old oak. He was dead before he struck and Kael decided to leave him there, to impress the locals with Bavmorda's puissance.

They'd gathered up the woman when a tremendous *crack* filled the air, accompanied by a gusting breeze of considerable force. Kael looked back at the oak and was thankful that none of his troops could see his face beneath his helm, for it was stamped with stark terror.

Where stood the man he'd slain now reared a dragon, a single sweep of its wings generating a veritable gale, while its great claws gouged trenches in the solidly packed earth and crumbled boulders big as houses to powder. Its tail lashed the ground with the force of an earthquake. It trumpeted its rage with a roar that shook the heavens.

Some of the troops made to run. Kael by contrast grabbed hold of the woman and crossed her throat with his dagger. The beast could kill him if it so desired, but it would see the woman it loved die as well.

To his delight, Kael realized the creature was running a monstrous bluff. Dragons were denizens of the Realm of Dreams; they were the stuff and product of the imagination. Its sole anchor to the tangible realm of the Daikini was the body that had just been murdered. It might be able to scare him to death in his sleep, but awake he was in no danger. Even as he watched, its ability to affect the physical world diminished, even as the dragon itself began to fade in the morning half-light.

The woman screamed his name: *"Calan!"*

Thorn let out a breath he hadn't been aware of holding and finished the name: "Calan Dineer." The dragon who had collected him in his sleep fifteen years ago and carried him to Tir Asleen, setting him on the path that would ultimately return him to this hateful place.

It was Elora, though, whose cry was most heartfelt and lost: *"Father!"*

She sank to her knees and repeated her cry, "Father," in the kind of broken voice a child uses to express its utter desolation of heart and spirit.

None save Khory noted the chimes at the door, or the monster who filled the doorway.

"At last," she said softly, drawing herself to her full height and still looking dwarfed by contrast with the Caliban. "You want one Elora or both, you want anything in this room, you must pass me."

The Caliban said nothing, neither word nor gesture. He loomed, creating the impression that he could demolish the entire castle without a second thought should the need arise.

Out of that supernal silence came a wriggling tangle of whips, possessing a perverse kind of animation, each topped with a fanged head and determined to be the one to capture Khory. None of them came close, as she disposed of the lot with a sideways sweep of her sword.

For the first time, the Caliban drew his own sword, a weapon sized and weighted for his massive, blockhouse form. Parrying such a weapon would be akin to deflecting a tower of solid iron. Yet when he attacked, Khory was there to meet him, teeth gritted, her own sword backed by all the reserves of her lean and wiry frame. In the comparatively close confines of Bavmorda's sanctum, the advantage in maneuverability lay with Khory and she pressed it to fullest advantage. Unfortunately, that also required her keeping the duel well clear of Elora and company, which severely limited her freedom of movement. Back and forth they went, she quicksilver, he ponderous, their blades clanging like hammers. Each of those terrible hits should have blown her arms from their sockets yet more than once she chose to stand her ground and have it out with her nemesis face-to-face.

The Resonator initiated another pulse and with it another timeslip, to the seminal moment of Elora's infancy, when Kael had stolen her away from Thorn and his companions and galloped her to Nockmaar to be sacrificed. True, an army had followed hot on his heels, composed of the survivors of those great castles who'd already fallen to Bavmorda's sorcery, the latest being gallant Galadoorn, but Kael gave it little thought. Nockmaar had never fallen that he knew of, and would never fall while he held command.

Of course, it did, the very next morning, as Kael's men were hoodwinked into chasing Thorn and Fin Raziel across the plain, only to have the army they believed transformed entirely into pigs rise up out of hidey-holes dug in the ground, fully restored and spoiling for vengeance.

The infant Elora meanwhile lay swaddled in her sacrificial cloth atop the altar in Bavmorda's sanctum, where now stood the Clockwork Resonator. Thirteen candles were arrayed about her, one for each of the Great Realms, and a bowl of foul brew stood ready to be mixed with her life's blood in consummation of the Ritual of Obliteration.

It was an epic battle, between Sorsha and her mother (Sorsha lost), between Fin Raziel and the woman who'd been her best friend (Fin lost), and finally between the Nelwyn who wanted to be a wizard and the greatest demon sorceress of her age. With a little bit of luck, some dexterous sleight of hand, and a fatal moment of clumsy footwork from the opposition, Thorn won the day and saved Elora's life. The Ritual intended for her consumed Bavmorda instead, utterly and completely.

That, thought all involved, was the end of it.

How was Thorn to know better? He was years removed from the wisdom and experience that would have prompted him to act and Fin, well, she was old and thankful to have emerged from the battle alive. None realized that Bavmorda's enchantment had opened gates between Elora and all the Great Realms, the better to sever all her connections with them when her soul was obliterated. They knew nothing of her parentage, of the husband who'd lost his bride, the father facing the annihilation of a child he'd never hold. Calan Dineer was Sovereign of the Dragons, Lord of the Great Realm of Dreams, the quintessence of everything known as magic.

So when Bavmorda acted to sever the link between the baby and the greatest of the Twelve Great Realms, Dineer reached out to shield his daughter from the spell's effects. He knew the limits of Bavmorda's power and of his, he felt he had a fair chance of success. Perhaps his efforts provided the moment's delay that allowed the heroes to arrive in time? He never said, and could not be asked. What he'd forgotten in his agitation and his fear was where this abominable act was taking place, the ancient seat of power of his most hated enemies.

As Bavmorda's ambitions went awry, so, too, did Calan's spear of destiny. In that moment, as the sorceress Queen's conjurations twisted back upon her and her body flared brighter than a dying star, consumed instantly and utterly, the road of time was split in twain.

Two paths, two destinies, two of everything mortal flowed forth from that accursed spot. Twice, Thorn watched himself carry Elora down to the cheering throng below, to be welcomed by Madmartigan and Sorsha. And then beheld them all ride off to vastly different destinies.

"The spell was never banished," he said, his voice growing hoarse with the enormity of the horror. "Its residue still taints this room. By the blessed Fates, what have we done? What have we done?"

He turned to Elora, but had no idea how to even begin to atone for this tragedy. Ignorance on his part might serve as an adequate explanation, but he would never accept it as an excuse.

Nothing prepared them for the wailing banshee shriek that tore from the Deceiver's throat, or her onslaught as she leaped from her place upon the floor to reach Elora in a single bound, the pair of them pitching headlong over a table to land in a messy sprawl hard against the Resonator. There was neither rhyme nor reason to the Deceiver's attack; these were the reactions of a child, purpose wholly without plan as she pummeled Elora again and again with her fists, her feet, her knees. It was fortunate for Elora that her hair had been cut too short for a decent handhold, else the Deceiver would have pulled that as well. At the same time, the Deceiver bombarded Elora with volley after volley of words—cruel, harsh insults cast forth for no other purpose than to do her harm. The sheer frenzy of the assault kept Elora on the defensive initially.

The others were torn over how to respond, for the duel between Khory and the Caliban was reaching its own climax, announced by Khory's body tumbling through the air from one end of the sprawling room to the other, to a pinpoint landing midway up the farthest wall.

Regrettably, she couldn't stick to that wall and therefore received another set of bumps and bruises when she flopped bonelessly to the floor. She was in rags by that stage, one bicep ringed with circles of angry purple shot through with darker shades of crimson where the Caliban had caught hold of her arm. She'd thought then that he would tear it from its socket. He had the strength, but to Khory's amazement it was his will that failed him. He hesitated—only for a moment, hardly enough time to notice, but more than enough for her to act. A kick, a stab, a wrench of the arm, and she was footloose once again.

There was blood, too, mainly hers, but while she was slow and careful about regaining her feet, the fire in her eye told all present this duel was in no way finished.

She still held Elora's sword, and as the Caliban lumbered past the others and full into the field effect thrown off by the Resonator, Khory returned once more to the attack. She struck with a masterful series of moves that left even Anakerie gasping in amazement. A double-handed diagonal strike across the body, reverse the sword and return it laterally and one-handed to open the belly, switch hands with the blade still reversed and rake it over the thorax along the opposite diagonal. Three strokes, executed with flawless precision in less than a half-dozen seconds, any one of them a mortal wound.

Yet it was Khory who was smashed to her knees by a bare-handed clout across the shoulders. She managed to turn that to her advantage, pushing off one leg and raking her sword across the Caliban's knees. With a blade that keen, by rights she should have amputated both legs; all she achieved was to make the creature stagger somewhat.

While they fought, with increasing ferocity, the Resonator continued generating pulsations of energy, blurring the boundaries between reality and imagination, scrambling those that separated then from now.

As Khory rose into a watchful, wary crouch, balanced on the balls of her feet, both she and the Caliban were struck by balls of fiery energy that seemed to burst outward from their own bodies. In Khory's case there was a flash from somewhere below her belly, while the Caliban's was hidden within the voluminous folds of its cloak, and the pair of them were suddenly painted in the most vibrant of colors. Light energy came alive, with the madcap effervescence of firedrakes, racing over and under their clothes in a race to see how quickly the whole body could be explored.

In their wake, both Khory and the Caliban began to change. Flashes of radiance illuminated different parts of their bodies in random order, revealing the person they'd been at the start of their lives. For Khory, there was little alteration in her actual appearance, save that Elora and the others gradually got a sense of the style of armor and costume worn in those bygone days. Only Elora noted that the raptor tattoo on Khory's face was casting forth a radiance of its own, completely distinct from the flashbursts triggered by the Resonator pulses. The difference for Khory was internal, a resurrection of the spirit that once had been.

The Caliban, however, underwent a far more striking transformation as each flash stripped away one after the other of its cloaks, as a chef might delicately peel an artichoke to reach its heart. What lay underneath was a figure that Elora recognized at once, possessed of a power and glory that was a match for any Monarch in the other Great Realms.

"Ard-righ," she breathed in wonderment as Eamon Asana was stripped at long last of all his disguises. "The High King of legend," she went on to say, "Eamon Asana himself!"

And yet . . .

The glimpse Elora had beheld in Khory's memory was of a man she'd willingly follow into any battle, against any foe, no matter the odds, solely on the strength of his word. This was more a ghost who happened to bear a close resemblance. There was a softness to the once-clean line of the jaw, a petulant twist to the edge of the mouth, a flatness to the eyes, that prompted Elora to turn her head to the Deceiver and back again, finding echoes in her other self of that same corrosive weariness. A sense of battles without number, so many that it no longer mattered whether they were won or lost because there would always be another. A nagging, caustic doubt that ate inexorably at the soul, with the question that if the High King was so gifted, so blessed, so *worthy,* why could he not bring this conflict to an end? Why was there *always* another battle? What was the point anymore?

"Your sacrifice bought the world peace, Khory" was what he said to Khory. The look she returned was as piercing as a well-shot arrow.

"Are we merchants then, to barter for what should have been— *could* have been—fairly won in battle?"

"At a cost of how many lives? Your one saved tens of thousands."

"The right decision then, the act of a statesman, courageous to the core. I'd salute you, Eamon Asana—if I weren't so curious about what brought you here. How many of those souls you putatively saved has the Caliban claimed over the generations since?"

"There's just one left to take, Khory. Then, at last, I can rest."

"You were our High King, my lord. How came you to this?"

"I betrayed my best friend and by so doing, myself."

Swords slashed the air with such speed they left trails of liquid silver in their wake. Despite the corruption that had claimed almost every decent part of him, Eamon Asana was still the man who'd faced the Monarch of Greater Faery in single combat and emerged without a scratch, to flesh or garments. He fought with the desperate strength of the damned and the brute confidence that came with an uncountable string of victories. There was a hunger in him as they fought too reminiscent of the Malevoiy and that look grew only more intense as he scored first blood, then second, then third. Slashing wounds, as messy as they were effective.

"She did better against the monster," noted Thorn.

"The Caliban had no need for skill. Force alone did the trick," said Anakerie. "There's movement outside," she reported.

Elora, too, had heard the skittering approach of the Malevoiy, as had the Deceiver. That sound effectively put an end to their own struggle and neither offered resistance as Thorn and Anakerie pulled them apart.

"It's this damnable machine, Drumheller," fumed the Princess Royal. "Is there nothing to be done to stop it?" She half raised her own blade, offering that as her best suggestion. Thorn shook his head, vehemently.

"Disrupting the matrix, that's the surest path to killing us all!"

"You still believe you're in control!" Anakerie sounded genuinely appalled.

Eamon Asana stood over Khory and smashed his sword down on hers again and again. There was no finesse to his attack, it was the kind of technique best used to chop through anvils. She was splayed on the ground, forced to brace her torso with one arm, while protecting herself one-handed with her sword. As a display of strength, she was pretty impressive herself for there wasn't the slightest quiver in her blade as his crashed down upon it. She met him on his terms and held her own.

Thing was, though, while the blade didn't waver, each strike moved it that much closer to Khory.

Then came the moment that took them all off guard. When it appeared that the next series of blows would decide the issue once and for all, Khory suddenly unfolded herself from where she lay. Up came the supporting arm, to catch hold of Asana's thick wrist just as the blades made contact.

He didn't mind. He immediately drew back both arms, which in turn hauled Khory upright. His intention was to break her hold and finish the matter but try as he might he couldn't make her release her grip. He put the full weight of his body and the force of every sinew to the task. She was as immovable as a mountain.

"Impossible," he sputtered. "There's no way Khory Bannefin—!"

"The Khory Bannefin you knew died at the hands of your new

friends, her lifelong foes." The woman spoke with Khory's voice but her stance told a different story.

"She was here!" He sounded strangely desperate.

"For a time, torn from her time and a sleep she'd earned. She's gone, Asana. I remain."

"Demon!"

The warrior smiled.

She shoved him back, just clear enough to give him room to raise his sword.

Their blades met with the sound of quick, staccato chimes and the occasional burst of sparks. Each contact made the raptor design etched onto Khory's face burn that much more brightly, the radiance touching her eye itself so that it, too, began to glow.

Asana punched her in the stomach and, when her head dropped, kneed her in the face. She staggered a few steps clear of him and before she could recover, he was on her, his sword slashing across the length of her body. It was a masterful ploy. It should have worked.

But his edge cut mostly air, though some more of her blood was spilled. Hers came up and under his attack, with the full force of her own powerful shoulders behind it, off-balance though she was and unable to provide a proper stroke to her swing. She cut him open to the spine and as he staggered past, the arrogance still on his face, she rose to her feet and pivoted. Her sword came down, his head came off, and the *ard-righ* of legend, the Caliban, was no more.

Elora caught Khory as she crumpled, the toll of battle finally exacting payment. The warrior tried to maintain hold of her sword but her fingers had lost all sensation. She couldn't close them around the haft.

"Second wave," Anakerie informed them, and Elora stood to face the Malevoiy.

There was only one, the manform who'd struck the bargain with her in Ch'ang-ja. It held the Caliban's broad-brimmed hat in hand, juggling it slightly, watching amused as an unending number of bells fell from their perches like snow, each sounding a delicate chime before vanishing in a puff of brimstone flame.

In an intentional parody of Court etiquette, the Malevoiy proffered the hat to Elora, who met its gaze but made no other move. It held the hat out to Anakerie, who responded with a sneer. It tossed the hat into the air and they all watched it settle in Khory's lap. The Malevoiy bowed.

Elora couldn't help herself. In a move that matched the Demon-Child for speed and sureness, she lunged for Khory's sword and slashed it back through the air toward the Malevoiy, meaning to deal with it as Khory had with Asana. Quick as she was, the Malevoiy was faster. It grabbed her blade, the shock of that contact giving her shoulder a painful wrench, and then, with its other hand, shattered it.

Good, thou art, Sacred Princess, it said to her. Sadly for thee and thine, just not good enough.

"There's got to be a way," she fumed, after the herald's departure, as the skittering of claws on stone in the hall outside marked the advance of Malevoiy reinforcements.

"That Bannefin, she had an army," said Khory.

Elora's eyes fell on her foe. The Deceiver sat in a huddle, her back to the solid frame of a table, staring at nothing, as divorced from the action as she could manage. She was like a pencil drawing, as each successive wave of energy from the Resonator stripped her of every semblance of humanity. Only a few layers of being remained to her, demarked by a dark silhouette as though she'd been outlined in ink. Once they were gone, once the contours had been frayed to nothingness, there would be no structure to anchor the energy that was her essence. It would drift apart and with it her consciousness. Elora had no idea how long the process would take, at what point the last thought would vanish. It wasn't something she ever wanted to experience and when she looked into the Deceiver's eyes she saw a reflection of that fear.

"I can't do it," Elora confessed. "I can't beat them." She almost laughed, although she felt no humor in her. "I mean, I can try, I *will* try, with all my heart. But it won't be enough, Drumheller, will it?"

"Not even with my help, Elora, no. I'm sorry."

"The Malevoiy represent the strength of ages. Me, I'm a teenager." Then her gaze settled on the Deceiver, where it had been heading all along. "But you're not. You wear their armor as a badge of conquest. You fought the Malevoiy and won!"

"For all the good that did me."

"Help us now."

"To what end? The salvation of your precious Realms? How do you know our actions won't make things worse, that we'll be upsetting the natural order?"

"Explain the prophecy; why else are we here?"

"What the hell d'you think I've been trying to do my whole life, you wretched child? Divine the meaning of some stupid story and apply it to the governance of the Realms. Great concept. Pity the execution left so much to be desired."

"Who said you were meant to rule the Realms?"

"Why bother with an Ascension then, eh? I tried and tried and tried, from this Epoch to the next, and it cost me—*everything*! You have no conception of the price. I was like you once, full of hope and ideals. Now I'm just tired. I'm like Asana. I'm done. Leave me to my fate."

"After all you've done, you just give up?"

"Can I win? Have you left me the thinnest reed of hope? You fought me from the start, as did you, Peck," she said to Drumheller with a snarl. Then she shrugged. "The hell with you both."

How's that for a joke, Elora thought. *Here am I, heart without a full complement of strength or of skill. Here is my enemy, the only one of us who's actually fought and beaten the Malevoiy, who possesses those qualities in abundance but without the heart to fight.*

"The last Realms," she said aloud, as though a herald had announced it from a watchtower.

"What's that, lass?" Thorn queried.

"Despair and hope." She knelt before Drumheller and Khory, and gently removed the dragon's egg from her pouch. "There isn't really time to explain," she said to them. "But I need you both to trust me."

"The binding spell?" Khory asked.

"I need it released."

"Have you considered that's what the Malevoiy are waiting for outside?" Thorn told her. "That's what they're counting on. The binding spell is the only protection the dragons have. Break it and the Malevoiy can seize the dragons for their own."

"I know the risk, Drumheller. I'm counting on you all to keep them clear."

"While you do what?"

"What *I* was born to do."

"Count us in," the brownies chimed in unison, followed by Anakerie, who said, "Maulroon and those others, they'll be right pissed to miss this little fracas, especially my brother."

"Hey hey," cried Franjean, "someone should live to tell the tale. What's the point of playing hero elsewise?"

"If I can help it, my friends," Elora said, "nobody dies today. My word on that."

She held out the egg. Khory stretched out her own hands, splaying the fingers wide enough to encompass much of its circumference so she could maintain direct contact with Elora and hopefully Drumheller.

"Please," Elora said, in the face of his reluctance.

With a nod of acquiescence, he joined his hands to theirs and spoke the correct enchantment. Elora felt a thrill of energy tickle the tips of her fingers.

"The Malevoiy," called Anakerie, watching the door. "I think they know what just happened. They're on the move!"

"A warding spell like this," said Thorn with pardonable pride, "they'd feel its neutralization in Sandeni." Then, seriously, to Elora, "All I ask of you, child, is that you know what you're doing."

"Hate to say it, but I'm making it up as I go along."

"Wonderful."

She faced the Deceiver.

"I'm beaten," her lifelong foe told her. "Congratulations. What's mine—what's left of mine—is yours, be welcome to it. I wish you better fate than I encountered."

"I don't want your damn' power. Taking it means your destruction."

"No less a fate than what I intended for you, my girl. Besides, wait a wee while longer, the whole question becomes moot. If that's your pleasure, be my guest, but you're wasting valuable resources you may yet need to save your pathetic, mayfly lives."

"I'm a healer, Elora," she told her older self, her use of the name serving as the final note of acceptance of this strange and frightening reality. *In all the years we've been at each other's throats,* she told herself, a bit bemusedly, *I never imagined that the person in my life most in need of that particular talent was—myself.*

She held out both hands, clasped around the dragon's egg, and the door plus a fair portion of the wall itself burst inward. Thorn met the Malevoiy with magic, the brownies with raw energy, the women and Luc-Jon with steel, and corpses quickly began to fall.

Visibly trembling, the Deceiver laid her own hands gently atop Elora's.

Elora's youth had been defined by bloodshed and disaster. The Deceiver's was one of unending joy. She had the most wonderful home, foster parents who loved her, and over time, siblings of a sort. The Shadow came later.

At the Deceiver's Ascension in Tir Asleen, she was given a crown and a throne and was subjected to speeches without number or, she suspected, any significant point at all concerning the practical limits of her power. She had other notions and quickly set them in place. She would bring order to the unruly, she would mandate peace throughout the Realms.

She should have waited. Someone should have counseled patience and a ferocious measure of discretion. She was dealing with Monarchs whose bloodlines went back to the dawning of life on the physical world. They viewed her as a slip of a girl who'd gotten lucky. Some obeyed, some objected, most waited for a sense of the eventual outcome.

When she tried to enforce her edicts, war was declared. The age-old pattern of bloodshed and betrayal once more reasserted itself, as it had since the banishment of the Malevoiy.

The Deceiver had been raised as a Princess, trained—as Anakerie was—to rule. Moreover, she had an intuitive sense of people, an awareness of the strengths of their individual characters and above all their weaknesses. As such, manipulating them became literally child's play. When she actually was a child, it was fun. A flip of the curls, a bat of the eyes, a dollop of irresistible charm, some cajolery, and she could get pretty much whatever she wanted. Only those who knew her longest, who'd known her in fact before her rescue from Bavmorda, appeared immune. Madmartigan, Sorsha, the brownies, and especially her champion, the Nelwyn wizard Willow Ufgood.

At first they were a welcome reality check, the only ones she knew who would treat her with the loving disrespect a child needs occasionally to remind her that she isn't quite the center of the Universe. They told her when she was wrong, offered a reprimand when she did wrong; they weren't afraid of her and therefore would challenge her when they felt there was a need. Since she had no living parents, they assumed that role for themselves and took that responsibility with total seriousness. Everyone else she encountered considered her the Sacred Princess—at best, royalty; at worst, some kind of living deity. In either case, utterly unapproachable on any level of normal human interaction.

The problem was, something always seemed to be missing from her life. She felt incomplete, that no matter what she achieved she would always judge herself lacking. It was a burr in her soul, it whispered nasties in her ear and made her wonder if others likewise saw this fundamental flaw in her. She thought of the child's tale of the Emperor's new clothes and dreamed of striding to her throne wholly unaware that she was stark naked, while her entire court burst their collective gut trying not to laugh. She began to look more closely at every face and ask herself if this one saw the joke or not.

Willow and the others noticed this change in her and tried to draw out the reason for it. She was of the age, though, where stubbornness becomes a primal character trait, up there with rebellion, and the last people she wanted to turn to for anything—as she fought to define and solidify her own unique identity—were her surrogate parents. In time, the mood might have passed. Or the others might have sat her down and had it out with her, as parents will when they see no better alternative. It was an adolescent phase, they told themselves. They trusted her judgment, her fundamental character.

The war changed that. From the beginning they argued against it, Willow most vehemently of all. They didn't accept her own position that a throne must be unassailable and that ultimately *she* knew best for the Twelve Realms. They didn't see what was obvious for Elora, which meant they *didn't* trust her, so she stopped listening. And when she grew tired of their disruptions of Council strategy sessions, she stopped inviting them. And when their encounters within the palace of Tir Asleen grew ever more strained, when the estrangement grew to the point where just thinking about them made her upset, she banished them from court.

She meant them no harm, she *loved* them. What drove her to distraction was the growing fear that they no longer loved her back. How could they, she wasn't worthy. It was the smallest of perceptual steps from that mark to the proposition that they'd never loved her, that they'd merely used her to further their own agendas—Madmartigan and Sorsha to gain a kingdom for themselves, Willow to become a sorcerer. That they'd never used their relationship for any personal gain only told her that they weren't very good at it, which again fit neatly into her growing worldview, diminishing them further in her eyes and doing much the same to her, for what did it say about the Sacred Princess herself that she would embrace such consummate losers?

By then, the Realms of the Circle of the World were going for each other's throats. Had she tried, the Deceiver might have found a diplomatic solution to the conflict, but she had no interest in compromise, only victory. Madmartigan and Sorsha, against type and nature, placed their lives and sacred honor at hazard and brokered a cease-fire and an eminently workable peace. Their Princess pretended to acquiesce and at the parley called to finalize the terms arrived with her newly established corps of assassins, the Black Rose, to decimate her rival Monarchs.

She took no action against Madmartigan and Sorsha; the elves saved her the trouble.

So it went, year after year, generation upon generation. Because she lost faith in her generals, she trained herself in all the warriors' arts. When she grew convinced that Willow was rousing the local wizards to rebellion, she mastered their arts as well. And remembering the breadth of Bavmorda's power, it was the most logical progression from the craft of white magic to that of black.

Each decision had its specific rationale. Each could be justified wholeheartedly. Each was necessary. Of that she was certain beyond all doubt.

But each led to further doubt, and that doubt led to the next decision, which cast forth the seeds of disaster, which in turn required yet another decision. Each was a dot of color in the canvas, pure and pristine.

Never once, though, did the Deceiver take the few steps required that would allow her to distance herself from her creation and view the canvas in its entirety, to see those apparently random dots within their whole context. Had she done so, she might have seen that the picture being created was altogether different from her intent.

She grew increasingly isolated and increasingly resentful. She was the Sacred Princess, the responsibility of the future of the world was on her shoulders; why did the populace refuse to understand, to cut her some slack, to accept that she knew best in everything?

Another pulse from the Resonator illuminated the Deceiver and Elora, pitting the heavy outline around the Deceiver's body even further. It changed the scene about them as well, transporting them to a place Elora knew only too well, the volcanic caldera that was hearth and home to the dragons.

Only this wasn't quite the place that Elora had left. There was a familiar emptiness, because the dragons of the Deceiver's history had reached the end of their life cycle, just as had those of Elora's. That aspect of time remained constant. The difference was that in the Deceiver's future, they simply died. There were eggs aplenty scattered about the ruins but no catalyst of spirit to inspire them to hatch. And the longer they lay dormant, the more imagination—the capacity to transcend the here and now in favor of something altogether new—fled from the Realms. That was why, as the war dragged ever onward, neither side could find a way to end it. Conflict became the accepted norm, no one could conceive of a world without it, a relationship that wasn't defined by it. The races of the Great Realms took their cues from the Sacred Princess. As she became more suspicious, so did they. As she embraced the concepts of deceit and betrayal—because the ends eternally justified the means—they did also.

In turn, the harshness of their behavior drove the Deceiver to greater extremes of her own, generating a wickedly self-perpetuating cycle that, with the best and most noble of original intentions, created a society that ultimately eclipsed the brutality and evil of Bavmorda's regime.

In Elora's imagination, she and the Deceiver were visiting a museum, strolling along a gallery past vast and complicated tapestries and paintings whose scale encompassed the totality of the Great Realms. A glance told Elora everything she needed to know, and the sight was like the clawed hand of a Malevoiy about her heart. By contrast, the Deceiver had her face up close to every piece, nattering justifications without end for the choice and placement of every strand of thread, every dot of paint. For her, every element was taken in isolation.

Until Elora yanked her other self back to stand beside her.

Elora thought before then she'd seen her share of grief. But she'd never seen a soul mourn an entire world, as the enormity of the tragedy crashed about them. Events could no longer be viewed by the Deceiver in abstract; they had suddenly and irrevocably become personal. Each strand of thread and pinpoint of paint represented a life. The Deceiver had placed them there for a purpose, as individuals; that was how she now found herself forced to relate to them and deal with their loss.

She wanted to die. Elora wanted to let her, because the crushing weight of such sorrow was more than she wanted to bear.

But she was incomplete as well. She lacked the ruthlessness, the indomitable strength of purpose, that had sustained the Deceiver throughout the whole of her long life.

She held out her hand.

"What?" the Deceiver asked of her.

"What you've always wanted," Elora said. "Me."

"This is some trick."

"I can't take from you, because that would be yielding to despair. Yielding myself, though, letting *you* win"—she gave a quirky, utterly charming smile that the Deceiver, though the structure of their features was identical, could never duplicate—"I guess that's embracing hope. Maybe this way we both win."

The Deceiver didn't respond at first, as she examined the offer for the hidden trick, the betrayal that was always lurking behind every generous impulse.

"It's your choice now, Elora Danan," Elora said to her. "I've made mine."

The Deceiver gripped Elora's hand in her own, clasping it between both of hers before pulling the other young woman into an embrace.

"This is the equinox," Elora whispered. "All things are in perfect balance. You have the world, you have the lever."

"Thank you," said her other self.

They finally understood how truly precious hope was, having lived through its utter extinction.

They understood how to dream what never was and inspire the best in folks to achieve that, because they had endured the worst.

To the others within the sanctum, their backs to a corner of the wall where the Malevoiy had driven them, it was like watching the first sunrise of spring. The pulses from the Resonator were coming so close together now that the visual din was continuous. The field effect began to coalesce, creating the portal Thorn and Anakerie had witnessed in Sandeni. Again, there was a fearful distortion of the structures of reality itself. Solid stone warped, turning malleable like soft wax before discorporating into blobs of matter that best resembled bubbles of varying sizes. Some of the Malevoiy were snared in the vortex that was forming, shrieking in unaccustomed terror as they found themselves in the grip of forces far beyond their ken and control.

A light more terrible than any present could remember flared from the Resonator and they all assumed the end was nigh.

They were right, but not in the manner they thought.

Through the body of the Resonator strode Elora and the Deceiver, in tandem step, each act and gesture a mirror image of the other. Each used a hand to support the dragon's egg. As they approached, their outlines lost coherent form, the boundaries between them blurring to insignificance, and Thorn was reminded of the image seen through the lenses of a pair of binoculars. Unfocused, the double-glass system would produce two distinct images. Turning the focusing ring gradually brought the view into strict alignment. That was what was happening here. The closer they came, the more two figures merged into one.

As Elora Danan cupped the egg in both her hands, and offered it a smile, there was a resounding *crack* as the eggshell broke apart.

To those outside, waiting for news, they thought the sun itself had been reborn on the surface of the world. The most terrible and beautiful of lights erupted outward from the Citadel, casting a glow sufficient to banish night from this entire hemisphere of the world, brighter by far than the most radiant star in the heavens. A light that would be seen and remarked on throughout the cosmos, from this time forth.

The energies of this explosion raced through the atmosphere, grappling with all the disharmonious elements they found in their path and setting them to rights. The storm that had raged over Angwyn since Elora's failed Ascension reached a peak so fierce it was fortunate there were none present to witness it, for their lives would surely have been forfeit. Lightning played across the city of Angwyn and where the bolts struck the earth, the icy substance of the Deceiver's enchantment fell away.

Life returned to that ensorcelled city. And a full measure of sanity to the world's weather.

In Nockmaar, as those encamped on the plain before the fortress scrambled for their horses and their lives, beating a headlong retreat to what they hoped was the safety of the mountains, their flight was halted, their attention transfixed by a trumpeting succession of roars.

A dragon reared into view, emerging from the core of the light, flexing its wings with the ineffable delight of a newborn experiencing the sensations of the world for the very first time. It leaped skyward and, as it rose from the ground, another appeared almost immediately to follow, and then another and another and another, until there seemed to be so many that the sky itself was filled from end to end, from top to bottom. All eyes were drawn back to the flaming ruin of Nockmaar itself, as the substance of the stone turned incandescent and to the amazement and delight of the onlookers actually began to cascade into gas. It was a variation on the Ritual of Oblivion, applied to a place rather than a person.

The dragons bugled, one and all, a cheer of celebration and thanksgiving, and then with their first breath of fire . . .

. . . they vanished.

With them went all evidence of their passing. The radiance vanished as well, revealing that day had spun inexorably into night. For the first time in Nockmaar's memory, stars were visible overhead. No more did clouds obscure the sky.

Then, the onlookers saw that Nockmaar's memory had reached an end, because that haunted, accursed stronghold was itself no more. The ground gleamed, like a polished tabletop, fused by the unimaginable heat of the dragons' flame into a ceramic glass. Of Elora Danan and her companions there was no sign, and the others immediately feared the worst.

Until they heard a young woman's laugh, rich with delight and merriment.

Still reeling from the events they scrambled to the center of the field, but all they found were Anakerie and Luc-Jon. They were laughing themselves, though Maulroon swore that wasn't the Princess Royal's voice he'd heard before. Of Elora Danan there was no sign, nor of Khory Bannefin, nor Thorn Drumheller, nor the brownies.

Actually, that wasn't quite true. In the precise center of the ceramic plain, where Bavmorda's sanctum had stood, and the altar and the Resonator—at the precise spot that marked the intersection of the greatest Magus Point in the Twelve Great Realms—was a clutch of flowers. A rose the likes of which no gardener had ever seen, nor would again, whose color was a silver so pure and polished the blossom might have been a casting of that precious metal. A little below were two more, one of burnished sungold, the other a wine-dark scarlet, companion stems of the same root. At the last, sneaking in and entangled around the main stem of both plants, a pair of miniature wild roses.

The others asked about Elora but neither Anakerie nor Luc-Jon had anything substantial to say right then. The scene, they felt, spoke most eloquently for her. The Deceiver was no more and the dread fortress of Nockmaar, a font of evil since time immemorial, likewise. Elora had prevailed, not through conquest but through faith. She had left the world better than it was, found a way to heal lasting wounds and restore the natural order of things.

She had brought life to a place that had never in its existence known any.

And in turn, given the people hope for a future radiant with promise.

The Shadow War was over. A new day, a brighter Epoch, was at hand.

CODA

THE YEAR TURNED. NOTHING CHANGED, AND EVERY-
thing.

Winter was normal, for the first time since the Deceiver's
enchantment had claimed Angwyn. With the breaking of
that curse, the infernal heat sink that had warped weather
patterns across the continent quickly dissipated, as though
Nature herself had decided the world had suffered enough.
There was cold aplenty, and snow, but there were warm
spells as well that hadn't been seen in years, and while the
elements might have been bitter and even harsh at times,
they could be survived. While the Deceiver reigned in
Angwyn, that hadn't been the case.

Angwyn itself faced the hardest test. True, the battle in
Nockmaar had ended both the threat of the Deceiver and the

sorcery that had sheathed the city in ice, but liberation proved bittersweet. The city was restored, buildings and people untouched
by the passage of years but beyond its walls the consequences of
that enchantment weren't so easily banished. Angwyn Bay
remained substantially frozen, which meant no trading vessels at
her wharves, nor any fishing. In effect, the city would be under
siege until the passage of the seasons once more gave it access to
both the land and the ocean. But the King and his Council had
reckoned without the Monarchs of the other Great Realms who'd
been ensorcelled with him. They had access to harvests that were
unaffected by the wild weather that had bedeviled the Daikini and
made an offer of them, free and clear. A gift to those in need, in
hopes that should circumstances warrant, the Daikini might do
the same in return.

As the days lengthened, and the vernal equinox aproached, the
storms that rolled across the great western prairie brought rain
more than snow, and with it a welcome gentleness. Parched fields
gratefully swallowed up the offered moisture and farmers and
ranchers from the Rampart Range to the Wall allowed themselves
to hope they might have decent crops and herds again, that the
lean times were behind them.

Of necessity, Daikini who'd never considered such a course of
action found themselves asking the help of the Veil Folk who
dwelled on or near their land. Naiads, to calm the streams and
guide the flow of irrigation channels so that fields and stock were
adequately cared for but also so that the water itself wasn't con-
taminated in the process. Dryads, for the restoration of wood-
lands. Pixies, nixies, and many of the lesser imps to help care for
the fields themselves. In return, the Daikini offered to share
whatever bounty resulted, for the benefit of all. Races that had
been bitter rivals found common cause in their own survival, and
ultimate prosperity.

The changes, though, were small and incremental. They were
personal. The greater whole of society proved more stubborn.
There were still mighty armies in the field, national ambitions to
be fulfilled. The winter that had plagued the heart of the continent
had also proved a formidable defensive redoubt, keeping military

operations almost nonexistent for weeks at a time, if not months. There was no point in waging war if the weather was more certain to kill you than your foe.

With the spring, with the climate gentling daily, those forces were expected to stir, like bears from hibernation, grumpy from enforced inactivity and spoiling for a fight.

At the vernal equinox, on the thoroughfare in the Sandeni district of Madaket once known as the Street of Lost Dragons but which had been renamed (unofficially and in the middle of the night with a brush of indelible paint) Street of *Young* Dragons, there was a gathering at Black-Eyed Susan's. No invitations were issued, nothing was done to indicate that this was any more than a normal evening, yet in its way it was uniquely special, for to the tavern came every principal in Elora's life and adventures. Many were strangers to one another, while some were old companions; what mattered in the end was the young woman who'd touched all their lives.

There were cheers and toasts, gossip and reminiscences.

Anakerie stepped over the threshold straight from the road, dressed much as she'd been the day years gone when Thorn Drumheller first beheld her in Angwyn. Trousers and riding boots, with a sand-colored blouse of such exquisite weave the cotton looked and felt more like silk. Over that went a sleeveless leather tunic, snug at the waist but slit below on both sides to allow for ease of riding. She wore earrings Thorn had made her, and a choker necklace of interwoven silver and gold. The hair she'd worn long her whole life was recently slashed to the nape of the neck; an attractive cut to be sure but one she was still getting used to. She thought herself quite daring, almost scandalous, until her return to Sandeni. Young girls wore their hair even shorter, in a rebellious brush cut that looked like it had been dipped in raven ink, the better to resemble the woman they claimed as their ideal, the Sacred Princess Elora Danan.

Anakerie wore two rings of significance on her left hand. One, on the traditional ring finger, was etched with the Great Seal of Angwyn, a representation of the seal itself. The other, on the thumb, served a similar office with the Maizan. They marked her office as plainly as any crown, for as Princess Royal of Angwyn, she stood first in governance beside her father, the King. The other, in its own way, was more important, for it was worn by the Castellan of the Maizan, making her undisputed leader of that nomad nation.

"I bid you welcome, Highness," said Renny Garedo in the reception foyer, as Anakerie unclipped her harness and divested herself of most of her weapons. She still wore the sword Elora had made, that Khory Bannefin had given her during the battle within Nockmaar. She hoped to pass it on to her own firstborn, when she had children. She hoped for a daughter.

Her reply to the Chief Constable was a smile and a moment when she stretched and twisted her body along the whole length of her spine, to work loose the kinks of too many days in the saddle.

"You're not expected till next week," the Constable continued pleasantly, referring to a scheduled summit conference between the Chancellor and representatives of the western powers over various bilateral relationships and mutual concerns. At the top of that agenda stood the Chengwei.

"Officially, my friend, I'm not here at all" was her cheery response, "so do me the courtesy of ignoring my escort outside. I promise they'll behave."

"Maizan, are they?"

"Lancers and a couple of Black Rose. It seems I can't travel anywhere alone anymore."

That prompted an outright laugh. "The price of responsibility, Highness." But then the Constable reverted to type and his voice and manner turned altogether serious. "Regarding your assassins, Highness. Have I your word you'll keep them on a tight leash?"

"If I have need of them during my stay, Renny, I'll tell you straight." It wasn't an absolute assurance but considering the source he found it acceptable.

Luc-Jon tried to greet her with a surprisingly courtly bow but Anakerie swept him into a comradely embrace instead.

"No ceremony, lad," she told him, as he led her through the press of tables to an alcove where other friends already awaited them. "We've fought and bled together, and seen our share of wonders. Whatever our rank, we're equals, you and I."

"You do me honor, Highness."

"Call me *Highness* again, you scut, it's the last thing you'll say for a while, I promise you that."

"As you wish, High—!" He grinned, the slip had been intentional. "Anakerie."

Giles Horvath headed the table, together with Ranulf DeGuerin and some others Anakerie couldn't make out at first, since they sat far back in the shadows. Not for the first time, she muttered about the fundamental unfairness that allowed some to possess Mage-Sight, so they could see in pitch-darkness, while most did not.

"Seems to me a grumpy sort of greeting," noted a familiar voice and she flushed at how transparent her thoughts could be. When she stepped around the table and into the shadow herself, where she could finally see Thorn Drumheller properly, she discovered the feeling was mutual.

The months hadn't made a difference in him. Being a Nelwyn, it was likely centuries wouldn't. His clothing looked rustic, until you noticed the extraordinary workmanship of its brownie tailors; the finest suits in Sandeni were no match. In style and substance, they were of a piece with the sorcerer, outwardly unassuming but with unexpected and delightful depths.

Susan herself, the proprietor, brought them a carafe of spiced mulled wine, Anakerie's favorite, and the perfect restorative after a long day's ride.

"You look well, Peck," she told Thorn.

"Responsibility becomes you, Anakerie," he replied. "How goes the world?"

"You ask me?"

"Monarchs and their surrogates are generally the folk you expect to know such things."

"Why not simply pour a scrying pool and see for yourself?"

He looked lost a moment, before telling her, "I've had my fill of magic. I've no great hankering to use it, at least for a while."

She nodded, understanding. "Plenty of war to go 'round, if that's what you're wondering. Bloodshed and betrayal, that I'm afraid hasn't changed. I wonder sometimes if we made any difference at all."

"It's only been six months; do you expect miracles?"

"Where Elora Danan is concerned, absolutely."

"In point of fact, ma'am," interjected Colonel DeGuerin, introducing his remarks with a tactful cough, "the Frontier's stabilized a fair piece since last fall."

"The Chengwei?"

He smiled, not pleasantly. "The army that came through Tregare was broken the night Elora Danan sent her WitchFires to chase them. When they heard the news from Ch'ang-ja, the commander was beside himself to arrange a truce and safe conduct to his own border. The eastern invasion force that decamped from the Tascara Sea remains intact. If they choose to advance they may prove troublesome but indications are unclear. There's every chance they won't."

"I have been out of touch."

"Incredibly busy, would be more like what I've heard," said Thorn.

"What have you heard, Peck?"

"After Nockmaar, you rode to the heart of the Maizan encampment, claimed Mohdri's sword and shield for your own, and challenged any and all comers to take them away from you."

"That's the Maizan way when a Castellan dies. The best man's supposed to win."

"I also heard you were unopposed."

She examined her left hand, watching the candlelight play on the precious metal of the two bands. "I'm Angwyn born," she said simply, before gesturing with her thumb, "but this is the ring I wear closest to my heart. The Maizan know this. I won't shed their blood if it can possibly be avoided, and I won't betray them."

"Spoken like articles of faith."

"For me, they are. Elsewise, what's the point?"

"Will they stay within Angwyn territory?" Thorn wondered, and she nodded.

"They may even settle."

"A Maizan putting down roots," marveled DeGuerin. "Who'd have thought to ever live to see such a day?"

"What about Chengwei?" Thorn asked, meaning the Empire itself rather than its armies.

"A disaster," the Colonel reported, as though he were briefing the Council of Ministers. "No place for the likes of you, Master Drumheller, that's certes. Because of what happened to Ch'ang-ja, there's precious little love for sorcerers of any stripe, by commons or crown. It's said the shock of that city's destruction devastated the Imperial Capital of Daido as well. Internally, the whole country's a mess, in near-total disarray. You have the Khagan trying to reestablish a central government, with some of the subordinate Khans remaining loyal but others striking out on their own. So, down the road, we'll have either a score of principalities to deal with or a land preoccupied for the better part of the next generation with setting its own house in order. Either way, a scenario the Republic welcomes. My sense is that the army at Tascara will likely disband. Even the harshest discipline won't hold men who believe their homes and families to be threatened. Whatever remains intact, the commander will offer either to the Khagan or to whichever local Khan looks the most promising. Or he might try to seize a province for his own."

"The more things change," Thorn said with a rueful shake of the head, "the more they stay the same."

"I think you're wrong there, Drumheller," said Anakerie. "More a case to me of old habits dying very hard."

"I've got a new Elora story," Luc-Jon announced excitedly, taking his seat at the table, with his wolfhound by his side.

"I beg your pardon?" This, from Anakerie.

"Haven't you heard? They're all the rage, everyone's telling them."

"Stories of how she won the Shadow War?"

Luc-Jon threw up his hands dismissively, buttressing the gesture with an outrush puff of breath. "Stories about *everything*!"

"The flight from Angwyn," bugled a brownie.

"The fire in Cherlindrea's forest," crowed Rool.

"The dance with the firedrakes."

"The romance with the Lord of the Dance."

"The death of the dragons!"

"The fall of Ch'ang-ja."

"The siege of Tregare!"

Then, together, delightedly, "And that's just the part that's true!"

They'd bounced titles back and forth with such giddy abandon that Anakerie had to laugh, and she was quickly joined by the others at the table.

"Did you know," Luc-Jon informed them, "that Elora Danan rode a dragon all the way to the sun and brought back a piece of its molten heart. Or that she crept into the castle where her true love was held captive and won him free from the Caliban itself!"

"Any description on that sweetheart, young scribe?" Anakerie asked.

"The usual," replied Luc-Jon, in the same humorous vein. "Tall, ridiculously good-looking, means well but dumb as the proverbial post. He exists, it seems, to be captured and rescued and to look superb on her arm. Otherwise . . . ?" He shrugged dismissively.

"No resemblance between art and life then, eh?" Anakerie teased.

"Not even close." He twisted a little on his seat, toward another figure sitting so deep in the shadows she might have been mistaken for one herself. "Something to ask of you, Khory?"

"You may ask, scribe," the warrior told him.

"What exactly happened in Ch'ang-ja?"

"I've been wondering that myself," said Anakerie.

"Elora Danan's version of Drumheller's 'disappearing pig' trick, you mean?" And Khory chuckled, but whether at the memory of the moment itself or the sheer audacity of Elora's improvised ploy, none could tell. "Sleight of hand," she told them with a shrug of her shoulders.

"You don't slip loose of our net quite that easily, my girl," warned Anakerie. "I was there, remember? With my sight bonded to Drumheller's. There's no way you could have escaped notice, even in that chaos. And how'd you get out of the city?"

"By the time it was destroyed, I was well clear."

"I ask again, on behalf of us all—*how?*"

"The flash was a handful of Chengwei thunderpowder. When we rolled out of sight of you and especially the Malevoiy, she asked the earth for help. She literally threw me through the floor, into the molten heart of the world."

Enough of the others had shared such an experience that a series of faint shudders passed around the table. It was a journey they'd all survived unscathed but which few wanted to repeat.

"She asked the earth to carry me safely to the place of my birth," Khory finished.

"Angwyn," said Drumheller.

"The catacombs, yes, beneath the old Palace Royal."

"Why there?"

"No one to harm me, for starters," she said with a slight quirk of the lips that passed with her for a smile. This was a shared secret between her and Drumheller, that she was a demon, cast forth in this human shell. "And the ploy also put me inside the Deceiver's citadel, allowing me the opportunity to reach her unnoticed."

"Why?" Anakerie asked.

"You saw what I did," Khory told her.

"How could Elora have anticipated what would happen between her and the Malevoiy, and what would come of it?"

"Reasonable deduction? Calculated risk? Blind instinct? If she became Malevoiy, she knew she would seek out her other self to end their rivalry once and for all. If she failed, the Deceiver would still have to be dealt with. If she succeeded, as she did, then she would become my target."

"She planned for you to kill her?"

"Drumheller," Khory explained patiently, "even I comprehend the significance of the Realms of Life and Death. One with *all* the Realms, that was the geas demanded of the Sacred Princess. That meant she had to perish and be reborn. Her sword did the one. Your Resonator provided the power for her resurrection, and the dragon's egg she gave to my charge allowed me to direct that power."

"And if you'd failed, Khory?"

"That wasn't an option," she told him, closing her hands with a soft clap to cap the discussion, only to think better of it and speak again. "She had to make a decision, that ultimately made the difference between victory and disaster, in a split second of time, without consultation or reassurance that she was doing the right thing, and without the opportunity to warn me of what was happening. And afterward, trust that I might deduce what else was required of me."

"That's a gamble you couldn't pay me to make," said Luc-Jon, shaking his head in wonderment.

"You misunderstand, scribe," Khory corrected him gently. "For Elora Danan it was no gamble."

She noticed the badge that anchored his cloak. "You've not worn that sign before," she told him.

Anakerie answered for the young man. "It means he passed his boards, his qualifying examinations." And she congratulated him on advancing from his status as an apprentice. He was a full-fledged scribe.

"An award as well deserved," said Giles Horvath, "as it is long overdue. You should be proud, my boy."

"Thank you, Master."

Anakerie noted that Luc-Jon was dressed for the road and commented on it. He grinned a little shamefacedly, as though caught with his hand in a cookie jar.

"I leave with Elora," he said, and actually blushed in the face of her raised eyebrow.

"There's a whole world to explore," he explained further. "Who knows what we'll find along the road, in the way of artifacts for Master Horvath's library. And"—he grinned wide—"considering how easily she attracts . . . trouble, those adventures ought to make for some exciting chronicles."

"She believes her work is done?"

"Don't you?" asked Giles Horvath. "Things *are* better, you know. Look about you, Anakerie, what do you see?"

"A tavern doing what it does best, providing a place for people to enjoy good means and good company."

"True enough. But look more closely. Did you know, for example, that the embassies on Veil Isle have been reopened?"

That was news and it made her straighten in her chair.

"The World Gate in its catacombs can evidently be accessed from the far side of the Veil. They can use it on a limited basis. We Daikini, regrettably, cannot. And while conditions on the isle are not ideal, they are bearable. Evidently, the Realms beyond the Veil, especially Greater and Lesser Faery, believe it worth the effort."

Mindful of the Master Scribe's earlier challenge, Anakerie searched the room once more and sat up even more straight in her seat. The crowd was mainly Daikini and mostly young—altogether to be expected given Madaket's proximity to University—but there was a broader smattering of mixed bloods, people like Renny Garedo, whose heritage crossed both sides of the Veil. Moreover, in one of the other alcoves, she saw figures too lean and tall to be Daikini, whose deceptively languid grace bespoke a single race.

"Elves?" She was incredulous.

"Walking the heartland of a Daikini city for the first time in living memory," said Giles with pardonable pride. "The Chancellor offered them a welcome and our Chief Constable guaranteed their safety."

"I know Renny's part elf himself but would they believe him? Or rather, *why* would they believe him?"

"Who can say, milady?" Thorn mentioned with a small grin. "Mayhap it's easier nowadays to trust?"

"How about you, Drumheller?" she asked, sitting close to him again and taking one of his hands in hers. She was near twice his height yet his hands were larger, his fingers longer and more delicate than her own. There was a strength in them that could crush her bones but she didn't fear it. Instead, while she waited for her answer and the ones to follow, she stroked his fingers, his palm; she caressed the calluses and gently touched the nicks and scars that were the legacy of his work as both farmer and sorcerer. One of them, she'd put there.

"Any word from home?" she asked.

He shook his head, quietly said, "No.

"My people are inherently cautious," he explained. "They'd want to be absolutely sure of a thing—in this case, that it's safe—before they commit and come out of their warrens."

"For how long?"

"As long as necessary."

"That could be—oh, Drumheller, I'm so sorry!"

"Nothing's lost, Highness, nor even mislaid. They're safe. And they'll stay there until they satisfy themselves that the world is. And that I am, too."

"That last, Drumheller," cautioned Rool, "is no picnic!"

"Still walk with the stench of a demon about you."

"That was the price demanded for bringing Khory Bannefin to life, and it's one I gladly paid. I've no regrets on that score, brownies. Of course," he said to Anakerie, "they don't mention I also carry the taint of the Malevoiy."

"How so?"

"Elora Danan is bound to them, I am bound to her. And I am a sorcerer."

"You have no sorcerers among the Nelwyn?"

He didn't actually reply in words, but the play of his lips, the tilt of his eyes, the emotions and conflicts she glimpsed in them, all combined with the InSight they shared to present Anakerie his answer. Sorcerers, yes. But Thorn Drumheller had wielded power beyond the scope of any Daikini and most of the Veil Folk themselves. He had stood as an equal among dragons, had seen one generation of those awesome creatures perish and helped bring their successors into being. For all his lack of physical stature, his imagination had always been limitless. As a mage, his reality now walked hand in hand with those dreams. That marked him more indelibly than any curse, and set him apart from his fellows as it did Khory Bannefin and Elora Danan herself.

"Why are you smiling, Princess?" he asked of her.

"Just pacing the trail of your thoughts. And thinking myself that if ever a way can be found to your true happiness, Drumheller, to the restoration of all you hold dear, you'll find it."

"You have more faith than I."

"Isn't that why we championed Elora's cause? For faith? For hope?"

She'd slipped onstage unnoticed, which was a revelation for Anakerie, for every time she'd seen Elora Danan in the spotlight it was impossible to take your eyes off her. Her skin still gleamed but the argent coloring was flushed with a pale rose that gave her more than a semblance of normal humanity. She looked in fact like a fair number of young women in the audience and hardly at all like the vision in chrome silver that was how most described the Sacred Princess. Her hair and brows were black but that word was an inadequate description of the color. It was as if that part of her retained a small vestige of the Malevoiy. Her eyes were so blue they registered even as far from the stage as the alcove, where Anakerie and the others welcomed their friend with applause. Her gown was a burgundy red so dark it was mostly black; only the warriors present recognized it as the color of blood, and only a few of those, that it was the color favored by the Black Rose. She wore it as a trophy. Having beaten those legendary, and rightly feared, assassins in fair combat, she thought it only fair to claim their colors as her own.

She paid no attention to the crowded room, hunched over her guitar as though she sat in her own parlor and was simply passing the time by improvising some tune or other. Only gradually did the shape of her ballad emerge, and it was a little longer before she began to sing.

Elora's voice was low and husky, far more suited to a tavern like this than the stage of a palace, where most troubadours preferred to play. Her first choice was a love song, about a man and a woman and a passion that transported them both. They were doomed, of course, because that was invariably the fate of the subjects of such songs, caught up in the machinations of an evil Monarch who had become so corrupted by foul ambition that the purity of the lovers was more painful to her than torture.

Anakerie remembered what she'd seen in Nockmaar, which was why she was taken off guard when Elora's ballad came to a happy ending. The lovers did not die. In fact, it was the strength of their bond that sustained them and allowed them to vanquish their foe. It was, for Elora, what should have happened.

She acknowledged the applause with a gracious bow and repaired to their table with a delightful skip-dance to her step.

"That was good," Anakerie told her.

"Work in progress."

"Is that what you plan to do with your life, Elora Danan? Sing for your supper?"

"It's an honorable profession, Anakerie."

"For some."

"Royal Highness," Elora chided, "you know better than that. The last thing any government wants on their hands right now is a living, breathing, active Sacred Princess. That goes for Cheng-wei, for Sandeni, for Angwyn. I'm far, far more useful to everyone as a symbol and a legend. Revealing myself as flesh and blood would spoil everything."

"You're far too glib for me, girl."

"I think you're just a little bit jealous." Anakerie had the grace to drop her eyes, she couldn't hold her gaze with Elora's, recognizing the truth in the younger woman's claim. There was jealousy in her, and resentment, that she felt bound to shoulder responsibilities that Elora gleefully cast aside. "But you're wrong. I'm not abandoning my duty or my responsibility. I'm not like you, or Drumheller for that matter. My role isn't to command, be it nations or magic. To work my will, I have to implore, to beseech, to entreat, to persuade. That's better done on the quiet, where nobody notices, or realizes what I'm doing. For that role, a song isn't so bad a choice of tools.

"In the face of the Sacred Princess, people generally tend to feel compelled to obey. That way lies disaster. For me, because it's an easy habit to fall into. For others, because they abrogate their own free will. Or worse, resent the usurpation of their authority.

"If there's a need, the legend can always come back to life. Otherwise, I think we're all better off if she remains a ghost and a mystery."

"So what will you do?"

"I've my whole life before me," said Elora Danan, as she

reached out with her right hand to Thorn Drumheller, with her left to Khory Bannefin. Perched in the hollows of her collarbones were a pair of brownies and on a beam a little above and behind her head, two great golden eagles. She flashed a smile that made Anakerie's heart ache.

"I can't wait to see what happens next."

The Shadow War was over.

The legend of the Princess, the Warrior, and the Mage has been born.

Their story—has only just begun.

CHRIS CLAREMONT is best known for his seventeen-year stint on Marvel Comics' *The Uncanny X-Men,* during which it was the best-selling comic in the Western Hemisphere for a decade; he has sold more than 100 million comic books to date. His novels *First Flight, Grounded!,* and *Sundowner* were science fiction bestsellers. Recent projects include the dark fantasy novel *Dragon Moon* and *Sovereign Seven*™, a comic book series published by DC Comics. He lives in Brooklyn, New York.

GEORGE LUCAS is the founder of Lucasfilm Ltd., one of the world's leading entertainment companies. He created the *Star Wars* and *Indiana Jones* film series, each film among the all-time leading box-office hits. Among his story credits are *THX 1138, American Graffiti,* and the *Star Wars* and *Indiana Jones* films. He lives in Marin County, California.